蔡志忠／编绘

[美]布莱恩·布雅
拉思杰博士 等／译

人生的滋味

菜根谭·心经

THE ROOTS OF WISDOM · HEART SUTRA

The Flavor of Life

中国出版集团
现代出版社

图字：01-2005-5957

图书在版编目（CIP）数据

菜根谭·心经 / 蔡志忠编绘；（美）布雅（Bruya, B.），（美）拉思杰（Rathje, W. L.）译. -- 北京：现代出版社，2013.9
（蔡志忠漫画中国传统文化经典：中英文对照版）
ISBN 978-7-5143-1762-6

Ⅰ. ①菜… Ⅱ. ①蔡… ②布… ③拉… Ⅲ. ①漫画—连环画—作品集—中国—现代 Ⅳ. ①J228.2

中国版本图书馆CIP数据核字（2013）第215084号

蔡志忠漫画中国传统文化经典：中英文对照版

菜根谭·心经

作　　者	蔡志忠　编绘
	［美］布莱恩·布雅（BRIAN BRUYA）
	拉思杰 博士（W L Rathje, PHD, &E E Ho, PHD.）等译
责任编辑	崔晓燕
出版发行	现代出版社
地　　址	北京市安定门外安华里504号
邮政编码	100011
电　　话	010-64267325　010-64245264（兼传真）
网　　址	www.1980xd.com
电子信箱	xiandai@cnpitc.com.cn
印　　刷	三河市南阳印刷有限公司
开　　本	710×1000　1/16
印　　张	17.25
版　　次	2013年10月第1版　2017年4月第4次印刷
书　　号	ISBN 978-7-5143-1762-6
定　　价	29.80元

目录
contents

菜根谭

The Roots of Wisdom 1

淡中知真味，常里识英奇 *Know the flavor within the plain,See the wonder within the common* 2

闲时吃紧，忙里悠闲 *Urgency in leisure,Leisure in toil* 3

澹泊明志，肥甘丧节 *In plainness is ambition realized, In richness is integrity compromised* 4

眼前放宽大，身后恩泽久 *Opened wide before you, Enduring kindness after* 5

路要让一步，味须减三分 *On a path, yield a step; In tasting, share a bite* 6

侠义交友，纯心做人 *Chivalry in making friends, Purity in living life* 7

退即是进，与即是得 *To retreat is to advance, To give is to receive* 8

骄矜无功，忏悔减罪 *Arrogance negates achievement,Repentance annuls misdeeds* 9

动静合宜，道之真体 *Movement and stillness in harmony are the,Dao's genuine body* 10

轩冕客志在林泉，山林士胸怀廊庙 *Those of coaches and crowns wish for woods and springs,Those of hills and woods yearn for halls and temples* 11

做事勿太苦，待人勿太枯 *Do not let industry become drudgery, Do not treat others with indifference* 12

知退一步之法，加让三分之功 *Know to retreat a step, Try to yield a bit* 13

对小人不恶，待君子有礼 *Do not despise the underling,Treat the gentleman with propriety* 14

超越天地之外，入于名利之中 *Transcending heaven and earth, Entering among fame and fortune* 15

修德须忘功名，读书定要深心 *Cultivating virtue takes forgetting*

fame,Acquiring knowledge requires a mind of depth 16

真伪之道，只在一念　*The ways of truth and deceit reside in a single thought* 17

忘功不忘过，忘怨不忘恩　*Forget achievement but not transgressions, Forget blame but not kindness* 18

恶人读书，适以济恶　*An evil person's learning, Serves to abet evil* 19

读书希圣讲学躬行，居官爱民立业种德　*Long for sageliness in learning, practice what you preach.Care for the people when in office, cultivate virtue in your career.* 20

苦中有乐，乐中有苦　*The delight of ioy is often found in the midst of hardship, The pang of disappointment come in times of fulfillment* 21

谦虚受益，满盈招损　*Modesty brings benefit,Complacency courts danger* 22

勿羡贵显，勿忧饥饿　*Do not envy eminence, Do not dread hunger* 23

阴恶之恶大，显善之善小　*A hidden evil is a cardinal evil,A flaunted good is a minor good* 24

忧劳兴国，逸豫亡身　*A country prospers through worry and toil, The self is lost through idle leisure* 25

一念贪私，万劫不复　*A single thought of selfish greed,A thousand pains without return* 26

心公不昧，六贼无踪　*If the master of the mind is on alert,The bandits six shall show no trace* 27

勉励现前之业，图谋未来之功　*Pushing the present enterprise, Planning for future success* 28

不着色相，不留声影　*Not caught up in material things,Not keeping the sounds and shadows* 29

动中静是真静，苦中乐见真乐　*Tranquillity amid tumult is genuine tranquillity, Pleasure amid hardship is genuine pleasure* 30

多种功德，勿贪权位　*Strive to cultivate achievement and virtue,Do not covet power and status* 31

文章极处无奇巧，人品极处只泰然　*A perfect essay takes no unusual skill, A perfect character is simply natural* 32

人生无常，不可虚度　*Life does not endure, So do not live in vain* 33

持盈履满，君子兢兢　*When grasping hold of plenty, A gentlemen treads lightly* 34

大处着眼，小处着手 *Turn your eyes to the big view,Turn your hands to the details* 35
爱重反为仇，薄极反为喜 *Love too heavy turns to hate, A meager jot can turn to joy* 36
对阴险者勿推心，遇高傲者勿多口 *Do not open up to the devious, Do not say much to the arrogant* 37
大量能容，不动声色 *Forbear much, Reveal little* 38
人乃天地之缩图，天地乃人之父母 *People are microcosms of the universe, The universe is the parent of people* 39
伦常本乎天性，不可任德怀恩 *Family ethics are innate, Without the need for pride or thanks* 40
不夸妍好洁，无丑污之辱 *Gone with the praise of beauty, Goes insult of the unsightly* 41
应以德御才，勿恃才败德 *Virtue should guide talent, Without talent shirking virtue* 42
穷寇勿追，投鼠忌器 *Do not pursue a desperate enemy, Careful the object you throw at a mouse* 43
趋炎附势，人情之常 *To flock to power and influence is common to human nature* 44
须冷眼观物，勿轻动刚肠 *Observe with a cool eye, Do not rashly vent your spleen* 45
人心惟危，道心惟微 *When the human heart is unresolved, The moral mind is indistinct* 46
自然造化之妙，智巧所不能及 *It is the wonder of natural transformations, That cannot be matched by human ingenuity* 47
云去而本觉之月现，尘拂而真如之镜明 *When the clouds are gone, the moon appears, When the dust is cleared, the mirror shines* 48
急流勇退，与世无争 *Bravely retreat in rapid currents, Struggle not against the world* 49
文华不如简素，谈今不如述古 *Better to have plain simplicity than elaborate embellishment, Better to recount the ancients than discuss the moderns* 50
修身种德，事业之基 *Cultivating virtue within yourself is the foundation*

of successful endeavor 51
心善而子孙盛，根深而枝叶荣 *With a good head, children and grandchildren prosper; With strong roots, leaves and branches flourish* 52
勿妄自菲薄，勿自夸自傲 *Do not be quick to belittle yourself, Do not boast or act arrogantly* 53
道乃公正无私，学当随时警惕 *The Dao is a public thing, Learning is a home cooked meal* 54
律己宜严，待人宜宽 *Be severe with yourself and lenient toward others* 55
人情冷暖，世态炎凉 *People's feelings are warm and cold, The world's attitude is hot and cool* 56
慈悲之心，生生之机 *A mind of compassion, A motive for life* 57
为官公廉，居家恕俭 *In office, fairness and integrity, At home, tolerance and thrift* 58
处富知贫，居安思危 *In prosperity, understand poverty, In stability, think about peril* 59
不得罪小人，不奉承君子 *Do not antagonize the petty one, Do not flatter the gentleman* 60
喜忧安危，勿介于心 *The vicissitudes of life are not worth dwelling on* 61
宴乐声色名位，三者不可过贪 *Parties and pleasure, music and lust, reputation and status, Several things to be approached with temperance* 62
冷静观人，理智处世 *Observe others coolly, Conduct affairs intelligently* 63
躁性偾事，和平徼福 *A frenzied nature injures the world Peace and harmony invite blessings* 64
恶不可即就，善不可急亲 *Do not immediately, accept rumored evil, Do not immediately approach rumored good* 65
酷则失善人，滥则招恶友 *Severity drives away good people,Carelessness invites wicked friends* 66
不轻诺，不生嗔，不多事，不倦怠 *Do not make blithe promises or lose your temper, Do not meddle in others' affairs or fail to finish* 67
守口须密，防意须严 *Closely guard the mouth, Staunchly check ambition* 68
不忧患难，不畏权豪 *Neither troubled in hardship, Nor fearful of authority* 69

菜根谭后集

The Roots of Wisdom 70
言行多不顾行，谈者未必真知 *Talkers rarely pay attention to actions, Debaters don't necessarily understand* 71
无为之作，优游清逸 *Doing nothing with nothing to do, Carefree playing in purest leisure* 72
世之广狭，皆由自造 *The confines of the world are created by us* 73
乐贵自然真趣，景物不在多远 *Taking joy in nature's delights, Stunning views are never far* 74
心静而本体现，水清而月影明 *The mind quiet, original substance appears, The water clear, the moon's reflection shines* 75
观形不如观心，神用胜过迹用 *Better to see the interior than know the exterior,The spirit employed always beats the form employed* 76
心无物欲乾坤静，坐有琴书便是仙 *The head free of desire quiets heaven and earth, A home with books and music becomes a magic kingdom* 77
知机真神乎，会趣明道矣 *The wonder of knowing the mysteries, The wisdom of seeing delight* 78
万象皆空幻，达人须达观 *The myriad appearances are empty illusions, The enlightened person must have comprehension* 79
泡沫人生，何争名利 *In the bubbl'e that is life, Why fight over fame and fortune* 80
广狭长短，由于心念 *Narrow or broad, short or long, they're all from the thoughts of the mind* 81
与闲云为友，以风月为家 *I make friends with the leisurely clouds and take the scenery as my home* 82
隐者无荣辱，道义无炎凉 *Recluses have no honor or disgrace,Morality knows neither hot nor cold* 83
隐者高明，省事平安 *The reclusive one is intelligent, Reducing tasks brings peace* 84
超越喧寂，悠然自适 *To transcend splendor and solitude, To be at comfort anywhere* 85
得道无牵系，静躁两无关 *Enlightened ones have no attachments, Quiet and calm make no difference* 86

理出于易，道不在远　*Understand ing is found in simplicity, Enlightenment isn't far away* 87

动静合宜，出入无碍　*Movement and stillness come with ease, Leaving and entering without obstruction* 88

执著是苦海，解脱是仙乡　*Holding on means a sea of suffering, Letting go means a land of paradise* 89

卧云弄月，绝俗超尘　*Sleeping and playing in nature, Escaping the dusty world* 90

云中世界，静里乾坤　*A world among clouds, A universe in tranquillity* 91

不希荣达，不畏权势　*No hope for splendor, No fear of power* 92

圣境之下，调心养神　*An inspirational environment, Attuning the mind, cultivating the spirit* 93

春之繁华，不若秋之清爽　*Better the brisk air of autumn than the vibrancy of spring* 94

得诗家真趣，悟禅教玄机　*Achieve the true sentiments of a poet, Realize the mysterious truths of Zen* 95

像由心生，像随心灭　*An image is born, issued from the mind An image is gone, following the mind* 96

来去自如，融通自在　*Coming and going at will, Dissolved in confident ease* 97

欲心生邪念，虚心生正念　*An acquisitive mind breeds deviant thoughts, A vacuous mind breeds decent thoughts* 98

富者多忧，贵者多险　*The wealthy have many worries, The noble have many dangers* 99

处世流水落花，身心皆得自在　*Live life like flowing water, drooping flowers, The body and mind must always be at ease* 100

处世忘世，超物乐天　*Living in the world, forget the world,Transcending things, enioy nature* 101

人生本无常，盛衰何可恃　*Life itself does not endure, How can prosperity be counted on* 102

宠辱不惊，去留无意　*Scorn or favor brings no surprise, Going or staying makes no difference* 103

苦海茫茫，回头是岸　*The sea of suffering is vast and far, Turn your head*

to the other shore 104
求心内之佛，却心外之法 *Seeking the Buddha on the inside, Spurning the dharmas on the outside* 105
野趣丰处，诗兴自涌 *In the charm of the wilds and places replete, Poetical springs well up from inside* 106
在世出世，真空不空 *Live in the world, transcend the world, The True Emptiness is not empty* 107
毁誉褒贬，一任世情 *Praise and slander, libel and fame, Resigned to all the world can give* 109
彻见自性，不必谈禅 *He who knows his original nature has no patience for talk of Zen* 110
真不离幻，雅不离俗 *The genuine leaves not the illusory, The refined leaves not the mundane* 111
布茅蔬淡，颐养天和 *A blanket of straw and vegetables plain nourish a natural harmony* 112
断绝思虑，光风霁月 *To cut off all your worries, A sunny breeze, an after-rain moon* 113
操持身心，收放自如 *Minding the body and mind, Freedom in indulgence and restraint* 114
自然人心，融和一体 *Nature and the mind, Harmonize as one* 115
雌雄妍丑，一时假相 *Winner and loser, beautiful and ugly are just momentary illusions* 116
祸福苦乐，一念之差 *Good and bad fortune, suffering and joy, There is only the difference of a single thought* 117
若要功夫深，铁杵磨成针 *With quiet patience and constant discipline,A foot of iron is ground into a pin* 118
雨后山色鲜，静夜钟声清 *After a rain, the mountains seem fresh; In the night, a bell rings clear* 119
雪夜读书夜清，登山远眺心旷 *Snowstorm studying purifies the spirit, Hilltop vistos expond the mind* 120
万钟一发，存乎一心 *A thousand gallons, a single hair, Each exists within the mind* 121
就身了身，以物付物 *Understand the self based on the self, Allow for things*

to take care of themselves 122
不可徒劳身心，当乐风月之趣 *Do not over work yourself, Enjoy the beauty of nature* 123
风迹留影，过而不留 *A passing wind, the moon's reflection, Leave and then are gone* 124
月盈则亏，履满者戒 *On reaching fullness, the moon wanes, One who reaches fulfillment abstains* 125
把握要点，卷舒自在 *Grasp the essentials and move about freely* 126
超越口耳之嗜欲，得见人生之真趣 *Transcend sensual desires Achieve life's delights* 127

附录·延伸阅读 *APPENDIX Further reading* 128

心经

THE HEART SUTRA OF PERFECT WISDOM 137
释义 DEFINITION OF TERMS 138
空 *Kong* 143
色AND空 *Material World & Kong* 147
心经 THE HEART SUTRA OF PERFECT WISDOM 152

《心经》漫画

THE HEART SUTRA ADDENDUM 168
工作时工作，休息时休息 *Work While You Work, Play While You Play* 169
各有特质 *Everyone Has Unique Qualities* 170
不问前生，只问今世 *Do Not Be Concerned about the Past; Only Care about the Present* 171
象牙·佛珠 *Ivory and the Buddhist Rosary* 172
蚕与蜘蛛 *The Silkworm and the Spider* 173
过分要求 *Asking for Too Much* 174
两只蛙 *Two Frogs* 175
蝉与狐 *The Cicada and the Fox* 176
银子与石头 *Silver and Rock* 177
不知足是病 *Discontent Is a Disease* 178

恶魔的帮手 *A Person's Worst Enemy* 179
铁杵磨针喻 *A New Interpretation for the Chinese Legend of Turning an Iron Rod into a Needle* 180
握在手上的才切实际 *Only What We Hold in Our Hands Is Meaningful* 181
自知之明好量力 *Know Yourself and Stay within Your Capabilities* 182
狐狸与葡萄园 *The Fox and the Grape Vine-yard* 183
每个人该有两个生日 *Everyone Should Have Two Birthdays* 184
野驴与家驴 *The Wild Donkey & the Domesticated Donkey* 185
捞过界的屠夫 *The Butcher Who Crossed His Level of Competence* 186
驴叫与蝉鸣 *The Cry of the Donkey & the Singing of the Cicada* 187
蚊与牛 *The Mosquito & the Ox* 188
人生就是过程 *Life Is in the Living* 189
何谓真"象" *What Is a True "Elephant"?* 191
小草的觉悟 *The Enlightenment of a Blade of Grass* 193
水与咖啡 *Water & Coffee* 195
人生没有对错 *There Is No Absolute Right or Wrong in Life* 197
道 *The Tao Road* 199
刻意 *Trying Too Hard* 201
小指的悲哀 *The Sadness of the Pinky Finger* 204
佛与粪 *Buddha and a Pile of Shit* 208
八风吹不动，一屁过江来 *The Eight Types of Emotional Winds Could Not Move Him; Yet, One Passing of Gas Blows Him across the River* 209
蜕变自己 *The Transformation of the Self* 210
谈禅令人呕吐 *Discussion of Zen Is Nauseating* 211
"是"而非"有" *"Being" and Not "Having"* 212
拥有与融入 *Ownership and Being A Part Of* 213
蜕变 *Metamorphosis* 214
扮演自己的角色 *Play One's Role in Life* 215
尽情做自己 *Be All You Can Be* 216
诞生自己 *Recovery of the Soul* 217
应无所住而生其心 *Do Not Be Attached and Let the Essence of the Heart Emerge* 218
真空妙有 *Ultimate Kong and Special Being* 219

输与赢　*Losing and Winning* 220

人生的牢狱　*The Prison of Life* 221

鱼与鸟　*The Fish and the Bird* 222

大与小　*Big and Small* 223

前生今世　*Past and Present* 224

有与无　*To Have and Not to Have* 225

孤寂与唠叨　*Loneliness and Nagging* 226

山不长脚，人长　*The Mountain Has No Feet, I Do* 227

自在地做一只都市的熊　*Be a Carefree Urban Bear* 229

实相看不见　*Not Able to See the Heart of Things* 231

两种观点　*Two Points of View* 234

你拥有自己吗？　*Do You Own Yourself ?* 236

大、小、多、少　*Big vs. Small & Abundant vs. Scarce* 238

人生的意义　*The Meaning of Life* 240

万物的本质　*The Spirit of Everything* 242

自省为先　*Self-Reflection as the First Priority* 244

云想衣裳花想容　*The Clouds Desire Pretty Attire and the Flowers Desire Pretty Faces* 245

轮回　*Reincarnation* 246

失即是得　*Loss Is Gain* 247

1的故事　*The Story of 1* 248

附录·延伸阅读　*APPENDIX Further reading* 251

菜根谭
The Roots of Wisdom

淡中知真味，常里识英奇

Know the flavor within the plain, See the wonder within the common

1
浓酒、美食、辣味、甜品不是自然的口味；
Strong, rich, spicy, and sweet are not genuine flavors;

2
真正自然的口味只是“淡”。
Genuine flavor is only plain.

3
具有神奇特异才能的人，不是最高超的人；
People with wondrous and unique skills are not perfect people;

4
最高超的人，言行只是“平凡”。
The most perfect people are only common.

刺激、新奇的事物不能长久，清淡平常才能保长。任何刻意成就的，往往失去了本来面目，自然才是真。
Exciting and novel things don't last very long. Only plain and common things endure over time. Anything that is too contrived has lost its original face. Only the natural is genuine.

闲时吃紧，忙里悠闲
Urgency in leisure, Leisure in toil

1
天地像是寂然不动，但气候变化从不停息；
Heaven and earth seem serene and still, though the seasons rest not for an instant;

日夜不停地交替，但日月的光明，却万古不变。
The sun and moon course along, though their brightness has always been constant.
2
所以，君子闲时应居安思危，
So a gentleman in leisure should keep urgent thoughts,
3
忙时应忙里悠闲。
And a leisurely humor when busy.
4
人要效法天地，不变中有变；变中有不变。平时心中不过于松懈，临事内心不可浮躁。
We should emulate nature, changing amid the constant, constant amid the changes. In leisure, the mind shouldn't be too relaxed, and in urgency, we shouldn't be too tense.

澹泊明志，
肥甘丧节
In plainness is ambition realized,
In richness is integrity compromised
1
能甘于粗茶淡饭的人，
One with pigweed in the mouth and amaranth in the gut,
2
心性必定玉洁冰清。
Is as pure as jade, as clear as ice.
3
追求繁华富贵、锦衣美食的人，
One who wears dragon robes and eats jade,
酒
4
往往会因利益，而像奴婢般地去谄媚权贵。
Will kneel like a maid-servant and grin like a slave...
5
甘于淡泊不为物役，抱负即能得以伸张，
Because aspirations are realized through plain simplicity,
6
贪图物欲，名节即因而丧失。
While integrity is compromised by the rich and sweet.
人不求人自然直，甘于粗茶淡饭的人，任何利益都不能使他改变立场。
People who don't seek favors from others are naturally upright. Someone who prefers to eat coarse food, like pigweed and amaranth, isn't moved by temptation

眼前放宽大，身后恩泽久

Opened wide before you, Enduring kindness after

1
眼前心胸要放得宽，
Open wide the fields before you,
2
才不会使人有所不满；
And others will have no grumblings against you.
他做人真好！
His conduct is impecca-ble!
真是无话可说。
I can't complain.
是！
What a guy!
3
死后留给后人的恩泽要能流得久远，
Leave kindness that endures behind you,
4
才能使后人有无尽的追思。
And others will remember you forever.
人应放开心田，对人体贴宽厚，就不会引起他人的不满；人应贡献己身，为大众谋求利益，自然会被人追思。
If you open up your heart to others in generosity and caring, no one will be dissatisfied with you. If you give of yourself for the benefit of others, you will naturally be remembered.

路要让一步，味须减三分

On a path, yield a step; In tasting, share a bite

走在狭窄的小路上，要让一步给人行走。
Where the path is narrow, step aside for others to pass.
你先请！
You go ahead.
谢谢。
Thank You.
遇到有利益的事，何妨分出三分让人同享。
When the flavor is rich, subtract a few parts for others to taste.
这是立身处世的一种安乐法则。
This is a very comfortable way of handling affairs.
“世事让三分，天空地阔；心田培一点，子种孙收。”你对人谦让几分，人也对你客气几分。
"In the affairs of the world, yield a few parts, for heaven is vast and the earth broad; in the field of the mind, cultivate a bit, that your descendants may reap from the seeds you sow." How much you yield to others determines how well others treat you.

侠义交友，纯心做人

Chivalry in making friends, Purity in living life

1
与朋友交往，要有三分侠义的心肠；
Making friends demands a little chivalry;

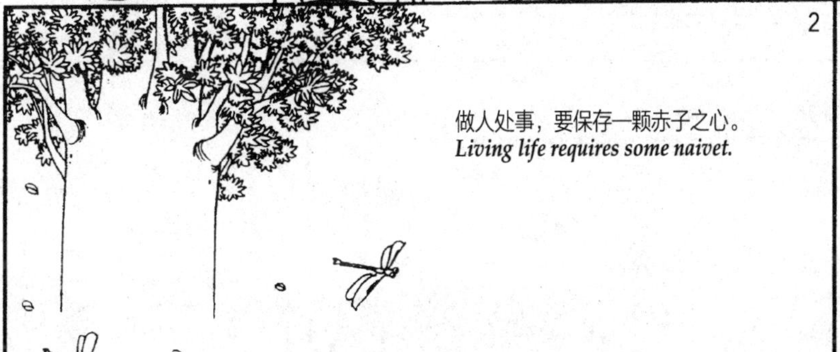
2
做人处事，要保存一颗赤子之心。
Living life requires some naivet.

朋友之间应互相勉励，有福同享、有难同当；为人处事应以真诚之心，坦诚待人，永远保持着善良的本性。
Good friends are supportive of each other, sharing the good times and working together through the hard times.In conducting ourselves, we should maintain a heart of natural simplicity, sincerity, and child-like naivet.

退即是进，与即是得

To retreat is to advance, To give is to receive

1
处世以能忍让为最可贵，
In handling affairs, take yieldingas supreme,
2
今日退一步就是日后进一步的本钱；
Retreating a step is the preparation for advancing a step;

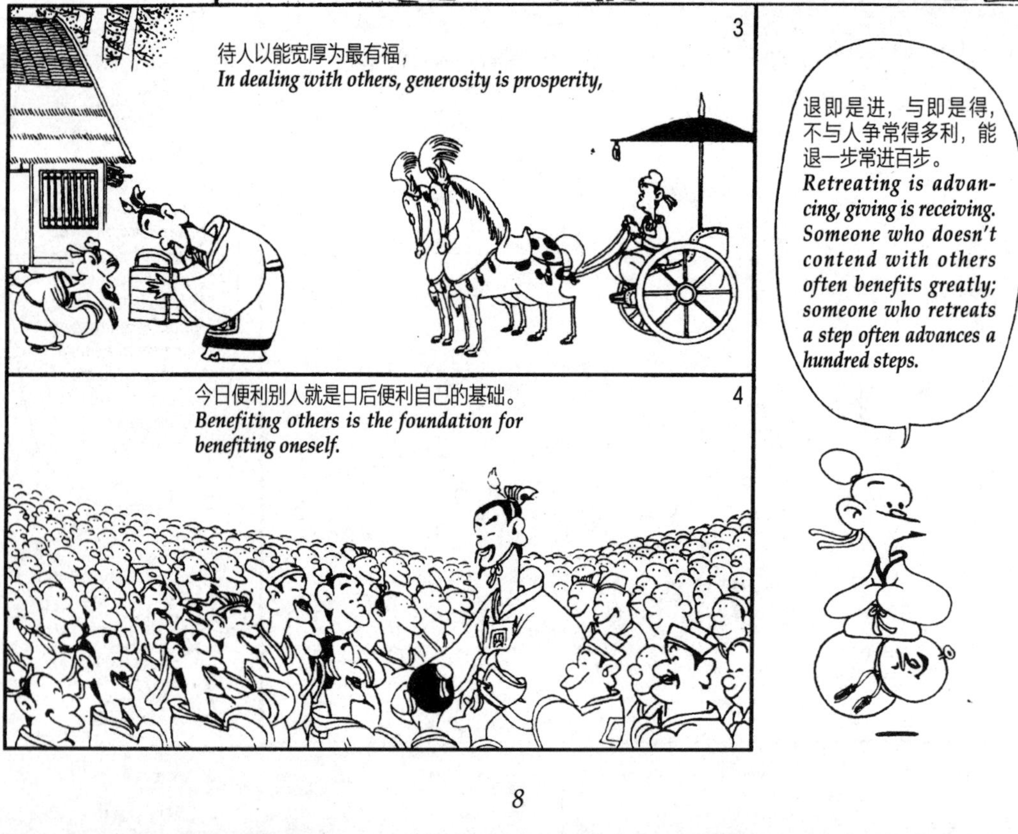
3
待人以能宽厚为最有福，
In dealing with others, generosity is prosperity,
4
今日便利别人就是日后便利自己的基础。
Benefiting others is the foundation for benefiting oneself.
退即是进，与即是得，不与人争常得多利，能退一步常进百步。
Retreating is advancing, giving is receiving. Someone who doesn't contend with others often benefits greatly; someone who retreats a step often advances a hundred steps.

骄矜无功，忏悔减罪

Arrogance negates achievement, Repentance annuls misdeeds

1
即使立下盖世的功劳……
The most distinguished deeds in the world...

2
也抵挡不过一个“矜”字的消磨；
Cannot bear up under the one word “arrogance”;

3
即使犯下滔天的罪恶……
The most ignominious crimes under the sun...

4
只要能及时悔悟也可立地成佛。
Cannot bear up under the one word “repentance”.

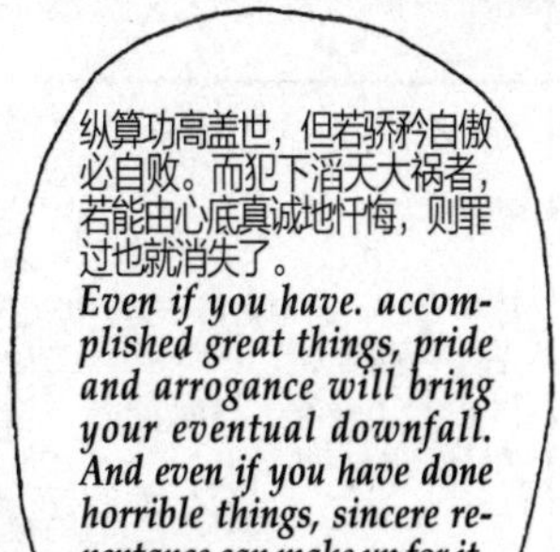
纵算功高盖世，但若骄矜自傲必自败。而犯下滔天大祸者，若能由心底真诚地忏悔，则罪过也就消失了。
Even if you have. accomplished great things, pride and arrogance will bring your eventual downfall. And even if you have done horrible things, sincere repentance can make up for it.

动静合宜，道之真体

Movement and stillness in harmony are the Dao's genuine body

1
好动的人，像风中的烛火摇摆不定。
An excessively active person is like lightning in the clouds, a flame in the wind.
2
好静的人，像冷却的灰烬、枯槁的树木死气沉沉。
An overly serene person is like dead ash, a dried up branch.
3
人的心应像在不动的浮云中有自由飞翔的鸢鸟；
One must instead be like a soaring kite among still clouds,
4
在静止的水流中有任意跳跃的鱼一样。
A leaping fish in placid water.
5
静中有动，动中有静，这才是有道者的心胸。
In order to possess the mind and body of the Dao.
动
Active
静
Tranquil
人生在世，唯有动中取静，静中取动，动静合宜才不失真趣。
The only way to maintain true delight is to be tranquil in action and active in tranquillity.

轩冕客志在林泉，山林士胸怀廊庙

Those of coaches and crowns wish for woods and springs,
Those of hills and woods yearn for halls and temples

1
身居高官显爵时，应有隐居山林淡泊名利的观念；
While abiding among coaches and crowns, do not let go the appeal of hills and woods;

2
大不了官不做，到山林隐居罢了。
If I can't succeed as an official, I can always retire to the forest.
3
而幽居山野泉林时，则应有出而治理国事的胸怀。
While residing amid woods and springs, aspire to the workings of the court.
4
有机会就尽一己之力，为国家社会做点事。
If I get the chance, I'll go out and do my best to serve society.
身负国家重任的人，须淡泊名利，以立立人，以达达人；而一般的平民百姓也应时时关心国事，尽自己的一份力量。
People in governmental positions should downplay reputation and profit in order to best serve society; Common people should always pay attention to government matters and be willing to do their part.

做事勿太苦，待人勿太枯
Do not let industry become drudgery, Do not treat others with indifference

1
尽心尽力地做事是一种美德，
Industry is a fair virtue,
2
但若是太过于操劳，就违反本性而使心情无法开朗愉快；
But sheer drudgery lends no joy to the spirit;

3
恬淡寡欲是一种高尚的节操，
Simplicity is of high merit,
4
但若是对事物过分冷漠，则将失去人生的意义。
But stark indifference helps no one and nothing.
为人处世应抱持着中庸之道不偏不倚，如此幸福快乐才会源源而来。
If in conducting all affairs we can maintain a balanced and unbiased attitude, our happiness and joy will be never-ending.

知退一步之法，加让三分之功
Know to retreat a step, Try to yield a bit

1
人情变化无常，
People's feelings flip-flop,
你好！
Hello!
你好！
Hello!
2
你浑蛋！
Miscreant!
什么？
Huh?
3
世路崎岖不平，
Roadways twist and turn,

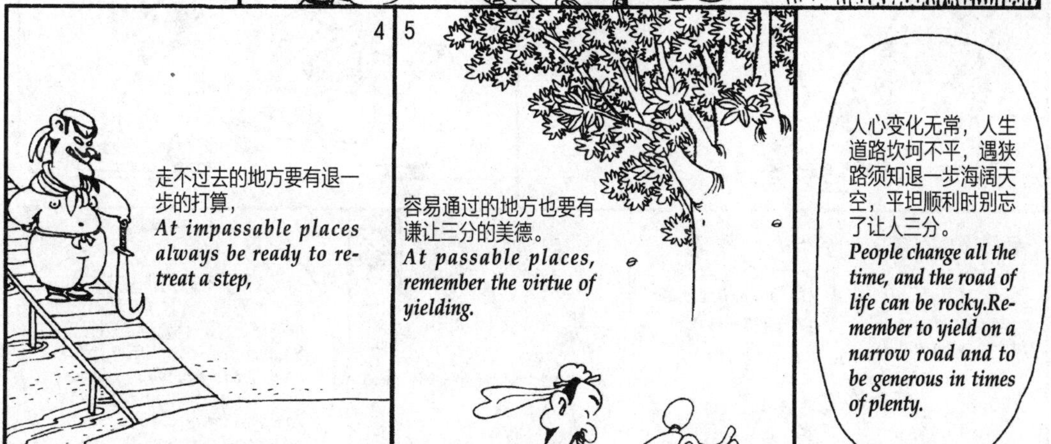
4
走不过去的地方要有退一步的打算，
At impassable places always be ready to retreat a step,
5
容易通过的地方也要有谦让三分的美德。
At passable places, remember the virtue of yielding.
人心变化无常，人生道路坎坷不平，遇狭路须知退一步海阔天空，平坦顺利时别忘了让人三分。
People change all the time, and the road of life can be rocky.Remember to yield on a narrow road and to be generous in times of plenty.

对小人不恶，待君子有礼

Do not despise the underling, Treat the gentleman with propriety

你看你又做错事了，又懒又笨！
You clumsy fool! You're lazy, and you're stupid!
对待小人严厉并不难，而难在不去厌恶憎恨他们。
It is not difficult to be strict with an underling; what is difficult is not despising him.

他不原谅我了……
I'm afraid he didn't forgive me...
对待高尚的君子恭敬并不难；
It is not difficult to respect a gentleman;
而难在掌握适度的礼仪表现。
What is difficult is maintaining propriety around him.
哈哈哈，好朋友，来干一杯！
Ha ha ha, Bottom's up, good buddy!
啮
clink!
待小人严厉不难，却难以包容的心去宽恕他。待君子恭敬不难，而难在如何表现得恰到好处。
Sometimes it is difficult for us to treat a person of lower station with appropriate compassion and to treat an admirable person with appropriate dignity.

超越天地之外，入于名利之中

Transcending heaven and earth, Entering among fame and fortune

1
别人虽然富贵而我仍坚守着仁德；
Though another is wealthy, still I am benevolent;
富
Rich
仁
Bene-volent
2
别人虽居高官显爵而我仍坚守着节义；
Though another is titled, still I am righteous;
爵
Titled
义
Righ-teous

3
一个君子绝不会被高官厚禄所笼络；
For a gentleman is not ensnared by illusions of nobility;
4
一个人若能坚决奋斗必能战胜环境；集中意志能变化气质。
A focused person transcends fate; a concentrated will stirs one's energy.
5
所以一个君子也不会为造物者所主宰。
For a gentleman is not restrained by the mold of the creator.
一个有为有守的君子，应以仁爱待人，以道德处世。不因别人而动摇心志。宁可做个自由人，何必为名利富贵所困？
Rather than being fettered by the expectations that are thrust upon us and giving in to desires that surround us, we should transcend our environment and live with dignity and integrity.

修德须忘功名，读书定要深心

Cultivating virtue takes forgetting fame, Acquiring knowledge requires a mind of depth

1
追求学问应集中精神，专心一致。
A student must gather his energies and concentrate on one path.
2
如果在潜修道德时仍去注意事功名誉，则必得不到真实的造诣。
If while cultivating virtue he daydreams about achievement and fame, surely there will be no fruition.

3
春有百花秋有月，夏有凉风冬有雪……
Springtime has the hundred flowers, autumn has the moon, Summer has a cooling breeze, and winter has the snow...
读书时偏好吟咏诗文……
If while studying he merely recites the elegant lines...
4
则必然不会用心思考问题。
Surely he will never have a mind of depth.
求学的目的是涵养道德，但若只重视学识的增进，或是附庸风雅地吟风弄月，这就失去了求学的意义。
The purpose of study is in cultivating virtue.If you emphasize only the advancement of knowledge or the beauty of literature, you've missed the significance of studying. Self-cultivation and study go hand in hand, and both require concentration and perseverance.

真伪之道，只在一念

The ways of truth and deceit reside in a single thought

1
人人都有慈悲心，维摩居士和屠夫刽子手的本心并没有两样。
Everyone possesses great mercy, and there is no difference between a saint or butcher.

处处都有自然的趣味，华宇和陋舍并没有不同。
All places have a touch of charm, and there is no disparity between a golden chamber and a thatched hut. 2
3
只是人心常被贪欲私情所蒙蔽，
It's just that our desires and passions often blind us,
4
一旦走偏了，咫尺之差便隔去千里之遥。
And at the point of departure, the difference of an inch can mean a thousand miles.
"羞恶之心，人皆有之；是非之心，人皆有之。"人心本善，却常有情欲所缚，正像光明的人忽然盲目失明，岂不可悲？
"Everyone has a sense of right and wrong." People are originally good but can be trapped by passions and desires. Isn't this astragic as a bright-eyedperson who suddenly goes blind?

忘功不忘过，忘怨不忘恩
Forget achievement but not transgressions, Forget blame but not kindness

1
我有好处在人家身上时不可以记在心上，
When I do good, I mustn't remember it,
2
但对人有了过失就不可以不记在心上。
When I do bad, I mustn't forget it.

3
从前你曾助我之恩，我没齿难忘。
I remember that time you did me a favor.
请别放在心上。
It was nothing.
别人有恩于我不可忘，
When someone helps me, I must remember it;
4
别人有怨于我不可不忘。
When someone blames me, I must forget it.
他们以前曾欺负你啊！
Remember when they were picking on you?
哈哈哈，我早就忘了。
Ha ha ha I must have forgotten.
事有可忘与不可忘，别人有恩于我或我有过于人不可忘，相反的我有恩于人或别人有过于我则不可不忘，这是与人相处和谐的基础。
Some things should be forgotten and some not. Other's kindness to you and your own wrongdoing must not be forgotten. Your own kindness to others and others'wrongdoing of you must be forgotten. This is the foundation for living in harmony with others.

恶人读书，适以济恶

An evil person's learning, Serves to abet evil

1
心地纯洁无瑕，才可以读圣贤书，学习古人的哲理，
One's heart must be pure before studying the ancients,
2
否则，看到古人的善行，就拿来用以达成私欲，
Otherwise, in learning good actions, one might usurp them for selfish ends,
这句写得真好，可以偷来用。
Well said!I can use this method myself,
3
听到古人的佳句，就借以掩饰自己的过失，
Or in learning good speech, one might use it to conceal one's shortcomings;
你瞧！古人也是这样说啊，证明我没错。
See, this ancient scholar said the same thing I did!
4
这就好比借武器给敌人，送粮食给盗贼一样啊！
This is like giving weapons to the enemy or grain to bandits.
这些武器粮食送给你！
These are for you!
嘻嘻
hee hee
古文
classic
粮
粮
学问如加以善用，则可修身治国。但心术不正者，反而会利用学问去做种种见不得人的事。
If put to good use, our studies can aid in cultivating the self and governing the country. But if our hearts are sullied, learning can also be used for all sorts of unmention able things.

读书希圣讲学躬行，居官爱民立业种德

Long for sageliness in learning, practice what you preach.Care for the people when in office, cultivate virtue in your career.

1
读书不探求圣贤的哲理，
If you do not meet the sages and worthies while studying,
2
有如摹写棐版的刻工。
You are like a printing plate engraver.

3
做官不爱护百姓，有如穿着衣冠的盗贼。
If you do not care for the people while serving in office, you are like a bandit in court robes.
4
谈学问却不身体力行，就像只会念经而不懂佛理的和尚。
To not practice what you preach is lip-service Zen.
南无阿弥陀佛
Namah Amitabha tock
南无阿弥陀佛
Namah Amitabha tock
南无阿弥陀佛
Namah Amitabha tock
南无阿弥陀佛
Namah Amitabha tock
5
事业有成却不积德，就像易凋的花朵。
To not plant seeds of virtue in establishing your career is to have blossoms fade in front of you.
世间的事理都有真实和假象。求学的目的在于书中的哲理，而不是表面的成绩。成就要与德业同行，才会有根基。
In all affairs, there are the genuine and the false. The goal of studying is to learn the principles, not to get the best grade.A virtuous career is the foundation on which accomplishment is built.

苦中有乐，乐中有苦
The delight of ioy is often found in the midst of hardship, The pang of disappointment come in times of fulfillment

1
陷于困境苦心思虑时，
In the midst of hardship,

2
往往会得到发自内心的喜悦；
A taste of delight is often found.
3
得意时，
In times of success,
4
则往往会产生失意的悲痛。
Disappointment is sure to follow.
失意时，发愤图强克服困境，当困境解除时，内心十分快慰。得意时，往往会因而忘形，乐极生悲。
In times of disappointment, we become determined to do better. When the hardship is overcome, we feel joyful and relieved. But success inevitably leads to complacency, and so joy eventually gives rise to grief.

谦虚受益，满盈招损

Modesty brings benefit, Complacency courts danger

1
欹器因装满了水而倾覆，
The qi*vessel topples over by being filled;
*A special vessel that fists to one side when empty,stands erect when half full, and overturns when full.Ancient kings kept them near at hand as reminders.

2
扑满因里面空无一物而保全。
The piggy bank remains whole by being empty.

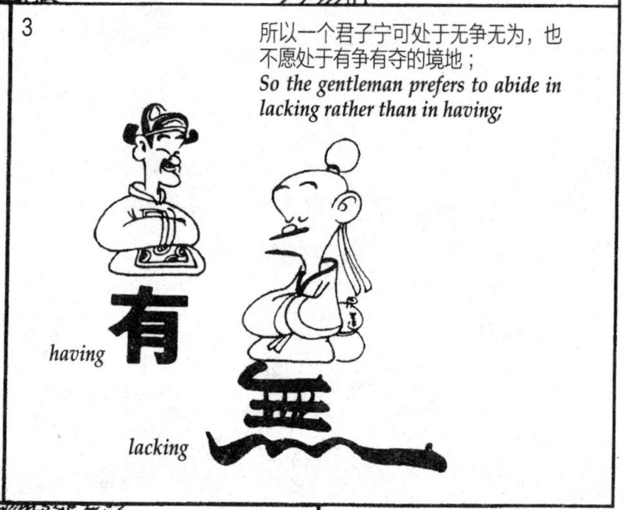
3
所以一个君子宁可处于无争无为，也不愿处于有争有夺的境地；
So the gentleman prefers to abide in lacking rather than in having;
having
有
lacking
無

4
宁可处于欠缺不完整的环境，也不愿事事要求完美无瑕。
To reside in deficiency rather than in perfection.

“弓满则折，月满则亏”，君子若能虚怀若谷，安贫乐道，则离正道不远矣。
"The bow breaks at full extension, the moon waxes then wanes."A gentleman should be as empty as a valley, take comfort in poverty, and rejoice in the Dao.
缺
deficiency

勿羡贵显，勿忧饥饿

Do not envy eminence, Do not dread hunger

1
人都以为拥有名利地位是一大乐事，
People know that fame and status are joyful things,
2
其实没有名利地位，才是真逍遥。
But they don't realize that having neither fame nor status is the most genuine joy.
3
人都为了吃不饱穿不暖的穷困而忧愁，
People know that being hungry and cold are dreadful things,
4
其实吃得饱穿得暖的富人忧愁更多。
But they don't realize that never being hungry or cold can be even more dreadful.
世事没有绝对的好坏善恶，都有其得失之处，只看你从哪个角度去看！
There's no such thing as absolute good or bad. Everything has its advantages and disadvantages, it all depends on how you look at it!

阴恶之恶大，显善之善小
A hidden evil is a cardinal evil, A flaunted good is a minor good

此路是我开，欲过此路者，留下买路财。
I'm the one who opened this road, so you'll have to pay to get through.
啊！Oh!
兄台做的是什么生意发财啊？
What fine business brings such good fortune?
1
2
做了坏事而深怕别人知道，是在恶性中还保留了一条向善之路。
To do evil and yet fear that others find out is to still have a path toward goodness.
哈哈哈，做点小买卖，开发道路收点路租啦！
Oh, just a bit of trading, you know. I opened up a road and accept a small toll from passersby!
3
我捐一文钱！
I'll donate a quarter!
4
做了好事就急于让别人知道，是在行善时便种下了罪恶之根。
To do good and ensure that others find out is the root of future evil.
我今天又行一善事，捐给寺庙一笔钱！
I did a good deed today. I donated quite a sum of money to a temple!
感谢状
Thank you
大善人
Philanthropist
好人好事
Benefactor
功德无量
Infinite Merits
好人好事
Good Deeds of a Good Man
为恶还怕人知，这种人还有良知，如给他机会改过，仍可走向正途。行善而急于让人知，这种人只为虚名，其实内心早就种下了恶根。
If a person who does wrong is afraid of other people finding out, at least he still has a con science and can change if given the opportunity. A person who wants others to know about his good deeds is looking for an empty reputa tion, and this is the root of future evil.
5

忧劳兴国，逸豫亡身

A country prospers through worry and toil, The self is lost through idle leisure

1
再顽劣凶悍的马也可以驾驭奔驰，
A violent horse can still be made to run;

2
溅出熔炉的金属最后还是会被注入模型。
Metal that leaps out of the smelt can still be returned to the mold.
3
但只要一贪图逸乐不肯振奋精神，终身便没有什么进步。
Play without effort means a life without progress.
嘿嘿！别再浑浑噩噩地虚度光阴了。
Hey, you guys, don't just sit there and dodge the world.
4
明朝陈献章说：
Chen Xianzhang once said:
一个人有很多缺点并不可耻，一生中没有缺点才是最值得担心的事。
To have many faults is not worth feeling ashamed about. What I worry about is going through life without having any faults at all.
5
这句话说得一点也没错啊！
How true!
一个人不怕有缺点有过失，只怕知道了自己的缺点仍不知悔改。
Don't be afraid of having faults.Be afraid instead of not making the effort to correct your faults.

一念贪私，万劫不复

A single thought of selfish greed, A thousand pains without return

人只要有一点贪求私利的念头，
A moment's selfish greed...
1
就会使刚毅正直变为柔弱无能；
Turns strength into weakness;
不应该据为己有啊，但是……
I know I shouldn't take what's not mine, but...
2
使聪明智慧变为昏昧无知；
Intelligence into confusion;
这么多钱，拿一点大概不要紧吧……
There's so much, it won't matter if I take a little...
3
使仁慈心肠变为阴狠毒辣；
Kindness into cruelty;
一不做二不休，统统独吞了！
Can't stop once you've started, might as well take it all!
4
使纯洁无瑕变为污秽肮脏！
And purity into pollution,
5
从此败坏了一生的品德。
Destroying one's character for life.
别逃！
Don't move!
6
所以古人以不贪求分外之物为最可贵，才能超越物欲的诱惑而顺利度过一生。
The ancients took uncovetousness as the most precious thing of all and so were able to transcend materialdesires for a lifetime.
7
人的贪念一动良知就被破坏了，于是就失去了辨别是非正邪的能力，聪明智慧也变成昏昧无知了。
When greed begins, the conscience is de stroyed, we lose our powers of discrimina tion, and intelligence turns into confusion and igno rance.

心公不昧，六贼无踪

If the master of the mind is on alert, The bandits six shall show no trace

1
耳闻目见的声色是外来的贼人，
What the eyes and ears see and hear become our outer bandits,
耳 ears
目 eyes

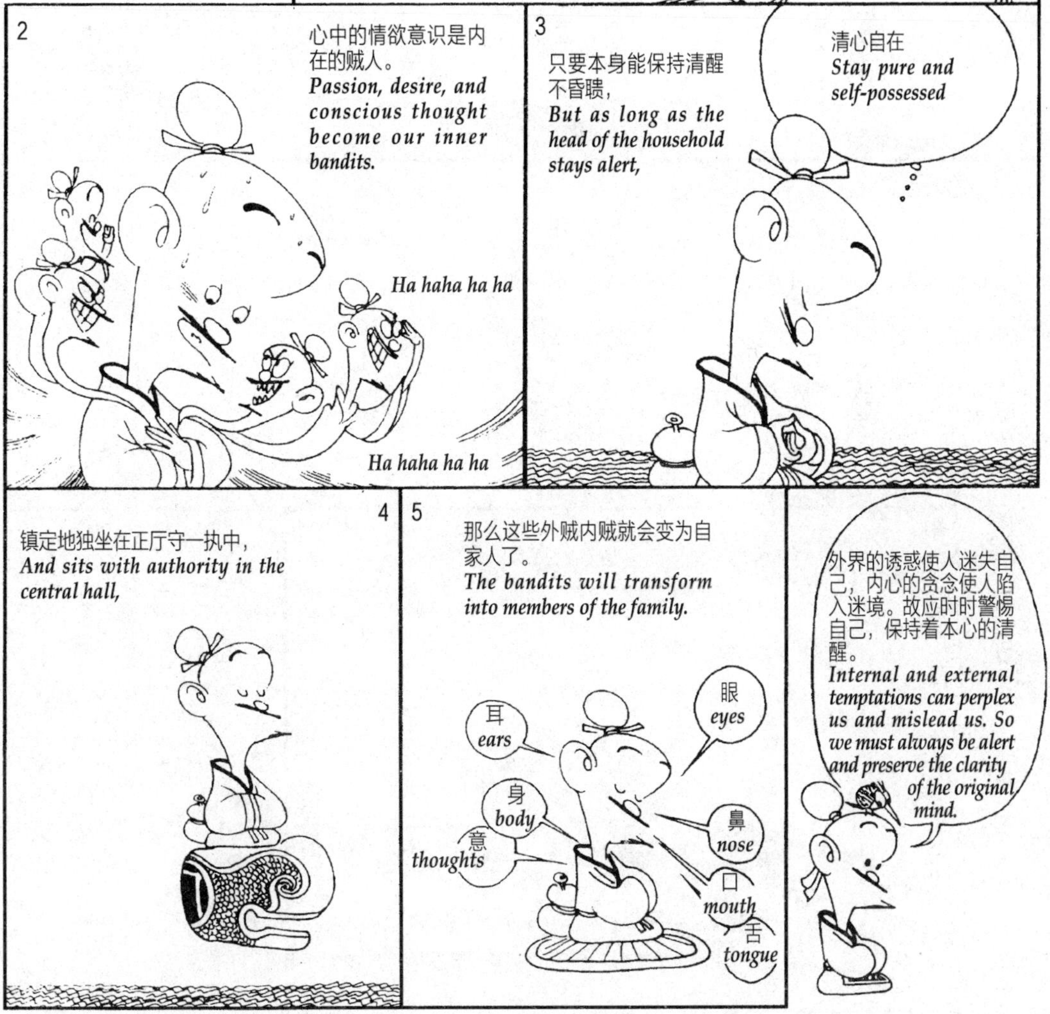
2
心中的情欲意识是内在的贼人。
Passion, desire, and conscious thought become our inner bandits.
Ha haha ha ha
Ha haha ha ha
3
只要本身能保持清醒不昏聩，
But as long as the head of the household stays alert,
清心自在
Stay pure and self-possessed
4
镇定地独坐在正厅守一执中，
And sits with authority in the central hall,
5
那么这些外贼内贼就会变为自家人了。
The bandits will transform into members of the family.
耳 ears
眼 eyes
身 body
意 thoughts
鼻 nose
口 mouth
舌 tongue
外界的诱惑使人迷失自己，内心的贪念使人陷入迷境。故应时时警惕自己，保持着本心的清醒。
Internal and external temptations can perplex us and mislead us. So we must always be alert and preserve the clarity of the original mind.

勉励现前之业，图谋未来之功
Pushing the present enterprise, Planning for future success

计划做没有把握的事，
Planning feats one is not yet capable of,
不如保守着目前既有的成就基础。
Is not so good as maintaining an already successful enterprise.
后悔已经过去的错误，
Regretting past losses,
不如提防将来可能会发生的过失。
Is not so good as preventing future mistakes.
要脚踏实地，从现有的稳定中求发展。若是失败了，要记取教训，不要活在悔恨中。
Stay practical and work outward from a stable foundation. If you fail, learn from your mistake without dwelling on it.

不着色相，不留声影

Not caught up in material things, Not keeping the sounds and shadows

1
风吹竹林，风一吹过，竹林并不再留下风声。
The wind sweeps through bamboo. The wind goes, and the bamboo keeps no sound.

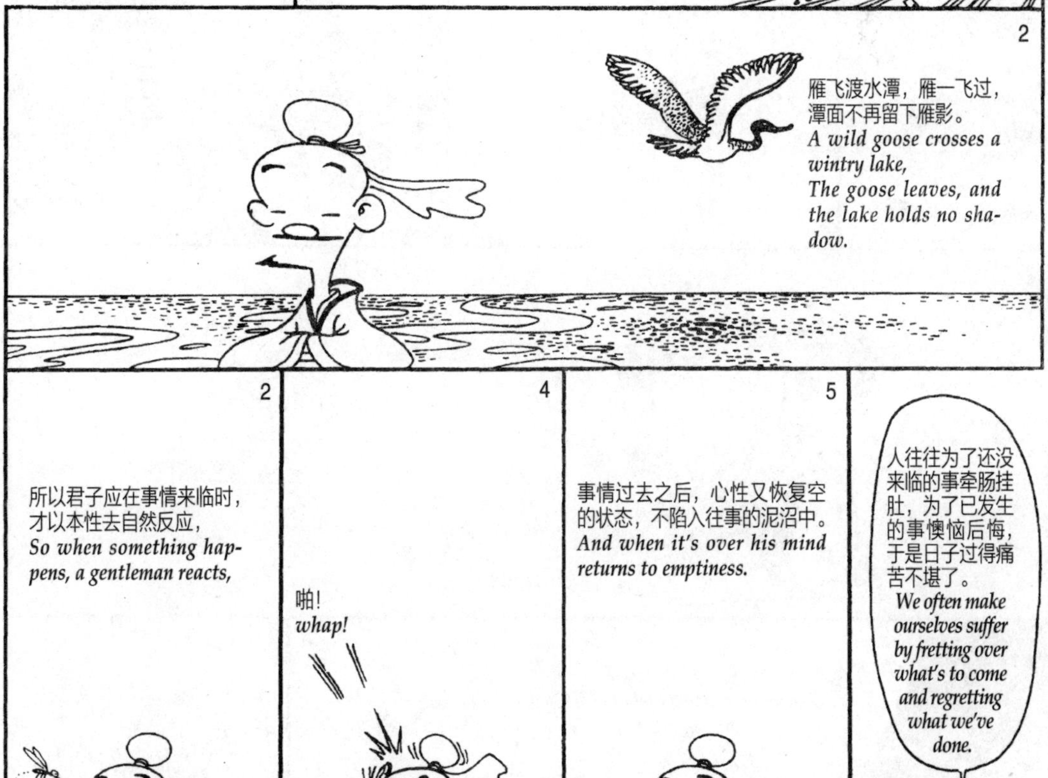
2
雁飞渡水潭，雁一飞过，潭面不再留下雁影。
A wild goose crosses a wintry lake,
The goose leaves, and the lake holds no shadow.
2
所以君子应在事情来临时，才以本性去自然反应，
So when something happens, a gentleman reacts,
4
啪！
whap!
5
事情过去之后，心性又恢复空的状态，不陷入往事的泥沼中。
And when it's over his mind returns to emptiness.
人往往为了还没来临的事牵肠挂肚，为了已发生的事懊恼后悔，于是日子过得痛苦不堪了。
We often make ourselves suffer by fretting over what's to come and regretting what we've done.

动中静是真静，苦中乐见真乐

Tranquillity amid tumult is genuine tranquillity, Pleasure amid hardship is genuine pleasure

1
在静寂无声中保持宁静，不算真正的静；
To find tranquillity amid tranquillity not genuine tranquillity;
2
能在喧嚷的环境中静得下来，才算真正达到静的境界。
Only tranquillity found in a tumultuous place is the spiritual realm of the genuine.

3
在快乐的境遇里感到快乐，不算真正的快乐；
To find delight in a delightful place is not genuine delight;
4
能在困苦的环境中体会到快乐，才是真快乐。
Only delight found amid hardship is the physical ground of the genuine.
人往往随着境遇而改变心境，能超越境遇不为境所迁，这时才是心体之真机。
Our attitude often changes with our surroundings, but if we can transcend our surroundings,we can attain spiritual an physical genumeness.

多种功德，勿贪权位
Strive to cultivate achievement and virtue, Do not covet power and status

施

一个老百姓如能行善积德；广施恩惠，
If a commoner is willing to cultivate virtue and extend kindness,
1

2
便是个没有爵位的公卿宰相。
Then he is an untitled noble.
救难的菩萨啊！
You're a savior!
3
一个官吏如果只贪图权势地位，而处处逢迎邀宠，
If a noble merely plots for power and curries favor,
圣上真是英明啊，了不起！
Oh, his majesty is so intelligent, so great!
4
不错，这官位施舍给你。
You're a good sycophant. Here's a new title for you.
便成了有官爵的乞丐。
Then is a titled beggar.
多谢圣上圣明，谢谢！谢谢！
Oh, I thank His Majesty. Thank you!Thank you!
人的尊卑高下，并不在于地位的高低，而在于德性的有无。位居高官恋栈权位而对上逢迎奉承，这与乞丐有何差别？
A person's value is determined not by his position but by his virtue.
What's the difference between a superior who goes around groveling to everyone m order to gain more power and a beggar on the street?

文章极处无奇巧，
人品极处只泰然

A perfect essay takes no unusual skill,
A perfect character is simply natural

1
好的文章没有什么奇特的地方，只是恰到好处；
There is nothing unusual about a perfect essay, it is simply done just right!

2
写得恰到好处，增一字则太多，减一字则太少。
Wow, it's just right. Not one word too many or one word too few.
好。Excellent.
太棒了！Wonderful!
3
好的人品没有什么和人不同的地方，只是尽了本性。
There is nothing unique about perfect character, it is simply natural.
4
他真是做到了尽仁尽义了。
His virtue is absolutely flawless.
处事应本着本性做自然的反应，不要有丝毫的勉强。夸强、虚假往往得不到好处。
Whatever the situation, just act naturally instead of trying to force things.
Boasting and pretending do not yield good results.

人生无常，不可虚度
Life does not endure, So do not live in vain

1
天地万古不变，可是人的这一生却不可再得。
Though the world has a thousand ages, I'll never get another self.

2
人生百年，日子很容易就匆匆而过。
Though a life has a hundred years, the days go by so fast.
3
人生在世，不可不知生命的乐趣。
One lucky enough to be born must come to know life's pleasures.
4
也不可不抱着虚度一生的忧虑。
And must harbor the worry of having lived in vain.
天地长久，但生命却有限。幸生为人，应随时随地体会周边美好的一切，才不会虚度此生。
The world is eternal, but life is limited. So since we have the good fortune to be alive, we should always try to experience the surrounding beauty, and then we will not have lived in vain.

持盈履满，君子兢兢

When grasping hold of plenty, A gentlemen treads lightly

1
咳
cough
咳
cough
年老时的疾病，都是年轻时不爱护身体所致。
Illnesses that come with old age are brought on from times of vigor.

2
衰败时的罪祸，都是得意时不知检点所造成。
Accusations after a downfall result from times of hubris.
3
所以君子在富贵得意时，
So when grasping hold of plenty,
4
言行举止要尤其谨慎小心。
A gentleman is particularly cautious.
一个君子在富贵得意时，应谨言慎行。年轻时，要多注意身体，一生才能安稳顺利。
When a gentleman is rich and powerful, he should speak softly and tread lightly. If he does this and takes care of himself when he is young, then he will have a smooth and stable life.

大处着眼，小处着手

Turn your eyes to the big view, Turn your hands to the details

1
细微的地方也不疏忽失误；
In small places, he doesn't seep;

2
别人看不见的地方也不欺骗隐瞒；
In dark paces, he doesn't cheat;
十目所视，十手所指，其严乎！
Careful! Ten eyes watch, and ten fingers point!
穷困失意的时候也不怠惰荒废；
And at the end of the road, he doesn't quit;
3
这样才能算是个真正的英雄。
This is a true hero.
4
“千里之堤，毁于一蚁之穴。”小事若不加注意往往是失败的祸源。
A true hero sees the big pictures, pays attention to details, always maintains his integrity, and doesn't give up in the face of setbacks.

爱重反为仇，薄极反为喜

Love too heavy turns to hate, A meager jot can turn to joy

1
即使以千金赠人，也很难获得别人的欢心，
A thousand gold pieces rarely bring a moment's favor,
这点小钱请笑纳。
A small gift for you.
旁边摆着吧！
Just set it right there.
2
有时一碗饭的恩惠，也能使人终身感激。
Yet a single meal can bring a lifetime of gratefulness;
这碗饭给你吃……
Take this bowl of rice...
谢谢！Thank you! 谢谢！Thank you!
3
因为过分的宠爱反而容易变成仇恨。
Because love too heavy turns to hate,
你忘恩负义！
You ungrateful wretch!
你偷鸡摸狗！
You underhanded-dirty dog.
4
而一点点的恩惠反而会使人感激不已。
While a meager jot can turn to joy.
想当年你曾救济我一碗米饭解饥。
I remember that time years ago when you gave me a bowl of rice to relieve my hunger.
爱并不是建立在物质条件上，而是给予适时的关心。锦上添花，何如雪中送炭来得实在？
Love should not be built on material things. Instead, care should be given at the proper times. What's more practical adding ornament to brocade or giving fuel on a snowy day?

对阴险者勿推心，遇高傲者勿多口

Do not open up to the devious,
Do not say much to the arrogant

1
遇到深沉阴险不太说话的人，不要急着和他推心置腹坦诚相交；
Do not open up to the inscrutable and reserved;

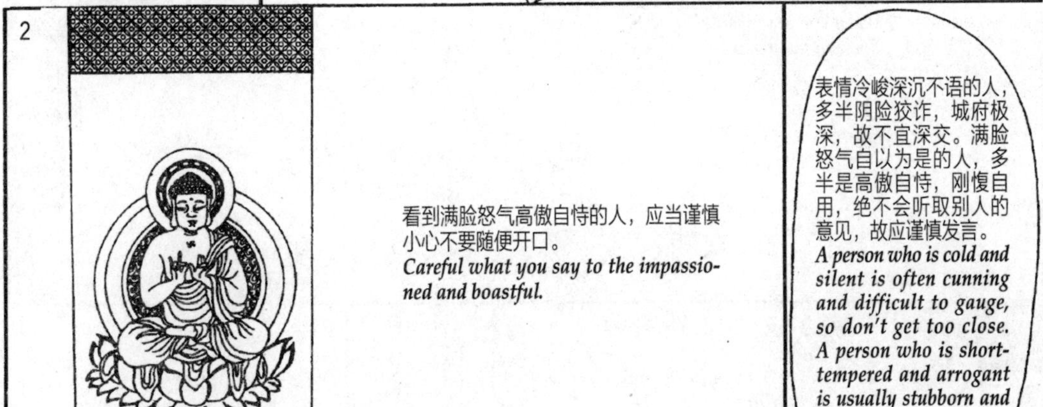
2
看到满脸怒气高傲自恃的人，应当谨慎小心不要随便开口。
Careful what you say to the impassioned and boastful.
表情冷峻深沉不语的人，多半阴险狡诈，城府极深，故不宜深交。满脸怒气自以为是的人，多半是高傲自恃，刚愎自用，绝不会听取别人的意见，故应谨慎发言。
A person who is cold and silent is often cunning and difficult to gauge, so don't get too close. A person who is short-tempered and arrogant is usually stubborn and close-minded, so be careful what you say.

大量能容，不动声色
Forbear much, Reveal little

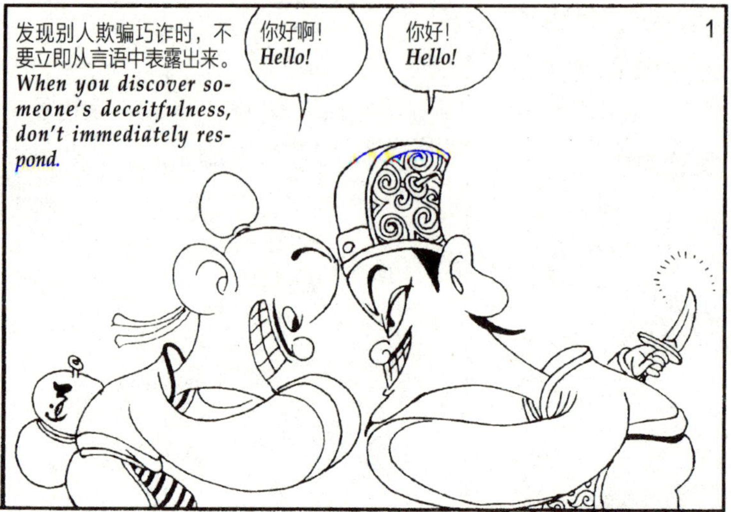
1
发现别人欺骗巧诈时，不要立即从言语中表露出来。
When you discover someone's deceitfulness, don't immediately respond.
你好啊！
Hello!
你好！
Hello!

2
受到别人侮辱时，不要立即表露在脸上。
When you are insulted by someone, don't immediately react.
酒
3
这里面含有无穷的意味，能使你一生受用不尽。
In this, there is infinite enjoyment and utility.
受别人侮弄欺骗时，应不动声色，以静制动观人入微，则别人也不敢再予欺骗侮弄了。
If you are deceived or insulted by someone, don't react right away.
This will confuse the other person, and he won't be so quick to do it again.

人乃天地之缩图，天地乃人之父母

People are microcosms of the universe, The universe is the parent of people

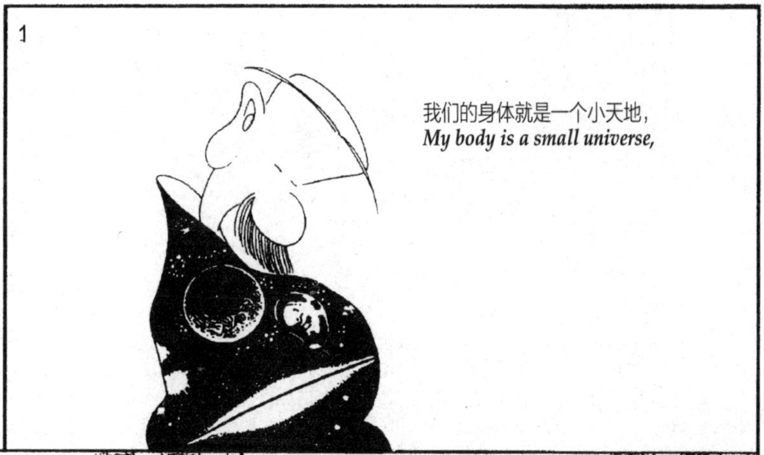
1
我们的身体就是一个小天地，
My body is a small universe,

2
能够在喜怒之间不犯过失，
So that my emotions lead not to transgressions,
3
使好恶之间有一定的标准，就是一种谐和调理的功夫。
And my predilections remain principled, this is its harmonizing skill.
天地是万物的父母，能使民众没有怨尤、使万物没有灾祸，也就是一种和睦的气象。
The universe is a great parent so that people have no complaints and things suffer no blight; this is its congenial atmosphere.
4
人心有喜怒哀乐之情和鉴别好恶的良知。喜怒好恶都有准则，行为举止才能合于法度，才能培养出健全的人格。
People are naturally endowed with emotions and personal biases, but we also possess the skill to balance these and conduct ourselves in a principled manner.

伦常本平天性，
不可任德怀恩
Family ethics are innate,
Without the need for
pride or thanks
1
父母对儿女慈祥，
Parents show affection for children,
2
儿女对父母孝顺，
And children are devoted to parents.
兄姐对弟妹爱护，弟妹对兄姐恭敬。
Older siblings look after younger siblings, and younger siblings show respect for older siblings.
3
4
这些亲情都是本来如此的，不必存有感激的念头。
This is how it should be, so there is no reason for even a shred of gratitude.
5
如果施予的一方以施舍恩惠的大恩人自任……
If the giving person thinks there is any special virtue in it,
真是大逆不道，也不想想我养育你之恩。
Who do you think you are?Don't you see how good I've been to you?
!
6
而接受的一方存着感恩图报的心理，
And the recipient thinks he should feel gratitude,
我小的时候你养我，你老的时候我养你，公平了吧?
You took care of me when I was young, and I take care of you now that you're old. Happy?!
7
那么彼此间便成了路人了，这种关系就像商业行为了。
Then the two might as well be mere passersby two people conducting daily business.
酒
父慈子孝兄友弟恭乃骨肉亲情的自然流露，不是勉强而来的。所以说：爱不需要说抱歉！
That members of a family should look after each other is the natural course of things, and it shouldn't be forced. That's why we say: love is not having to say you're sorry.

不夸妍好洁，无丑污之辱
Gone with the praise of beauty, Goes insult of the unsightly

1
有美好就有丑陋和它成对比；
Where there is refinement, there is the unrefined as its counterpart.
美 refined
丑 unrefined
2
我诗书棋画样样都出色，人品修养无人能比。
I'm talented, intelligent, handsome, virtuous. I'm just an overall great person.
如果我不自夸美好，有谁会认为我丑陋呢？
If I do not praise refinement, who can call me unrefined?
Hmph
吹牛大王！
Braggart!
好臭美！
Blow hard!
3
有洁净就有污秽和它成对比，
Where there is purity, there is the blemished to stand in contrast;
洁 pure
污 impure
4
我纯洁无瑕，一生都没有污点。
I'm pure as the driven snow,with not a blemish on me.
如果我不偏好洁净，有谁能污秽我呢？
If I am not preju diced toward purity, who can call me blemished?
5
!
现在有污点了！
Now you re blemished! pitooey!
为人处世该谦冲为怀，不要自夸自傲，自然就不会招致无谓的毁谤和侮辱了。
If we are humble and unassuming rather than boastful and arrogant, then naturally no one will slander or insult you.

应以德御才，勿恃才败德

Virtue should guide talent, Without talent shirking virtue

才能
Talent

1
道德是才能的主人，才能是道德的奴仆。
Virtue is the master of ability, ability is the servant of virtue.
道德
Virtue
才能
Talent

2
有才能而无道德，就好比一个家没有主人而任由奴仆当家管事。
Talent without virtue is like a household without a head and the servants handling all the affairs.
是。
Yes, master.
我要你向东！我要你向西！
Do this!Do that!
才能
Talent
道德
Virtue

向前一直走，一直走！
Go forward, and keep walking!
是。
Yes, master.
这样一来，怎能不使妖魔鬼怪恣意而行呢？
Is this not a monster out of control?
才能
Talent
道德
Virtue
3

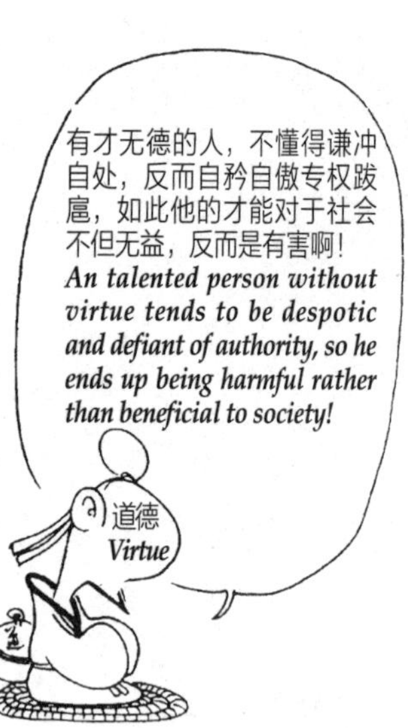
有才无德的人，不懂得谦冲自处，反而自矜自傲专权跋扈，如此他的才能对于社会不但无益，反而是有害啊！
An talented person without virtue tends to be despotic and defiant of authority, so he ends up being harmful rather than beneficial to society!
道德
Virtue

穷寇勿追，投鼠忌器
Do not pursue a desperate enemy, Careful the object you throw at a mouse

1
铲除奸恶之徒，要留给他一条生路。
When trying to root out evil, you must leave a route for escape.
把钱留下，放你一条生路，你走吧！
Just put the money down and get out!

2 如果使他没有容身之地，
Because if you leave no other choice,
不成！除恶务尽，别想开溜！
Now I've got you
可恶！与你拼命了！
All right! Come on!
反了！反了！
Oh no!
3
4
就像堵塞老鼠进出的洞穴一样……
It's like plugging up a rat's hole...
5
你无路可逃了！
Now let's see you get away!
6
结果室内所有的器物都会被咬破。
And everything in sight will be bitten or broken.
反了！反了！
Oh no!
除恶应留给他们一条生路，如不给他们一个改过自新的机会，逼其陷于绝境，则必使之铤而走险，造成更大的不幸。
If you force someone into a comer rather than giving him a chance to change, he'll feel trapped and come at you tooth and nail, creating a much bigger problem in the end.

趋炎附势，人情之常
To flock to power and influence is common to human nature

饥饿时就依附别人，
To flock to others when hungry,
吃饱了便远走高飞，
And fly away when fed,
看见别人富贵就急着想攀附，
To cling to someone who is hot,
看到别人贫贱就鄙弃不顾。
And mm away when he is cold.
这是一般人共有的毛病啊！
This is an ailment across human nature!
人往往因自己的际遇不同，而改变自己的态度；往往因别人的情况不同，而改变对别人的态度，这是一般人的通病！
It is so common for us to treat wealthy and powerful people differently from poor and weak people.
Indeed, it seems to be an illness that everyone has!

须冷眼观物，勿轻动刚肠
Observe with a cool eye, Do not rashly vent your spleen

1
君子应保持冷静的态度来观察事物，
A gentleman should wipe clean his cool eyes,
2
呜……
Ooooh...
3
太不像话了！
I can't believe this!
4
可恶！你们太过分了！
You scoundrels! How dare you!
5
你对我们不满意？
Do you have a problem?
你胆敢有意见？
Is there something you would like to say?
谨慎小心不要轻易表现刚直的性格。
Be cautious, and not rashly vent his spleen.
处事时应冷静、小心、谨慎，不要轻率地表现出刚直的个性，才不致招来怨尤与灾祸。
We should handle all affairs with calm and caution. We should have a sense of justice but not act rashly when it is violated, which can bring disaster.

人心惟危，道心惟微
When the human heart is unresolved, The moral mind is indistinct

1
在微弱的灯光下，天地万物都已悄然无声，这就是我们身心要安息的时候；
In the soft glow of a lamp, when all noises cease;

2
清晨醒来，万物都还未开始活动，这是我们刚从迷蒙中醒觉的时候。
This is when we begin to go into repose.

3
如能趁这时反身内省，在理性光辉的照耀下，
Coming out of dreams at dawn, before the hosts begin to stir this is when we begin to leave a groggy state,

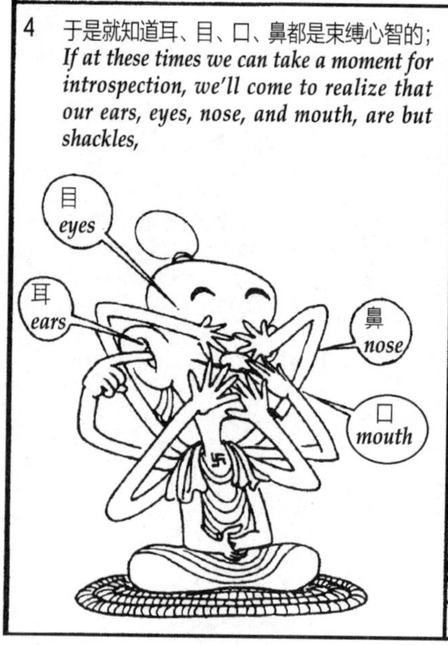
4
于是就知道耳、目、口、鼻都是束缚心智的；
If at these times we can take a moment for introspection, we'll come to realize that our ears, eyes, nose, and mouth, are but shackles,
目 *eyes*
耳 *ears*
鼻 *nose*
口 *mouth*

5
而情欲嗜好都是使人性堕落的机器。
And that our passions, desires, and infatuations are mechanisms of downfall.

人在就寝前、清醒后，是头脑最清明的时刻，如能利用此时作自省的功夫，将获益良多。
Just before going to sleep and just after waking up are when the world is quiet and the mind is clear. If we can take advantage of this time for introspection, we will reap great benefits.

自然造化之妙，智巧所不能及

It is the wonder of natural transformations, That cannot be matched by human ingenuity

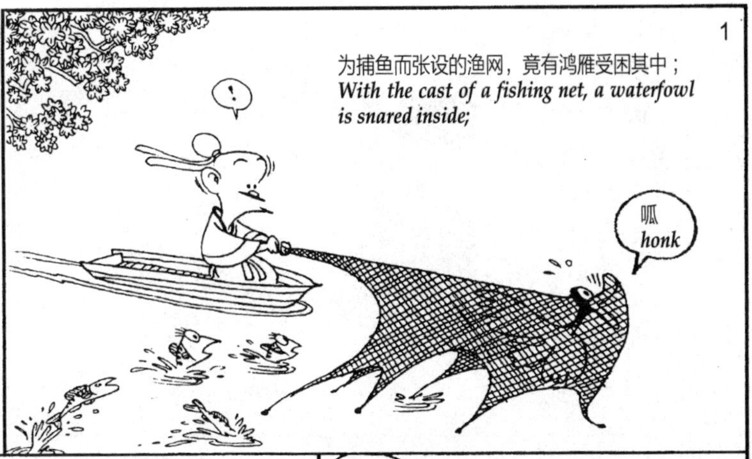
1
为捕鱼而张设的渔网，竟有鸿雁受困其中；
With the cast of a fishing net, a waterfowl is snared inside;
!
呱
honk

2
螳螂捕蝉……
With the greed of the mantis...
!
3
却不知黄雀在后窥伺。
A sparrow pounces from behind.
嘻嘻
Hee hee
4
玄机之中藏着玄机，变化之外又生变化。智慧技巧再高明也不足以依赖呀！
Within every trap lies another trap; outside every change springs another change. How can ingenuity be counted on?
人不可过于自恃，须知人外有人，天外有天。凡事应明察秋毫，瞻前顾后，方能减少错误灾变的发生。
One shouldn't be too presumptuous of one's abilities. In everything you do, carefully observe even the smallest details. Go boldly forward, but watch your back. Only in this way can you reduce the chance of disaster pouncing on you from behind.

云去而本觉之月现，尘拂而真如之镜明

When the clouds are gone, the moon appears, When the dust is cleared, the mirror shines

1
水不起波浪自然就平静；
Water undisturbed is naturally calm;
2
镜子不受遮掩自然就明亮。
A mirror uncovered is naturally bright.
3
所以人心没有什么可清洗的，只须去除使心绪混乱的杂念，自然清心自在。
So the mind cannot be made clear; just eliminate delusion, and the mind will naturally be clear.
4
快乐不须往外寻求，
Happiness need not be sought after;
5
只须去除使身心痛苦的根源，快乐自然存在。
just eliminate suffering, and happiness will naturally exist.
人心本是清净，但往往被妄想杂念所遮蔽，因此只要拭去妄念，清净光明的本心自然就会出现。
The mind is naturally clear, but it is often obscured by delusions and distractions.If we can just eliminate these, the clarity of the original mind will naturally shine through.

急流勇退，与世无争

Bravely retreat in rapid currents, Struggle not against the world

1
引退当在事业巅峰的时候；
In retiring, retire at a time of highest achievement;

2
处身最好是在与人无争的地方。
In residing, reside in a place of solitary retreat.

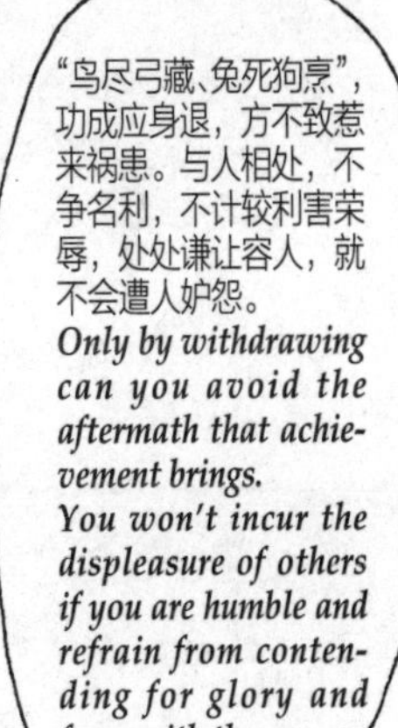
"鸟尽弓藏、兔死狗烹"，功成应身退，方不致惹来祸患。与人相处，不争名利，不计较利害荣辱，处处谦让容人，就不会遭人妒怨。
Only by withdrawing can you avoid the aftermath that achievement brings.
You won't incur the displeasure of others if you are humble and refrain from contending for glory and fame with them.

文华不如简素，谈今不如述古

Better to have plain simplicity than elaborate embellishment, Better to recount the ancients than discuss the moderns

1
与其结交城市中人，不如和隐居山野的老翁做朋友；
Better to befriend a mountain recluse than interact with a city man;

2
与其攀交权贵人家，不如亲近贫贱人家；
Better to chat with a commoner than meet with a magnate.
3
与其听那毫无凭据的里巷传闻，不如听听樵夫牧童的歌唱；
Better to hear the songs of woodcutters and shepherd boys than listen to the gossip of streets and alleyways;
4
与其谈论周围人物的过失，不如讲述先人的嘉言善行。
Better to recount the great words and actions of the ancients than discuss the transgressions and wrongdoing of the moderns.
古
结交富贵，不如亲近隐士、凡人；听是非之句不如听樵歌牧咏；谈人是非不如传述古人善行；趋祸当然不如修德。
Mountain recluses seek tranquillity, commoners are mild, shepherd boys' songs are heartwarming, and recounting the ancients can inspire us.

修身种德，事业之基

Cultivating virtue within yourself is the foundation of successful endeavor

1
道德是建立事业的基础，
Virtue is the foundation of any endeavor;
道德
Virtue

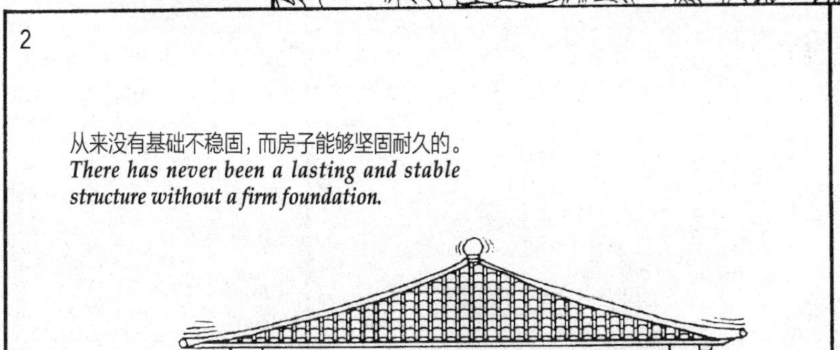
2
从来没有基础不稳固，而房子能够坚固耐久的。
There has never been a lasting and stable structure without a firm foundation.

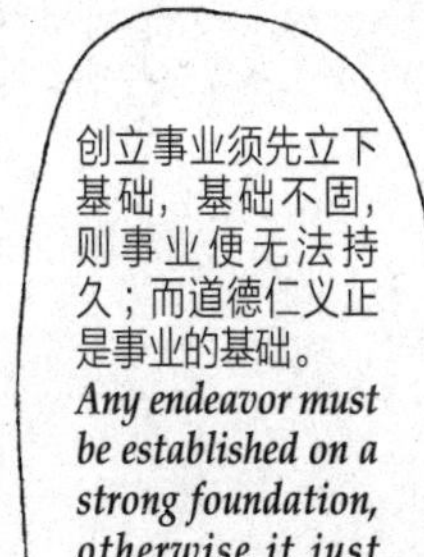
创立事业须先立下基础，基础不固，则事业便无法持久；而道德仁义正是事业的基础。
Any endeavor must be established on a strong foundation, otherwise it just won't last; and the strongest foundation of all is virtue.

心善而子孙盛，根深而枝叶荣

With a good head, children and grandchildren prosper; With strong roots, leaves and branches flourish

1
善良的本性是后世子孙昌盛的根苗；
A good heart is the rootstock for one's descendants;

2
没有不栽种根苗而枝叶能繁荣茂盛的道理。
There has never been a plant that flourished without healthy roots.
根本坚固则枝叶必然茂盛，所以身心健全，子孙才能绵延不绝；心地善良纯正处处积德行善，子孙才能获得更多的恩泽。
A good heart allows for decency and kindness toward others, which will be repaid over and over to one's children and grandchildren.

勿妄自菲薄，勿自夸自傲

Do not be quick to belittle yourself, Do not boast or act arrogantly

1
古人说：
Someone once said:
不要随意放弃自家无穷无尽的宝藏不用，而去向别人乞讨。
Abandoning one's very own inexhaustible treasure, door to door with bowl in hand, just like the needy ones.

2
古人又说：
It is also said:
不要向人夸耀自己的才华与财富，你所拥有的别人未必比你少。
Oh, needy one, with newfound riches, do not speak of dreams,for in whose hearth that sits at home is fire without the smoke?
3
前一句是规诫人：不要忽视自己所拥有的，
The first verse advises us not to overlook what we possess,
后一句是规诫人：不要夸耀自己所拥有的。
And the second to not boast of what we possess.
4
这是做学问的人应该深切警惕的。
They are both good precepts for the student.
天下万物，每个个体都是独一无二有其存在价值的，不必跟人比较，不要妄自菲薄，自傲自夸。
Everything under the sun is unique and possesses it's own worth. Don't compare yourself with others, don't belittle your own worth, and don't think too highly of yourself.

道乃公正无私，学当随时警惕

The Dao is a public thing, Learning is a home cooked meal

1
道是一种人人都可追求的事，
The Dao is a public thing,
2
应当随着个人的性情去引导。
And we should approach it individually.

3
学问就像家常便饭一样简易，
Learning is a home-cooked meal,
4
看到好的我学习，看到坏的我警惕。
I learn from people's good points and bad points.
应当随着事物的变化而随时警戒惕励自己。
And we should always be alert.
学问只是人人都可求得的东西，只要虚心向学，则处处皆是学问。
Learning is as simple as a home-cooked meal and is something that everyone can pursue. As long as weare open-minded,there is something to learn in every situation.

律己宜严，待人宜宽
Be severe with yourself and lenient toward others

1
别人有了过错应该宽恕，
Pardon the transgressions of others,
这次原谅你希望你能改过。
I'll forgive you this time, and I hope you'll do better next time.
是的。
I'll try.
2
但自己有了过错则不可宽恕。
But not your own.

3
自己遭受困窘应该要忍耐，
Forbear in your own hardships,
忍耐、忍耐、忍耐……
You can do it, you can do it...,
4
但别人若遭受困窘则不可忍心不顾。
But not in others'.
与人相处应该严以律己宽以待人。自己遭困境时要以毅力恒心来突破，别人遭困境时应及时伸出援手。
We should always be strict with ourselves and lenient towards others. When you have difficulties, strive to work through them; and when others have difficulties, lend a helping hand.

人情冷暖，世态炎凉
People's feelings are warm and cold, The world's attitude is hot and cool

1
我富贵时，别人来奉承我，只是奉承我的权势地位而已。
When I have a high status, people show respect, but what they respect are my high hat and broad belt.
2
我贫贱时别人来侮辱我，
When I am destitute, people insult me,
3
只是侮辱我的贫困、寒酸罢了。
But what they insult are my coarse clothes and straw sandals.
4
然而，根本不是尊奉我本人，我何必高兴？
So since it is not me they respect, why should I feel happy?
根本不是轻视我本人，我何必生气呢？
And since it is not me they insult, why should I feel angry?
名利地位原是身外之物，得之不足为喜，失之不足为忧。表面虚伪的事物，不能换取真情至性的流露。
Reputation, wealth, and status are all external things, so there is no reason to be happy when you get them or sad when you lose them.Superficial things cannot bring genuine happiness.

慈悲之心，生生之机
A mind of compassion, A motive for life

1
“为了怕老鼠饿死，而经常留下点米饭。”
"To leave some food for the sake of the mice."

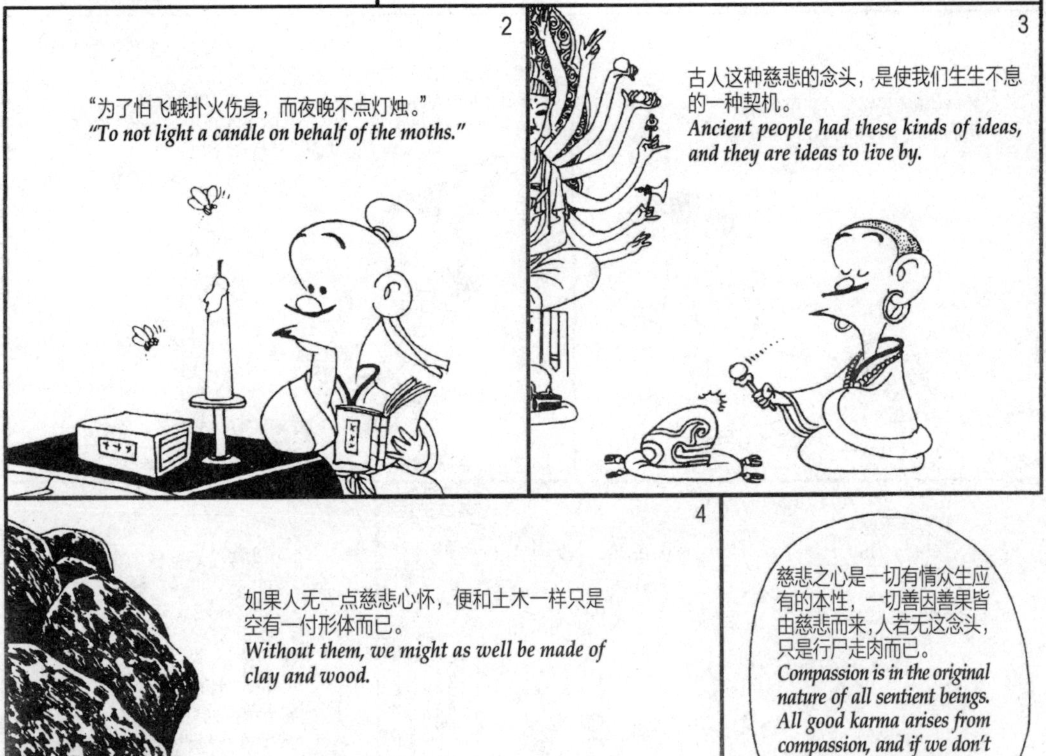
2
“为了怕飞蛾扑火伤身，而夜晚不点灯烛。”
"To not light a candle on behalf of the moths."
3
古人这种慈悲的念头，是使我们生生不息的一种契机。
Ancient people had these kinds of ideas, and they are ideas to live by.
4
如果人无一点慈悲心怀，便和土木一样只是空有一付形体而已。
Without them, we might as well be made of clay and wood.
慈悲之心是一切有情众生应有的本性，一切善因善果皆由慈悲而来，人若无这念头，只是行尸走肉而已。
Compassion is in the original nature of all sentient beings. All good karma arises from compassion, and if we don't live by it, we are nothing more than walking corpses.

为官公廉，居家恕俭
In office, fairness and integrity, At home, tolerance and thrift

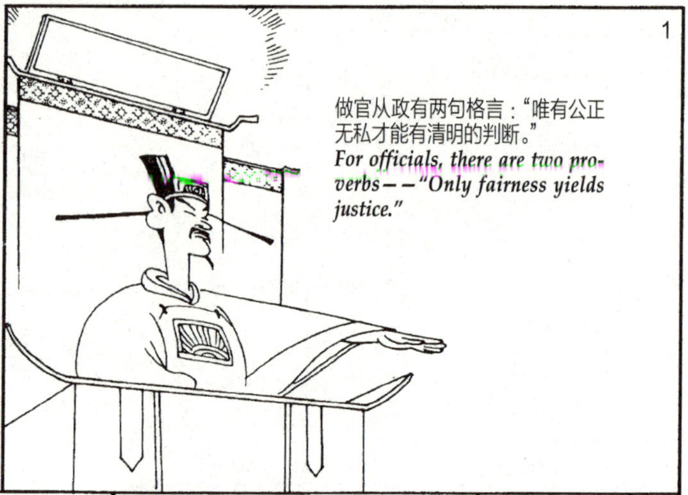
1
做官从政有两句格言：“唯有公正无私才能有清明的判断。”
For officials, there are two proverbs——“Only fairness yields justice.”

2
“唯有廉洁不受贿赂才能保持威严。”
“Only integrity yields authority.”
3
治理家务也有两句格言：
For the household, there are also two proverbs:
唯有宽恕包容才能平和安乐。
“Only tolerance brings peace.”
4
唯有节俭朴实才能使家用充足不虞匮乏。
“Only thrift brings plenty.”
5
居官当以公廉持身，才能受人尊敬仰慕。治家当以恕俭持身，才能使家庭和乐安康。
An official is just and wields authority only by being impartial and upright. A household is peaceful and prosperous only if the family members are tolerant and frugal.

处富知贫，居安思危

In prosperity, understand poverty, In stability, think about peril

1
再挥霍下去，家财必会散尽……
If we go on squandering money like this, we'll all be destitute soon...
富贵时，要知道贫穷的痛苦。
When living in prosperity, understand the suffering of poverty.

2
再放纵下去，将来必成个老酒鬼……
If I keep goofing off like this, I'll end up an old drunk...
少壮时，要想到年老时的悲楚。
When young and strong, think about the bitterness of being old.
人无远虑，必有近忧，处富知贫，居安思危。
Without distant worries, trouble will be near at hand.

不得罪小人，不奉承君子

Do not antagonize the petty one, Do not flatter the gentleman

1
不要和小人敌对结仇，
Keep from becoming a petty person's enemy,

2
小人自然会有他的对头。
A petty person naturally has his adversary.
3
不要对君子逢迎取媚，
Keep from trying to curry a gentleman's favor;
4
君子不会因而给你特别的恩惠。
A gentleman does not hold to personal favors.
跟小人计较，只会增加更多的困扰。向君子取悦讨好，只会招致对方的轻蔑。
Getting mixed up with a petty person will only increase your troubles. Ingratiating yourself with a gentleman will only bring disdain.

喜忧安危，勿介于心
The vicissitudes of life are not worth dwelling on

1
不要为了不如意的事烦恼；
Ponder not in discontent;
不要为了一时称心如意而高兴！
Take no joy in good's advent!
哇哈哈，我得到一大笔横财了！
Woo hoo!I'm in the money!
2
3
不要因为长久的安定而有恃无恐；
Complacence none in long stability;
4
不要因起步困难而畏缩不前。
Do not stop at first adversity.
一个人当坚持信心和毅力，不可为了一时的安定喜悦而松懈了勤奋的精神，只有勇往直前才能不断地突破和进步。
When you've made up your mind to do something, don't get distracted by momentary joys or disappointments. Whether you are stable or having difficulty, continue boldly forward.

宴乐声色名位，三者不可过贪

Parties and pleasure, music and lust, reputation and status, Several things to be approached with temperance

1
喜欢华美淫靡歌声的人，不是个好读书人。
A man who is too accustomed to music and splendor is not a man of learning.

2
经常宴客作乐的家庭，不是个好家庭。
A man who takes too much pleasure in drink and banquets is not a man of the family.

3
名利权位观念太重的人，不是个好臣子。
A man who thinks too much about reputation and status is not a man of the people.
声色、宴乐、名位虽然都为人所好，但必须懂得节制，不可过分贪求，否则必遭灭顶。
It's all right to occasionally indulge in one's desires, but don't let pleasure control you.

冷静观人，理智处世
Observe others coolly, Conduct affairs intelligently

1
以冷静的眼，观察人的行为；
Observe with a cool eye;
2
以冷静的耳，细听人的话语；
Listen with a cool ear;

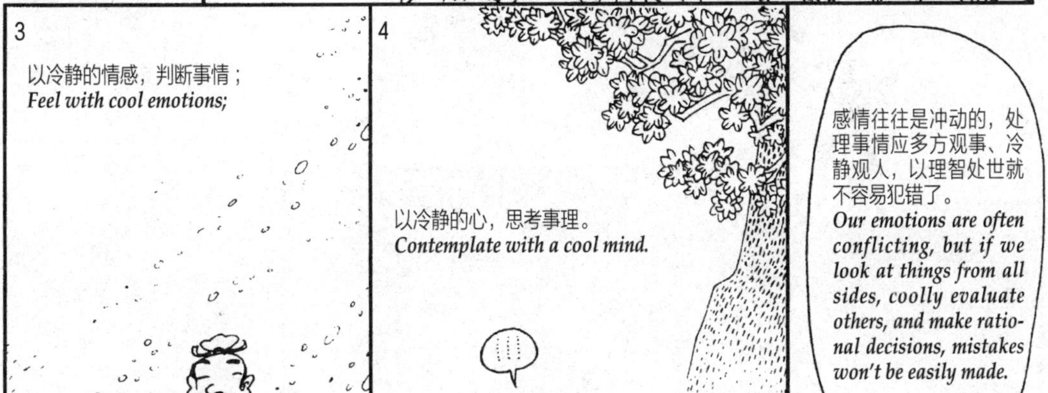
3
以冷静的情感，判断事情；
Feel with cool emotions;
4
以冷静的心，思考事理。
Contemplate with a cool mind.
感情往往是冲动的，处理事情应多方观事、冷静观人，以理智处世就不容易犯错了。
Our emotions are often conflicting, but if we look at things from all sides, coolly evaluate others, and make rational decisions, mistakes won't be easily made.

躁性偾事，和平徼福

A frenzied nature injures the world Peace and harmony invite blessings

1
性情急躁粗心大意的人，做什么事都不会成功；
A person of frenzied nature and rash thoughts shall never accomplish anything;

2
又搞砸了……
I've failed again...
3
性情温和平静的人，
A person of mild thoughts and peaceful temperament,
4
所有的吉祥幸福自然会降临在他身上。
Shall accumulate good fortune.
考虑周密的人处事谨慎细心按部就班，自然能成功；急躁粗心的人，凡事都未经审慎思虑，便匆忙付诸行动，必然容易失败。
Someone who is cautious and thorough in everything will naturally succeed, while someone who carelessly plunges into any old thing will usually fail.

恶不可即就，善不可急亲

Do not immediately, accept rumored evil, Do not immediately approach rumored good

这个人坏得一无是处。
That guy is utterly despicable.
听到别人坏，不可立刻产生厌恶的心理，
When you hear about someone's wickedness, don't be quick to despise him,
1

不会啊……看来挺不错的。
Doesn't look that way to me...
2
因为这可能是小人为泄恨而搬弄的是非。
For it may just be that some calumnious fellow is venting his anger.
3
听到别人好，不可立即去亲近他，
When you hear about someone's excellence, don't be quick to accept him,
这个人好得一塌糊涂。
This man is truly outstanding.
4
!
谢了。
Thank you.
多谢你美言，这是你的报酬。
Your compliments are much appreciated. Here is our agreed upon sum.
因为这可能是小人用以跻身致仕的伎俩。
For it may just be that some wretched fellow is advancing his own interests.
为人固要忠厚诚恳，但不可因而随便轻信人言，必须冷静地思索、客观地验证，才不落人圈套。
Of course it's good to be honest and sincere, but don't believe everything people say. If you consider and verify things calmly and objectively, you won't fall into someone else's trap.

酷则失善人，滥则招恶友

Severity drives away good people, Carelessness invites wicked friends

1
用人不能过于苛酷，
In employing others, don't be too severe,
笨笨笨笨蛋！通通是一群白痴！
Fools fools fools fools! You're all a bunch of idiots!

2
苛酷就会使想来为你效力的人因而离去。
Otherwise even the ones who wanted to help will leave.
咦？通通走光了……
Hey, where's everybody going?...
3
交友不应太过于轻率，
In making friends, don't be careless,
4
轻率就会使逢迎取媚的人因而到来。
Otherwise there will be those who will come to flatter you.
"要怎么收获先怎么栽"，人与人相处，如同镜子的两面，你怒它也怒，你笑它也笑！
"Sow what you wish to reap." Interacting with others is like looking in a mirror if you're angry, they're angry; if you smile, they smile.

不轻诺，不生嗔，不多事，不倦怠

Do not make blithe promises or lose your temper, Do not meddle in others' affairs or fail to finish

1
放心吧！这件事包在我身上。
Don't worry! You can count on me!
不可因一时高兴而轻许诺言。
Do not make blithe promises on account of being joyful.
谢谢。
Thank you!

2
不可借醉装疯，乱发脾气，
Do not lose your temper due to inebriation,
3
不可乘一时之快而多管闲事。
Do not meddle in other people's affairs on account of indignation.
4
不可因力疲倦而有始无终。
Do not fail to finish due to your own exhaustion.
在高兴时、酒醉时、冲动时、困倦时应把持自身随时留意，不要轻率地做出使自己懊悔的事。
When joyful, drunk, indignant, or tired, give yourself some room to think. Don't do something rash that you'll regret later.

守口须密，防意须严
Closely guard the mouth, Staunchly check ambition

1
口是传达心意的大门，守口不密就会泄露心中的秘密。
The mouth is the portal of the mind. If you do not guard it well, it will reveal your inner secrets.
2
啊！说漏了嘴。
Oops!Let the cat out of the bag.
嘻嘻
Hee hee.
3
意欲是表现心意的双脚，
Ambition is the locomotion of the mind.
4
5
6
提防意欲不够严密，就会走进邪路歪道。
If you do not keep it in check, it will take you down the path of evil.
哇！
Ahhh!
不要逞一时的口舌之快而招惹是非，不要放任自己的意欲，以免兴起邪念，因而走入歪道。
Be prudent in what you say and don't give free reign to your desires. A momentary lapse can mean a lifetime of regret.

不忧患难，不畏权豪
Neither troubled in hardship, Nor fearful of authority

1
君子处在患难中，并不忧虑担心；
A gentleman is not apprehensive in the midst of trouble;

2
在宴饮游乐时，反而会戒慎忧虑。
It is during feasts and merrymaking that he worries.
3
君子遇到有权势地位而强横无理的人，并不感到畏惧；
He does not fear in the face of the powerful and brutal;
4
对于孤苦无依的人，则会油然而起同情心。
It is toward the man without a family that he feels alarmed.
君子处变不惊，不沉湎于声色酒肉中；君子济弱扶倾，不恃强凌弱、欺善怕恶。
A gentleman is courageous and steadfast. He is not concerned with other people's opinions of him, he does not immerse himself in carnal pleasures, and he helps the needy.

菜根谭后集
The Roots of Wisdom

言行多不顾行，谈者未必真知

Talkers rarely pay attention to actions, Debaters don't necessarily understand

我希望能遁世隐居，享受山野林泉的生活。
Oh, how I'd like to get away from it all and be a recluse, enjoying the mountain wilds and the forest springs.
那就去隐居啊！
Well, why don't you?
1
2
经常谈论隐居山林的人，不一定真能领略隐居的乐趣。
Those who discuss the pleasures of mountains and forests do not necessarily appreciate the delight of them.
唉，好寂寞哦……
Sigh. I'm so lonely.

3
不喜欢谈论功名利禄的人，不一定真能忘却功名利禄。
Those who dislike talk of fame and fortune do not necessarily try so hard to forget them.
我最恨谈这些俗不可耐的话题了。
I detest talking about such vulgar topics.
名利。
Fame and fortune.
名利。
Fame and fortune.
4
真能体会山林逸趣者，不会将之形于色表于言；真能淡泊名利者，早已超脱名利的观念，心中无所谓的好恶。
People who really find delight in being a mountain recluse don't go around talking about how great it is. People who have no desire for fame and fortune have long since transcended even the thought of them, so there is no liking or disliking of the two.

无为之作，优游清逸

Doing nothing with nothing to do, Carefree playing in purest leisure

1
2
死了！
He's a goner!
太小了，放它一马吧。
Too small, I guess I'll throw it back.
3

4
钓鱼本是清逸的事，但却含有生杀的权力。
Fishing is a leisurely activity, yet it wields the baton of life and death.
活了！
You're alive!
plunk!
5
下棋本是清雅的游戏，但却含有胜败的争斗心理。
Chess is a refined game, yet it requires a warring mind.
胜！
Check-mate!
负……
Dam
6
因此可见多事不如无事来得舒适自在。
So we see that joyous affairs are less easeful than having no affairs at all.
7
多才不如无才能够保全纯真的本性。
And many talents are less genuine than having no talents at all.
庄子说："至乐无乐。"不需要借助于任何的逍遥，才是真逍遥。
Zhuangzi said: "The ultimate pleasure is having no pleasures. "True carefree leisure is found in doing nothing at all, not in this or that pastime or amusement.

世之广狭，皆由自造
The confines of the world are created by us

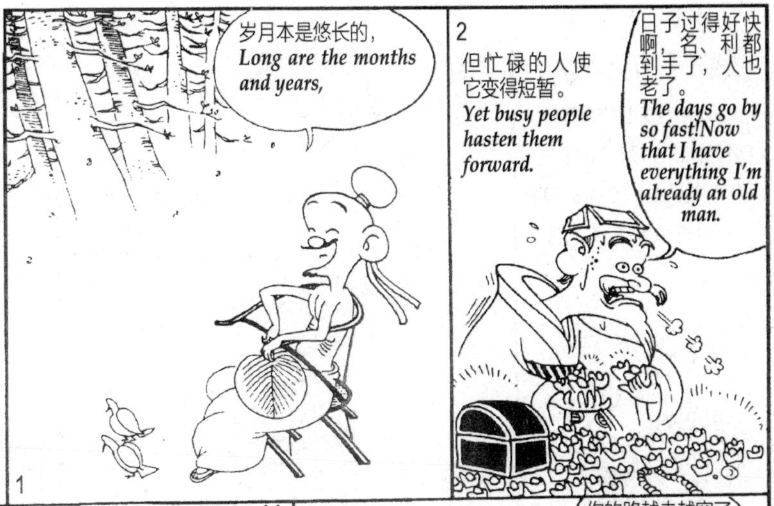
1
岁月本是悠长的，
Long are the months and years,
2
但忙碌的人使它变得短暂。
Yet busy people hasten them forward.
日子过得好快啊，名、利都到手了，人也老了。
The days go by so fast!Now that I have everything I'm already an old man.

3
天地本是宽阔的，
Vast are heaven and earth,
4
但心胸窄小的人使它变得狭隘。
Yet vulgar people narrow their confines.
你的路越走越窄了。
You're walking a fine line, buddy.
5
风花雪月本是很美的，
Leisurely are the breeze, the flowers, the snow, and the moon,
6
但劳虑的人使它变得多余。
Yet toilers see them as superfluous
那些花花草草有什么好看？
What's so great about silly old flowers?
若心中充满了物欲，于是精神变成了肉体的奴隶。人生的目的难道仅是名和利吗？
If your mind is full of material desires, your spirit becomes a slave to the body. It seems ridiculous to say that the goal of life is to achieve fame and fortune.

乐贵自然真趣，景物不在多远

Taking joy in nature's delights, Stunning views are never far

能使人获得乐趣的事务，并不在于多寡。
Delight lies not in quantity;
即如脸盆般的水池，如拳头大的石头间，山水的意趣都已具备。
Among a tiny pool and small rocks a landscape is complete.
一花一世界，一叶一如来。
A single blossom is a world. A single leaf is the Buddha.
能使人领会自然景色的地方不必向外远求，
Vistas lie not in distant places,
草窗竹屋下，同样可以邀纳明月清风。
Within a humble window and bamboo hut a vantage is replete.
"参禅何须山水，灭却心头火亦凉。"懂得体悟欣赏人生的人，随处都能识得生命的真谛。
"In practicing Zen, what need for hills and streams? Extinguish the mind, and fire becomes cool. "If we understand how to enjoy life, we can find the truth in any place.

心静而本体现，水清而月影明

The mind quiet, original substance appears, The water clear, the moon's reflection shines

1
倾听深夜里的钟声，能够唤醒迷境中的人。
Hearing the toll of a bell on a quiet night, you wake from a dream within a dream.
!
咚咚
bong bong

2
静观明潭上的月影，能够看见自己的本性。
Looking at the moon's reflection on a clear lake, you see the self outside the self.

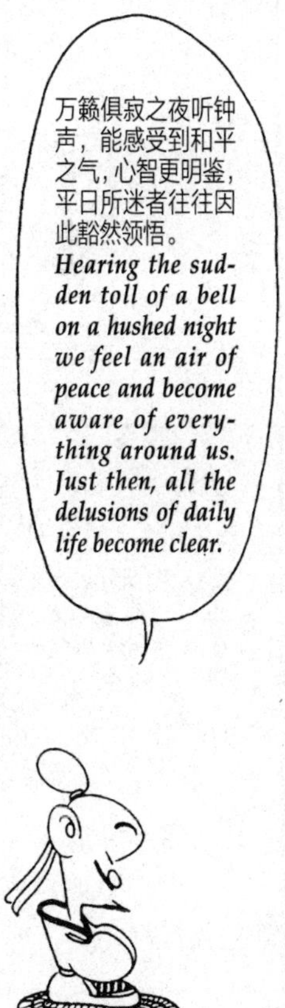
万籁俱寂之夜听钟声，能感受到和平之气，心智更明鉴，平日所迷者往往因此豁然领悟。
Hearing the sudden toll of a bell on a hushed night we feel an air of peace and become aware of everything around us. Just then, all the delusions of daily life become clear.

观形不如观心，神用胜过迹用

Better to see the interior than know the exterior, The spirit employed always beats the form employed

1
人往往只会读有字的书，
People try to understand books with words,
2
却看不见世上的无字书。
But not the wordless books.
善读书者，无之非书；山水亦书也，棋酒亦书也，花月亦书也。
For the good student, everything is a book. Landscapes are books; amusements are books, nature's details are books.

3
人往往只会弹有弦的琴，
People try to appreciate zithers with strings,
4
却听不见天地间的无弦琴者。
But not the stringless zithers.
天地间的琴音，处处可闻，有心的人即可听到。
There is music everywhere if you just have the mind to hear it.
5
只会运用有形的形体，而不懂得无形的神韵，哪能够真正得到读书弹琴的乐趣？
If we employ the form but not the spirit, how will we ever know the delight of books and zithers?
用心去看，用心去听，你便能发现天地间到处都是无字书，无弦琴音。
If you see and hear with the mind, you'll discover that everywhere there are wordless books and stringless zithers.

心无物欲乾坤静，坐有琴书便是仙

The head free of desire quiets heaven and earth,
A home with books and music becomes a magic kingdom

1
能做到对物质欲望不再贪求，
If the heart is free of material desires,
2
胸襟自然就能像秋天的天空一样晴朗，碧绿的海洋一样开阔。
It is an autumn sky, a vast sea.
3
能体会琴书生活的乐趣，
If the home has music and books,
4
周边即能变成山林石室一样的清静；有如生活在海外仙境的快乐自在。
It is a rocky hideaway, a magic kingdom.
心无物欲，方寸之间都是海阔天空。淡泊生活而能自得其乐，即能体会周边每一事物的美妙之处。
If you free yourself Of material desires, a square inch can be as vast as the sea and the sky. If you maintain a simple lifestyle, subtle joys can be found in everything around you.

知机真神乎，会趣明道矣

The wonder of knowing the mysteries, The wisdom of seeing delight

1
能体会周边微小事物的情趣，
To know the delight all around me,

就像五湖景色全都纳入我胸中。
Is to have the vistas of the world in a single inch.
2

能看透眼前的道理，千古以来的英雄都归我掌握。
To solve the mysteries before me, is to hold the heroes of the past in the palm of my hand.
3

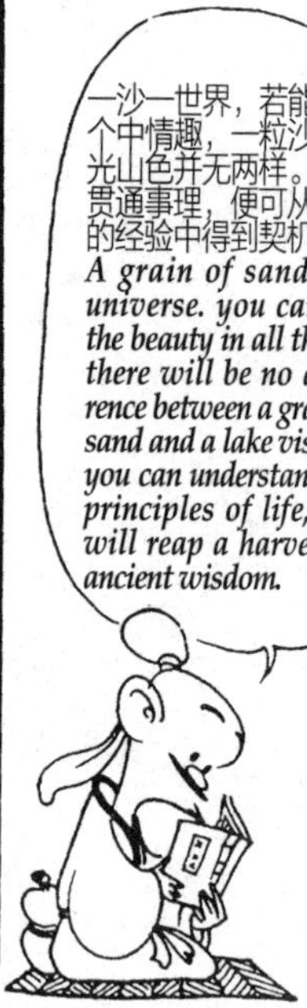
一沙一世界，若能体会个中情趣，一粒沙与湖光山色并无两样。若能贯通事理，便可从先人的经验中得到契机。
A grain of sand is a universe. you can see the beauty in all things, there will be no difference between a grain of sand and a lake vista. If you can understand the principles of life, you will reap a harvest of ancient wisdom.

万象皆空幻，达人须达观

The myriad appearances are empty illusions, The enlightened person must have comprehension

1
小河大地只不过是宇宙中的一粒微尘。
The structures of the earth reside in a speck of dust.
2
而人更是处在微尘中的微尘。
Let alone a speck with in a speck.

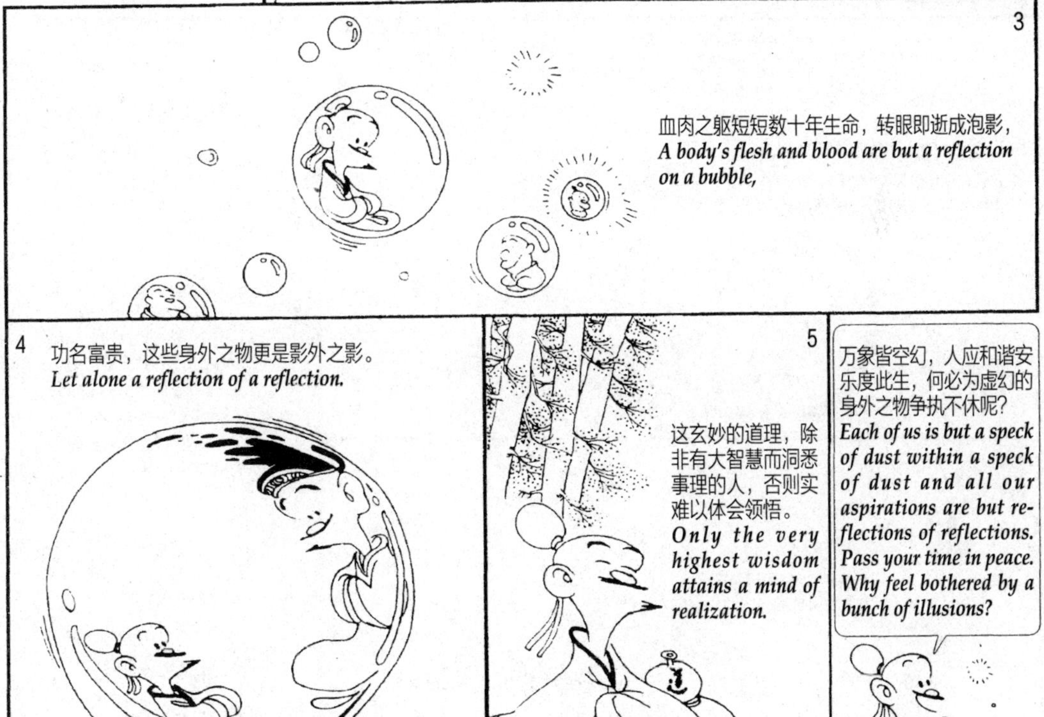
3
血肉之躯短短数十年生命，转眼即逝成泡影，
A body's flesh and blood are but a reflection on a bubble,
4
功名富贵，这些身外之物更是影外之影。
Let alone a reflection of a reflection.
5
这玄妙的道理，除非有大智慧而洞悉事理的人，否则实难以体会领悟。
Only the very highest wisdom attains a mind of realization.
万象皆空幻，人应和谐安乐度此生，何必为虚幻的身外之物争执不休呢？
Each of us is but a speck of dust within a speck of dust and all our aspirations are but reflections of reflections. Pass your time in peace. Why feel bothered by a bunch of illusions?

泡沫人生，何争名利

In the bubbl'e that is life, Why fight over fame and fortune

石火光中争长竞短，
To argue about who's best in the light of a flint spart,
我的气质比你高。
I've got character.
我的才华比你好。
I've got talent.
1
能有多少光阴可用?
How long will the light endure?
胡说!
You do not!
我赢了。
I win.
2

我才是真正的强者。
I'm tougher than you are.
我比你还强。
Are not.
在小如蜗牛角般的狭小空间争雌雄，
To fight about who's stronger while standing on a snail's antennae...
3
地球，在宇宙中只是一粒生埃；人生，在宇宙中只是一刹那。在短暂的人生中，应好好体会生的美妙，而不是把时间花在竞长短、争雌雄。
The earth is but a speck in the universe, and life is but an instant in eternity. In your short time here, do your best to see the subtle beauties of life instead of arguing about who's best and who's strongest.
4
嘻嘻嘻嘻
Hee hee hee hee.
能有多大世界可争?
How big is your world?

广狭长短，由于心念

Narrow or broad, short or long, they're all from the thoughts of the mind

1
日子过得好快哦！
The days go by so quickly!
日子过得好慢哦……
Easy for you to say...
时间的长短全在于个人的想法；
Duration and brevity stem from a thought.

2
好宽好大的房子哦！
What a huge manor!
我还是觉得太小了点。
It still seems a little too small...
空间的宽窄全在于个人的感觉。
Broad and narrow are related to the mind.

3
能够忙里偷闲的人，一天比千年还长久；
For one who finds leisure in work, a single day is a thousand ages;

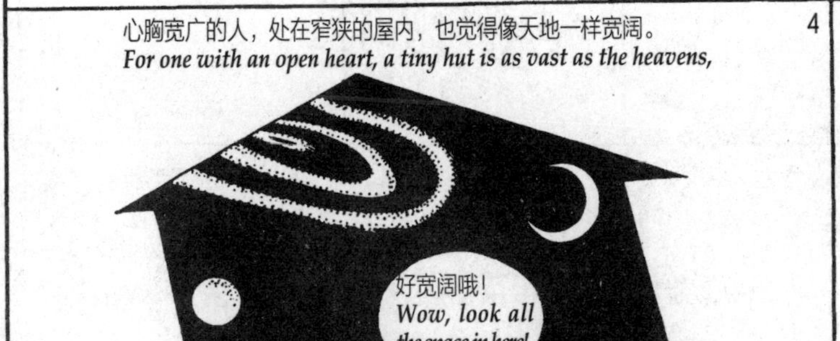
4
心胸宽广的人，处在窄狭的屋内，也觉得像天地一样宽阔。
For one with an open heart, a tiny hut is as vast as the heavens,
好宽阔哦！
Wow, look all the space in here!

时空的感受因人而异。心境若能修闲，则事事从容有余；心胸若能宽平，则海阔天空任我遨游。
The perception of time and space differs from person to person. If you are relaxed inside, there will be time enough for everything. If you keep an open mind the entire breadth of the world is yours fo renjoying.

与闲云为友，以风月为家

I make friends with the leisurely clouds and take the scenery as my home

1
长满松树的山涧边，拄着手杖独自散步；
With cane in hand, he walks alone along a pine-covered valley;
2
所站立的地方，云雾围绕着破旧的衣袍。
And where he stands, clouds gather to his tattered clothes.
3
在竹影稀疏的窗户外，枕着书本高卧而眠；
Beneath a bamboo window, he sleeps deeply with books for a pillow;
4
醒来时月光的寒意已侵入破旧的毛毡里。
And when he wakes, the moon penetrates his chilly blanket.
“与闲云为友，以风月为家”这种极美的情趣，不需要什么条件，任何人都能获得。
Little is needed to enjoy the subtle charm of nature. Anyone can experience it.

隐者无荣辱，道义无炎凉

Recluses have no honor or disgrace, Morality knows neither hot nor cold

宠辱不惊……
Sticks and stones may...
退隐山林的高士没有虚荣得失的心理。
Living alone in the forest, there is no honor or disgrace;
1

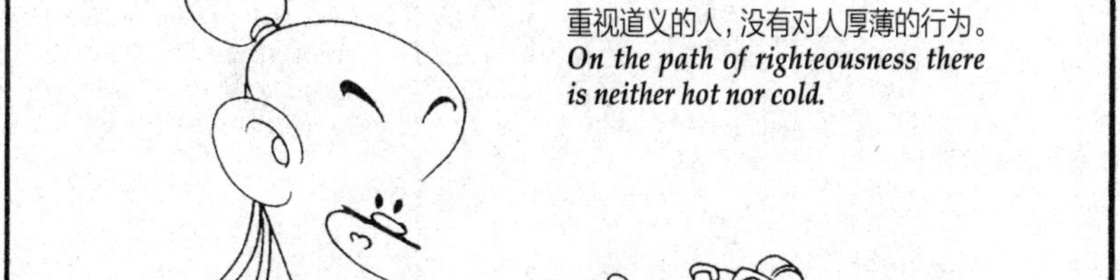
2
有钱的没钱的都一视同仁，通通是我的好朋友！
Rich or poor, you are all my good friends!
重视道义的人，没有对人厚薄的行为。
On the path of righteousness there is neither hot nor cold.

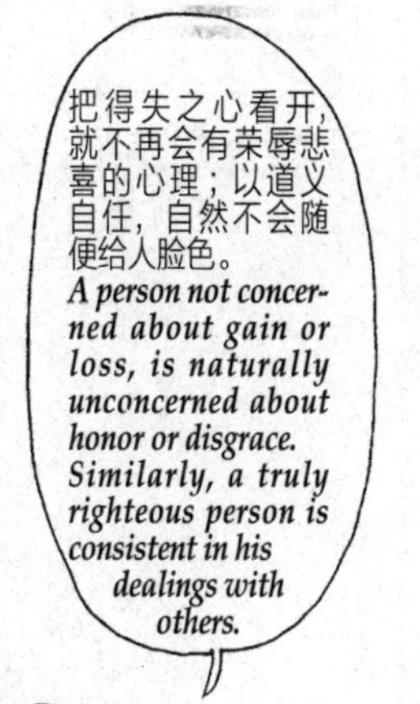
把得失之心看开，就不再会有荣辱悲喜的心理；以道义自任，自然不会随便给人脸色。
A person not concerned about gain or loss, is naturally unconcerned about honor or disgrace. Similarly, a truly righteous person is consistent in his dealings with others.

隐者高明，省事平安

The reclusive one is intelligent, Reducing tasks brings peace

1
夸耀自己的名声不如避讳自己的名声来得意味深长。
Fleeing fame is more delightful than promoting it;
我才高八斗，诗、书、画样样都很行。
There is really nothing I can't do well.
¡¡¡
2
好。
Sure.
这个拜托你写吧。
Could you copy this in your fine calligraphy please?
3
我也劳驾您代为效劳了。
I have one as well. Would you mind?
行行行，没有问题。
No, no, not at all.

4
熟练事理，不如省事来得安闲自在。
Reducing tasks is more relaxing than being skilled at tasks.
我文思如涌，下笔如流，马上就写好了。
Not only am I good, but I'm fast. Be done in just a moment.

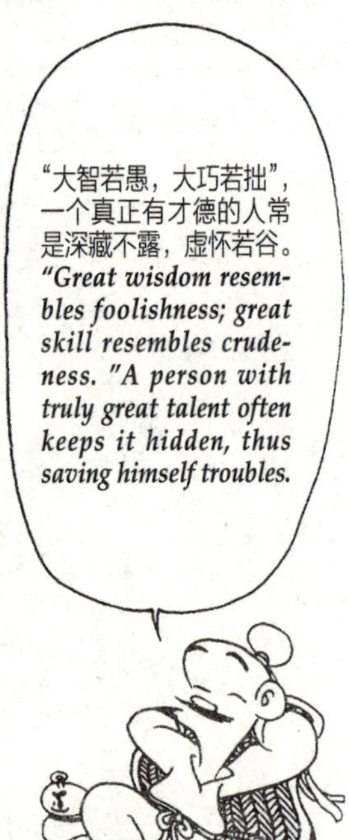
"大智若愚，大巧若拙"，一个真正有才德的人常是深藏不露，虚怀若谷。
"Great wisdom resembles foolishness; great skill resembles crudeness. "A person with truly great talent often keeps it hidden, thus saving himself troubles.

超越喧寂，悠然自适

To transcend splendor and solitude, To be at comfort anywhere

1
爱静的人，观赏白云和奇石，即能悟出宇宙玄妙的哲理。
A lover of solitude sees the wonder in white clouds and curious rocks.
2
喜欢繁华富贵的人，听到美妙的歌声，看到婀娜的舞蹈，就会忘了所有的疲倦。
A seeker of splendor forgets his cares in clear singing and clever dancing.

3
只有了悟天地之道怡然自得的人，没有喧闹或寂寞，也没有繁华或衰败，所到之处无不是能悠然自得的天地。
Only the self-sufficient man is without splendor or solitude, so wherever he goes is a comfortable patch of the sky.
这个很不错。
This is nice.
能了悟事理的人，凡事处之泰然，怡然自得，心不为境所迁，是逍遥的至高境界。
Being carefree and at ease means not letting circumstance influence you. If you are happy inside, you will be happy anywhere.
这个也非常好。
This isn't bad, either.

得道无牵系，静躁两无关

Enlightened ones have no attachments, Quiet and calm make no difference

一片孤云从山谷中飘出，它的去留毫无牵系；
Lonely cloud emerging from cliffs, no attachment to going or staying;
1

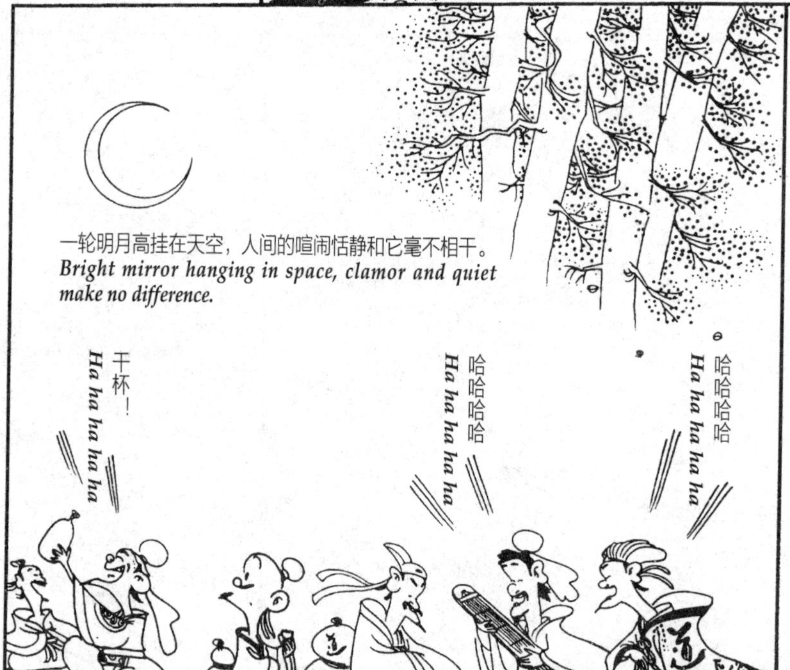
一轮明月高挂在天空，人间的喧闹恬静和它毫不相干。
Bright mirror hanging in space, clamor and quiet make no difference.
干杯！
Ha ha ha ha ha
哈哈哈哈
Ha ha ha ha
哈哈哈哈
Ha ha ha ha
2

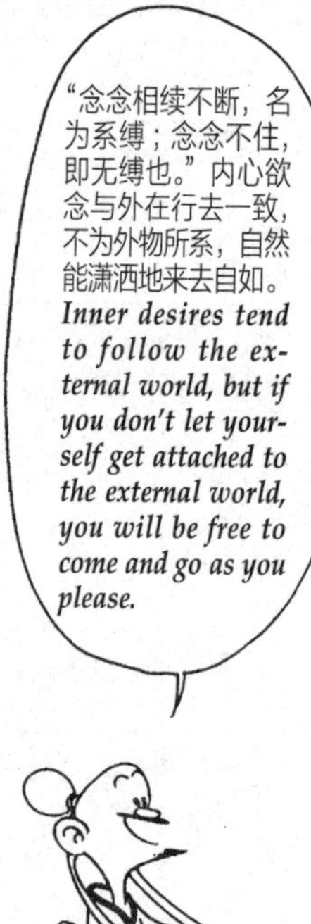
"念念相续不断，名为系缚；念念不住，即无缚也。"内心欲念与外在行去一致，不为外物所系，自然能潇洒地来去自如。
Inner desires tend to follow the external world, but if you don't let yourself get attached to the external world, you will be free to come and go as you please.

理出于易，道不在远
Understanding is found in simplicity, Enlightenment isn't far away

1
禅师说：
In Zen, it is said:
饿了就吃饭，累了就睡觉。
When hungry come and eat some food, when tired come and sleep.
2
论作诗要旨的人说：
In poetry, it is said:
眼前的景致要描写得平易顺口。
Intricate scenes before the eyes are set in common tongue.
3
最平凡的事物往往藏着最高深的道理。
The highest profundity is hidden in the most mundane;
4
最困难的事物往往须从最简易的地方着手。
The utmost difficulty should be approached from utmost simplicity.
日常生活即是道，把握眼前所见所接触的一切事物，体会其中的道理，所获得的启发即是最真切的学问。
The Dao is found in daily life. Grasp the things near at hand and experience their inherent principles. The insights thus gained are the most genuine kind of learning.
5
有意求道者反而离道远；
The one of ambition goes seeking far away;
Dao
6
无心道者反而离道近。
The one of no-mind, finds it right nearby.

动静合宜，出入无碍

Movement and stillness come with ease, Leaving and entering without obstruction

1
水淙淙不停地流着，而四周却悄然无声……
Water flows, yet the place is without a sound;
2
使人得到处于喧闹之中而感到寂静的趣味。
In coming to a boisterous place, one finds the charm of solitude.
嗨！
Hey!
哗
Ha ha
肉

3
山势高耸而云雾犹能来去自如，
The hill is high, yet the clouds do not obstruct,
4
使人领悟从有我进入无我境界的玄机。
In realizing external being, one enters the wonder of nothingness.
若心能定静，就不会执著于外相，则万物万象随心转，这就达到了物我合一，无我忘我的超然境界。
If you can still your mind, you won't be at the mercy of the external world, and instead, all things will revolve around you.
This is becoming one with the external world, a transcendent realm of self-forgetting.

执著是苦海，解脱是仙乡

Holding on means a sea of suffering, Letting go means a land of paradise

1
山林本是胜地，但一迷恋便成了庸俗喧闹的地方；
Mountains and forests are wonderful places, but with attachment, they become a market or court;
2
书画本是高雅的技艺，但一耽溺迷恋便有市侩气。
Calligraphy and painting are elegant tasks, but with infatuation, they become products for sale.
3
心灵若能不受外物污染，则在充满欲望的境地仍犹如人间仙境；
So to an unpolluted mind, the world of desire is a city of angels;
4
心里若有系恋，则快乐幸福的人间仙境也会变成苦海。
But to a mind with attachments, the realm of pleasures becomes a sea of suffering.
欲得净土，当净其心；随其心净，即佛土净。若内心能保持纯净无染，则所到之处无不是人间仙境。
To reach the pure land, purify your mind. When the mind is pure, the Buddha-realm is pure. If you can maintain a pure mind, everywhere you go will be a paradise.

卧云弄月，绝俗超尘

Sleeping and playing in nature, Escaping the dusty world

1
在芦花纷飞下，以雪地为床而卧，以浮云为帐而眠，
Reclining beneath a cover of reed flowers, with a bed of snow and a canopy of clouds...
2
可以保全得一颗清明纯净的本心。
Preserves in one a store of refreshing air.

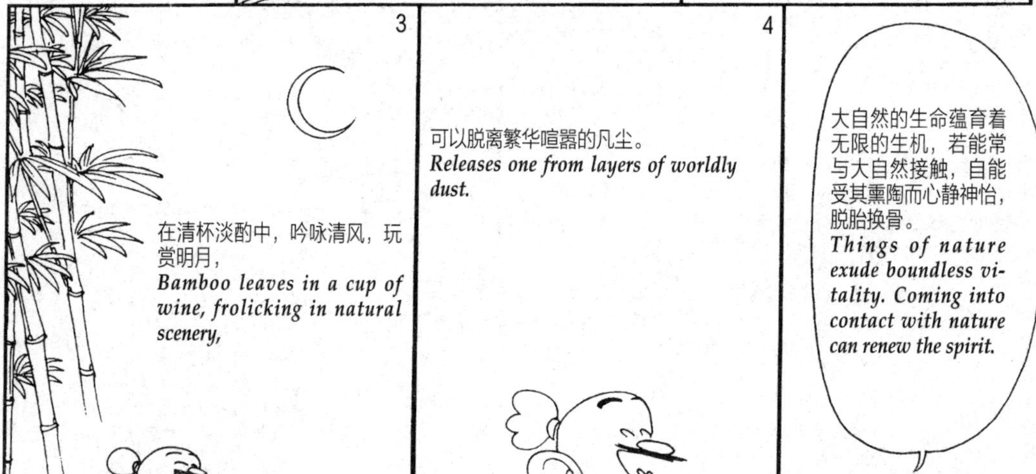
3
在清杯淡酌中，吟咏清风，玩赏明月，
Bamboo leaves in a cup of wine, frolicking in natural scenery,
4
可以脱离繁华喧嚣的凡尘。
Releases one from layers of worldly dust.
大自然的生命蕴育着无限的生机，若能常与大自然接触，自能受其熏陶而心静神怡，脱胎换骨。
Things of nature exude boundless vitality. Coming into contact with nature can renew the spirit.

云中世界，静里乾坤

A world among clouds, A universe in tranquillity

1
在竹篱旁听到鸡啼狗叫，恍如置身仙境。
Beneath a bamboo fence, I heard the barking of dogs and cackling of chickens and suddenly seemed to be in a world among clouds.

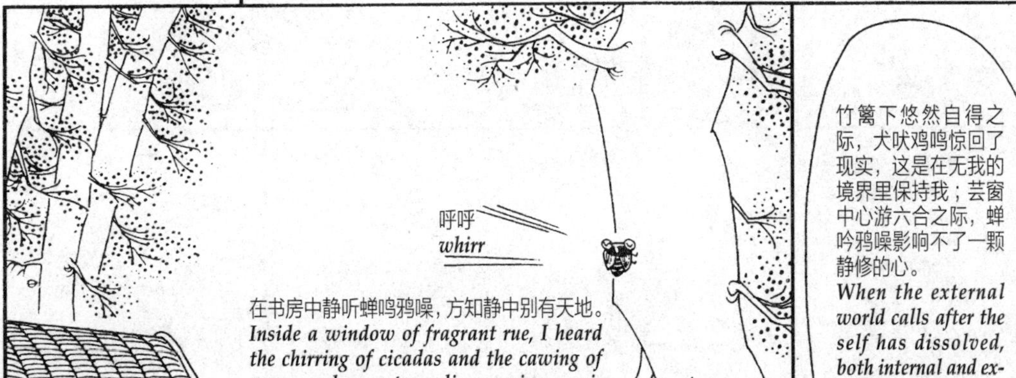
呼呼
whirr
在书房中静听蝉鸣鸦噪，方知静中别有天地。
Inside a window of fragrant rue, I heard the chirring of cicadas and the cawing of crows and came to realize a universe within tranquillity.
2
竹篱下悠然自得之际，犬吠鸡鸣惊回了现实，这是在无我的境界里保持我；芸窗中心游六合之际，蝉吟鸦噪影响不了一颗静修的心。
When the external world calls after the self has dissolved, both internal and external worlds come sharply into focus.

不希荣达，不畏权势

No hope for splendor, No fear of power

我不希冀获得荣华富贵，
I do not hope for splendor,
1
2
则何必担忧利禄的诱惑呢?
So why worry of the bait of emolument and status?

我不与人争逐名利权位，则何必畏惧仕途上的重重危机呢?
I do not contend for advancement, so why fear the pitfalls of officialdom?
3

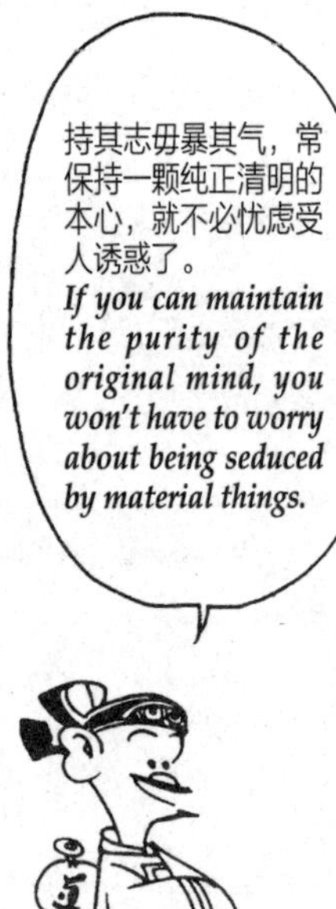
持其志毋暴其气，常保持一颗纯正清明的本心，就不必忧虑受人诱惑了。
If you can maintain the purity of the original mind, you won't have to worry about being seduced by material things.

圣境之下，调心养神

An inspirational environment, Attuning the mind, cultivating the spirit

1
徜徉在山林泉石之间，世俗名利之心就会渐渐忘去。
Wandering among mountains, springs, and rocks, my worldly mind gradually ceases to be.
2
潜心研求于诗书图画之内，庸俗的气质就会消失无形。
Lingering in poetry, calligraphy, and paintings, my vulgar side slowly dissolves.
3
所以君子虽不会沉迷于所好的事物，而丧失本来的志气，
So although a gentleman does not damage his character through material amusements,
4
也常要借所遇的事物来调养身心。
Yet he uses his environment to reattune his mind.
自然美景可荡涤尘心，诗书图画可开阔视野，使气质品格提升。
The beauty of nature cleanses the spirit; poetry, calligraphy, and paintings expand our horizons and elevate our character.

春之繁华，不若秋之清爽

Better the brisk air of autumn than the vibrancy of spring

1
春天的景色繁华美丽，令人心神安详舒适；
The scene on a spring day is vibrant and thriving, opening the mind and freeing the spirit;

2
不过却不如秋天云淡风清，兰花芬芳，桂花清香，
But how much better the crisp breeze and white clouds of an autumn day infused with the fragrance of orchids and sweet osmanthus,

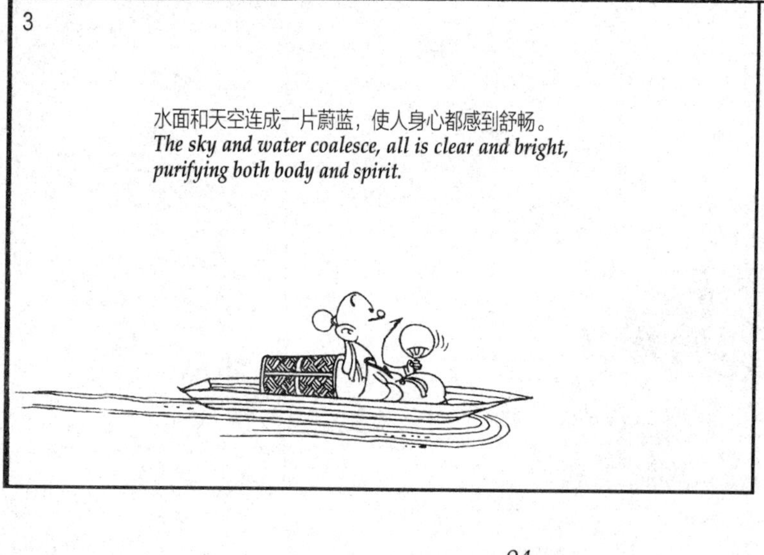
3
水面和天空连成一片蔚蓝，使人身心都感到舒畅。
The sky and water coalesce, all is clear and bright, purifying both body and spirit.

春之繁华不若秋之清爽；年轻时为了物欲而冲刺奋斗，不若中年后突破俗情而淡泊。
The spring is vibrant, but how much better the briskness of autumn. In youth, we struggle in the fight for material things, but how much better the refinement and simplicity of old age.

得诗家真趣，悟禅教玄机

Achieve the true sentiments of a poet, Realize the mysterious truths of Zen

不识字但说起话来却有诗意的人，可说是领悟了诗人作诗的真正趣味。
To be illiterate and yet possess the spirit of poetry is to have achieved the tree sentiments of a poet;
春天月夜雨声蛙！
You should hear the flogs on a spring night beneath the moon!
1

不曾参过禅偈但说起话来却有禅机的人，可说是已领悟了禅宗教义的高深哲理。
To have never studied a verse and yet possess the spirit of Zen is to have realized the mysterious troths of Zen.
你度人成佛，我度石头成佛！
You turn people into Buddhas, and I turn rocks into Buddhas!
2

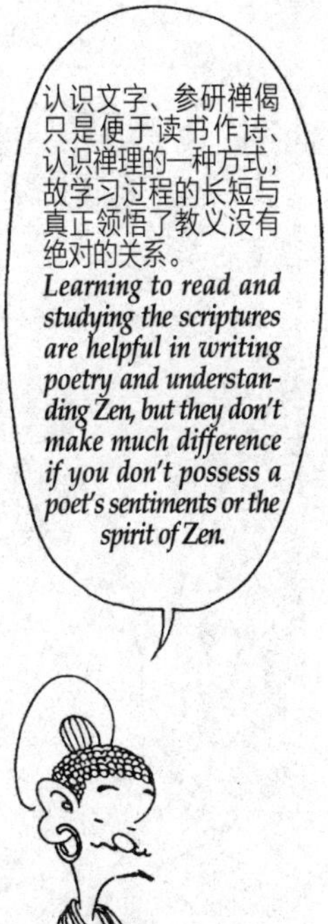
认识文字、参研禅偈只是便于读书作诗、认识禅理的一种方式，故学习过程的长短与真正领悟了教义没有绝对的关系。
Learning to read and studying the scriptures are helpful in writing poetry and understanding Zen, but they don't make much difference if you don't possess a poet's sentiments or the spirit of Zen.

像由心生，像随心灭

An image is born, issued from the mind
An image is gone, following the mind

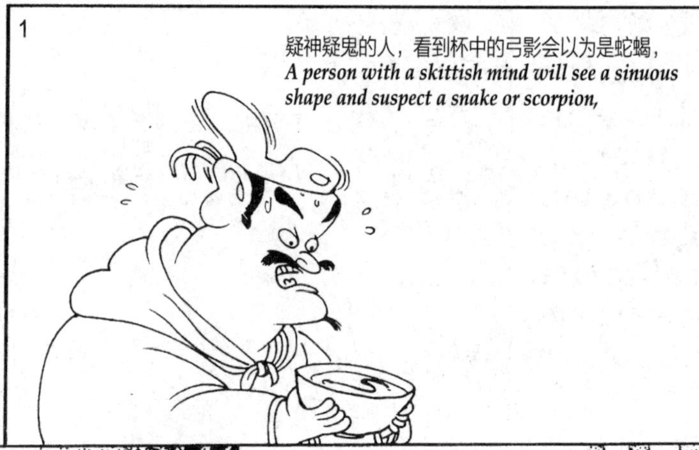
1
疑神疑鬼的人，看到杯中的弓影会以为是蛇蝎，
A person with a skittish mind will see a sinuous shape and suspect a snake or scorpion,

2
看到暗处的石头会以为是老虎，他的周边充满着疑惧杀机。
See a slanted rock and think it a crouching tiger.
All around him is a murderous atmosphere.
3
内心安闲和平的人，石虎与他相处也会像海鸥一样温驯，
For a person with a tranquil mind, the vicious Shi Hu can be a harmless seagull,
4
蛙声可当成悦耳的音乐，他所接触之处，到处都是祥和之地。
The sound of frogs can be an orchestra. Everywhere he goes, he sees the harmony of things.
心念若不能定静，见风吹草动即生疑惧。心念若能静定不动，则不为物所惑而能洞见真相。
If you cannot quiet your mind, the rustling of the wind and swaying of the grass will fill you with suspicion and terror. But if your mind is tranquil and at ease, you will see the harmony of everything around you.

来去自如，融通自在
Coming and going at will, Dissolved in confident ease

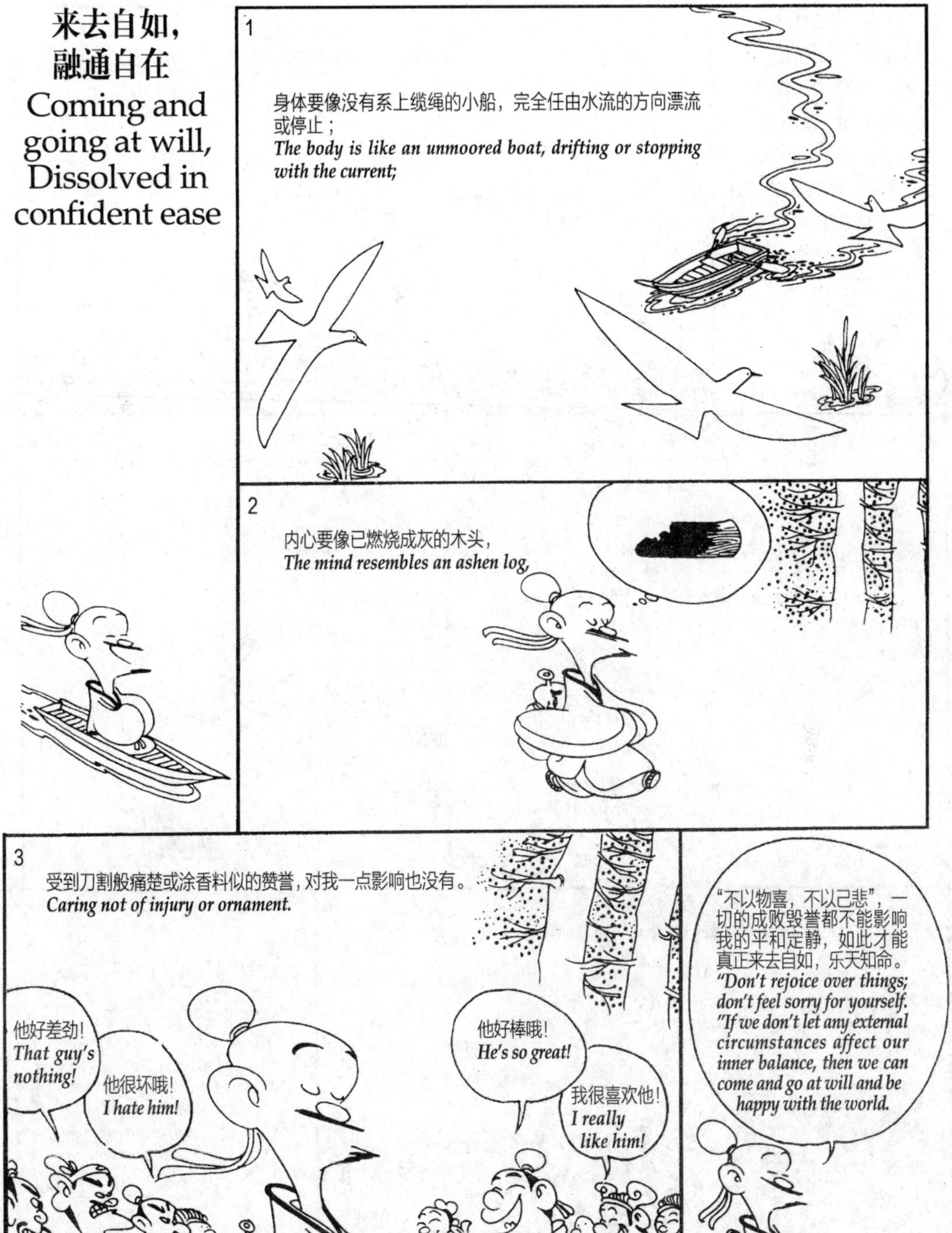
1
身体要像没有系上缆绳的小船，完全任由水流的方向漂流或停止；
The body is like an unmoored boat, drifting or stopping with the current;
2
内心要像已燃烧成灰的木头，
The mind resembles an ashen log,
3
受到刀割般痛楚或涂香料似的赞誉，对我一点影响也没有。
Caring not of injury or ornament.
他好差劲！
That guy's nothing!
他很坏哦！
I hate him!
他好棒哦！
He's so great!
我很喜欢他！
I really like him!
"不以物喜，不以己悲"，一切的成败毁誉都不能影响我的平和定静，如此才能真正来去自如，乐天知命。
"Don't rejoice over things; don't feel sorry for yourself." If we don't let any external circumstances affect our inner balance, then we can come and go at will and be happy with the world.

欲心生邪念，虚心生正念

An acquisitive mind breeds deviant thoughts, A vacuous mind breeds decent thoughts

1
心中充满欲望的人，他的心湖波涛汹涌……
One with desires inside is a billowing wintry lake,

2
即使处在山林中也感受不到寂静之趣。
And even in the mountain forests he finds no tranquillity.
真无聊啊……
This is so boring...
3
心中没有物欲的人，在酷热中，心田也能感觉清凉，
One with vacuity inside is cool amid scorching heat,
静
Cool

4
即使处在喧哗中也不会感到扰攘。
And even in the market and court he knows no clamor.
哗哗
Ha ha
哗哗
Ooo hoo
哗哗
Wa ha
哗！
Yap yap
心中宁静祥和，不生物欲贪念，虽处朝市也不觉喧闹，虽处污晦的名利场中也不受侵染。
If your mind is serene and calm, that is free of greed and yearnings, then even among crowds you won't feel bothered, and even in vile places you won't be tainted.

富者多忧，贵者多险
The wealthy have many worries, The noble have many dangers

1
财富愈多的人，愈怕失去财物；
He who keeps much has much to lose;
2
由此可知富有的人不如贫穷的人无忧无虑。
So We see that poverty holds fewer worries than wealth.
两袖清风不怕抢也不怕偷。
With empty hands and an empty heart I go.
3
地位爬得愈高的人愈容易跌倒；
He who climbs high has far to fall;
哇！
Ahhh!
4
由此可知显贵的人不如卑贱的人能常保平安。
So we see that lowliness holds more stability than status.
钱财愈多愈容易招惹祸端，“树大招风、名高丧身”，所以地位尊贵反而不如卑贱的人常保自在无虑。
The more wealth you have, the more you invite disaster. "A tall tree invites typhoons, a big name destroys the self."

处世流水落花，身心皆得自在

Live life like flowing water, drooping flowers, The body and mind must always be at ease

1
有位高僧说：“竹影扫台阶，但尘土并不因而扬起。”
A virtuous monk of old once said, “Bamboo shadows sweep across the steps, but the dust doesn't move.
2
“月影深入沼泽，而水面并不因而起波纹。”
“The lunar orb penetrates a pond, but the water shows no trace.”
3
有位儒者说：“任由水流湍急，而四周环境依然安详宁静。”
One of our Confucians said, “Flowing water rushes along, but the surroundings remain still;”
4
“花瓣虽然纷纷凋落，而意兴依然安闲自在。”
“Flowers droop and the petals flutter, but my thoughts are all at ease.”
5
人若常抱这种意念来待人处事，则身心将是多么地自在啊！
If a person can maintain this frame of mind in dealing with the world and handling affairs, how carefree life will be!
君子应随缘而居，事情来了就全力以赴，事情过去了也要平心静气，勿患得患失，才不失本性。
We should change with circumstances but not be at the mercy of our surroundings, only in this way can we preserve our original natures.

处世忘世，超物乐天

Living in the world, forget the world, Transcending things, enioy nature

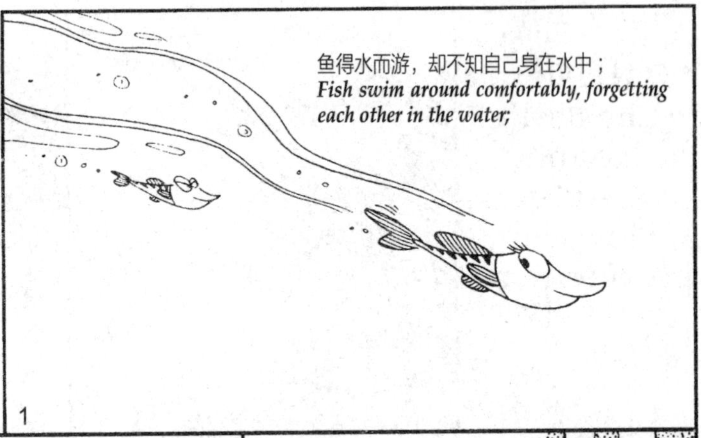
1
鱼得水而游，却不知自己身在水中；
Fish swim around comfortably, forgetting each other in the water;

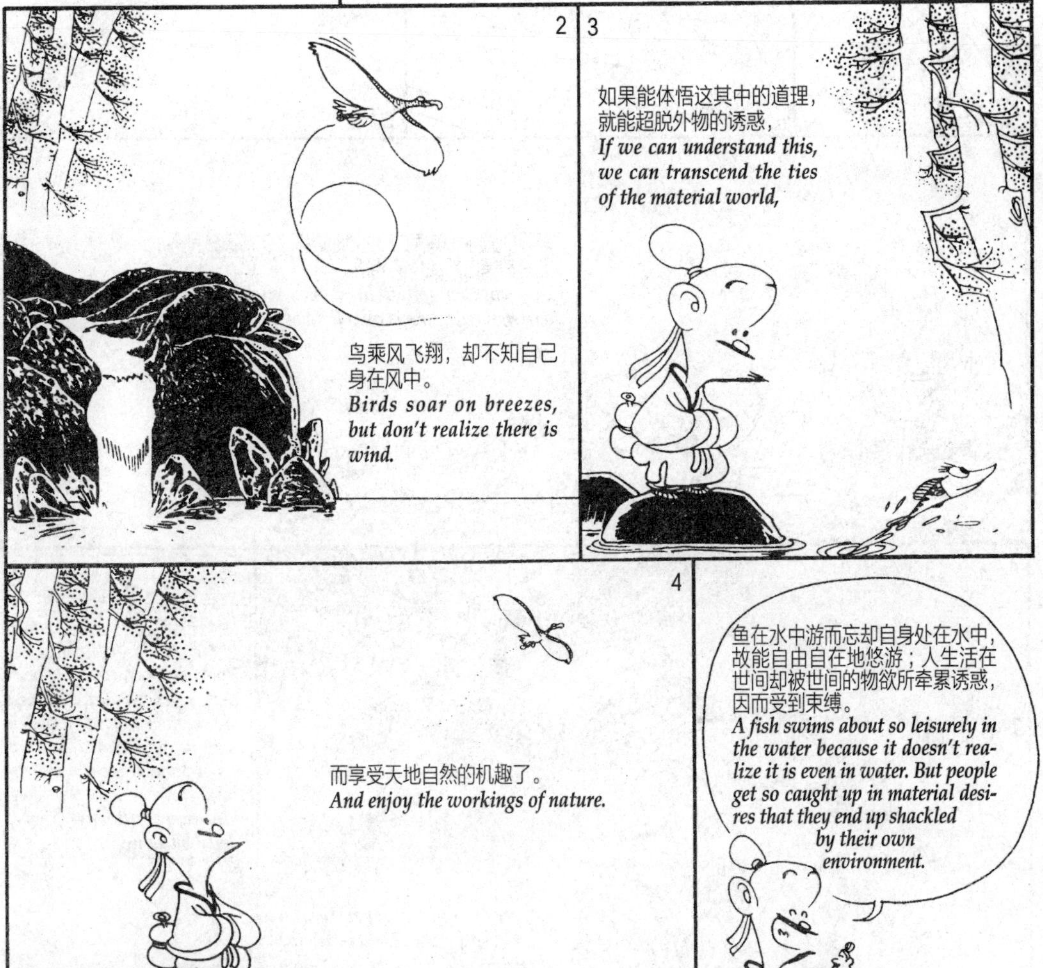
2
鸟乘风飞翔，却不知自己身在风中。
Birds soar on breezes, but don't realize there is wind.
3
如果能体悟这其中的道理，就能超脱外物的诱惑，
If we can understand this, we can transcend the ties of the material world,
而享受天地自然的机趣了。
And enjoy the workings of nature.
4
鱼在水中游而忘却自身处在水中，故能自由自在地悠游；人生活在世间却被世间的物欲所牵累诱惑，因而受到束缚。
A fish swims about so leisurely in the water because it doesn't realize it is even in water. But people get so caught up in material desires that they end up shackled by their own environment.

人生本无常，盛衰何可恃

Life itself does not endure, How can prosperity be counted on

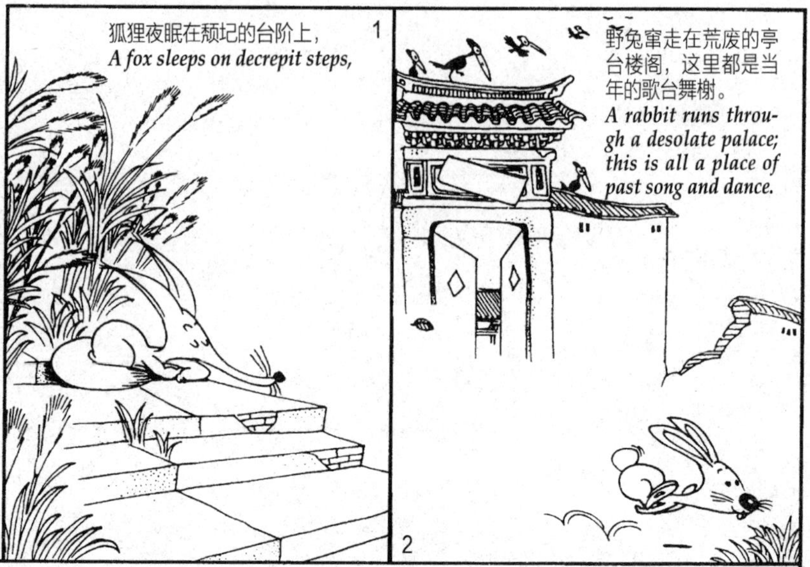
1
狐狸夜眠在颓圮的台阶上，
A fox sleeps on decrepit steps,
2
野兔窜走在荒废的亭台楼阁，这里都是当年的歌台舞榭。
A rabbit runs through a desolate palace; this is all a place of past song and dance.

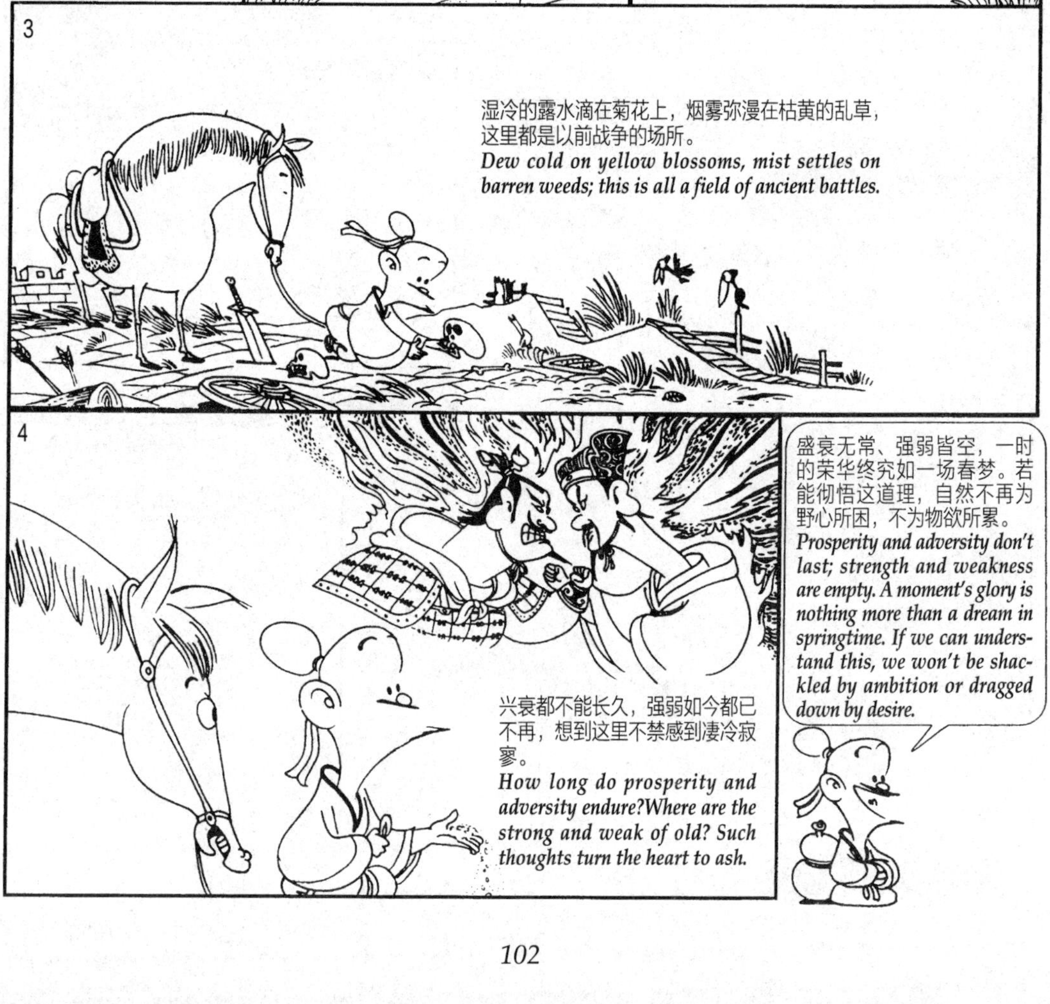
3
湿冷的露水滴在菊花上，烟雾弥漫在枯黄的乱草，这里都是以前战争的场所。
Dew cold on yellow blossoms, mist settles on barren weeds; this is all a field of ancient battles.
4
兴衰都不能长久，强弱如今都已不再，想到这里不禁感到凄冷寂寥。
How long do prosperity and adversity endure? Where are the strong and weak of old? Such thoughts turn the heart to ash.
盛衰无常、强弱皆空，一时的荣华终究如一场春梦。若能彻悟这道理，自然不再为野心所困，不为物欲所累。
Prosperity and adversity don't last; strength and weakness are empty. A moment's glory is nothing more than a dream in springtime. If we can understand this, we won't be shackled by ambition or dragged down by desire.

宠辱不惊，去留无意

Scorn or favor brings no surprise, Going or staying makes no difference

1
你好棒哦！
You're wonderful!
是吗？
Is that right?
2
你好菜哦！
You're despicable!
是吗？
Is that right?
3
!
受到荣宠或屈辱勿喜也勿悲，依旧闲看庭前花。
Favor or scorn brings no surprise, leisurely watching the flowers blossom and fade before the court.

4
恭喜你又升官了。
Congratulations, you've been promoted!
是吗？
Really?
5
你被开除了。
You're fired!
是吗？
Really?
6
升官或贬谪勿介意，因为富贵就像浮云一样，时聚时散。
Going or staying makes no difference, peacefully watching the clouds curl and unfold in the sky.
!
不要被外来的毁誉、荣辱改变了心性。职位的去留升迁就像浮云般有聚有散，毫不执著留恋。
Don't let being honored or disdained affect your mood.
Positions come and go like floating clouds and aren't worth dwelling on.

苦海茫茫，回头是岸

The sea of suffering is vast and far, Turn your head to the other shore

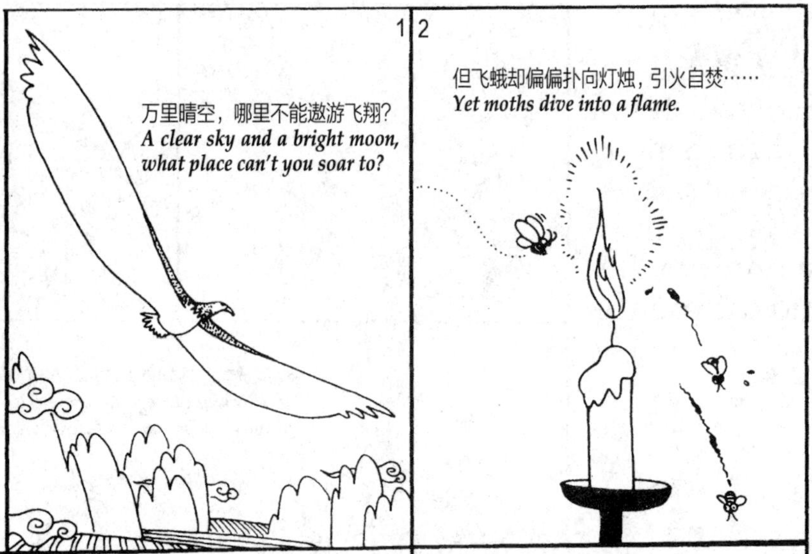
1
万里晴空，哪里不能遨游飞翔？
A clear sky and a bright moon, what place can't you soar to?
2
但飞蛾却偏偏扑向灯烛，引火自焚……
Yet moths dive into a flame.

3
清泉绿草，哪种不能饮食果腹？
A clear spring and green herbs, what can't you eat or drink?
4
但鸱鸮却偏喜欢吃腐臭的鼠肉……
Yet crows prefer putrid rats...
5
唉！世上能不成为飞蛾、鸱鸮的人有几个呢？
Alas!How many in the world do not become moths or crows?
海阔天空可任人翱游，而一般人却把自己紧锁在狭小的空间里，盲目追求名位利禄，就如同飞蛾引火自焚。
With the world so vast, you can soar off to anywhere at all, yet most people lock themselves in a tiny little space, blindly pursuing wealth and status just hke the moth attracted to a flame.

求心内之佛，却心外之法

Seeking the Buddha on the inside, Spurning the dharmas on the outside

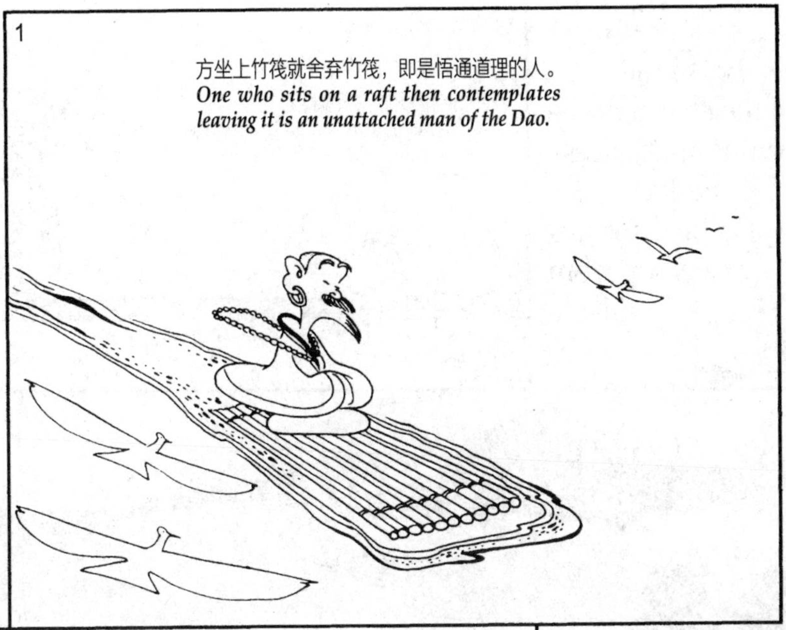
1
方坐上竹筏就舍弃竹筏，即是悟通道理的人。
One who sits on a raft then contemplates leaving it is an unattached man of the Dao.

2
若是骑在驴上却又在找驴，终究成不了开悟的禅师。
One who rides a mule then goes seeking a mule will never be a master of Zen.

船筏只是借以到达目的的工具，故应得鱼忘筌、得兔忘蹄、得意忘言。人的自身，一切俱足，往外去追觅真理，往往是愈追愈远了。
A raft is simply a tool to get you to your destination. After getting the fish, forget the net; after getting the rabbit, forget the snare, after getting the meaning, forget the words. The truth is right in front of you, so there's no need to go off in search of it.

野趣丰处，诗兴自涌

In the charm of the wilds and places replete, Poetical springs well up from inside

1
作诗的灵感在灞陵桥上，
Poetic thoughts on Ba river bridge,

2
只要略起诗兴，山林峰峦即是广大的题材。
Softly voicing lines, woods and summits expand before me.
3
大自然的趣味就在湖边，
Charm of the wilds at a Jing lake bend,
4
一个人独自前往，便能体会到山川相映的美景。
Roaming all alone, the hills and rivers reflect back and forth.
敞开胸襟，纳入大自然之趣；山水花月，唯有心者得之。
Open you heart and let nature in, because only someone with an open heart can appreciate the mountains, waters, flowers, and moon.

在世出世，真空不空

Live in the world, transcend the world, The True Emptiness is not empty

1
能超越一切色相意识不为色相所迷惑，不一定能看透一切，
The Tree Emptiness is not empty;
2
是什么？
What's that?
执著于事物外在的形象，不能看清事物的本真，
Maintaining illusions is not the truth.
浪。
Waves.
3
错了，不是浪而是水！
Wrong. It's water!
4
对啊……浪只是假象，它的本真是水啊……
That's right.., it's just water appearing as waves...
破除事物形象的迷惑，也不一定能看清事物的本真。
Destroying illusions is also not the truth.

5
请问我佛如何解释这个道理呢：
Ask Sakyamuni for his opinion:
6
那就是身在世俗，但要有超脱世俗的胸怀，
Live in the world, but transcend it.
7
苦心营求私欲固然是一种痛苦，
Following desires is suffering,
8
而断绝一切欲念也是一种痛苦，
Severing desires is also suffering.
9
如何能执两用中，就端赖自己的体会和修持了。
Do what we do: rely on your own understanding and ability.
执著于物相或偏执于虚幻，都是违反自然真理，只有身在世俗中，而心怀超脱世俗之外，才是最高妙的处世之道。
Both living in illusions and emphasizing the unreality of illusions are contrary to the truth. To simultaneously live in the world and transcend it is the best way to get along.

毁誉褒贬，一任世情

Praise and slander, libel and fame, Resigned to all the world can give

1
饱经世故的人，完全任由人情世态反复无常，
One who has had his fill of the tastes of the world resigns himself to the vicissitudes of life...
我非你帮忙不可，请你替我做事。
I really need you. You must come out and work for me.
2
他总是懒得睁眼计较。
Too wearied to open his eyes.
现在不需要你了，请你滚！
I don't need you anymore. Get out of here!
3
看透人情冷暖的人，任随别人毁誉褒贬，
One who completely understands human sentiment accepts both praise and slander...
你好棒！
You're wonderful!
是吗？
Really?
4
你好差劲！
You're despicable!
是吗？
Really?
他自己只是点头称是而不动气。
With just a nod of his head.
一个人历经沧桑饱经人情冷暖，便能看透世情，对人情的反复无常、毁誉褒贬都能无动于衷。
One who has been tossed about in life comes to understand how people think and fortunes change.
Be at peace with yourself, and the world will be peaceful.

彻见自性，不必谈禅

He who knows his original nature has no patience for talk of Zen

1
本性证明的人，就是饿了吃饭，渴了喝水的人，
One whose original nature is crystal clear eats when hungry and drinks when thirsty...
什么是禅？
What is Zen?
肚子饿了就吃饭，疲倦了就睡觉。
Eating when hungry, sleeping when tired.

2
也都是为了调剂保持自己身心的健康。
Balancing body and mind.
3
而心地沉迷物欲的人，纵使是谈论禅理、推敲佛偈，
One whose mind is confused discusses Zen and expounds on scripture,
溪声便是广长舌，山色岂非清净身。
The sound of the valley is a long, broad tongue; how is the color of mountains not a purified body?
4
愈参愈不明白……
The more I read the less I understand...
也只是在玩弄浪费自己的精神智力。
Making a mess of his spirit.
不能从内在澄清自己的意念，而端求外在的潜修以参悟禅理，无异是缘木求鱼。
You can't purify the mind by attempting to crack the truths of Zen. That's like climbing a tree to get a fish.

真不离幻，雅不离俗

The genuine leaves not the illusory, The refined leaves not the mundane

1
黄金是从矿穴中挖掘出来的，宝玉是从石头中雕琢而成的，
Gold comes from mines, and jade is found in rock;
2
如果不经过幻化，就无法求得真实。
One can only seek the genuine in the illusory.
3
在饮酒的场合中，可遇着有道德的人，
The Dao is found in wine,

4
在声色场所也可能遇到神仙，虽是高雅也不能脱离凡俗。
And gods are met in flowers, the refined cannot be separated from the mundane.
弃绝俗世，则流于偏颇乖僻，结果难免随入世俗；应处身在世俗中而不坠入世俗。
Forsaking the mundane world and living an eccentric life on the edges of so ciety, it's difficult to avoid falling right back into the mundane. If, however, you choose to place yourself in the mundane world, you can rise above the mundane.

布茅蔬淡，颐养天和

A blanket of straw and vegetables plain nourish a natural harmony

1
能在粗布被窝里睡得香甜，
To slumber deeply under a blanket of coarse cloth,
2
即能体会天地中和平的气象。
Is to know the harmony of heaven and earth.

3
能在粗茶淡饭中感到满足，
To relish the taste of rice and pigweed soup,
4
即能体会淡泊生活的美妙。
Is to know the genuineness of a simple life.
能将物质生活降到最低，即能在精神生活中得到最大的满足，因为再无人有能力令你去做你不想做的事了。
If you can reduce material needs to their lowest level, you can achieve the greatest heights of spiritual happiness, because then no one can make you do what you don't want to do.

断绝思虑，光风霁月

To cut off all your worries, A sunny breeze, an after-rain moon

1
在狭小的屋中，若能捐弃一切思虑，
Inside a tiny hut, a thousand womes are gone;

2
哪还管他什么雕梁画栋，高耸入云的华厦？
Who cares about painted mansions as high as the clouds or beaded curtains as perfect as raindrops?
3
浅酌三杯后，心中或许能领会某些真趣，
After three cups, the truth complete has come,
酒
4
此时只知以素琴对月弹弦，
All I know are a plain zither playing to the moon...
5
短笛迎风吹奏，哪还管他那些烦人的俗务？
And a short flute singing to the breeze.
对酒当歌，人生几何？譬如朝露，去日苦多！人若能抛开思虑，即能真切体会享受人生。
If we can get rid of all our worries, we'll be able to experience and enjoy hfe to the fullest.

操持身心，收放自如

Minding the body and mind, Freedom in indulgence and restraint

人生要放任自己的身心，一切听由自然造化。
It's best to release the mind and body and blindly follow creation.
白居易说：
Bai Juyi oncc said:
1
人生要收敛自己的身心，寂静不动使之归于寂定。
It's best to restrain the mind and body and wholly return to tranquillity.
晁补之说：
Chao Buzhi said:
2

但过于放任而不加检束，则易流于狂妄放荡；
An indulgent person can slide into recklessness;
3
过于收敛而不知调剂，则易流于枯寂死沉。
A restrained person can lapse into boorishness.
4
只有善于操持自己身心，掌握重点，才能达到收放自如的境界。
Only the person who can manage his body and mind well can be as indulgent or tranquil as he pleases.
5
过于放任或过于收敛身心都失于偏颇乖违。执其中道而行，不偏不倚才能超凡入圣。
Overindul gence and too much restraint are both extreme behavior. Only by walking the middle path and not straying to either extreme can you transcend the ordinary and enter sageliness.

自然人心，融和一体
Nature and the mind, Harmonize as one

1
在雪花纷飞的夜晚，
On seeing a snowy night...
2
皎洁的明月高挂天空，使人的心境清明澄澈。
Or the moon in the sky, one's mood seems purified.
3
春风送暖天气和爽时，使人的意念平和融洽。
On feeling a springtime wind or warm air, one's thoughts seem harmonized.
4
由此可见，融为一体，没有间隙。
Creation and the mind interfuse with no space in between.
天地造化与人心原为一体，境随心转，心随物化，心中却除物欲则能得自然之趣。
Nature and the mind are origi nally one body; the environ ment changes with the turnings of the mind, and the mind changes with the trans formations of things. By elim inating material desires, we can get at the charm of nature.

雌雄妍丑，一时假相

Winner and loser, beautiful and ugly are just momentary illusions

1
演戏的人傅粉施朱，在化妆笔下赛美丑，
The players apply mascara and rouge, becoming pretty or ugly at the tip of a brush.

2
歌舞完毕观众散去，美丑在什么地方？
Finally the songs end and the crowds disperse; where are the pretty and ugly now?
3
对弈的人争前恐后，在下子之间比胜负，
The competitors vie for first and last, becoming winner or loser as the pieces fall,
胜！Checkmate!
负……Dam!
4
棋局赛完，棋子收了，胜败又在哪里？
Finally the games end and the pieces are collected; where are the winner and loser now?
戏台前扬扬得意，幕落后不过是位靠演戏维生的优人；棋盘上无往不利，局尽后仍须面对世俗的拂逆。
On stage, they are proud and elegant, but behind the curtain they are just actors trying to make a living. At the game board he beats all comers, but when the games are over, he still has to face the mundane world.

祸福苦乐，一念之差

Good and bad fortune, suffering and joy, There is only the difference of a single thought

1
人生的福祸都是由人的念头想法所造成的。
All good and bad fortune in life are created by the mind.

2
名利欲望太强烈就是火坑，贪婪爱恋之心太强烈就是苦海；
If desire for profit is too intense, it becomes a fiery pit, if gree attachment is too strong, it become a sea of suffering.
若抱持着一个澄净的念头就可使火海变成水池，得一念惊醒就可脱离苦海而到达极乐世界。
A single thought of purity, and the searing flames become a pond; a single thought of realization, and the boat ascends the Other Shore.
因此世尊说：
Therefore, Sakyamuni said:

3
念头稍有不同，所处的境界就有差别，人能不小心谨慎吗？
If one's thoughts change slightly, one's realm changes drastically. So can one not be but cautious?!
内心沉溺于贪爱，名利欲念太重，就易陷于罪恶的深渊，引火烧身。只要及时醒觉，就能脱离无边的苦海！
If the mind is mired in acquisitiveness, an desires for profit are too strong, it's easy to fall into the depths of vice. If we awaken to the truth in time, we can escape the boundless sea of suffering.

若要功夫深，铁杵磨成针

With quiet patience and constant discipline, A foot of iron is ground into a pin

1
绳子可以锯断木头，
A rope saw severs a log;
2
水滴可以穿透石头，
Drops of water penetrate rock a person studying the Dao must be persevering.

3
求学论道的人，若能有恒心毅力，凡事顺其自然而不强求，则必然水到渠成，瓜熟蒂落。
Water flows into existing channels; melons ripen then drop from the vine.

4
悟得真道的人都是能完全听任自然。
One who has attained the Dao follows the natural processes.
求学问道须勤加努力探求，泉水流到自然成为沟渠，瓜果成熟自然会脱蒂落下。
Pursuing enlightenment requires patience and perseverance. After enlightenment everything comes naturally.

雨后山色鲜，静夜钟声清

After a rain, the mountains seem fresh; In the night, a bell rings clear

1
雨后观看山色，会觉得景象更为清新美丽；
Observing mountain scenery after a ram, the wew seems freshly beautiful;

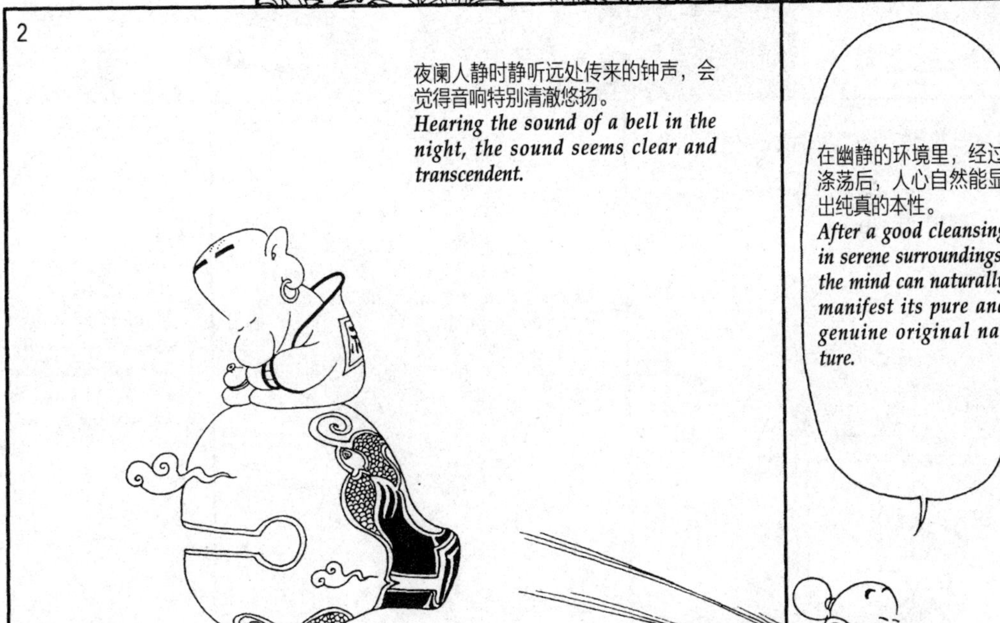
2
夜阑人静时静听远处传来的钟声，会觉得音响特别清澈悠扬。
Hearing the sound of a bell in the night, the sound seems clear and transcendent.
在幽静的环境里，经过涤荡后，人心自然能显出纯真的本性。
After a good cleansing in serene surroundings, the mind can naturally manifest its pure and genuine original nature.

雪夜读书夜清，登山远眺心旷

Snowstorm studying purifies the spirit, Hilltop vistos expond the mind

1
爬上高山远眺可以使人心胸开阔；
Climbing up high expands the mind,
2
面对着溪流可以使人意念悠远；
Studying on a snowy night purifies the spirit;

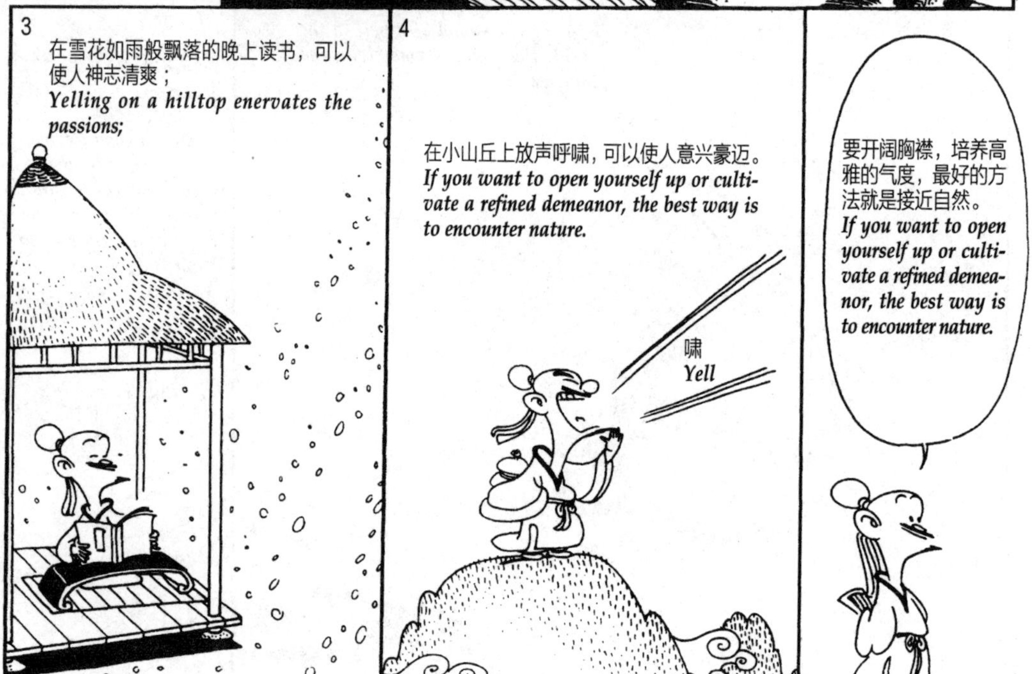
3
在雪花如雨般飘落的晚上读书，可以使人神志清爽；
Yelling on a hilltop enervates the passions;
4
在小山丘上放声呼啸，可以使人意兴豪迈。
If you want to open yourself up or cultivate a refined demeanor, the best way is to encounter nature.
啸
Yell
要开阔胸襟，培养高雅的气度，最好的方法就是接近自然。
If you want to open yourself up or cultivate a refined demeanor, the best way is to encounter nature.

万钟一发，存乎一心
A thousand gallons, a single hair, Each exists within the mind

1
心胸宽阔，
If the mind is expansive,
!
2
3
则万钟的财禄也会视如破坛瓦罐一样没有什么价值。
A thousand gallons is but a jugful.
酒
4
心胸狭隘……
If the mind is narrow...
5
则即使是毫发小事，也会视如车轮般重大。
A single hair is like a wagon wheel.
6
你滚开！别挡我的路！
Get out of my way!
心胸豁达开朗的人，凡事看得高远，不会被眼前利所蒙蔽。心胸狭隘的人，处处与人计较，所以往往成不了大事。
People with expansive minds are visionary and talented and aren't blinded by profit and gain. Narrow-minded people bicker over every little thing and will never accomplish great things.

就身了身，以物付物

Understand the self based on the self, Allow for things to take care of themselves

1
了然彻悟己身非我所能长久保有的人，
Only those who understand the self based on the self,

2
就不会任意要求天地万物都依顺自己的意思行事。
Can let the myriad things take care of the myriad things.

3
凡事皆能顺其自然，使天地万物各适其性自由发展，
Only those who return nature to nature,

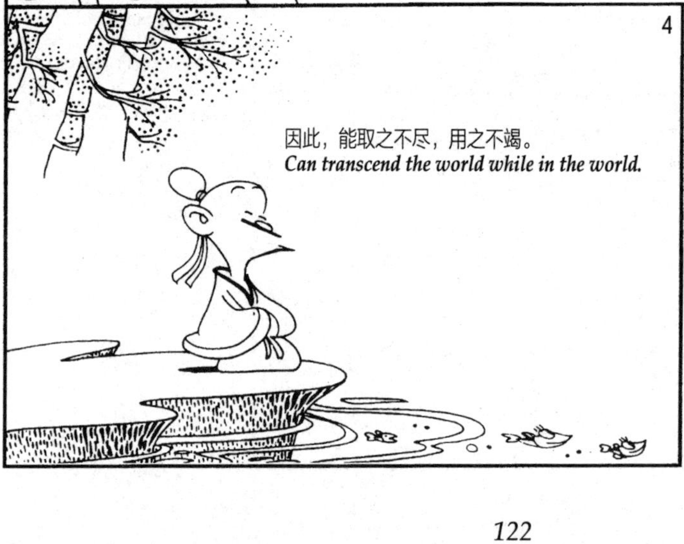
4
因此，能取之不尽，用之不竭。
Can transcend the world while in the world.

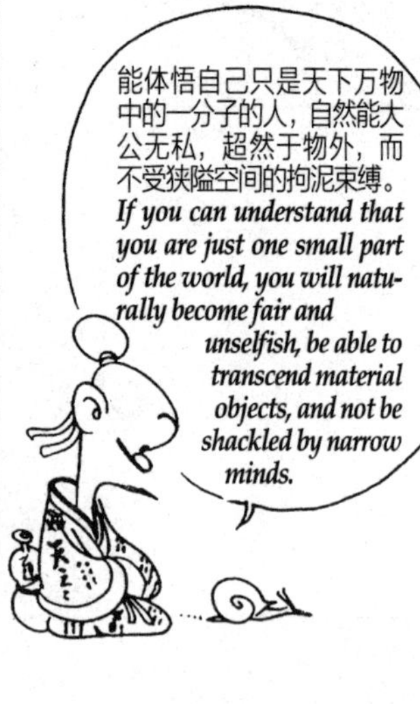
能体悟自己只是天下万物中的一分子的人，自然能大公无私，超然于物外，而不受狭隘空间的拘泥束缚。
If you can understand that you are just one small part of the world, you will naturally become fair and unselfish, be able to transcend material objects, and not be shackled by narrow minds.

不可徒劳身心，当乐风月之趣

Do not over work yourself, Enjoy the beauty of nature

1
一个人生活得太闲散，就容易心生妄想邪念。
If life is too leisurely, extraneous thoughts will usurp it.
忙得像部工作的机器一样……
I'm so busy I feel like some kind of a machine...
太过于忙碌，则易失去人生的乐趣，
If too busy, one's genuine nature won't get out.
2
所以有才德的君子，不可不多加注意自己身心的健康；
So a gentleman must look after his body and mind,
3
4
也不可不多接近大自然，品赏风花雪月的趣味。
And mustn't fail to indulge in the beauty of nature.
健康的人生，应持守其中庸之道，不使自己无所事事，也不宜过于劳碌，导致身心的疾病。
For a healthy life, we must walk the middle path. Don't let yourself have nothing at all to do, and don't let yourself get too busy.

风迹留影，过而不留

A passing wind, the moon's reflection, Leave and then are gone

1
耳朵要像山谷，疾风呼啸而过什么也未留下，
If one's ears resemble the whistling sound of a valley wind that when it leaves is gone,
2
他很坏！ *He's terrible.*
他好差！ *He's a lout.*
他很好啊， *He is quite good.*
那么所有的是非黑白都会消逝。
Then right and wrong will go as well.

3
心境要像月亮倒映在水面上，虽然月色沉浸在水里，却空灵而不着痕迹，
If one's mood resembles the floating sight of a moonlit pond, still and undisturbed,
4
那么就会忘了物我的存在。
Then self and other will be forgotten.
能无视于毁誉，心境方能清。居心要像月亮倒映在水面般空寂而不着痕迹，如此便不会有忧愤烦恼了。
If you can pay no heed to praise and blame, you can maintain purity of mind. Our normal frame of mind should be like water reflecting the moon: still and undisturbed. If we can do this, our troubles and worries will disappear.

月盈则亏，履满者戒
On reaching fullness, the moon wanes, One who reaches fulfillment abstains

1
欣赏花朵要在半开放的时候，喝酒只能喝到略带醉意的程度，
To view flowers just blossoming, to drink until slightly tipsy,
2
这时候才能享受其中的微妙趣味。
In the midst of these is wonderful delight.
3
如果等到花开绚烂或喝得酩酊大醉，
But if continued to the point of dazzling flamboyance or delirious intoxication,
4
就易陷入窘恶的境地了。
It all becomes a vulgar scene.

5
处境圆满事业到达巅峰的人，应该多想想其中的道理。
One who has reached the point of fulfillment should consider this.
过满则易衰，不及则易败，凡事做到七八分处才能体会其中的妙趣。所以“不持盈、不履满”才是处世应有的态度。
Only by doing and having just enough can you enjoy the charms of life.Do not upset the balance of life by striving for more than enough.

把握要点，卷舒自在
Grasp the essentials and move about freely

1
人生就像一场傀儡戏，
Life is like a marionette,
2
只要将丝线机纽掌握住，不要让任何一条丝线紊乱，收放自如，
But as long as you hold the sticks, and the strings remain untangled, you can move around as you please.
行动或停止完全操在我手中，一点也不受他人的干涉；
And with no one to interfere, you can freely leave the stage.
先走一步啦！
One foot in front of the other!
3
再见！
Bye bye!
我身不由己啊……
I can't control myself...
如此就可以超脱于这场戏外了。若能掌握自己的本心，不受外在环境的影响，不受他人左右，自然收放自如。
If you can grasp your own nature and not be influenced by your surroundings or other people, you can come and go as you please.

超越口耳之嗜欲，得见人生之真趣

Transcend sensual desires Achieve life's delights

1
饮茶不必求精，只要茶壶不干涸就成；
I don't expect the best tea, yet my pot is never dry;
2
喝酒不必求酒味香醇，只要酒杯不空就成；
I don't expect strong drink, yet my cup is never empty;
3
素琴虽弹不出曲调，却能调和身心；
My plain zither lacks a string, but still it reattunes me;
4
短笛虽吹不出动人的音乐，却能使心胸舒畅。
My short flute lacks a hole, but still it comforts me.
5
纵使不能像伏羲那样清静恬淡，
Although it's difficult to out-do the ancient sage Fu Xi in purity and non-action,
6
也可以媲美嵇康和阮籍那样潇洒飘逸。
Yet I can match the worthies Ji Kang and Ruan Ji in their casual elegance.
凡事只要能自得其乐，就不必讲究精美的品味、着重外在的形式，一切但求怡然自适，随遇而安。
In all affairs, it's enough to find a little enjoyment for yourself. There's no need to be a connois seur of everything and emphasize outward appearances.
Just enjoy simple pleasures and take comfort in your surroundings.

附录·延伸阅读

APPENDIX Further reading

此部分为本书图画页的延伸阅读，各段首所示的页码与图画页对应。

P2 酞肥辛甘非真味，真味只是淡；神奇卓异非至人，至人只是常。

P3 天地寂然不动，而气机无息稍停；日月尽夜奔驰，而贞明万古不易。故君子闲时要有吃紧的心思，忙处要有悠闲的趣味。

P4 藜口苋肠者，多冰清玉洁；衮衣玉食者，甘婢膝奴颜。盖志以澹泊明，而节从肥甘丧也。

P5 面前的田地要放得宽，使人无不平之叹；身后的恩泽要流得久，使人有不匮之思。

P6 径路窄处，留一步与人行；滋味浓的，减三分让人尝。此是涉世一极安乐法。

P7 交友须带三分侠气，做人要存一点素心。

P8 处世让一步为高，退步即进步的张本；待人宽一分是福，利人实利己的根基。

P9 盖世功劳，当不得一个矜字；弥天罪过，当不得一个悔字。

P10 好动者，云电风灯；嗜寂者，死灰槁木。须定云止水中，有鸢飞鱼跃气象，才是有道的心体。

P11 居轩冕之中，不可无山林的气味；处林泉之下，须要怀廊庙的经纶。

P12 忧勤是美德，太苦则无以适性怡情；澹泊是高风，太枯则无以济人利物。

P13 人情反复，世路崎岖。行不去处，须知退一步之法；行得去处，务加让三分之功。

P14 待小人，不难于严，而难于不恶；待君子，不难于恭，而难于有礼。

P15 彼富我仁，彼爵我义，君子固不为君相所牢笼；人定胜天，志一动气，君子亦不受造物之陶铸。

P16 学者要收拾精神，并归一路。如修德而留意于事功名誉，必无实诣；读书而寄兴于吟咏风雅，定不深心。

P17 人人有个大慈悲，维摩屠刽无二心也；处处有种真趣味，金屋茅簷非两地也。只是欲闭情封，当面错过，便咫尺千里矣。

P18 我有功于人不可念，而过则不可不念，人有恩于我不可忘，而怨则不可不忘。

P19 心地干净，方可读书学古。不然，见一善行窃以济私，闻一善言假以覆短，是又藉寇兵而赍盗粮矣。

P20 读书不见圣贤，如铅椠佣；居官不爱子民，如衣冠盗；讲学不尚躬行，为口头禅；立业不思种德，为眼前花。

P21 苦心中，常得悦心之趣；得意时，便生失意之悲。

P22 攲器以满覆，扑满以空全。故君子宁居无不居有，宁处缺不处完。

P23 人知名位为乐，不知无名无位之乐为最真；人知饥寒为忧，不知不饥不寒之忧为更甚。

P24 为恶而畏人知，恶中犹有善路；为善而急人知，善处即是恶根。

P25 泛驾之马可就驰驱，跃冶之金终归型范。只一优游不振，便终身无个进步。白沙云："为人多病未足羞，一生无病是吾忧。"真确论也。

P26 人只一念贪私，便销刚为柔，塞智为昏，变恩为惨，染洁为污，坏了一生人品。故古人以不贪为宝，所以度越一世。

P27 耳目见闻为外贼，情欲意识为内贼。只是主人翁惺惺不昧，独坐中堂，贼便化为家人矣。

P28 图未就之功，不如保已成之业；悔既往之失，不如防将来之非。

P29 风来疏竹，风过而竹不留声；雁渡寒潭，雁去而潭不留影；故君子之事来而心始现，事去而心随空。

P30 静中静非真静，动处静得来，才是性天之真境；乐处乐非真乐，苦中乐得采，才是心体之真机。

P31 平民肯种德施惠，便是无位的公相；士夫徒贪权市宠，竟成有爵的乞人。

P32　文章做到极处，无有他奇，只是恰好；人品做到极处，无有他异，只是本然。

P33　天地有万古，此身不再得；人生只百年，此日最易过。幸生其间者，不可不知有生之乐，亦不可不怀虚生之忧。

P34　老来疾病，都是壮时招的；衰后罪孽，都是盛时造的。故持盈履满，君子尤兢兢焉。

P35　小处不渗漏，暗处不欺隐，末路不怠荒，才是个真正英雄。

P36　千金难结一时之欢，一饭竟致终身之感。盖爱重反为仇，薄极翻成喜也。

P37　遇沉沉不语之士，且莫输心；见悻悻自好之人，应须防口。

P38　觉人之诈，不形于言，受人之侮，不动于色，此中有无穷意味，亦有无穷受用。

P39　吾身一小天地也，使喜怒不愆，好恶有则，便是燮理的功夫；天地一大父母也，使民无怨咨，物无氛疹，亦是敦睦的气象。

P40　父慈子孝，兄友弟恭，纵做到极处，俱是合当如此，着不得一丝感激的念头。如施者任德，受者怀恩，便是路人，便成市道矣。

P41　有妍必有丑为之对，我不夸妍，谁能丑我？有洁必有污为之仇，我不好洁，谁能污我？

P42　德者才之主，才者德之奴。有才无德，如家无主而奴用事矣，几何不魍魉猖狂？

P43　锄奸杜倖，要放他一条去路。若使之一无所容，譬如塞鼠穴者，一切去路都塞尽，则一切好物俱咬破矣。

P44　饥则附，饱则飏，燠则趣，寒则弃，人情通患也。

P45　君子宜净拭冷眼，慎勿轻动刚肠。

P46　一灯萤然，万籁无声，此吾人初入宴寂时也；晓梦初醒，群动未起，此吾人初出混沌处也。乘此而一念回光，炯然返照，始知耳目口鼻皆桎梏，而情欲嗜好悉机械矣。

P47　鱼网之设，鸿则罹其中；螳螂之贪，雀又乘其后。机里藏机，变外生变，智巧何足恃哉。

P48　水不波则自定，槛不翳则自明。故心无可清，去其混之者，而清自现；乐不必寻，去其苦之者，而乐自存。

P49 谢事当谢于正盛之时，居身宜居于独后之地。

P50 交市人不如友山翁，谒朱门不如亲白屋；听街谈巷语，不如闻樵歌牧咏；谈今人失德过举，不如述古人嘉言懿行。

P51 德者事业之基，未有基不固而栋宇坚久者。

P52 心者后裔之根，未有根不植而枝叶荣茂者。

P53 前人云："抛却自家无尽藏，沿门持钵效贫儿。"又云："暴富贫儿休说梦，谁家灶里火无烟。"一箴自昧所有，一箴自夸所有，可为学问切戒。

P54 道是一重公众物事，当随人而接引。学是一个寻常家饭，当随事而警惕。

P55 人之过误宜恕，而在己则不可恕；己之困辱宜忍，而在人则不可忍。

P56 我贵而人奉之，奉此峨冠大带也；我贱而人侮之，侮此布衣草履也。然则原非奉我，我胡为喜；原非侮我，我胡为怒。

P57 "为鼠常留饭，怜蛾不点灯"，古人此等念头，是吾人一点生生之机。无此，便所谓土木形骸而已。

P58 居官有二语，曰："唯公则生明，唯廉则生威。"居家有二语，曰："唯恕则情平，唯俭则用足。"

P59 处富贵之地，要知贫贱的痛痒；当少壮之时，须念衰老的辛酸。

P60 休与小人仇仇，小人自有对头；休向君子谄媚，君子原无私惠。

P61 毋忧拂意，毋喜快心，毋恃久安，毋惮初难。

P62 饮宴之乐多，不是个好人家；声华之习胜，不是个好士子；名位之念重，不是个好臣士。

P63 冷眼观人；冷耳听语；冷情当感；冷心思理。

P64 性躁心粗者，一事无成；心和气平者，百福自集。

P65 闻恶不可就恶，恐为谗夫泄怒；闻善不可即亲，恐引奸人进身。

P66 用人不宜刻，刻则思效者去；交友不宜滥，滥则贡谀者来。

P67 不可乘喜而轻诺，不可因醉而生嗔，不可乘快而多事，不可困倦而鲜终。

P68 口乃心之门，守口不密，泄尽真机：意乃心之足，防意不严，走尽邪蹊。

P69 君子处患难而不忧，当宴游而惕虑；遇权豪而不惧，对茕独而惊心。

P71 谈山林之乐者，未必真得山林之趣；厌名利之谈者，未必尽忘名利之情。

P72 钓水，逸事也，尚持生杀之柄；奕棋，清戏也，且动战事之心。可见喜事不如省事之为适，多能不若无能之全真。

P73 岁月本长，而忙者自促，天地本宽，而卑者自隘，风花雪月本闲，而劳者自冗。

P74 得趣不在多，盆池拳石间，烟霞俱足：会景不在远，蓬窗竹屋下，风月自赊。

P75 听静夜之钟声，唤醒梦中之梦；观澄潭之月影，窥见身外之身。

P76 人解读有字书，不解读无字书。知弹有弦琴，不知弹无弦琴。以迹用，不以神用，何以得琴书之趣。

P77 心无物欲，即是秋空霁海；坐有琴书，便成石室丹丘。

P78 会得个中趣，五湖之烟月尽入寸里；破得眼前机，千古之英雄尽归掌握。

P79 山河大地已属微尘；而况尘中之尘；血肉身躯且归泡影，而况影外之影。非上上智，无了了心。

P80 石火光中争长竞短，几何光阴？蜗牛角上较雌论雄，许大世界？

P81 延促由于一念，宽窄系之寸心。故机闲者，一日遥于千古；意广者，斗室宽若两间。

P82 松涧边，携杖独行，立处云生破衲。竹窗下，枕书高卧，觉时月侵寒毡。

P83 隐逸林中无荣辱，道义路上无炎凉。

P84 矜名不若逃名趣，练事何如省事闲。

P85 嗜寂者，观白云幽石而通玄；趋荣者，见清歌妙舞而忘倦。唯自得之士，无喧寂，无荣枯，无往非自适之天。

P86 孤云出岫，去留一无所系；朗镜悬空，静躁两不相干。

P87 禅宗曰：“饥来吃饭倦来眠。”诗旨曰：“眼前景致口头语。”盖极高寓于极平，至难出于至易。有意者反远，无心者自近也。

P88 水流而境无声，得处喧见寂之趣；山高而云不碍，悟出有入无之机。

P89 山林是胜地，一营恋便成市朝：书画是雅事，一贪痴便成商贾。盖心无染著，欲境是仙都；心有系恋，乐境成苦海矣。

P90 芦花被下，卧雪眠云，保全得一窝夜气；竹叶杯中，吟风弄月，躲离了万丈红尘。

P91 竹篱下，呼闻犬吠鸡鸣，恍似云中世界：芸窗中雅听蝉吟鸦噪，方知静里乾坤。

P92 我不希荣，何忧乎利禄之香饵？我不竞进，何畏乎仕宦之危机？

P93 徜徉于山泉石之间，而尘心渐息，夷犹于诗书图画之内，而俗气潜消。故君子虽不玩丧志，亦常借境调心。

P94 春日气象繁华，令人心神骀荡，不若秋日云白风清，兰芳桂馥，水天一色，上下空明，使人神骨俱清也。

P95 一字不识，而有诗意者，得诗家真趣；一偈不参，而有禅味者，悟禅教玄机。

P96 机动的，弓影疑为蛇蝎，寝石视为伏虎，此中浑是杀气；念息的，石虎可作海鸥，蛙声可当鼓吹，触处俱见真机。

P97 身如不系之舟，一任流行坎止；心似既灰之木，何妨刀割香涂。

P98 欲其中者，波沸寒潭，山林不见其寂；虚其中者，凉生酷暑，朝市不知其喧。

P99 多藏者厚亡，故知富不如贫之无虑；高步者疾颠，故知贵不如贱之常安。

P100 古德云：“竹影扫阶尘不动，月轮穿沼水无痕。”吾儒云：“水流任意急境常静，花落虽频意自闲。”人常持此意，以应事接物，身心何等自在。

P101 鱼得水逝，而相忘乎水；鸟乘风飞，而不知有风。识此可以超物累，可以乐天机。

P102 狐眠败砌，兔走荒台，尽是当年歌舞之地；露冷黄花，烟迷衰草，悉属旧时争战之场。盛衰何常，强弱安在，念此令人心灰。

P103 宠辱不惊，闲看庭前花开花落：去留无意，漫随天外云卷云舒。

P104 晴空朗月，何处不可翱翔，而飞蛾独投夜烛；清泉绿草，何物不可饮啄，而鸱鸮偏嗜腐鼠。噫！世之不为飞蛾鸱鸮者，几何人哉？

P105 才就筏便思舍筏，方是无事道人；若骑驴又复觅驴，终为不了禅师。

P106 诗思在灞陵桥上，微吟就，林岫便已浩然；野兴在镜湖曲边，独往时，山川自相映发。

P107 真空不空，执相非真，破相亦非真，问世尊如何发付？

P108 在世出世，循欲是苦，绝欲亦是苦，听吾侪善自修持。

P109 饱谙世味，一任覆雨翻云，总慵开眼；会尽人情，随教呼牛唤马，只是点头。

P110 性天澄徹，即饥餐渴饮，无非康济身心；心地沉迷，纵谈禅演偈，总是播弄精魂。

P111 金自矿出，玉从石生，非幻无以求真；道得酒中，仙遇花里，虽雅不能离俗。

P112 神酣布被窝中，得天地冲和之气；味足藜羹饭后，识人生淡泊之真。

P113 斗室中，万虑都捐，说甚画栋飞云，珠帘卷雨；三杯后，一真自得，唯知素琴横月，短笛吟风。

P114 白氏云:“不如放身心，冥然任天造。”晁氏云:“不知收身心，凝然归寂定。”放者流为猖狂，收者入于枯寂。唯善操身心者，把柄在手，收放自如。

P115 当雪夜月天，心境便尔澄彻；遇春风和气，意界亦自冲融。造化，人心，混合无间。

P116 优人傅粉调朱，效妍丑于毫端，俄而歌残场罢，妍丑何存？奕者争先竞后，较雌雄于著子，俄而局尽子收，雌雄安在。

P117 人生福境祸区，皆念想造成。故释氏云:“利欲炽然即是火坑，贪爱沉溺便为苦海；一念清净烈焰成池，一念惊觉船登彼岸。”念头稍异，境界顿殊，可不慎哉！

P118 绳锯木断，水滴石穿，学道者须加力索；水到渠成，瓜熟蒂落，得道者一任天机。

P119 雨余观山色，景象便觉新妍；夜静听钟声，音响尤为清越。

P120 登高使人心旷，临流使人意远；读书于雨雪之夜，使人神清；舒啸于丘阜之巅，使人兴迈。

P121 心旷，则万钟如瓦缶；心隘，则一发似车轮。

P122 就一身了一身者，方能以万物付万物；还天下于天下者，方能出世间于世间。

P123 人生太闲，则别念窃生；太忙，则真性不现。故士君子不可不抱身心之忧，亦不可不耽风月之趣。

P124 耳根似飙谷投响，过而不留，则是非俱谢；心境如月池浸色，空而不着，则物我两忘。

P125 花看半开，酒饮微醉，此中大有佳趣。若至烂漫酕醄，便成恶境矣。履盈满者，宜思之。

P126 人生原是一傀儡，只要根蒂在手，一线不乱，卷舒自由，行止在我，一毫不受他人提掇，便超出此场中矣。

P127 茶不求精而壶亦不燥，酒不求冽而樽亦不空，素琴无弦而常调，短笛无腔而自适。纵难超越义皇，亦可匹俦嵇阮。

心 经

THE HEART SUTRA OF PERFECT WISDOM

色 AND 受想行识
Material World and Sensations, Perceptions, Decisions & Awareness*

想 Perceptions
受 Sensations
行 Decisions
识 Awareness

** Sensations, Perceptions, Decisions & Awareness belong to the inner world or inner mind.*
受，想，行，识都属于人的内心世界或内在思想。

释 义
DEFINITION OF TERMS

色 Material World
受 Sensations
想 Perceptions
行 Decisions
识 Awareness
空 Kong
自佛教于东汉传入中国以来，从南北朝开始，佛经被大量翻译过来。
Buddhism was introduced to China during the Eastern Han Dynasty (A.D.25-220). In the subsequent years of the Southern/Northern Dynasties (A.D.317-581),a large number of Buddhist sutras were translated into Chinese.
因此很多用语都是文义含量很大的古文，今天的人们很难精确地理解其中之义。
As a result, some words commonly used in translations of sutras are very old and loaded with ancient meanings which are difficult for people today to fully understand.
没错。
That's right.
所以我们在开始先将几个重要的文字做详细的说明，而内文中就不再翻译这几个字了。
In this translation, we will define major terms at the beginning and not translate them again when they appear in the text.
这办法很好！
Good idea!

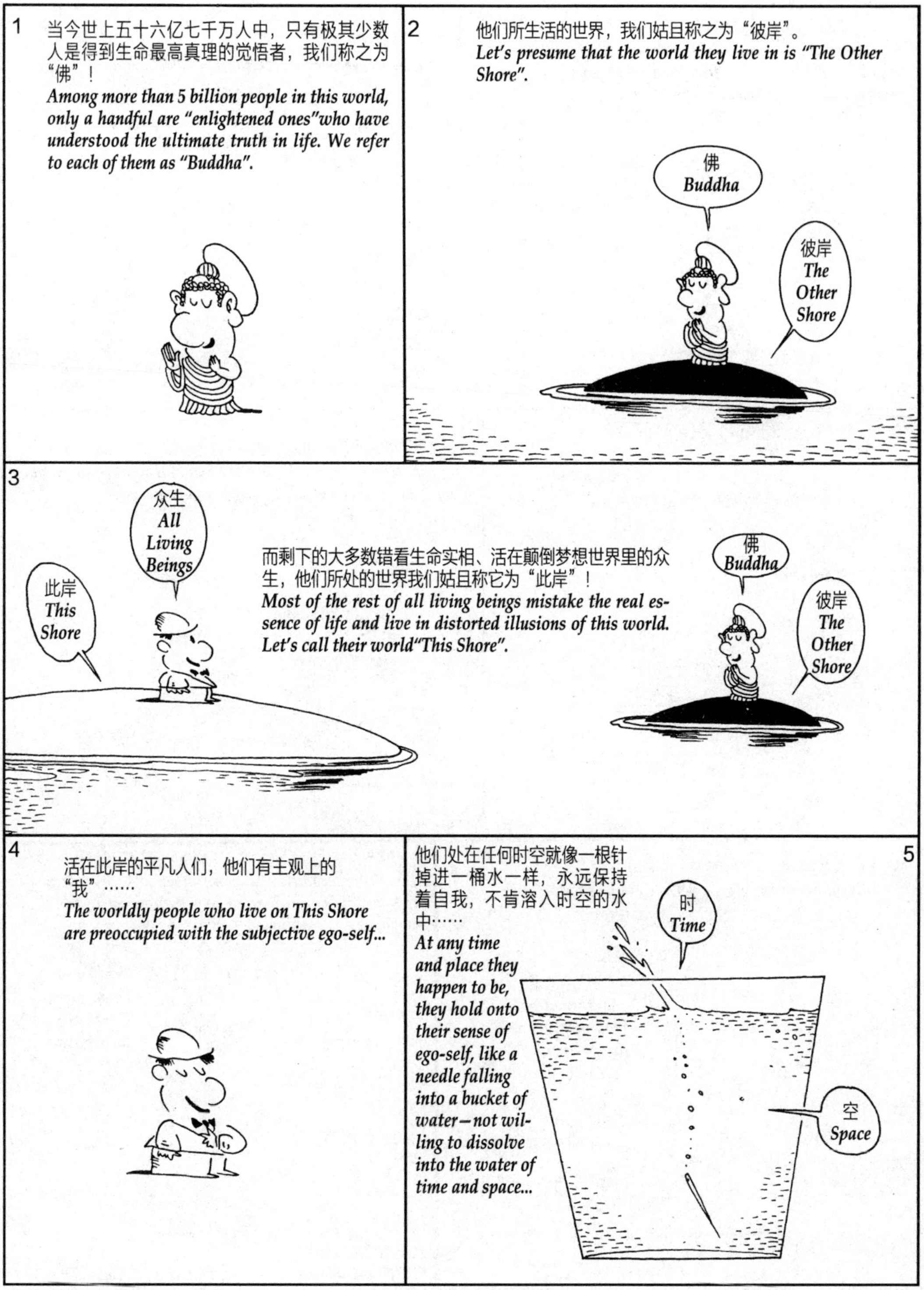
1
当今世上五十六亿七千万人中，只有极其少数人是得到生命最高真理的觉悟者，我们称之为“佛”！
Among more than 5 billion people in this world, only a handful are "enlightened ones"who have understood the ultimate truth in life. We refer to each of them as "Buddha".
2
他们所生活的世界，我们姑且称之为“彼岸”。
Let's presume that the world they live in is "The Other Shore".
佛 Buddha
彼岸 The Other Shore
3
众生 All Living Beings
此岸 This Shore
而剩下的大多数错看生命实相、活在颠倒梦想世界里的众生，他们所处的世界我们姑且称它为“此岸”！
Most of the rest of all living beings mistake the real essence of life and live in distorted illusions of this world. Let's call their world"This Shore".
佛 Buddha
彼岸 The Other Shore
4
活在此岸的平凡人们，他们有主观上的“我”……
The worldly people who live on This Shore are preoccupied with the subjective ego-self...
5
他们处在任何时空就像一根针掉进一桶水一样，永远保持着自我，不肯溶入时空的水中……
At any time and place they happen to be, they hold onto their sense of ego-self, like a needle falling into a bucket of water—not willing to dissolve into the water of time and space...
时 Time
空 Space

有我就有与时空对比出来的好、坏、贵、贱……
As long as the ego-self exists, there are judgements which contrast "I"with time and space–such as good vs. bad, high status vs. low class...
重要 Important
渺小 Insignificant
伟大 Great
卑微 Lowly
6
7
有了我，就有它们……
As long as the ego-self exists, there is "they"...
外在世界 EXTERNAL WORLD
8
他通过他自己的辨识工具、眼、耳、鼻、舌、身、意……
Through a person's own tools of recognition–eyes, ears, nose, tongue, body, mind...
意 Mind
耳 Ears
眼 Eyes
鼻 Nose
舌 Tongue
身 Body
六识 Six Senses
9
接收到了外在世界所传回来的信息：色、声、味、触、法……
Information is received from the external world–form, voice, smell, taste, touch and all other phenomena ....
法 Phenomena
声 Voice
味 Smell
香 Taste
色 Form
触 Touch
六尘 Six Observations
10
于是这些资料进入了他的内心世界里……
This information enters a person's inner world...
受 Sensations
信息识别与记忆。 Information Identification and Memory.
眼 Eyes
鼻 Nose
舌 Tongue
身 Body
耳 Ears
意 Mind
信息传进人的大脑后先存入资料中心，并进行比较……
After the information is communicated to the cortex of the brain, it is stored in the information centre and then compared and contrasted...
信息比较 Comparing and Contrasting Information
想 Perceptions
PS：想是心之相。
PS:Perceptions are the manifestation of the ego-self.
11

12 用原本存有的资料与新信息比较，并加上自己一直在改变的感情标准进行分析、推理、决策，最后发出行为的指令。

New information is compared to existing information and the ego-self's everchanging emotional values are added to analyze, deduce and reason. Finally, comes the decision to act.

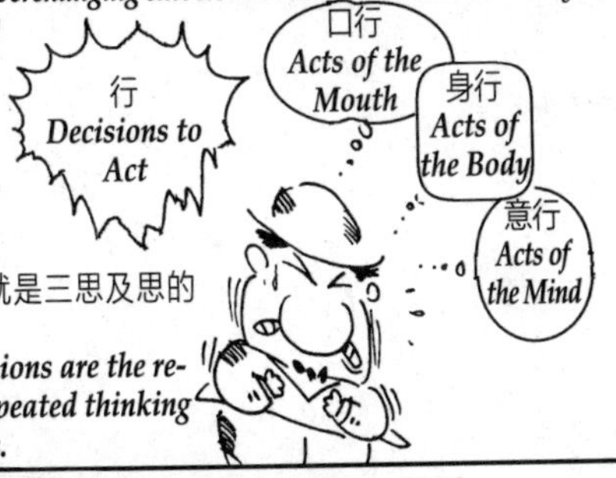
行
Decisions to Act
口行
Acts of the Mouth
身行
Acts of the Body
意行
Acts of the Mind

PS：行就是三思及思的结果。

PS: Decisions are the result of repeated thinking processes.

13 而这些内心所产生的反应与行为作用也因而造成了结果。

Thereafter, these inner responese and decision-making processes produce their results.

识 Awareness

PS:如果没有让口、身行动，也会存入想的部分，变成意识形态。

PS: Even if there are no acts by the mouth or the body, these decision-making processes still become part of anyone's awareness.

14

这个会因外在而起变化的内心世界，就叫做——受、想、行、识。

This inner world is ever-changing in response to external stimuli and is referred to as sensations, perceptions, decisions and awareness.

受
Sensations
想 Perceptions
识 Awareness
行 Decisions

15

色

MATERIAL WORLD

而内心世界以外的所有外在世界（包括自己的肉身）就叫做——色。

All of the external world (including the self's physical body) which is outside of the inner mind is referred to as the material world.

好
Good
坏
Bad
美 Beautiful
丑
Ugly
大
Big
小
Small
贵 Prestigious
贱
Lowly
长
Long
短
Short

16

五蕴
The Five Aspects Of Existence

外在世界的色与内心世界的受、想、行、识合称为——五蕴。
The external material world and the sensations, perceptions, decisions, and awareness of the inner world are referred to as "the five aspects of existence".

17 众生处在有我、有对象的相对世界里，于是就有大、小……
All living beings exist in the relative world of ego-self and objects.Therefore,there is the contrast of big vs. small...

大 Big.
小 Small.

18 有美、丑……
beauty vs. ugliness ...

美 Beauty.
丑 Ugliness.

19 有顺、逆的分别心……
The mind distinguishes things that are my will and not my will ...

逆 Not My Will.
顺 My Will.

20 他们持有这种把自己独立起来与时、空对立的生活态度，我们称它为活在——色境。
When people live with this attitude of separating ego-self from time and place,we refer to it as living in the "REALM OF MATERIAL WORLD".

空
KONG

无诸相曰空。
不著世间如莲华，
常善入于空寂行。
No observation of any phenomena is kong.
Like a lotus blossom which comes out of the dirt of the world but is not touched by it.
Allow your true self to freely unfold on the spiritual journey of detachment and calmness.
因缘所生之法，
究竟而无实体，曰“空”！
All phenomena are manifested through chance variations.They are distorted by each ego-self's mindset and have no real essence of their own. This is kong.

1
而活在彼岸的觉悟者们，他们活在世界的态度是不一样的……
The enlightened ones who live spiritually on The Other Shore have a different attitude toward their lives in this world...
佛 Buddha
彼岸 The Other Shore
2
他们活在任何空间，就无我地把自己融入那个空间……
Whatever time they happen to live in,they dissolve themselves into that time without any ego involvement either...
3
他们活在任何时间，就无我地把自己融入任何时间……
Whatever place they happen to live in, they dissolve themselves into that space without any ego involvement...
热得过瘾，正好做日光浴……
A nice hot day. Perfect for sun bathing...
4
他观花时……
When an enlightened one watches flowers...
我即是花，我即是香……
I am the flower, I am the fragrance...
5
他听雨时……
When an enlightened one listens to the rain...
沥沥沥
Pitter-Patter, Pitter-Patter
我即是雨，我即是雨声。
I am the rain, I am the sound of the rain.

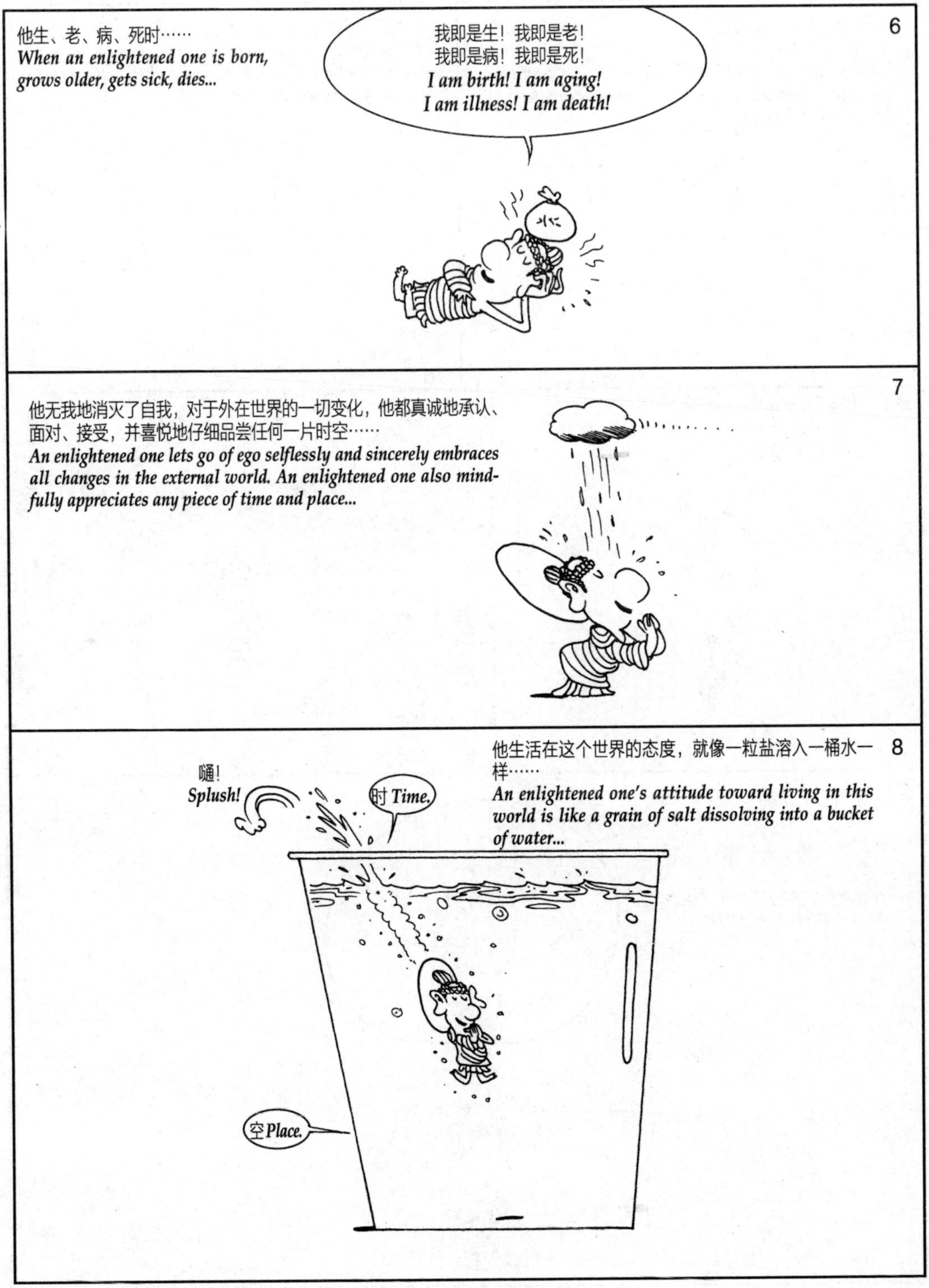
6
他生、老、病、死时……
When an enlightened one is born, grows older, gets sick, dies...
我即是生！我即是老！
我即是病！我即是死！
I am birth! I am aging!
I am illness! I am death!
7
他无我地消灭了自我，对于外在世界的一切变化，他都真诚地承认、面对、接受，并喜悦地仔细品尝任何一片时空……
An enlightened one lets go of ego selflessly and sincerely embraces all changes in the external world. An enlightened one also mindfully appreciates any piece of time and place...
8
他生活在这个世界的态度，就像一粒盐溶入一桶水一样……
An enlightened one's attitude toward living in this world is like a grain of salt dissolving into a bucket of water...
嗵！
Splush!
时 Time.
空 Place.

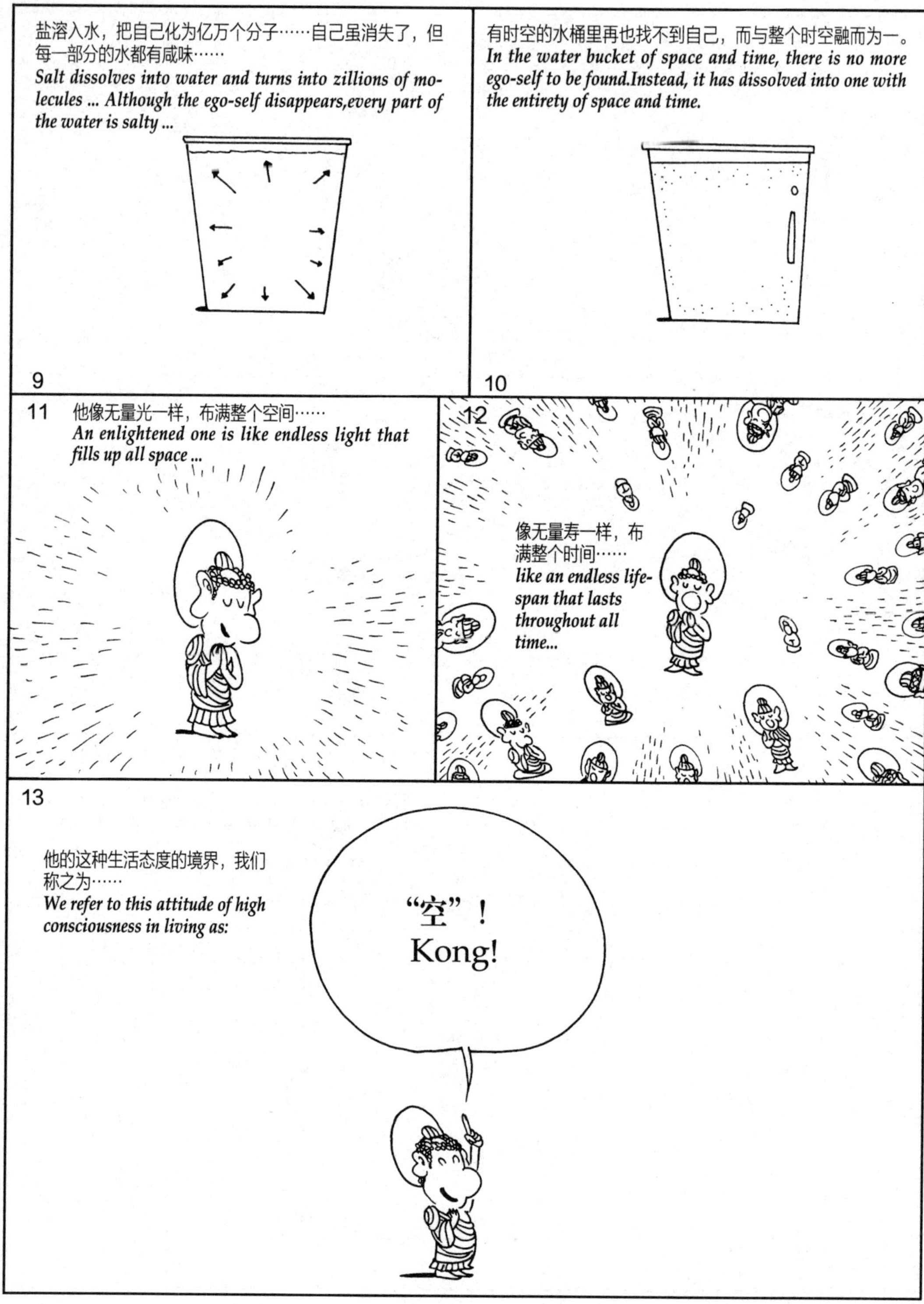
盐溶入水，把自己化为亿万个分子……自己虽消失了，但每一部分的水都有咸味……
Salt dissolves into water and turns into zillions of molecules ... Although the ego-self disappears,every part of the water is salty ...
9
有时空的水桶里再也找不到自己，而与整个时空融而为一。
In the water bucket of space and time, there is no more ego-self to be found.Instead, it has dissolved into one with the entirety of space and time.
10
11
他像无量光一样，布满整个空间……
An enlightened one is like endless light that fills up all space ...
12
像无量寿一样，布满整个时间……
like an endless life-span that lasts throughout all time...
13
他的这种生活态度的境界，我们称之为……
We refer to this attitude of high consciousness in living as:
“空”！
Kong!

色 AND 空
MATERIAL WORLD & KONG

色
Material
World

"色"是被心造成的形相；
而因缘所生之法，究竟而无实体，曰"空"。

Material World refers to all phenomena of the outer world observed by the ego-mind which separates itself from any particular time and place.
Kong implies that all phenomena appear because of chance variations,have no real essence,and are distorted by each ego-self's mindset.

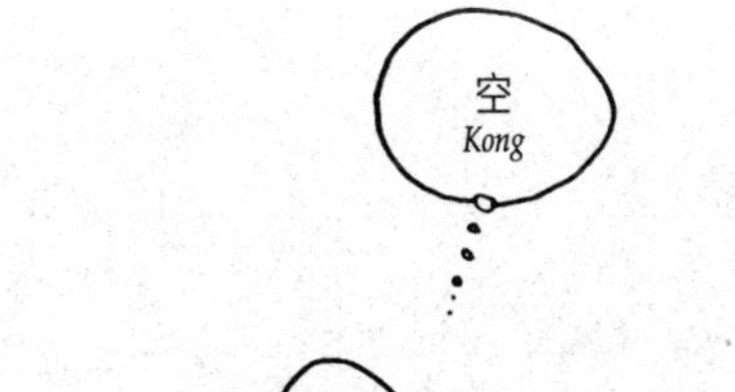
空
Kong

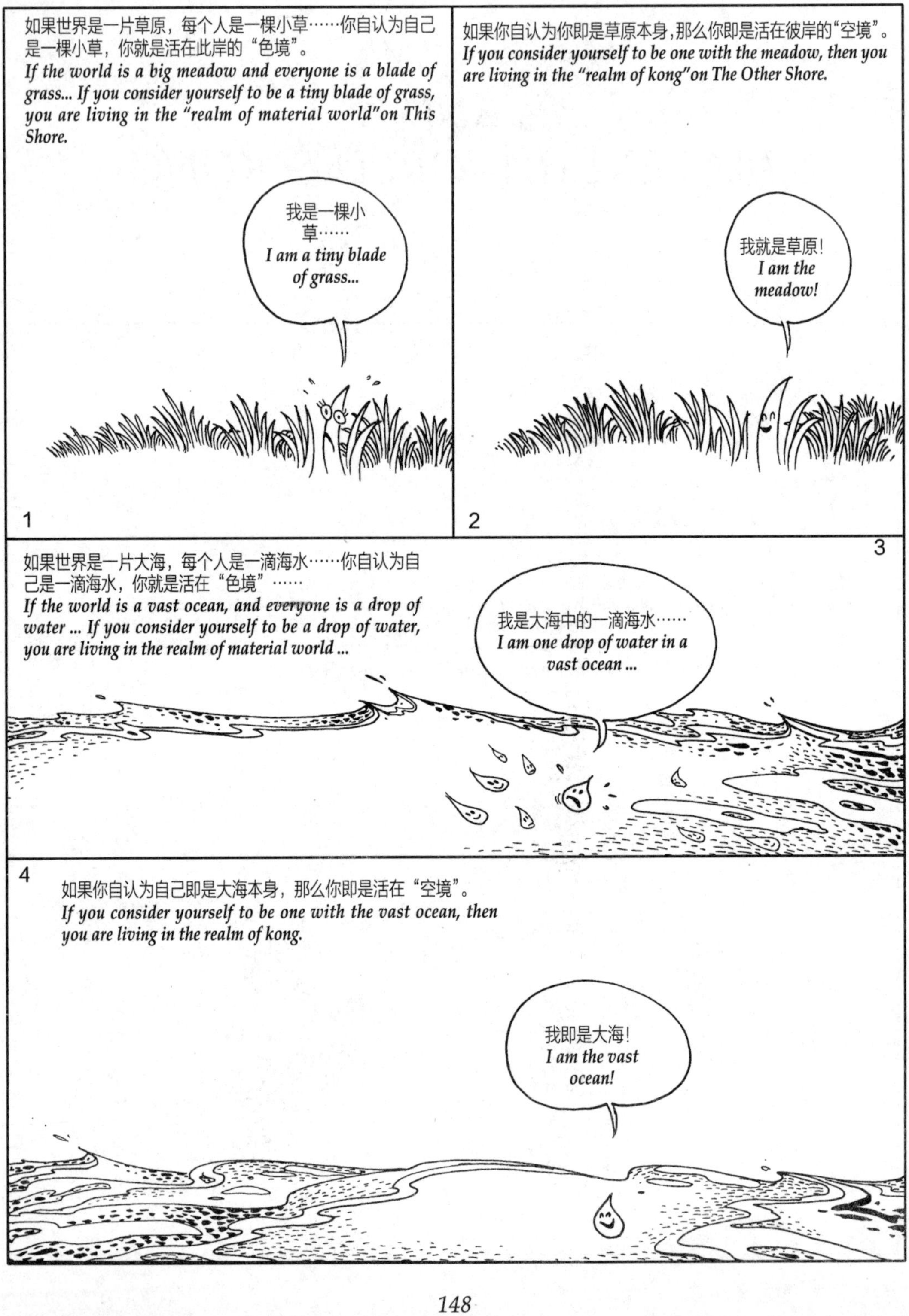
如果世界是一片草原，每个人是一棵小草……你自认为自己是一棵小草，你就是活在此岸的“色境”。
If the world is a big meadow and everyone is a blade of grass... If you consider yourself to be a tiny blade of grass, you are living in the "realm of material world"on This Shore.
我是一棵小草……
I am a tiny blade of grass...
1
如果你自认为你即是草原本身,那么你即是活在彼岸的“空境”。
If you consider yourself to be one with the meadow, then you are living in the "realm of kong"on The Other Shore.
我就是草原!
I am the meadow!
2
3
如果世界是一片大海，每个人是一滴海水……你自认为自己是一滴海水，你就是活在“色境”……
If the world is a vast ocean, and everyone is a drop of water ... If you consider yourself to be a drop of water, you are living in the realm of material world ...
我是大海中的一滴海水……
I am one drop of water in a vast ocean ...
4
如果你自认为自己即是大海本身，那么你即是活在“空境”。
If you consider yourself to be one with the vast ocean, then you are living in the realm of kong.
我即是大海!
I am the vast ocean!

5

这个此岸与彼岸其实是同一个时空……
The so-called This Shore and The Other Shore are, as a matter of fact, in the same physical space and time ...

好清静。
How serene.
好无聊……
How boring...

只是处于这时空中的人的态度不同，活的境界便有所不同。
The only difference is in the mindset (This Shore or The Other Shore) used by those living in any particular place and time. The quality of life for those two mindsets ends up significantly different.

好好听！
What a delightful sound!
好吵……
How noisy...

6

7

所以，佛陀说：
Therefore,the Buddha Shakyamuni says:

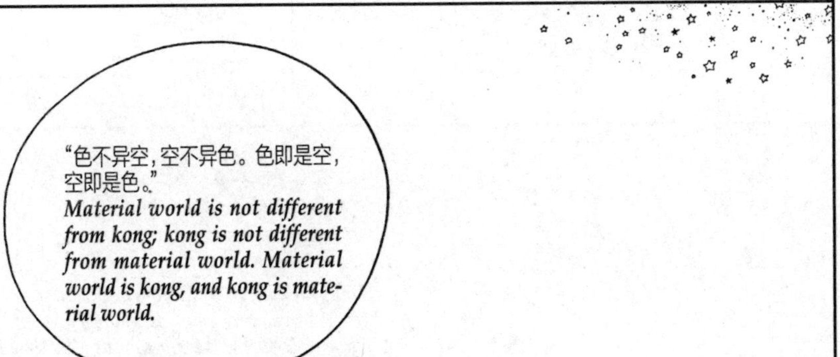
“色不异空，空不异色。色即是空，空即是色。”
Material world is not different from kong; kong is not different from material world. Material world is kong, and kong is material world.

8
一个人处在任何时间，空间中，要像一粒盐溶入一桶水一样……
A human being in any time and place should be like a grain of salt dissolving into a bucket of water ...
此时 This Moment.
此地 This Place.
当下 Right Here.
一粒盐刚掉入一桶水时，有我有水……
Right at the time a gain of salt falls into a bucket of water, there is ego-self and there is water ...
我是一粒盐…… I am a grain of salt ...
9
当它溶入水之后，便无我无水，消失了自己，无我地把自己融入了时空的每一部分。
After it dissolves into the water, there is no more pure salt or pure water. The identity of ego disappears as self dissolves into every part of that particular time and place.
我即是水！ I am one with the water.
水的每一部分都有我。 Every part of the water has me.
10
11
把自己溶入一桶水，你就拥有了整桶水……把自己融入所处的时空中，你就拥有了整片时空。
Dissolve the ego-self into a bucket of water. You therefore own the whole bucket of water ... Dissolve the ego-self into the time and place you happen to be, and you own that whole time and place.

12
大多数人都老是背负着过去，期盼着将来，而没有活在现在……
Most people are always carrying the burden of the past, anticipating the future, while missing life in the present ...
现在
PRESENT
过去 *PAST*
将来 *FUTURE*

13
要做一个融入于当下的人啊……别当一个背负过去与企盼着未来的奴隶啊！要像一艘随时空而流的船啊……
Be a person who dissolves into the present ... Yeh!... Do not be a slave who carries the burden of the past and anticipates the future.Yeh! Be like a boat that flows in time and space ...Yeh! ...

14
“水到那里，船就到那里；船到那里，人就到那里；人到那里，心就到那里。”
“Wherever the water goes, the boat is; wherever the boat goes, the body is; wherever the body goes, the mind and heart are.”

心 经
THE HEART SUTRA OF PERFECT WISDOM

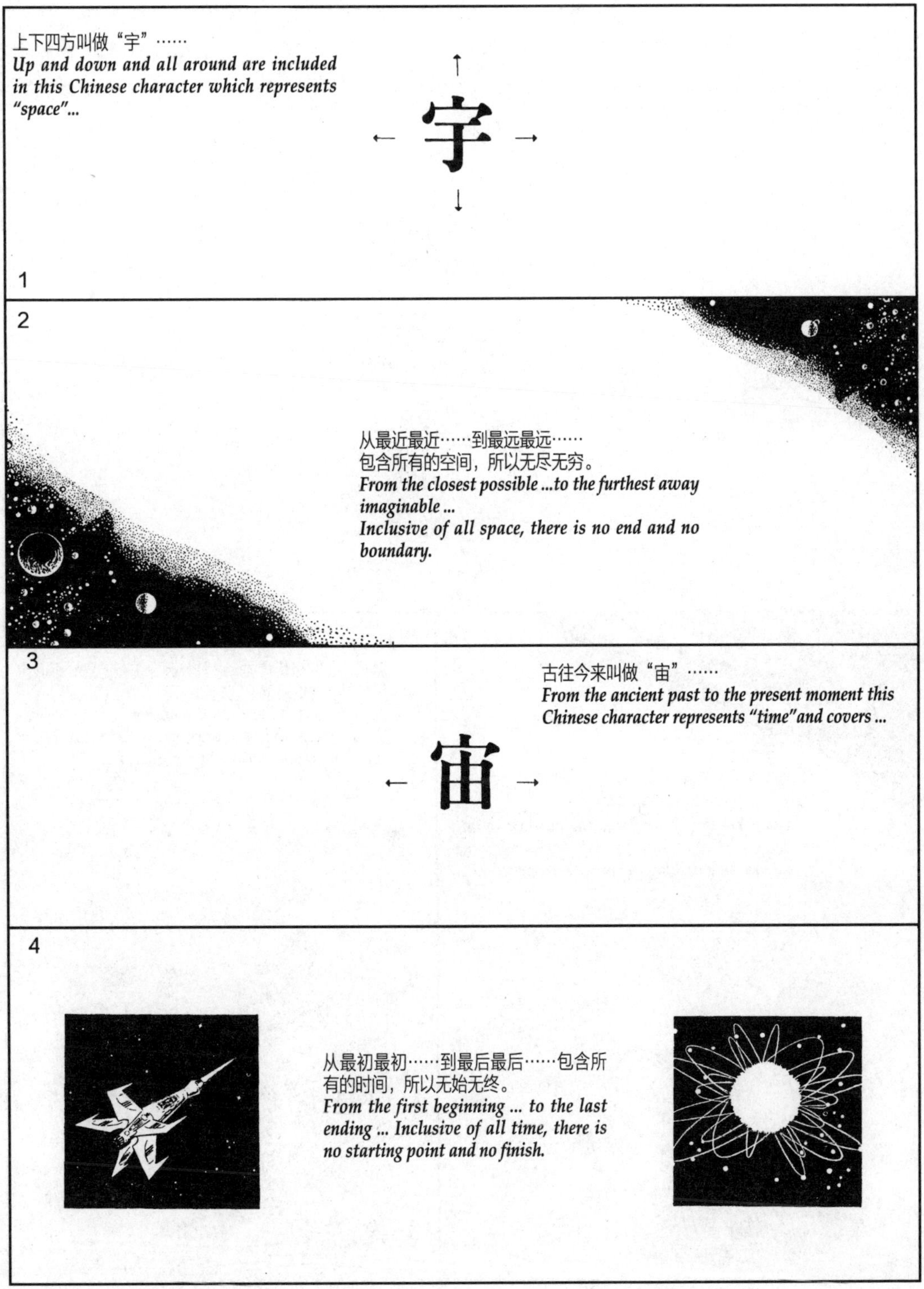
上下四方叫做“宇”……
Up and down and all around are included in this Chinese character which represents “space”...
宇
从最近最近……到最远最远……
包含所有的空间，所以无尽无穷。
From the closest possible ...to the furthest away imaginable ...
Inclusive of all space, there is no end and no boundary.
古往今来叫做“宙”……
From the ancient past to the present moment this Chinese character represents “time”and covers ...
宙
从最初最初……到最后最后……包含所有的时间，所以无始无终。
From the first beginning ... to the last ending ... Inclusive of all time, there is no starting point and no finish.

当“观自在菩萨”用无我的观点做最彻底深永的沉思时……
Bodhisattva Quan Yin used the selfless point of view to obtain the most perfect wisdom ...
5
6
他清澈地领悟到宇宙的一切一切都是一体的，没有任何东西能独立于宇宙之外……
Quan Yin then brought us the wisdom to understand that everything in this universe is one essence, and nothing can be truly independent ...
7
世间外在的一切物质、名利与自己内在的身心感受也都是随时随地流变不定的……
The external material world and one's inner sensations, perceptions, decisions, and awareness all flow and change constantly in time and space.

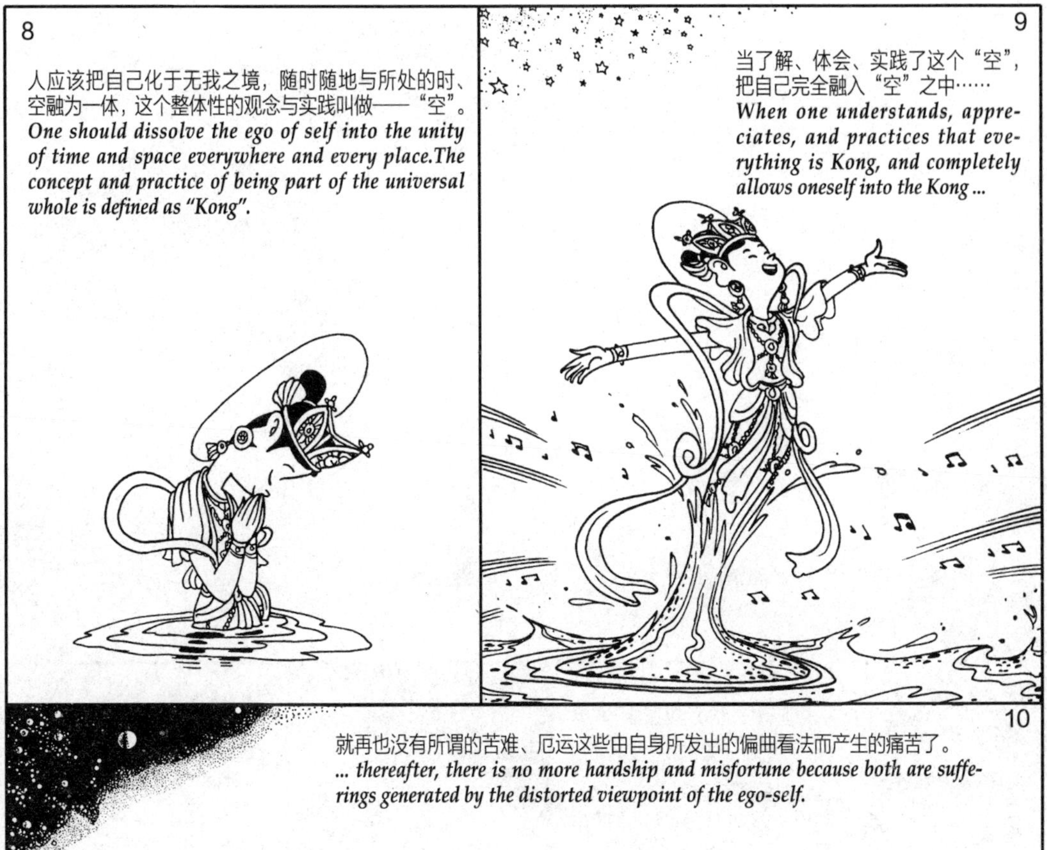
8
人应该把自己化于无我之境，随时随地与所处的时、空融为一体，这个整体性的观念与实践叫做——“空”。
One should dissolve the ego of self into the unity of time and space everywhere and every place.The concept and practice of being part of the universal whole is defined as “Kong”.
9
当了解、体会、实践了这个“空”，把自己完全融入“空”之中……
When one understands, appreciates, and practices that everything is Kong, and completely allows oneself into the Kong ...
10
就再也没有所谓的苦难、厄运这些由自身所发出的偏曲看法而产生的痛苦了。
... thereafter, there is no more hardship and misfortune because both are sufferings generated by the distorted viewpoint of the ego-self.

11
佛陀对他的学生舍利弗说：
Buddha Shakyamuni said to his disciple Sariputra:
舍利弗啊！如果我们用自己的观点去看自身以外的所有对象，其实这些对象也同时是本体，本体也同时是对象啊！
Sariputra, we often look at external objects as completely separate from us. In reality, all objects are one with the ultimate essence, and this essence is inseparable from any object.
12
因为没有任何东西能独立于本体之外，包括你自己，包括你的心灵，包括发自你心灵的感受，这些也都包含在这本体之内。
Nothing can be independent of this ultimate essence. Your entire body, mind, and spirit are all a part of this essence.
13
这个本体我们姑且称它为“空”……
This ultimate essence of the universe is kong.
14
一切你所看到的对象我们称它为“色”！
All objects you see may be referred to as material world.

15
如此一来你就知道空跟色并不是两回事。色即是空，空即是色，没有不同。
As a result, kong and the material world are not separate. Material world is kong, and kong is material world. They are not different from each other.
16
人的感受、知觉、判断、意识、观念等一切精神作用也是如此，都涵盖在这个“空”里面。
This is also the case for our sensations, perceptions, decisions and awareness. They are all included in the kong essence.
17
舍利弗啊，一切事物、一切观感都是因为你站在自己的立场才产生的啊！
Sariputra, all of your observations and opinions originate at the point of the ego-self!
18
所谓生、死、美、丑、多、少，都是以你的立场才会有的感受啊！
Phenomena such as life and death, beauty and ugliness, abundance and scarcity are all generated from one's individual point of view!

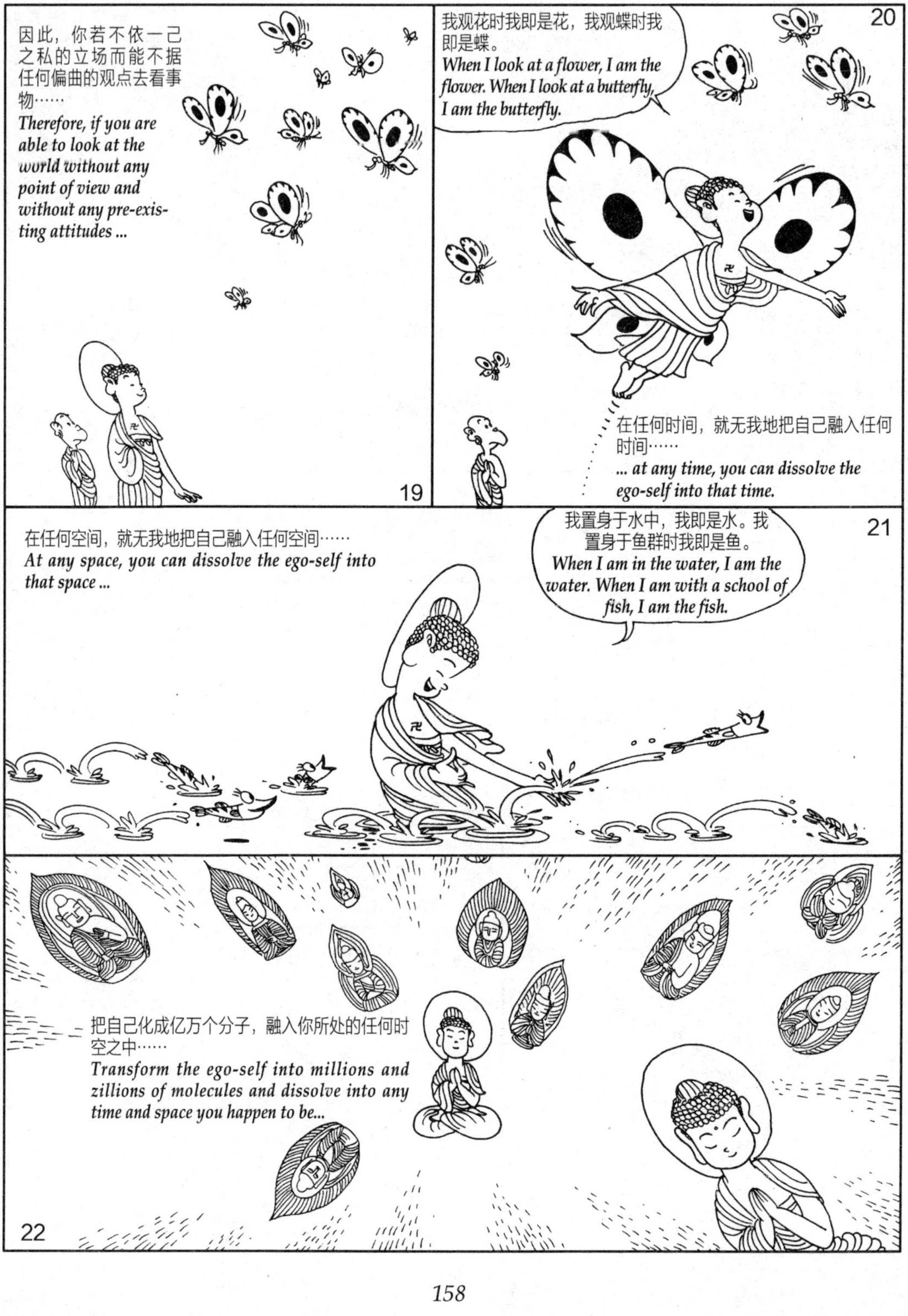
因此，你若不依一己之私的立场而能不据任何偏曲的观点去看事物……
Therefore, if you are able to look at the world without any point of view and without any pre-existing attitudes ...
19
20
我观花时我即是花，我观蝶时我即是蝶。
When I look at a flower, I am the flower. When I look at a butterfly, I am the butterfly.
在任何时间，就无我地把自己融入任何时间……
... at any time, you can dissolve the ego-self into that time.
21
在任何空间，就无我地把自己融入任何空间……
At any space, you can dissolve the ego-self into that space ...
我置身于水中，我即是水。我置身于鱼群时我即是鱼。
When I am in the water, I am the water. When I am with a school of fish, I am the fish.
22
把自己化成亿万个分子，融入你所处的任何时空之中……
Transform the ego-self into millions and zillions of molecules and dissolve into any time and space you happen to be...

23
这时就再也没有我……也没有宇宙、法相、时间、空间这些对象了……
At this time,there is no more separate ego-self ... and no more separate universe, phenomena, time, space ...
就像一粒盐溶入一桶水一样，盐消失了，但水的每一部分都有咸味。
This is like a grain of salt dissolved into a bucket of water, Every part of the water is now a bit salty.
进入没有盐也没有水，完完全全溶入的境界。
No more pure salt, and no more pure water. They became one complete whole.
24
也就没有所谓自身的感受、知觉、判断、意识了。
There are no more activities of the ego-self ...
行 decisions
想 perceptions
受 sensations
识 awareness
25
不据自己的立场用眼睛、耳朵、鼻子、舌头、身体、心灵去侦测……
... no more use of the six senses to monitor the external world from the point of view of ego-self ...
意 Mind
眼 Eyes
耳 Ears
鼻 Nose
舌 Tongue
身 Body
26
就不会产生这些感官所看、所听、所闻、所尝、所触、所感受的一切偏曲的信息。
One will not have all of the distorted information generated from human senses.
香 Smell
声 Sound
味 Taste
法 Phenomena
嗡 !Buzz!
触 Touch
色 Material World

27
不站在"生"去看待"死"，不站在"无"去想望"有"……
No attempt to understand "death"from the point of view of "life,"no illusion of "presence"from the viewpoint of "absence"...
死 Death
生 Life
没有偏曲的观点，就不会产生各种差异的分别心……
Without distorted viewpoints, there will be no more sense of separateness ...
28
无所谓"因"，也无所谓因的形成……
There is no such thing as "cause"and, therefore,no such thing as"planting a seed"...
因 Cause
29
果 Effect
无所谓"果"，也无所谓果的来不来临……
There is no such thing as "effect"and, therefore, no such concern as"harvesting the fruit"...
30
生命的意义在于完全地融入，在于过程而不在于目的。
The meaning of life is found in completely dissolving into the process of living and not in specific goals.
31
明白了这些，就不会再被老、死的问题所困扰而忧心痛苦！
With such an understanding, one will no longer be troubled by the problems of aging and death.

苦 Suffering
集
Causes of Suffering
灭
Cultivation to End Suffering
道
The State of No Ego-Self and No Suffering
人生的痛苦……发觉苦的原因……进行消除苦的修行治疗……
而达到最终的无我无苦的境界……这四个阶段我们称之为苦、集、灭、道。
There are four phases in cultivation—Experiencing the suffering in life ... Discovering the causes of suffering ... Using cultivation to be rid of suffering ... and Reaching the ultimate state of no self and no suffering.
32

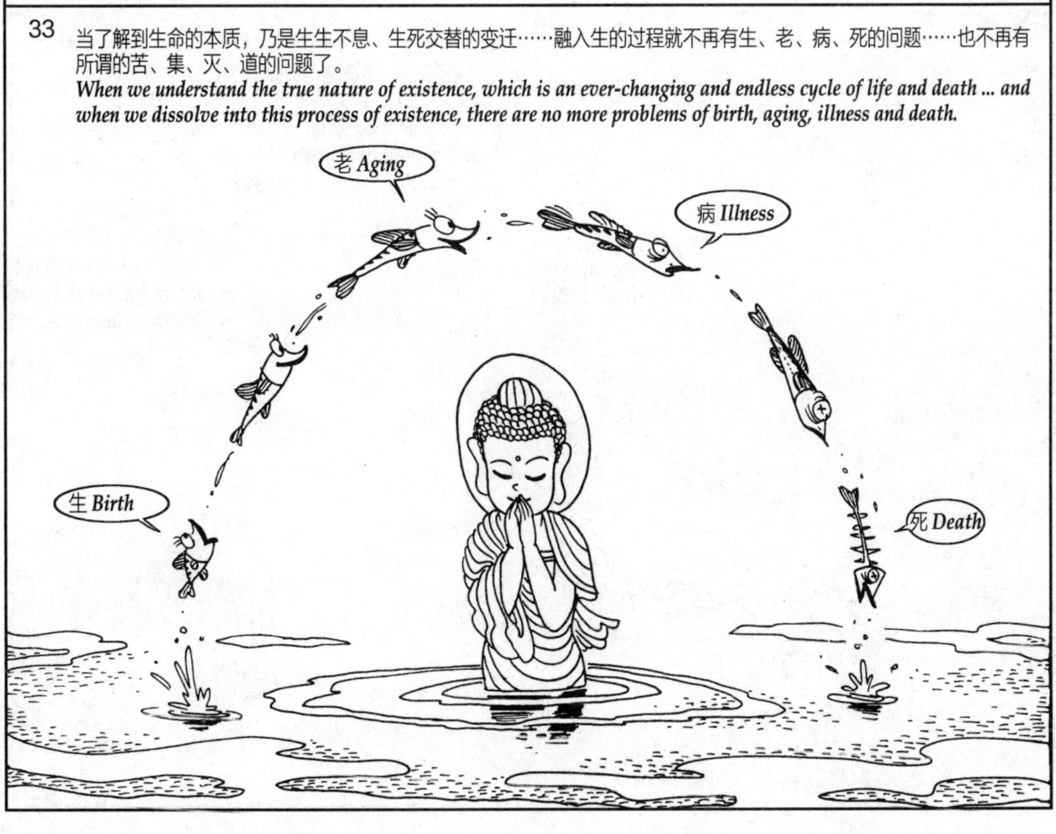
33
当了解到生命的本质，乃是生生不息、生死交替的变迁……融入生的过程就不再有生、老、病、死的问题……也不再有所谓的苦、集、灭、道的问题了。
When we understand the true nature of existence, which is an ever-changing and endless cycle of life and death ... and when we dissolve into this process of existence, there are no more problems of birth, aging, illness and death.
老 Aging
病 Illness
生 Birth
死 Death

34
能了解这个道理看起来很聪明，其实哪有什么聪明之处？
Being able to understand this principle appears to be wise. But what's so wise about it?
35
这个道理明明白白地摆在那里而已，只是一般人迷惘而看不到。
This principle clearly lies in front of everyone's eyes. Unfortunately, most people are too confused to see it.
36
能实践这个道理看来像深有所获，其实哪有得到什么？
Someone who practises this principle would appear to have a lot to gain. But what is to be gained?
这个道理原本如此，只是一般人不懂得取用……
This principle is most natural, and yet,most people don't know how to use it.

37
悟者们都想通了这些，清澈地看清一切事物原本的样子。
The enlightened ones have thought through these principles and clearly see everything as it truly is.
38
他的心也就豁然开朗，不再被偏曲的错误观点所左右……
The enlightened heart is therefore wide open and no longer led everywhere by distorted points of view.
39
舍弃自我，舍弃心灵所产生的差别……
于是他不再有恐惧、渴望与幻想，不再活在颠倒错误的观念中。
After letting go of one's ego-self and the sense of separation ...
one no longer has fear, desire and fantasy, and no longer lives by a distorted point of view.
40
因为他知道这些错误的观点，都是人自己站在一己之私的立场才产生的呀。
Because one knows that all distortions of existence are generated from ego's selfish viewpoint.

因此，他的心像一潭湖水，由浊而慢慢地澄清……直达清澈平静，这就是彼岸！
Therefore, an enlightened one's mind is like the water in a lake which gradually settles down from muddiness to complete clarity and quietness ... This is what is meant by The Other Shore.
41

42
过去、现在、未来的一切悟者们，也都是依照这种能达彼岸的智慧而得到最高的觉悟。
All enlightened ones—from the past, present, and future—follow this kind of wisdom to reach from This Shore of worldly life to The Other Shore of highest consciousness.

43
摆脱了发自一己身心的偏曲看法与幻象，而直达彼岸。
Cleansing oneself of all distorted attitudes and illusions means fully reaching The Other Shore.
44
是至高无上的方法，是超绝无比的方法。
a method of supreme excellence and an outstanding method without peers!
45
所以我们应该知道，到达彼岸的智慧是伟大的方法，是大彻大悟的方法。
Therefore, we should know that such utmost and perfect wisdom is a method of grand power and ultimate illumination.

46
它能消除一切因偏曲看法而产生的妄想和痛苦。这个方法是真实的、可行的，每个人都可以采用并因它达到彼岸。
This approach can rid you of all illusion and suffering generated from distorted viewpoints.This method is realistic and practical. Everybody can adopt it to reach The Other Shore.

47
让我们为采用这方法走在半路上的悟者们唱首歌鼓励一下吧。
Let us sing a song to encourage those soul mates who are half-way to enlightenment.
彼岸
The Other Shore!

48
走在半路中的同道呀！
走在半途中的同道呀！
走往彼岸的悟者们呀！
Hey! Comrades who are half way!
Hey! Friends in the middle of the road!
Hey! Soul mates moving toward The Other Shore of enlightenment!
49
走向彼岸！
登向彼岸！
Move onto The Other Shore!
Climb onto The Other Shore!
50
哈哈哈！
登上彼岸后多快乐呀！
La, la, la!
How joyful it is to be on The Other Shore!
呵呵
Yeh!...
Yeh!...
《般若波罗蜜多心经》
The End of THE HEART SUTRA of PERFECT WISDOM.

【心经】漫画
THE HEART SUTRA ADDENDUM

工作时工作，休息时休息
Work While You Work,Play While You Play

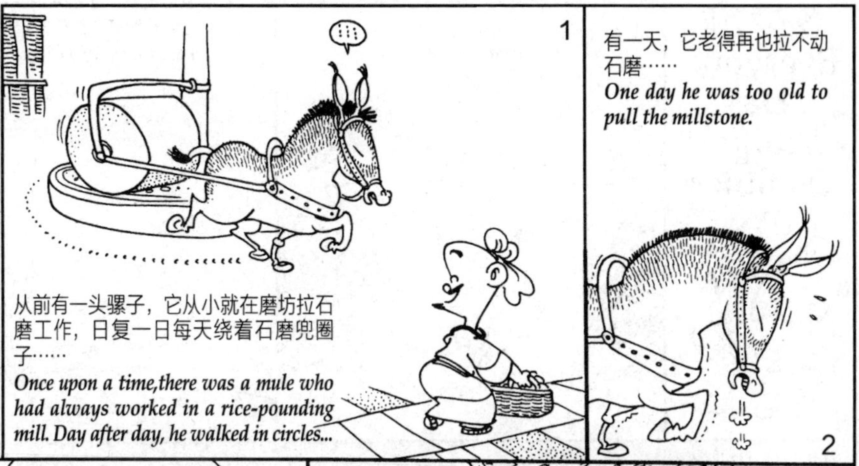
1
从前有一头骡子，它从小就在磨坊拉石磨工作，日复一日每天绕着石磨兜圈子……
Once upon a time,there was a mule who had always worked in a rice-pounding mill. Day after day, he walked in circles...
有一天，它老得再也拉不动石磨……
One day he was too old to pull the millstone.
2

3
你工作了一辈子，现在老了也该退休不必再工作了。
You have worked all your life. Now you are old and should retire from work.
从今起你每天就躺在这里吃草、睡觉、呼吸新鲜空气。
From now on, you will eat tender grasses, sleep long, and breathe fresh air.
4
5
可是，这样的日子骡子活不下去，它每天还是绕着树兜圈子，日复一日……
The mule, however, could not handle living like this. He would walk in circles around the tree, day after day ...
诸君莫笑骡子傻，也许有一天……你也是笨骡之一！
Don't you readers laugh at the stupidity of the mule. Maybe one day ... you will be one of the stupid mules!

各有特质 Everyone Has Unique Qualities

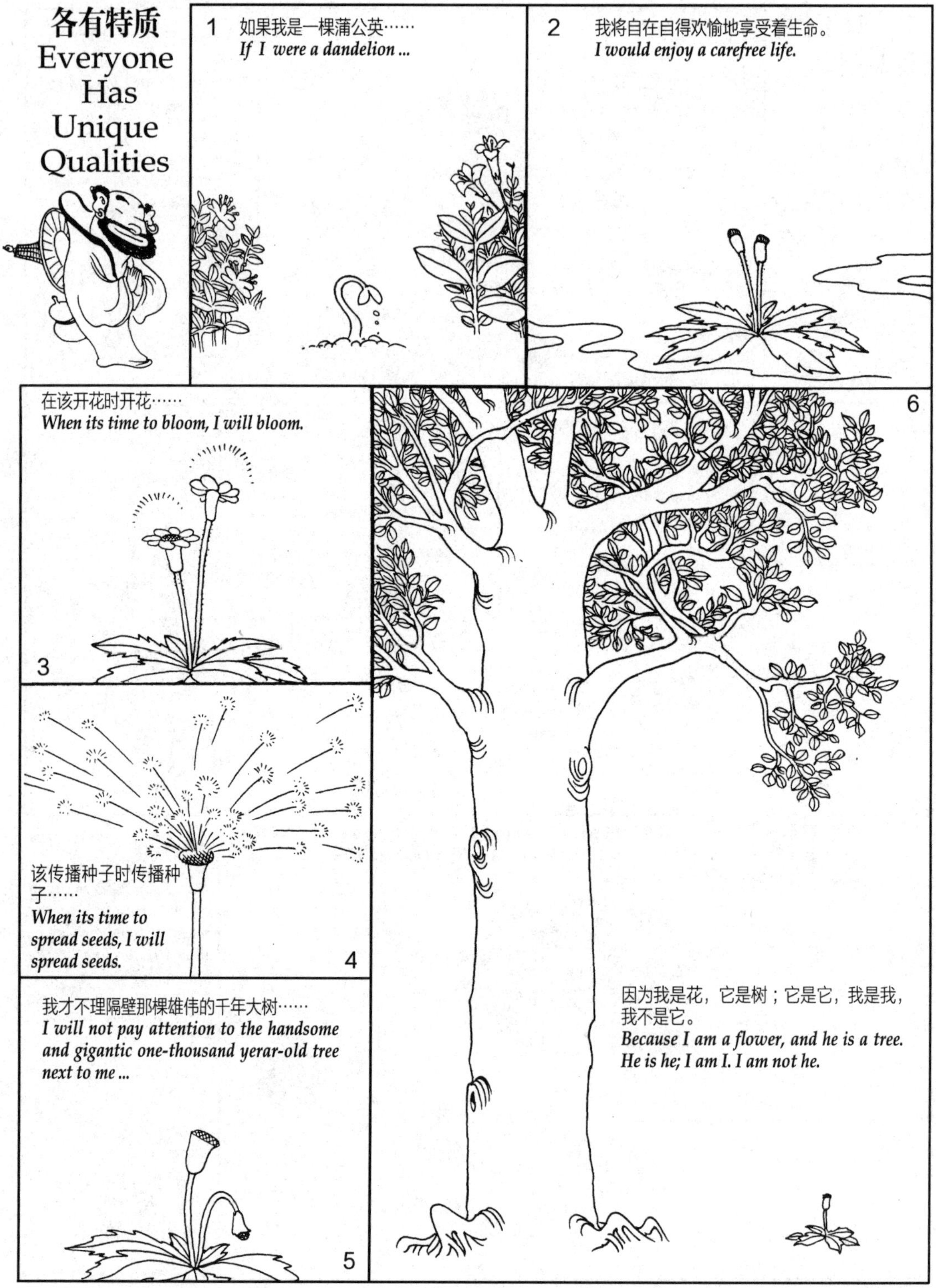
1
如果我是一棵蒲公英……
If I were a dandelion ...
2
我将自在自得欢愉地享受着生命。
I would enjoy a carefree life.
在该开花时开花……
When its time to bloom, I will bloom.
3
该传播种子时传播种子……
When its time to spread seeds, I will spread seeds.
4
我才不理隔壁那棵雄伟的千年大树……
I will not pay attention to the handsome and gigantic one-thousand yerar-old tree next to me ...
5
6
因为我是花，它是树；它是它，我是我，我不是它。
Because I am a flower, and he is a tree. He is he; I am I. I am not he.

不问前生，只问今世
Do Not Be Concerned about the Past; Only Care about the Present

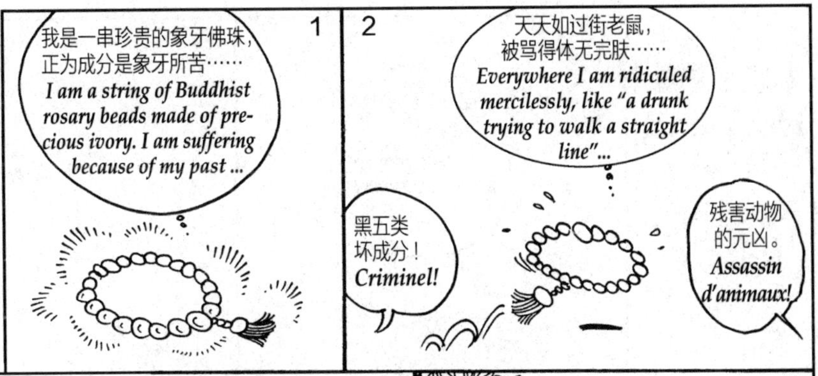
1
我是一串珍贵的象牙佛珠，正为成分是象牙所苦……
I am a string of Buddhist rosary beads made of precious ivory. I am suffering because of my past ...
2
天天如过街老鼠，被骂得体无完肤……
Everywhere I am ridiculed mercilessly, like "a drunk trying to walk a straight line"...
黑五类坏成分！
Criminel!
残害动物的元凶。
Assassin d'animaux!

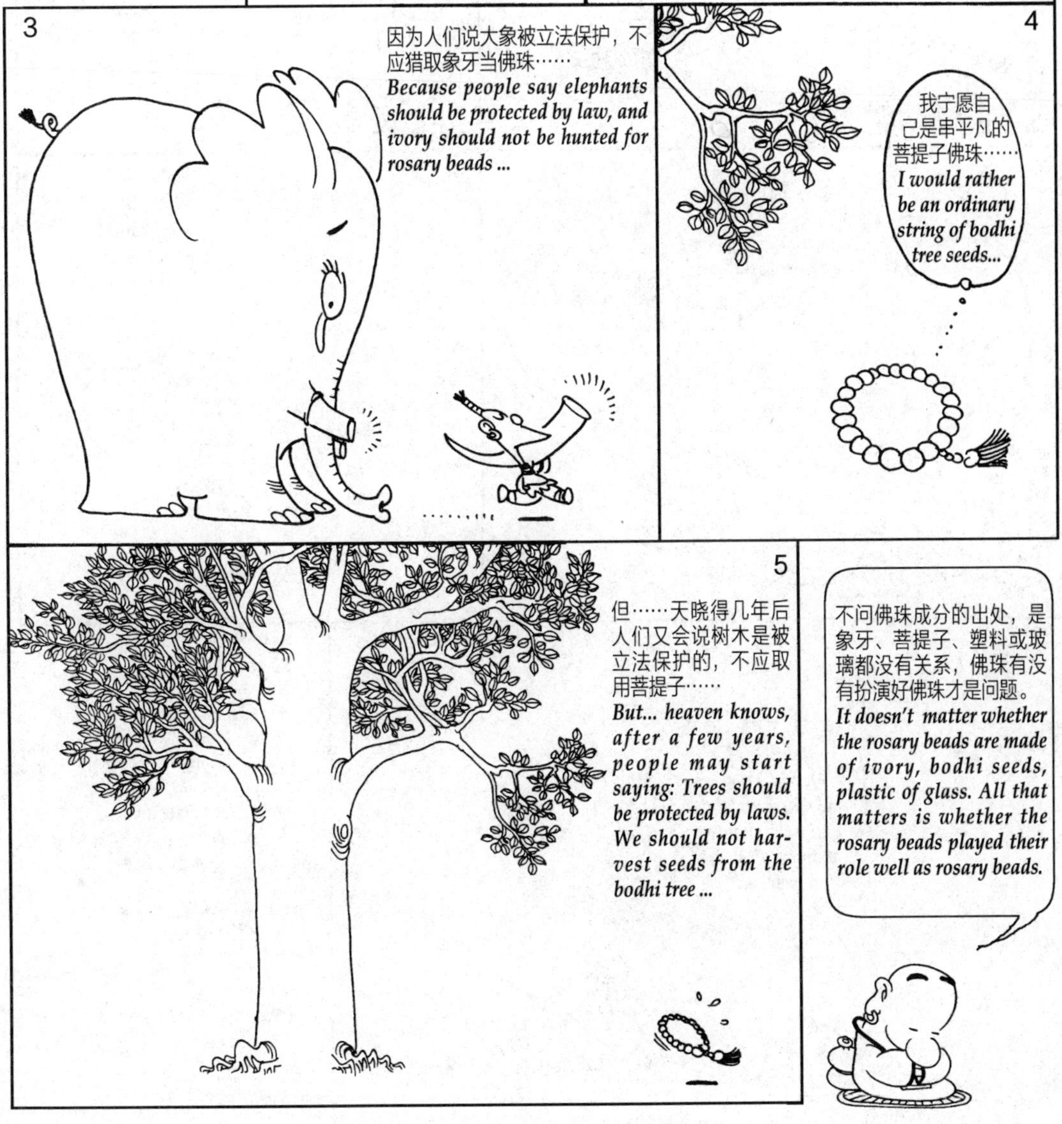
3
因为人们说大象被立法保护，不应猎取象牙当佛珠……
Because people say elephants should be protected by law, and ivory should not be hunted for rosary beads ...
4
我宁愿自己是串平凡的菩提子佛珠……
I would rather be an ordinary string of bodhi tree seeds...
5
但……天晓得几年后人们又会说树木是被立法保护的，不应取用菩提子……
But... heaven knows, after a few years, people may start saying: Trees should be protected by laws. We should not harvest seeds from the bodhi tree ...
不问佛珠成分的出处，是象牙、菩提子、塑料或玻璃都没有关系，佛珠有没有扮演好佛珠才是问题。
It doesn't matter whether the rosary beads are made of ivory, bodhi seeds, plastic of glass. All that matters is whether the rosary beads played their role well as rosary beads.

象牙·佛珠
Ivory and the Buddhist Rosary
我是一串象牙佛珠……
I am a string of rosary beads made of ivory.
以前我是牙……
I used to be tusks ...
无用，但能使象信心十足。
which were not particularly useful, but I enabled the elephant to be full of confidence.
阿弥陀佛
阿弥陀佛
Amitabha!
Amitabha!
现在我是珠……
Now I am a rosary ...
无用，但能使诵者无念安详。
Which is not particularly useful, but I help the chanters stay mindful and peaceful.
生前生后面貌不同，是牙是珠各司其职。
Although my appearances differed before and after death, I served my purpose well in both phases.

蚕与蜘蛛 The Silkworm and the Spider

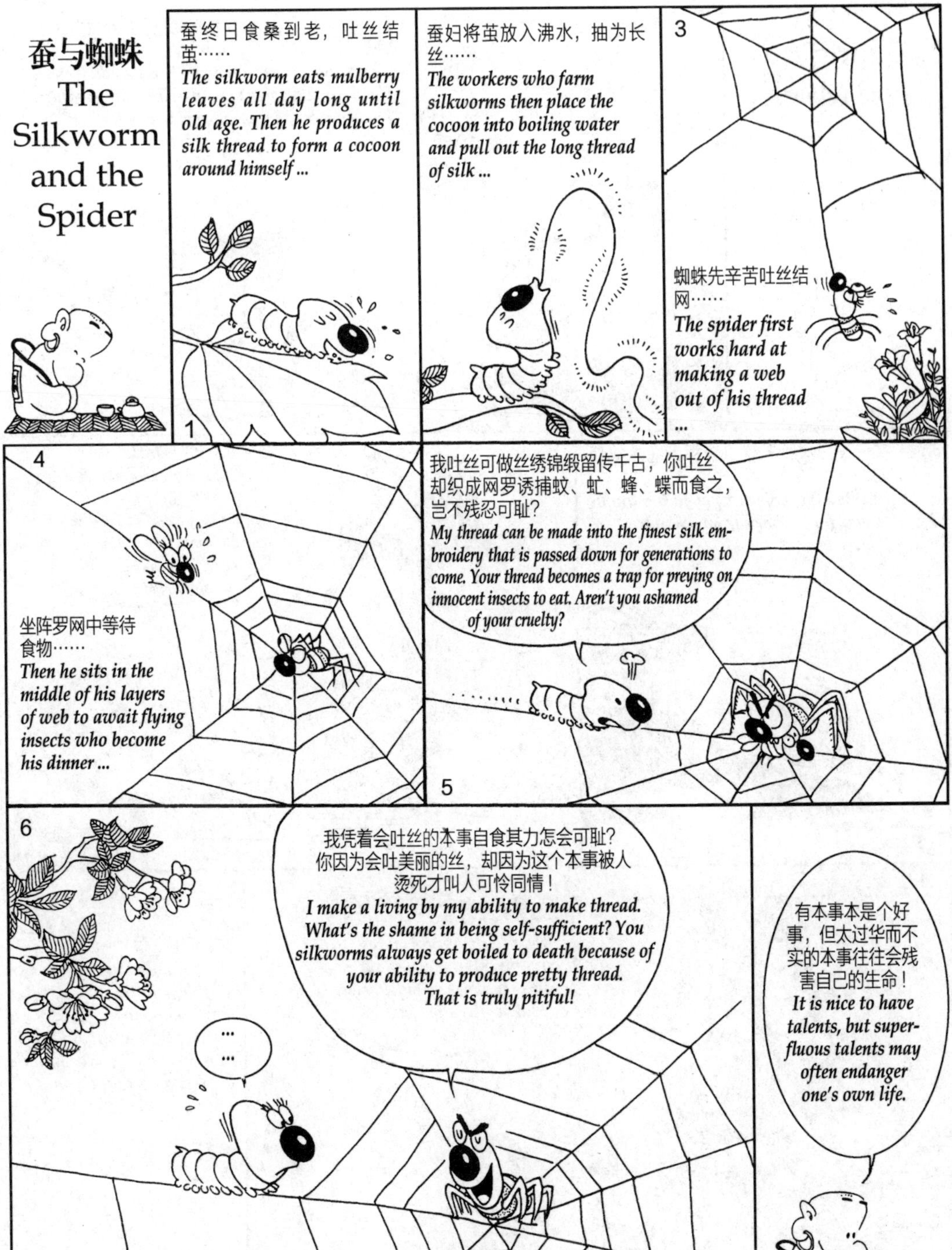
1
蚕终日食桑到老，吐丝结茧……
The silkworm eats mulberry leaves all day long until old age. Then he produces a silk thread to form a cocoon around himself ...
蚕妇将茧放入沸水，抽为长丝……
The workers who farm silkworms then place the cocoon into boiling water and pull out the long thread of silk ...
3
蜘蛛先辛苦吐丝结网……
The spider first works hard at making a web out of his thread ...
4
坐阵罗网中等待食物……
Then he sits in the middle of his layers of web to await flying insects who become his dinner ...
我吐丝可做丝绣锦缎留传千古，你吐丝却织成网罗诱捕蚊、虻、蜂、蝶而食之，岂不残忍可耻？
My thread can be made into the finest silk embroidery that is passed down for generations to come. Your thread becomes a trap for preying on innocent insects to eat. Aren't you ashamed of your cruelty?
5
6
我凭着会吐丝的本事自食其力怎会可耻？你因为会吐美丽的丝，却因为这个本事被人烫死才叫人可怜同情！
I make a living by my ability to make thread. What's the shame in being self-sufficient? You silkworms always get boiled to death because of your ability to produce pretty thread. That is truly pitiful!
...
...
有本事本是个好事，但太过华而不实的本事往往会残害自己的生命！
It is nice to have talents, but superfluous talents may often endanger one's own life.

过分要求
Asking for Too Much

1
某人有两个女儿，大女儿嫁给花匠，小女儿嫁给陶瓷匠。
Once upon a time, a woman had two daughters. The older daughter was married to a gardener. The younger one was married to a potter.
2
有一天，她到寺庙里烧香祈福求神保佑……
One day the woman went to the temple to pray for blessings from the gods ...
3
神啊！求您施法让天持续下雨，使我大女儿的花朵开得更美丽……
Dear Deity, please let the weather keep on raining, so that my older daughter's flowers will bloom better ...
4
神啊！求您施法让天持续好天气，让阳光能晒干我小女儿的陶瓷器。
Dear Deity, please let the weather stay sunny, so the sunshine will dry up my younger daughter's pottery.
世间没有完美的事物，到野外踏青，游客希望阳光亮丽；农夫则希望下雨……
There is no perfect solution for all things in this world. When city folks go to the countryside to hike, they wish for a bright sunshiny day ... while the local farmers wish for rain for their crops ...

两只蛙
Two Frogs

1
两只蛙同住在水塘，夏天池里的水被炎阳晒干……
Once two frogs lived together in a pond. One summer, the scorching sun dried up all water in the pond ...
没水住不下去……
We can't stay here any longer without water ...
2
鸟择林而栖，蛙择水而居。
Birds look for forests to live in, while us frogs look for water to live around.
3
哈！前面有一口水井！
Look! Right in front of us there's a well!
4
哼。
Mmmm.
我们跳进去吧，这里可供我们居住和吃食呢！
Let's hop right in. This is a fine place to live and eat.
5
现在住进去当然很好，问题是将来怎能够出来？
Yeh, right! It's fine to move in now, but the problem is ... how will we ever be able to get out again!
!
井 WELL

做事情需顾到结果，你的机会或许只是一口水井……跳进去容易，出来可难！

We need to consider the consequences of our decisions. Sometimes an attractive opportunity may be just water in a well ... easy to hop in, but impossible to climb out!

蝉与狐
The Cicada and the Fox
从前有一只狐饿了三天肚子，它四处发狂地找食物……
Once there was a miser who sold all of his property for silver and hid his silver in a secret place ...
1
2
没东西吃，吃只蝉也不错……
Without any other options, having a cicada for dinner is not a bad idea ...
3
伟大的歌手啊，请下来接受我的礼赞吧。
Oh, great singer, please come down here and accept my admiration perso nally.
4
哈！
Ha!
5
你中计了！
You've been tricked
6
咦？竟只是一片叶子，被骗了……
What? Just a leaf? I've been fooled ...
7
从狐狸大便中的蝉翼我看到同伴犯错的下场。相同的错误不能犯两次，有时连犯一次也不可以。
From the wings of cicada in the faeces of foxes, I have seen the consequences of my friends' mistakes. The same mistake should not be repeated twice. Sometimes, one mistake in a lifetime is too many.
聪明的家伙……
Smart guy...
智者，能从自己的错误经验中得到教训；上智者，能从别人的错误中得到教训。
The smart ones can learn lessons from their own mistakes; the smartest ones learn lessons from the mistakes of others.

银子与石头
Silver and Rock
从前有个守财奴，把财产全兑成银子藏在一个隐秘的地方……
Once there was a miser who sold all of his property for silver and hid silver in a secret place...
1
他天天去探望这些财富，每天看得美滋滋的……
Everyday he would visit his fortune and he always enjoyed himself very much ...
2
有一天一个小偷知道这秘密，就把银子偷了……
One day a thief found out about his secret and stole his silver ...
3
嘻嘻嘻!
Hee,hee, hee!
啊！银子不见了……
Oh, no! My silver is gone!
4
我全部的财产五百两银子全给偷走了！
All my fortune of 500 Chinese hectograms of silver has been stolen.
5

6
?
silver
你把这石头当做银子不就行了，因你未充分利用银子的功能，这与石头又有何两样？
Isn't it the same for you to see this rock as silver? You never put your silver to any use. What's the difference between your silver and the rock.
silver
7

守财奴之所以守财是因为他不识钱财的真正价值，人不甘于扮演自己是因为他对自己没认识清楚。

A miser is obsessed about keeping his fortune because he does not recognize the real value of money. A person who does not know his true self-worth will not be satisfied with playing his role in life.

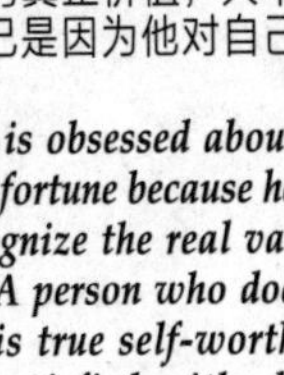

不知足是病
Discontent Is a Disease

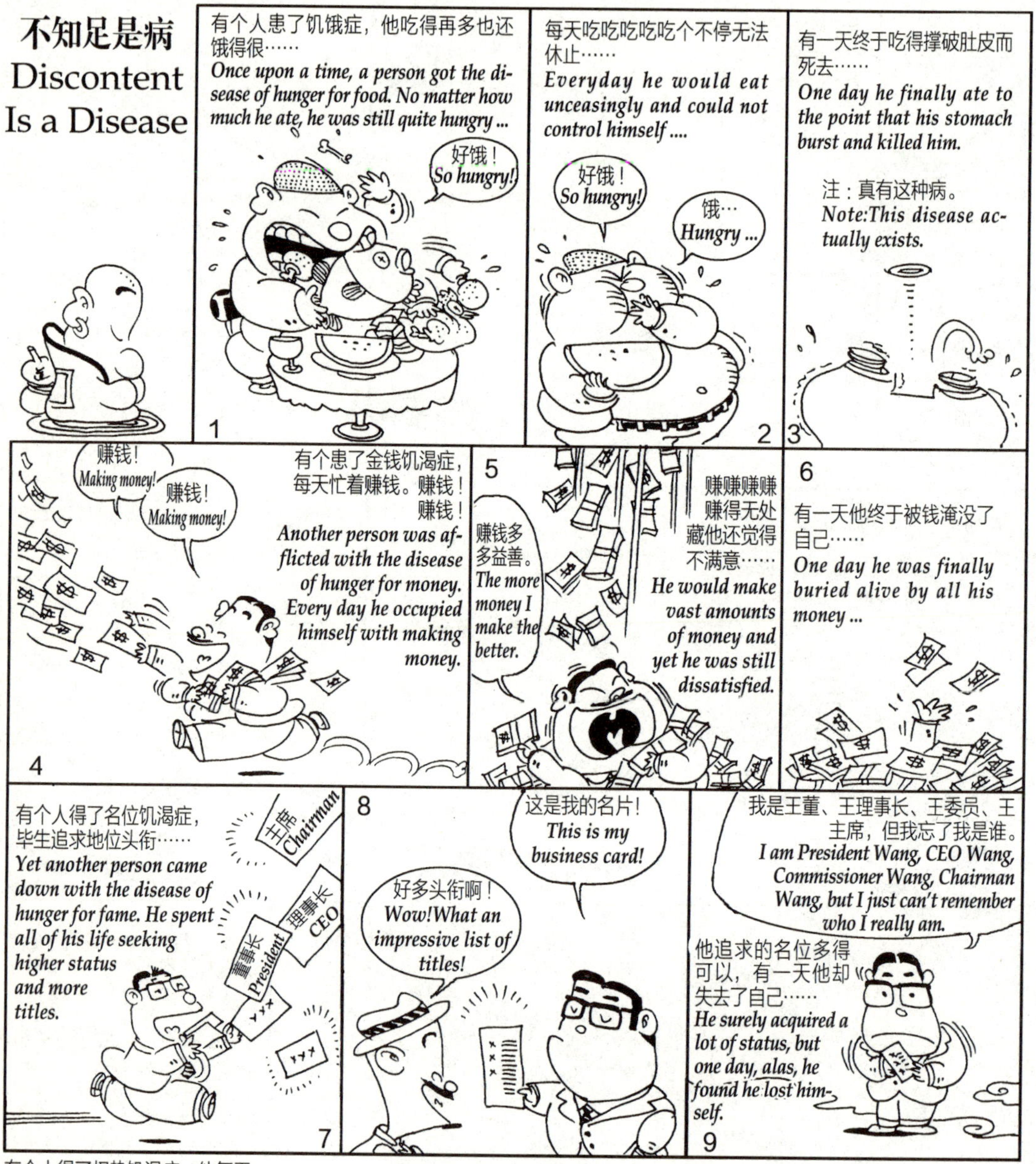
有个人患了饥饿症，他吃得再多也还饿得很……
Once upon a time, a person got the disease of hunger for food. No matter how much he ate, he was still quite hungry ...
好饿！
So hungry!
1
每天吃吃吃吃吃个不停无法休止……
Everyday he would eat unceasingly and could not control himself ....
好饿！
So hungry!
饿…
Hungry ...
2
有一天终于吃得撑破肚皮而死去……
One day he finally ate to the point that his stomach burst and killed him.
注：真有这种病。
Note:This disease actually exists.
3
赚钱！
Making money!
赚钱！
Making money!
有个患了金钱饥渴症，每天忙着赚钱。赚钱！赚钱！
Another person was afflicted with the disease of hunger for money. Every day he occupied himself with making money.
4
5
赚钱多多益善。
The more money I make the better.
赚赚赚赚赚得无处藏他还觉得不满意……
He would make vast amounts of money and yet he was still dissatisfied.
6
有一天他终于被钱淹没了自己……
One day he was finally buried alive by all his money ...
有个人得了名位饥渴症，毕生追求地位头衔……
Yet another person came down with the disease of hunger for fame. He spent all of his life seeking higher status and more titles.
主席
Chairman
理事长
CEO
董事长
President
7
8
这是我的名片！
This is my business card!
好多头衔啊！
Wow!What an impressive list of titles!
我是王董、王理事长、王委员、王主席，但我忘了我是谁。
I am President Wang, CEO Wang, Commissioner Wang, Chairman Wang, but I just can't remember who I really am.
他追求的名位多得可以，有一天他却失去了自己……
He surely acquired a lot of status, but one day, alas, he found he lost himself.
9

有个人得了权势饥渴症，他每天……
……
有个人得了古董饥渴症，他每天 收集收集……
……
有个人他得了工作饥渴症，他每天……
……
有个人得了……
……
有个人……

One person got the disease of hunger for power.
Every day he would ...
...
One person got the disease of hunger for antiques.
Every day he would collect more and more ...
...
One person got the disease of hunger for work.
Every day he would ...
...
One person got the disease ...
...
One person ...

恶魔的帮手
A Person's Worst Enemy

1
当世上发现了铁的时候，大树们就忧虑着未来的命运……
When the world discovered iron, the trees started worrying about their future fate ...
当当！
clang! clang!

2
可怕！
Despicable!
既生树何生斧，是谁发明了这种恶魔的凶器？
Why are there axes in this world to create a holocaust for trees? Who invented this murderous tool of the devil?
3

4
如果不是树提供了斧柄，光是这块铁怎能伤害得了你们？
If the tree did not provide the handle for the axe, how could this mere piece of iron hurt you much?

厄运形成的缘起，往往是因为自己，最大的敌人往往是自身。

The origin of bad luck can often be traced back to the self. In fact, a person's worst enemy may often be himself.

铁杵磨针喻

A New Interpretation for the Chinese Legend of Turning an Iron Rod into a Needle

1
有恒心为成功之本，凡事只要坚持认真去做必能得到成果。
Persistence is the basis of success. Anything can be accomplished so long as you seriously persist in doing it.
从前有个妈妈教训她的儿子说：
Once there was a mother who taught her son:
2
只要有恒心，铁杵也能磨成绣花针。
So long as you are persistent, even a big iron rod can be turned into a small needle for embroidery...
3
二十年后……
Twenty years later...
4
瞧！铁杵磨成针证明只要有毅力没有任何事不能达成。
Look! The iron rod is now a needle. This proves that so long as there is endurance, there is no ambitious goal that cannot be reached.
5
但成果只是一根绣花针，失去的却是整个青春。
You invested your valuable years of youth, but your only accom- plishment is a small needle.
铁杵磨针固然没错，但用功既重所期甚轻，失去的比得到的还多。
There is nothing wrong with turning an iron rod into a needle ...but a small return on a major invest- ment does not pay off.

握在手上的才切实际

Only What We Hold in Our Hands Is Meaningful

1
一只熊在溪边苦等了一天……
A bear once waited patiently for a whole day by a stream...
2
终于捕到一条小鱼。
Finally, he caught a tiny fish.

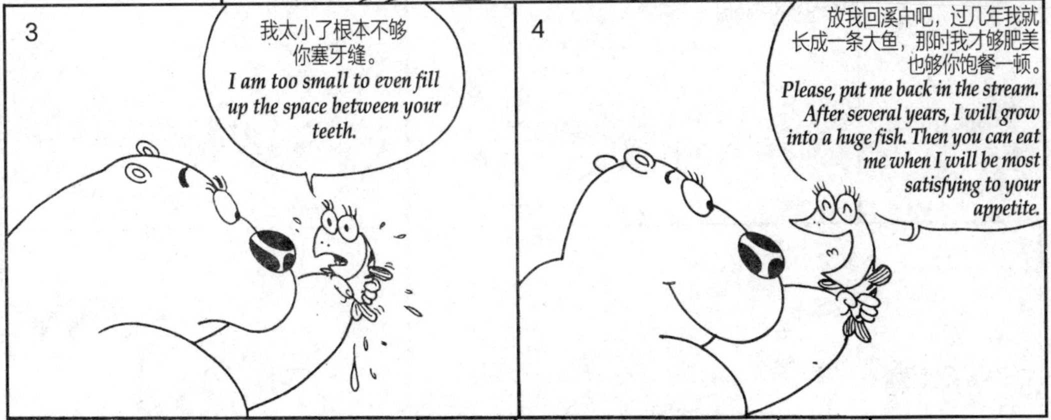
3
我太小了根本不够你塞牙缝。
I am too small to even fill up the space between your teeth.
4
放我回溪中吧，过几年我就长成一条大鱼，那时我才够肥美也够你饱餐一顿。
Please, put me back in the stream. After several years, I will grow into a huge fish. Then you can eat me when I will be most satisfying to your appetite.

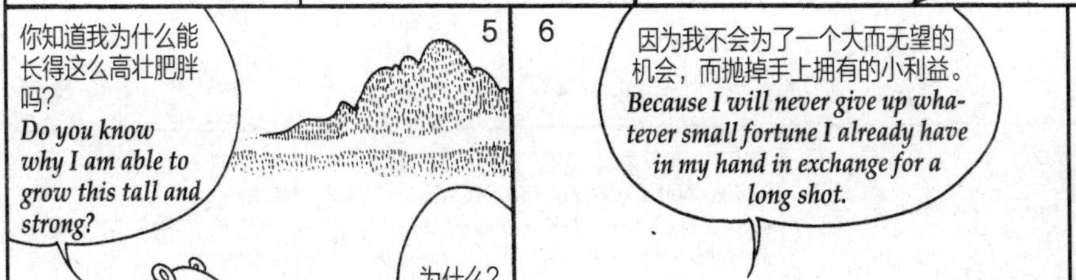
5
你知道我为什么能长得这么高壮肥胖吗？
Do you know why I am able to grow this tall and strong?
为什么？
why?
6
因为我不会为了一个大而无望的机会，而抛掉手上拥有的小利益。
Because I will never give up whatever small fortune I already have in my hand in exchange for a long shot.
完了……
OOPS!

人多怀念着过去，期盼着将来，而没有在过现在。能掌握目前拥有的，真切地过着现在，才算是体会人生的人。

Most people hold onto the past, look forward to the future, and do not embrace the present. Only those who can appreciate what they have now live fully.

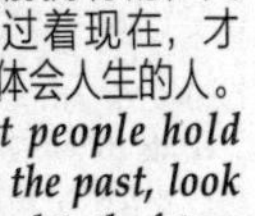

自知之明好量力
Know Yourself and Stay within Your Capabilities

从前有个人很崇拜英雄侠义……
Once there was a man who loved worshipping heroes.
水浒*
*The Lives of 108 Heroes
我要效法武松打虎的勇气。
I should model my life after the courage of Wu Song who was famous for fighting tigers.
来上三杯出发找虎去！
Let me have three toasts and set out to look for tigers!
哈！发现虎迹了！
Ha! I found the footprints of a tiger!
你千里而来为的是想与我比一比？
So you came from thousands of miles away in order to fight me?
不不不！我只是找您的足迹，不敢真正找您……
No!No!No! I was only interested in finding your footprints. I dare not even think of approaching anyone as highly respected as you ...
幻想往往不切实际。未能达成目标，十之八九都只能怨自己不了解自己的能力。
Fantasized ideals often do not work in real life. When people cannot reach their preset goals, most of them can only blame themselves for not knowing the limits of their own capabilities.

狐狸与葡萄园
The Fox and the Grape Vine-yard

1 有一只狐狸看到一个葡萄园结满了果实……
Once there was a fox who saw a vineyard full of scrumpitions grapes...
进去饱餐它一顿。
I'llget in there and enjoy a big meal.
2 可是它太胖了穿不过栅栏……
But he was too fat to squeeze through the fence...
3 于是它三天三夜不饮不食使身体消瘦下去……So he starved himself for three days and three nights in order to slim down.
4 终于能够进来了！
Finally! I can squeeze myself through.
5 好吃！好吃极了！
Yum! Delicious!
6 吃得真过瘾，回去吧。
What a wonderful treat. Now its time to go home.
7 哇！又钻不出去了……
Wow! I can't get out anymore...
8 只好重施故技，又三天三夜不饮不食……
So he had to repeat his old trick again. He went without food for three days and three nights...
9 结果是出来了没错，但肚子不是跟进去时一样。
I finally got out, but my stomach is as hungry as ever.
人生何尝不是如此？赤裸裸地诞生，又孑然而死去。人死之后遗留下善行才值得称颂，无人能带走自己一生经营的财富与盛名。
Isn't life like this too? We were born naked and take nothing with us when we leave. Only good deeds that benefit humanity are worthwhile praising after a person dies. You can't take with you the fame or fortune that were the result of your lifetime pursuit...

每个人该有两个生日
Everyone Should Have Two Birthdays

每个人都是生自于父母，但是……
Everyone is given birth by his parents, but...
1
我从哪里来？
Where did I come from?
我要去哪里？
Where am I going?
2

3
我是谁？
Who am I?
4
我到底是什么？
What exactly am I?
我有能力做什么？
What am I capable of doing?
我想做什么？
What do I want to do?
我就是我，我不是他！
I am myself. I am not Him!
5

我找到了自己是什么！
I have found my own heart!
6
7
8
我明白自己是何物，我破茧而出了！
I understand what my heart is now. I have broken my cocoon and am reborn!

每个人都生自于父母……重要的是自己还要让自己再诞生一次。
Everyone is given birth by parents . The important thing is to allow the heart to be born again.

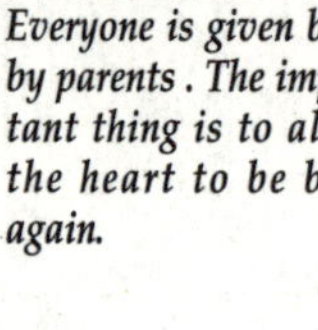

野驴与家驴
The Wild Donkey & the Domesticated Donkey

从前有只住在山林的野驴，它每天为了三餐找食物找得很苦……
Once there was a wild donkey who lived in the woods on a mountain. He worked extremely hard every day just searching out enough food for three meals...
呼！呼！
1
2
一天，它看到了一只饲养的驴吃得又好，住得也舒服……
One day, he saw a domesticated donkey who ate really well and lived in quite a comfortable place...

3
你有吃不完的粮食吃得肥嘟嘟，真是幸福。
You have an endless supply of food to eat to make you chubby. How lucky!
!
4
吃饱了还不快去工作，站在这里发什么呆？
You have finished your meal. Go! Hurry to work! What are you standing around for?
咩！
Meeaaaah!

用自由换来幸福，终究是得不偿失……
If freedom is exchanged for fortune, all the gain is not worth the price...
5

以条件交换得来的利益，多是不值得羡慕的。失去的往往多过得到的，这笔生意做得糊涂。

Profits gained by giving up your valuables are often not worth envying; the loss may often outweigh the gain. This is not a shrewd business deal.

捞过界的屠夫
The Butcher Who Crossed His Level of Competence

1
有只饿狼有天遇到一头驴……
One day a hungry wolf ran into a donkey...
2
哈哈！今天可饱餐一顿驴肉料理。
Ha! Today is the day for a feast-the special cuisine of donkey meat!
3
我脚扎到一根刺，要吃我最好先把刺拔出来，免得不小心伤了你的喉。
My foot was stuck by a thorn. Before you eat me, you had better pull it out so you won't hurt your throat by accident.
4
是这里吗？
Is it here?
对对对没错！
Yeh, yeh, yeh. That's right!
5
砰！
KA-WACK!
你中计了！
You got tricked!
6
是我不对，父亲教我处理肉的技术，可是我偏去做医生的事。
It's my own fault. My father taught me the techniques of butchering, and yet I chose to operate like a surgeon.
专精一味是好事，别逞强捞过界去做自己不熟悉的事……
It is a good thing to be specialized in what you do. Don't show off beyond your level of competence by doing things that are not familiar to you...

驴叫与蝉鸣
The Cry of the Donkey & the Singing of the Cicada

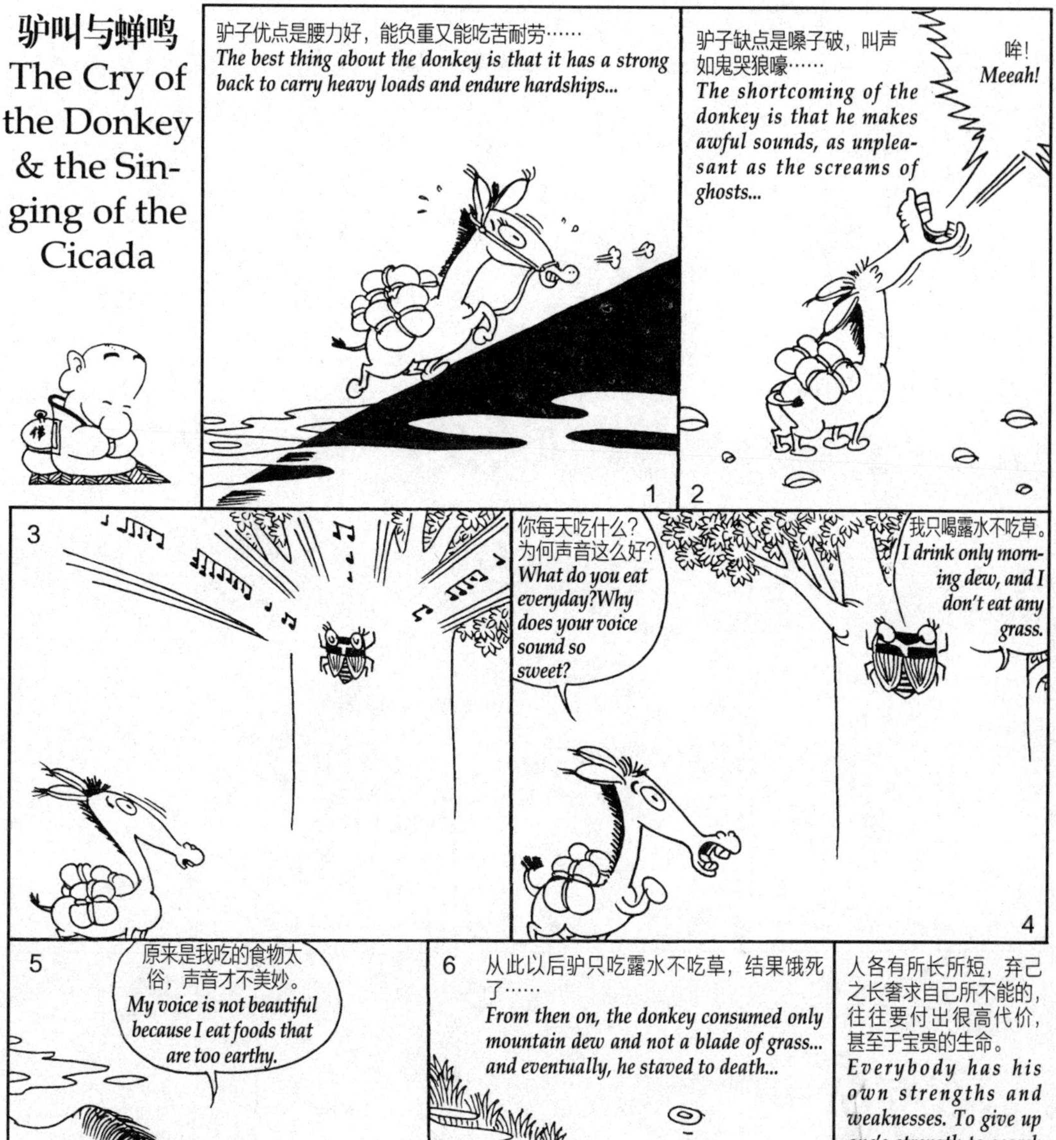
驴子优点是腰力好，能负重又能吃苦耐劳……
The best thing about the donkey is that it has a strong back to carry heavy loads and endure hardships...
1
2
驴子缺点是嗓子破，叫声如鬼哭狼嚎……
The shortcoming of the donkey is that he makes awful sounds, as unpleasant as the screams of ghosts...
咩！
Meeah!
3
你每天吃什么？为何声音这么好？
What do you eat everyday?Why does your voice sound so sweet?
我只喝露水不吃草。
I drink only morning dew, and I don't eat any grass.
4
5
原来是我吃的食物太俗，声音才不美妙。
My voice is not beautiful because I eat foods that are too earthy.
6
从此以后驴只吃露水不吃草，结果饿死了……
From then on, the donkey consumed only mountain dew and not a blade of grass... and eventually, he staved to death...
人各有所长所短，弃己之长奢求自己所不能的，往往要付出很高代价，甚至于宝贵的生命。
Everybody has his own strengths and weaknesses. To give up one's strength to search for what is beyond one's capabilities often requires paying a high price—even to the extent of one's own life.

蚊与牛 The Mosquito & the Ox

1
从前有一只蚊子停在一头牛的角上……
Once there was a mosquito who landed on the horn of an ox...
2
良久……
After a long while...
3
良久……
After a very long while...
4
走啦！
I am leaving!
5
嘿！我要走了不再陪你，希望你别介意。
Hey, I've got to go and can't keep you company any longer.
6
我不知道你来，也没感觉到你的存在，你要走跟我有何关系？
I didn't know when you came. I never even felt you there. What does it have to do with me that you're leaving?
人往往过度膨胀高估自己，自己看自己比别人看自己更重要一些。
People often overly inflate their selfimportance. They are more important in their own eyes than in the eyes of others.

人生
就是过程
Life Is in the Living
1
如果我是黄河——河的源头是我生之时；出海口是我死之刻……
If I were the Yellow River of China – the origin of the river represents when I was born; the entrance into the ocean is when I die ...
生 Birth
死 Death
2
我从疏细的小水慢慢汇聚成流，再慢慢形成大河……
I gather myself from scattered small creeks into large streams and then slowly into this major river ...
3
在我的旅途中时而狭逆……
During my journey, sometimes the path is narrow and twisted...
4
时而宽畅……
Sometimes it's wide and open...
5
时而汹涌澎湃……
Sometimes it's rough and turbulent...
6
时而平静安详……
Sometimes it's calm and peaceful...

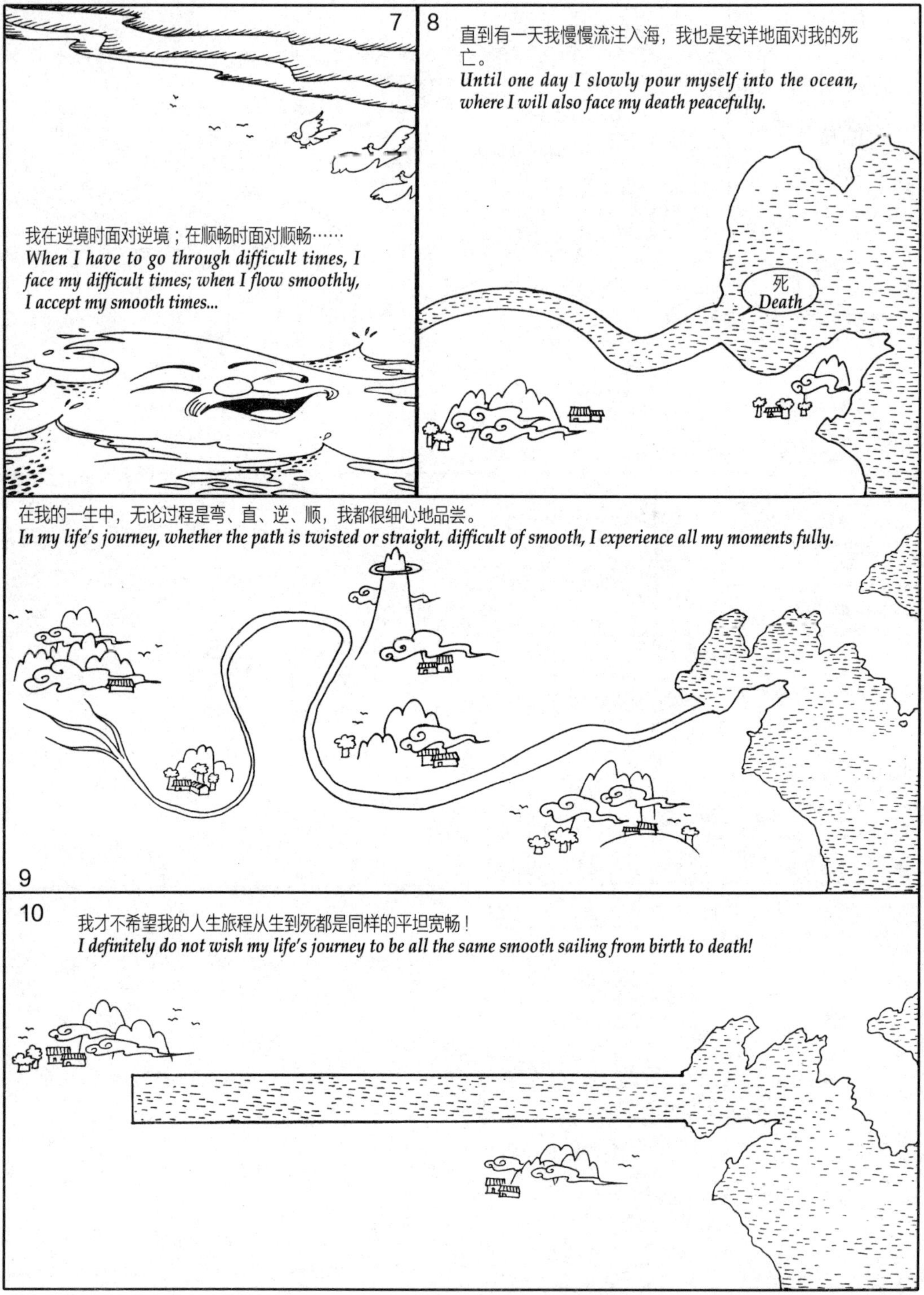
7
我在逆境时面对逆境；在顺畅时面对顺畅……
When I have to go through difficult times, I face my difficult times; when I flow smoothly, I accept my smooth times...
8
直到有一天我慢慢流注入海，我也是安详地面对我的死亡。
Until one day I slowly pour myself into the ocean, where I will also face my death peacefully.
死
Death
在我的一生中，无论过程是弯、直、逆、顺，我都很细心地品尝。
In my life's journey, whether the path is twisted or straight, difficult of smooth, I experience all my moments fully.
9
10
我才不希望我的人生旅程从生到死都是同样的平坦宽畅！
I definitely do not wish my life's journey to be all the same smooth sailing from birth to death!

何谓真“象”
What Is a True “Elephant”?

从前有七个瞎子，他们从没看过象，更不知道象长得像什么样……
Once there were seven blindmen. None of them had ever seen an elephant, and none had any idea what an elephant looked like...
象?
Elephant?
1
2
一天，他们终于有机会碰到了一只象，于是大家急忙用手去端详……
One day, they had a chance to meet a live elephant, so everyone hurried to find out what an elephant was like with their hands...
扇
A fan
岩
A rock
墙
A wall
棒
A stick
绳
A rope
柱
A column
管
A hose
3
我们都知道了什么是真“象”！
Now we all know what a true elephant is!
4
象像一根柱子。
An elephant is like a column!

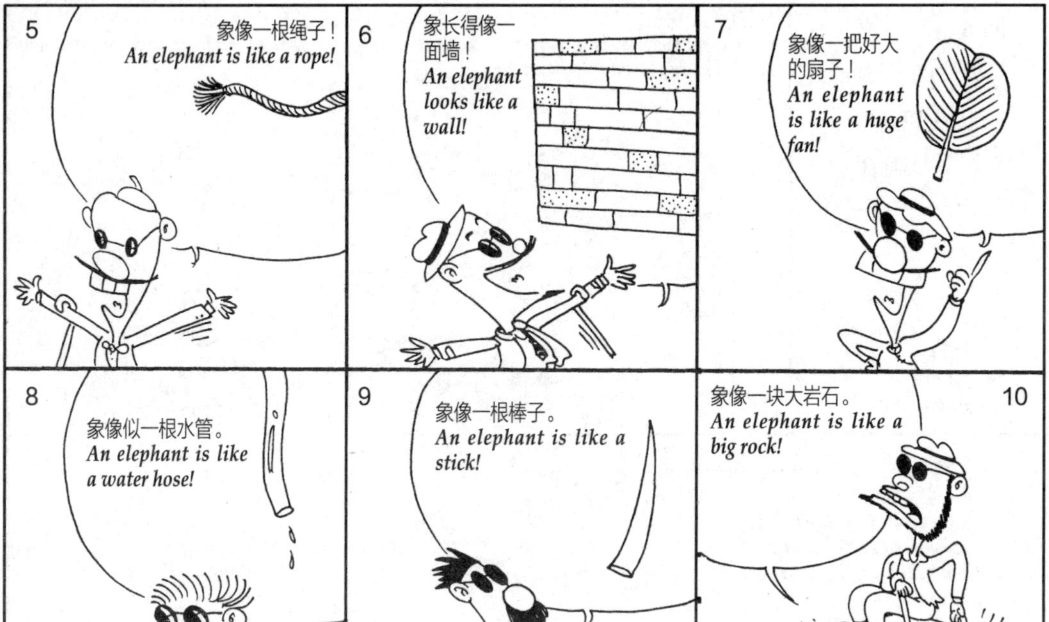
5
象像一根绳子！
An elephant is like a rope!
6
象长得像一面墙！
An elephant looks like a wall!
7
象像一把好大的扇子！
An elephant is like a huge fan!
8
象像似一根水管。
An elephant is like a water hose!
9
象像一根棒子。
An elephant is like a stick!
10
象像一块大岩石。
An elephant is like a big rock!
11
象像柱子。A column.
象像绳子。A rope.
象像一块岩石。A rock.
错了！象像扇子才对！You're all wrong!It is like a fan!
不对，象像一面墙！A wall!
象像水管。A water hose.
象好像一棒子。A stick.
象不像柱、绳、墙、扇、管、棒、岩，象就是象。
An elephant is not like a column, rope, wall, fan, hose, stick,or rock. An elephant is an elephant.
你们都站在片面的角度观象，怎能看到真"象"！
Each of you has touched only one part of the elephant. How could you possibly understand the whole truth of an elephant.
12

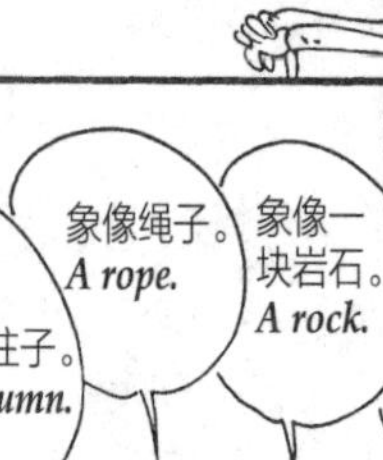

人有了立足点就不能看到真相！
人不应据自己的观点用眼耳鼻舌身意去看对象，而应全然地投入对象之中化二元为一元。
无论你置身于任何时间，就与时间同为一体；置身于任何空间，就与空间同为一体；面对任何对象就与对象同为一体，完完全全融入其中。
不要站在自己的立场看对象，不要站在昨天的你看今天！

Once people have their points of view, they are blocked from understanding the truth. Whatever time it happens to be, you are one with time; whatever space it happens to be, you are one with space; whoever you are with, you are both an integral part of the universal essence. People should not use the perspective of the ego-self to judge objects with eyes, ears, nose, tongue,body and mind. Do not judge today from the ego-self of yesterday.

小草的觉悟
The Enlightenment of a Blade of Grass

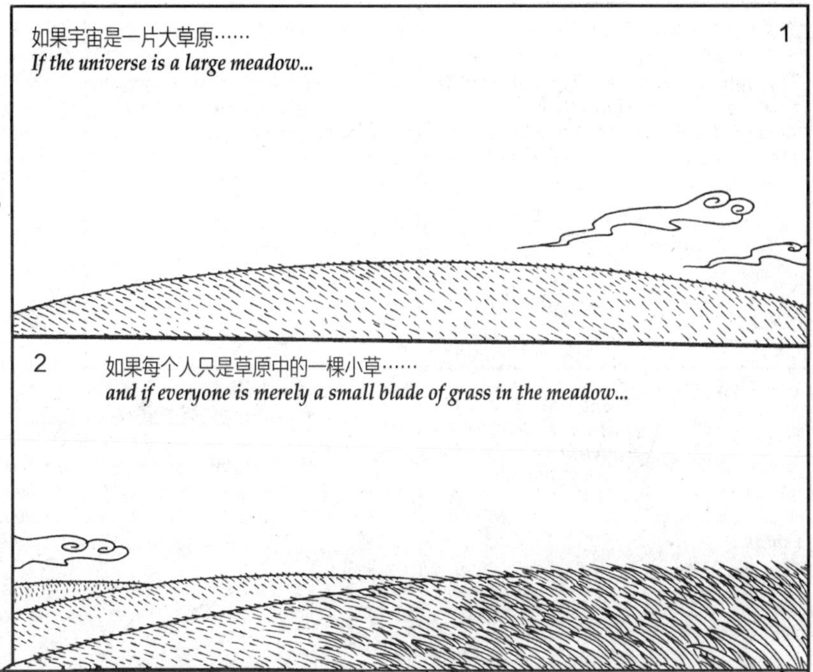
如果宇宙是一片大草原……
If the universe is a large meadow...
1
2
如果每个人只是草原中的一棵小草……
and if everyone is merely a small blade of grass in the meadow...

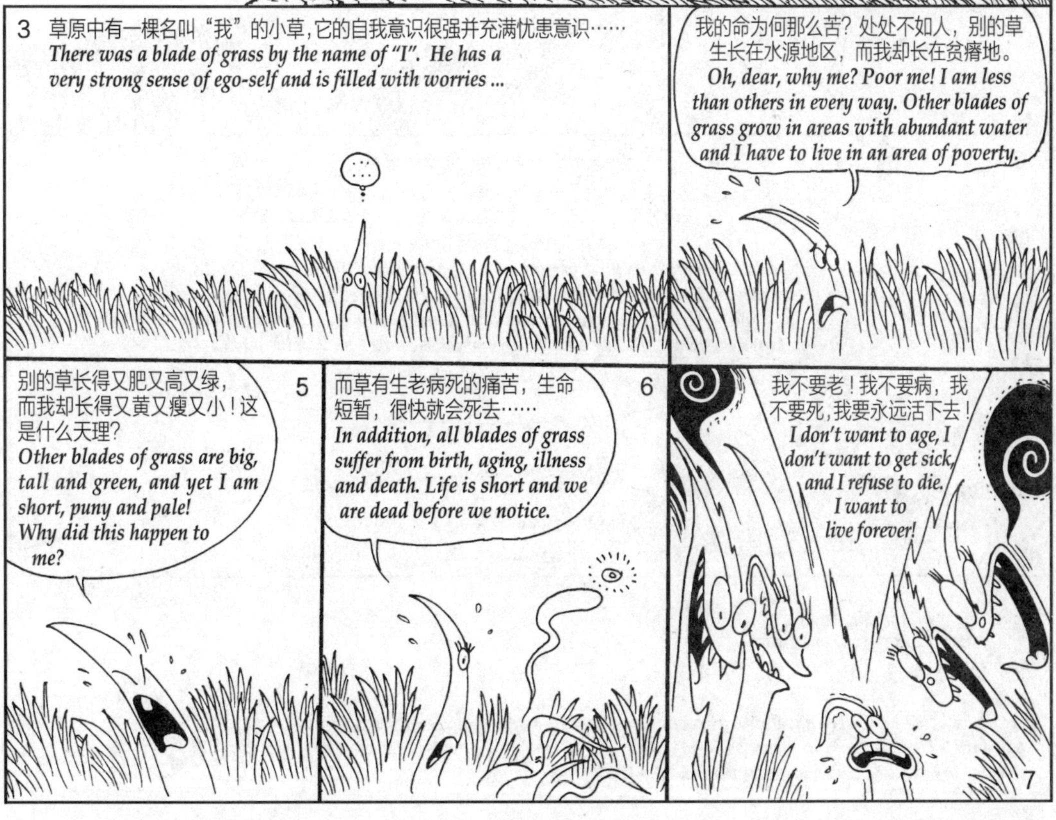
3
草原中有一棵名叫“我”的小草，它的自我意识很强并充满忧患意识……
There was a blade of grass by the name of "I". He has a very strong sense of ego-self and is filled with worries ...
我的命为何那么苦？处处不如人，别的草生长在水源地区，而我却长在贫瘠地。
Oh, dear, why me? Poor me! I am less than others in every way. Other blades of grass grow in areas with abundant water and I have to live in an area of poverty.
5
别的草长得又肥又高又绿，而我却长得又黄又瘦又小！这是什么天理？
Other blades of grass are big, tall and green, and yet I am short, puny and pale! Why did this happen to me?
6
而草有生老病死的痛苦，生命短暂，很快就会死去……
In addition, all blades of grass suffer from birth, aging, illness and death. Life is short and we are dead before we notice.
我不要老！我不要病，我不要死，我要永远活下去！
I don't want to age, I don't want to get sick, and I refuse to die. I want to live forever!
7

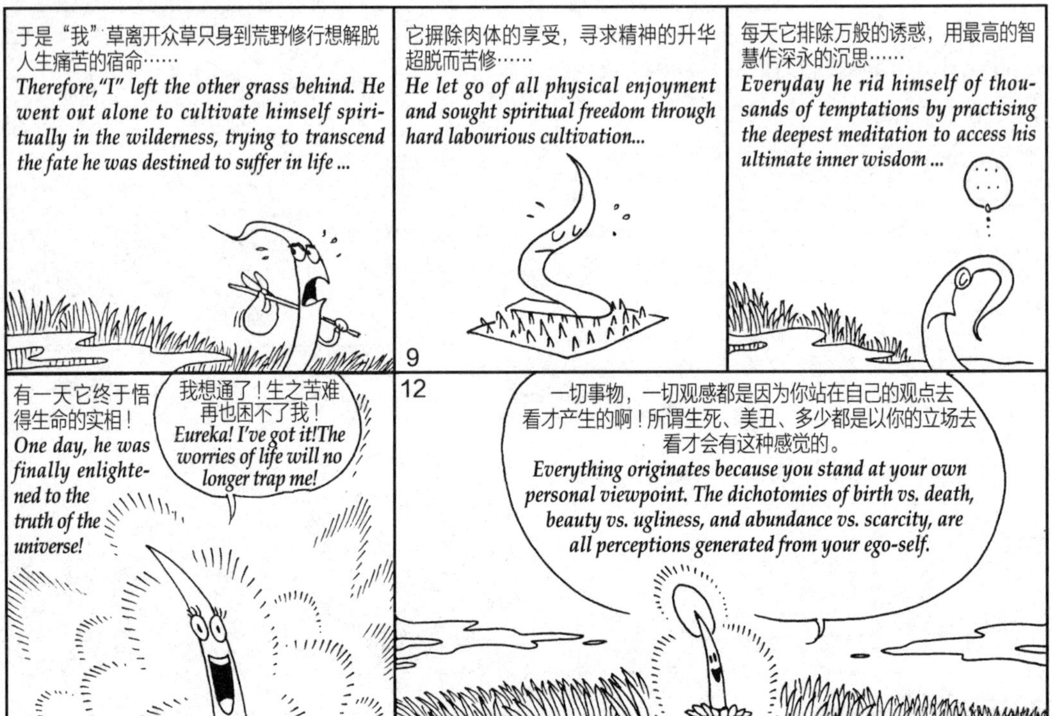
于是“我”草离开众草只身到荒野修行想解脱人生痛苦的宿命……
Therefore,“I” left the other grass behind. He went out alone to cultivate himself spiritually in the wilderness, trying to transcend the fate he was destined to suffer in life ...
它摒除肉体的享受，寻求精神的升华超脱而苦修……
He let go of all physical enjoyment and sought spiritual freedom through hard labourious cultivation...
每天它排除万般的诱惑，用最高的智慧作深永的沉思……
Everyday he rid himself of thousands of temptations by practising the deepest meditation to access his ultimate inner wisdom ...
有一天它终于悟得生命的实相！
One day, he was finally enlightened to the truth of the universe!
我想通了！生之苦难再也困不了我！
Eureka! I've got it!The worries of life will no longer trap me!
一切事物，一切观感都是因为你站在自己的观点去看才产生的啊！所谓生死、美丑、多少都是以你的立场去看才会有这种感觉的。
Everything originates because you stand at your own personal viewpoint. The dichotomies of birth vs. death, beauty vs. ugliness, and abundance vs. scarcity, are all perceptions generated from your ego-self.
不据自己的立场去侦测就不会感受到这一切偏曲信息，也就不产生各种差异的分别心。也就无所谓“因”，也无所谓“果”。也无所谓因果的来不来临，也不再为老、死的问题所困扰而痛苦忧心……
If you don't observe from your personal standpoint, you will not generate all sorts of mental separations from the essence of the universe. Therefore, there is no so-called “cause” and “effect.”There is no concern over whether any causal effect will arrive of not, and no more suffering over the troubles associated with aging and death ...

如果宇宙是一片大草原……
如果每个人只是草原中的一棵小草……
那么草就是草原的一分子，草也是草原本身……虽然草生死交替，但草原本身却依然生生不息。

If the universe is a large meadow... If everyone is merely a small blade of grass in the meadow .. Then each blade of grass is one with the meadow ... Although there are alternations of birth and death in grass, the meadow itself is forever alive.

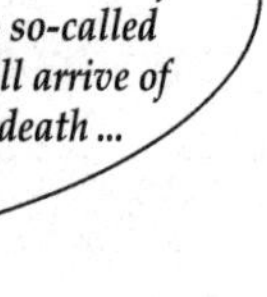

水与咖啡
Water & Coffee
1
别瞧我小小一杯咖啡，价钱可是不少，一杯可要一百元！
Don't you underestimate a small cup of coffee like me. I am worth a lot of money. Each cup will cost you $100!
2
喝了我可得神效，提神解劳又不打瞌睡。
People who drink me get magical results. Their spirits get lifted and their tiredness is left behind so they are no longer sleepy.
3
咖啡哪有醇酒好？酒才是世上最棒的饮料，喝了气氛好。
How could coffee be on a par with a good liquor like me? Alcoholic drinks are the best beverages in the world. After a drink, people become friendly and romantic.
4
况且酒的身价也高过咖啡，一杯八百元还不包括小费！
Besides, liquor also costs more than coffee, $800 per glass, not including tip.
XO
5
比上不足、比下有余，最少我还赢过这杯清水。
Although I am not the best, I am much better than some others.At least I beat this glass of clear water for sure.
6
桌上唯一免费的饮料，价值最低。
He is the only free drink on this table. He costs almost nothing.
笑死人啦！
What a clown!
7
别瞧不起人了，在此我的价值不如你们，但在沙漠中我却是最珍贵的东西。
Don't look down on me. Although I am worth less than you in this restaurant, in the desert I am the most precious beverage.
是没错……
Well, that is correct …

8
清水说得没错，
且听我冻顶乌龙茶来为各位说道。
Clear water makes sense. Please allow me, specialty brand Oolong tea, to explain to you.
9
天下万物没有好坏贵贱之分，
每样东西都有它的价值，都有它的好！
In this world, there is no absolute difference in the worth of anything. Everything is valuable and beautiful in its own way!
10
若论价值我冻顶乌龙茶一两二千元可不比两位贱……
In terms of monetary value, good tea leaves, like myself, cost S20 per ounce. I am definitely not cheaper than the two of you ...
11
很多人不爱咖啡、醇酒独喜欢喝我。
Many people don't care for coffee and alcohol, but have a special preference for me.
12
写作思考来杯咖啡当然不错。
To write andthink, a cup of coffee is often a good companion.
是啊！
Absolutely!
13
喜庆交际醇酒一杯却是最适宜。
During social occasions and celebrations, a glass of good liquor may be quite desirable.
当然。
Of course.
14
解渴补充水分，清水是生命不可或缺的。
To satisfy thirst and to rehydrate the body, clear water is vital to the survival of all life.
就是说嘛！
That's right!
15
所以说天下万物各有其特性，不需要同他人比较，
你是水就扮演水；是咖啡就扮演咖啡。
Therefore, everything in this world has its own unique quality. There is no need to compare yourself with others. If you are water, play the role of water well. If you are coffee, play the role of coffee well.
是啊。
Correct.
正确。
Right.
我同意！
I agree.
物本身并无好坏善恶之分，君若是一杯清水时且莫自卑——清水自有清水的好。
Everything by itself needs no judgment of good vs. bad. If you are a glass of clear water, don't feel inferior—water has its own significance.

人生没有对错 There is No Absolute Right or Wrong in Life

1
从前有一群菜鸭每天在池边游水寻欢，日子过得惬意得不得了……
Once there was a flock of domesticated ducks. Everyday they would swim in the pond and enjoy themselves. Their days were quite carefree and joyous ...
2
其中有只灰鸭特别与众不同，因为它自视甚高。
Among them was a grey duck who stood out from the crowd because of his high regard for himself.
3
我才不要像它们一样醉生梦死，让宝贵的光阴溜掉枉过一生。
I am not going to live an indulgent, meaningless life like they do. They are wasting their lives and letting precious time slip away.
4
1234
1234!
ABCD
灰鸭为了高人一等，它每天晨跑做体操学电脑终日读书学语文，勤奋得不得了……
In order to be better than the rest of the flock, everyday he would diligently jog in the morning, do aerobic exercise, take computer courses, and study foreign languages all day long ...
5
有一天终于苦学有成，学问做得实在好！
One day he finally achieved the goal of all his hard work. His outstanding academic achievement was recognized by all!
6
春去秋来，秋收季节终于来到……
Spring passed and Autumn arrived, the season of the harvest had finally come ...
A
B
C

7
各位的时辰已到，我送你们到电宰场报到！
It is now time for you to say good-bye to the world. I am taking you to report to the butcher's block!
呱！呱！
Quack! Squawk!
呱！呱！
Quack! Squawk!
我勤奋了一辈子，怎可以这样死去？
I've worked diligently all my life, how can I die like this?
8
9
宿命难逃！
It's hard to escape your destiny!
救命啊！
HELP!
菜鸭的下场就是如此，别怨天尤人！
This is always the end for domestic ducks, don't blame fate or accuse others for your natural path of life!
10
11
咔嚓！
12
你的下场还不是与我们一样！
See, you ended up in the same place we did!
不及时行乐才是枉过一生啊……
What a waste of life—to not enjoy the pleasures of it while you could!
我不喜欢玩乐，喜欢读书做学问过一生难道也错了？
I didn't like to play around. I liked to spend my time studying and learning. Was that so wrong?
13
14
选择怎样过一生是每个人的权利，悠闲过一生没有错；勤奋过一生也没错！
To choose a lifestyle is everyone's right. There is nothing wrong with having an easy life, and there is nothing wrong with a diligent life!
明白！
Now I understand!

道
The Tao Road
1
这是一条漫长而沉寂的道。
This is a long and quiet road.
2
我走在漆黑中颠踬！
I stumble in pitch darkness!
跌了又起来，我茫然行走……
After the fall, I get up again and walk on and on uncertainly ...
3
脚底踩着寂寥的石子和枯叶。
Under my feet are lonely little rocks and dried leaves.
沙！
Sha!
4
背后某人也踩着石子枯叶……
Somebody behind me is also stepping on little rocks and dried leaves ...
Sha!
5
6
我慢下来。他也放慢脚步；
I slow down. His footsteps also slow down;
沙！
Sha!
沙！
Sha!
7
我跑，他也跟着跑。
I run, and he runs after me.
沙！
Sha!
沙！
Sha!
8
我转身！
I turn around!
9
无人。
Nobody to be seen.

10
万物幽暗无门，
All the buildings are dark and it look like there's no way to get to them.
11
只有脚步声回应我，
Only the sound of footsteps is aware of my existence.
沙！ Sha!
沙！ Sha!
12
在这些弯处我转着转着永远通向街道，
Along the winding road I turn around over and over again. I am always moving in the direction of distant city streets.
沙！ Sha!
沙！ Sha!
13
那里无人等候，无人跟踪我，
Over there nobody awaits me, nobody follows me.
14
那里我追逐一个跌踬的人，
Over there I chase a running person;
沙！ Sha!
沙！ Sha!
15
他起身来说他看见我。
He turns around claiming to have seen me.
16
——改写自奥克塔维欧 · 帕斯作品。
–adapted from the work of Octavio Paz.
无人！ Nobody to be seen.
腾出自己与时空对立将会迷失自己。生之旅，应与时间空间化为一体。因为……环境是你，时空是你；前人是你，后人也是你！
If one raises oneself up against time and space, one will lose oneself. The journey of life should be such that we are one with time and space. Because the environment is you, time and space are you, the person before you is you, the person after you is you!

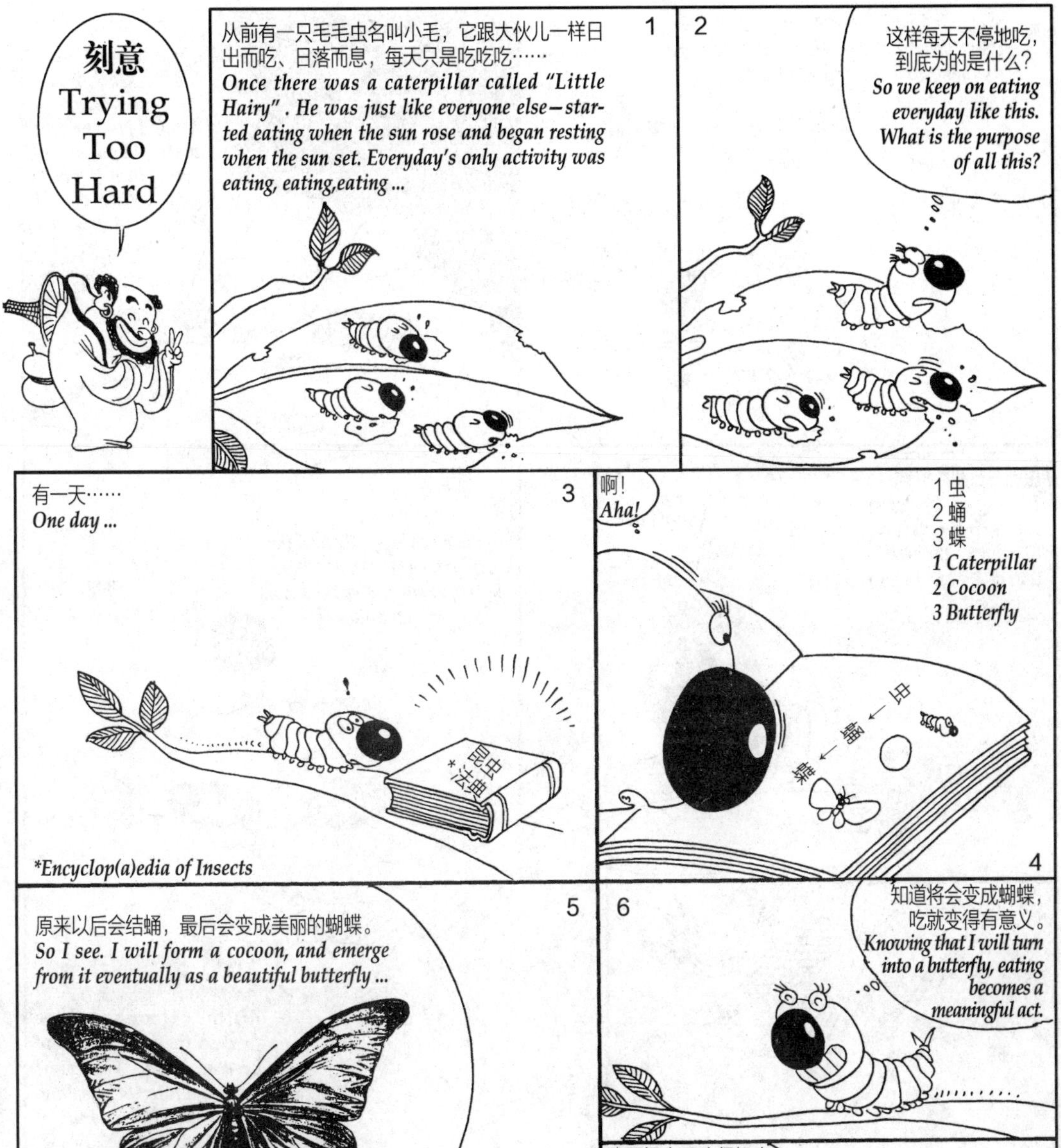
刻意
Trying Too Hard
1
从前有一只毛毛虫名叫小毛，它跟大伙儿一样日出而吃、日落而息，每天只是吃吃吃……
Once there was a caterpillar called "Little Hairy". He was just like everyone else—started eating when the sun rose and began resting when the sun set. Everyday's only activity was eating, eating,eating ...
2
这样每天不停地吃，到底为的是什么？
So we keep on eating everyday like this. What is the purpose of all this?
3
有一天……
One day ...
昆虫法典*
*Encyclop(a)edia of Insects
4
啊！
Aha!
1 虫
2 蛹
3 蝶
1 Caterpillar
2 Cocoon
3 Butterfly
虫 ← 蛹 ← 蝶
5
原来以后会结蛹，最后会变成美丽的蝴蝶。
So I see. I will form a cocoon, and emerge from it eventually as a beautiful butterfly ...
6
知道将会变成蝴蝶，吃就变得有意义。
Knowing that I will turn into a butterfly, eating becomes a meaningful act.
7
我要把自己吃得好大好大，将来可变成大蝴蝶赢过别人。
I am going to eat so much and become so big that I will turn into a giant butterfly and be better than all the others.

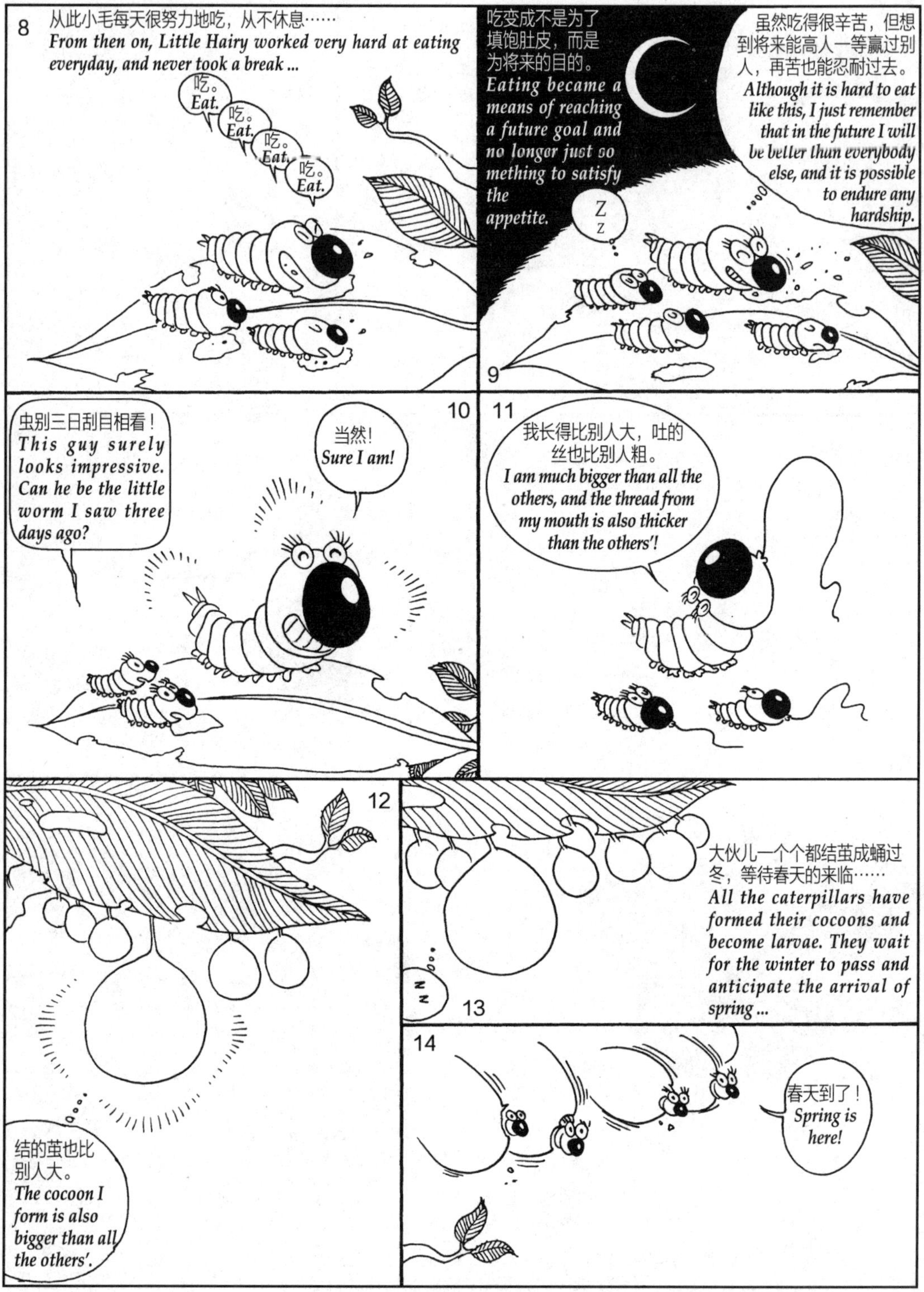
8
从此小毛每天很努力地吃，从不休息……
From then on, Little Hairy worked very hard at eating everyday, and never took a break ...
吃。Eat.
吃。Eat.
吃。Eat.
吃。Eat.
吃变成不是为了填饱肚皮，而是为将来的目的。
Eating became a means of reaching a future goal and no longer just so mething to satisfy the appetite.
虽然吃得很辛苦，但想到将来能高人一等赢过别人，再苦也能忍耐过去。
Although it is hard to eat like this, I just remember that in the future I will be better than everybody else, and it is possible to endure any hardship.
Z Z
9
10
虫别三日刮目相看！
This guy surely looks impressive. Can he be the little worm I saw three days ago?
当然！
Sure I am!
11
我长得比别人大，吐的丝也比别人粗。
I am much bigger than all the others, and the thread from my mouth is also thicker than the others'!
12
结的茧也比别人大。
The cocoon I form is also bigger than all the others'.
大伙儿一个个都结茧成蛹过冬，等待春天的来临……
All the caterpillars have formed their cocoons and become larvae. They wait for the winter to pass and anticipate the arrival of spring ...
13
14
春天到了！
Spring is here!

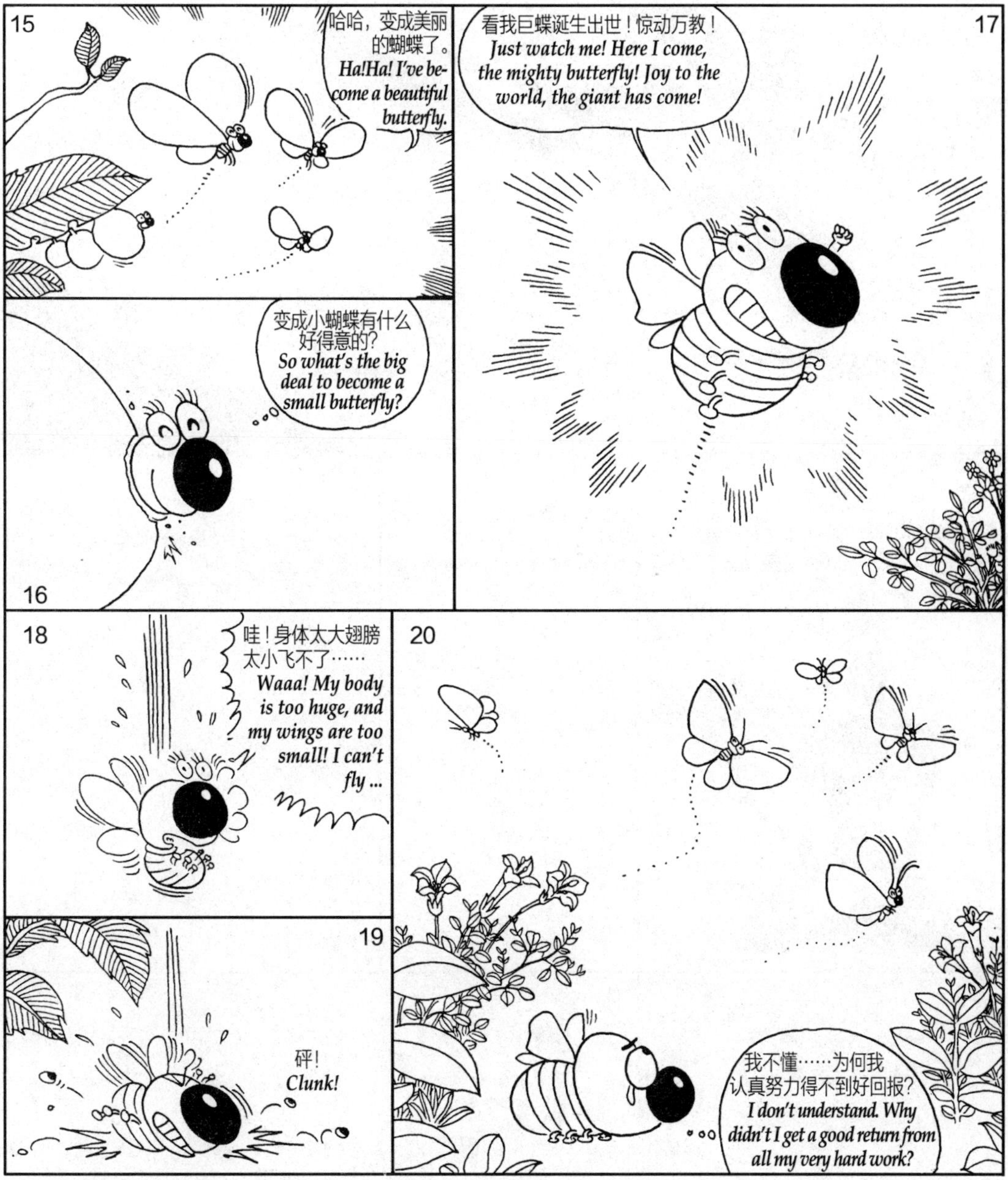
15
哈哈，变成美丽的蝴蝶了。
Ha!Ha! I've become a beautiful butterfly.
16
变成小蝴蝶有什么好得意的？
So what's the big deal to become a small butterfly?
17
看我巨蝶诞生出世！惊动万教！
Just watch me! Here I come, the mighty butterfly! Joy to the world, the giant has come!
18
哇！身体太大翅膀太小飞不了……
Waaa! My body is too huge, and my wings are too small! I can't fly ...
19
砰！
Clunk!
20
我不懂……为何我认真努力得不到好回报？
I don't understand. Why didn't I get a good return from all my very hard work?

一分努力不见得有一分收获，刻意强求不见得能得好成果。
人生在世过的是一分一秒，童年就以童年过；成年就以成年过；老年就以老年过；平常心是道！
Honest effort does not always promise a reward. Trying too hard does not necessarily mean a good outcome. The important part of living is to live every minute and every second. Live childhood as childhood, adulthood as adulthood, and your later years as later years. To maintain a steady mind which is not excited by out-of-the-ordinary events is "the way"(Tao).

小指的悲哀
The Sadness of the Pinky Finger

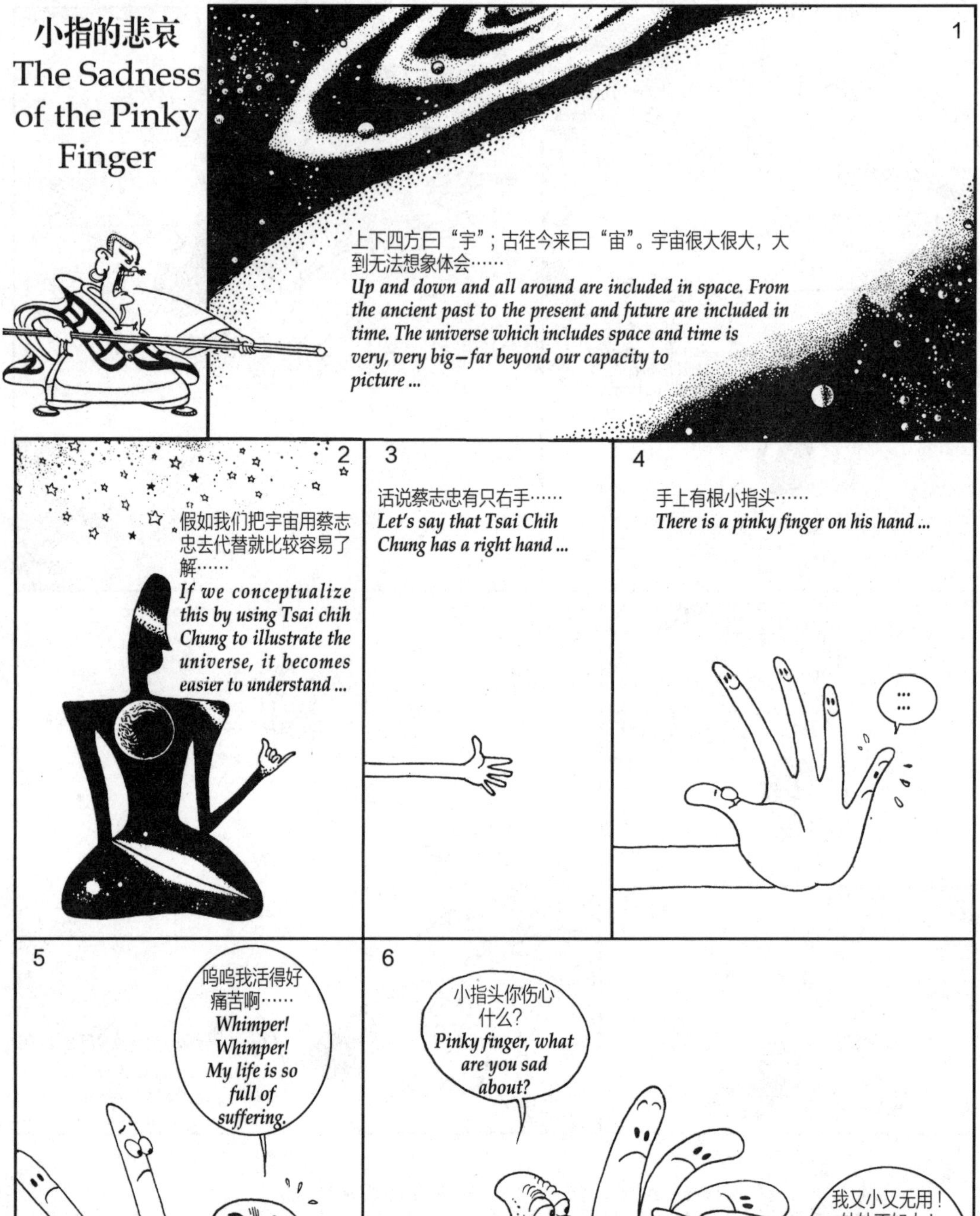
1
上下四方曰“宇”；古往今来曰“宙”。宇宙很大很大，大到无法想象体会……
Up and down and all around are included in space. From the ancient past to the present and future are included in time. The universe which includes space and time is very, very big—far beyond our capacity to picture ...
2
假如我们把宇宙用蔡志忠去代替就比较容易了解……
If we conceptualize this by using Tsai chih Chung to illustrate the universe, it becomes easier to understand ...
3
话说蔡志忠有只右手……
Let's say that Tsai Chih Chung has a right hand ...
4
手上有根小指头……
There is a pinky finger on his hand ...
5
呜呜我活得好痛苦啊……
Whimper! Whimper! My life is so full of suffering.
6
小指头你伤心什么？
Pinky finger, what are you sad about?
我又小又无用！处处不如人！
I am so small and so useless. I am less than everybody in every way!

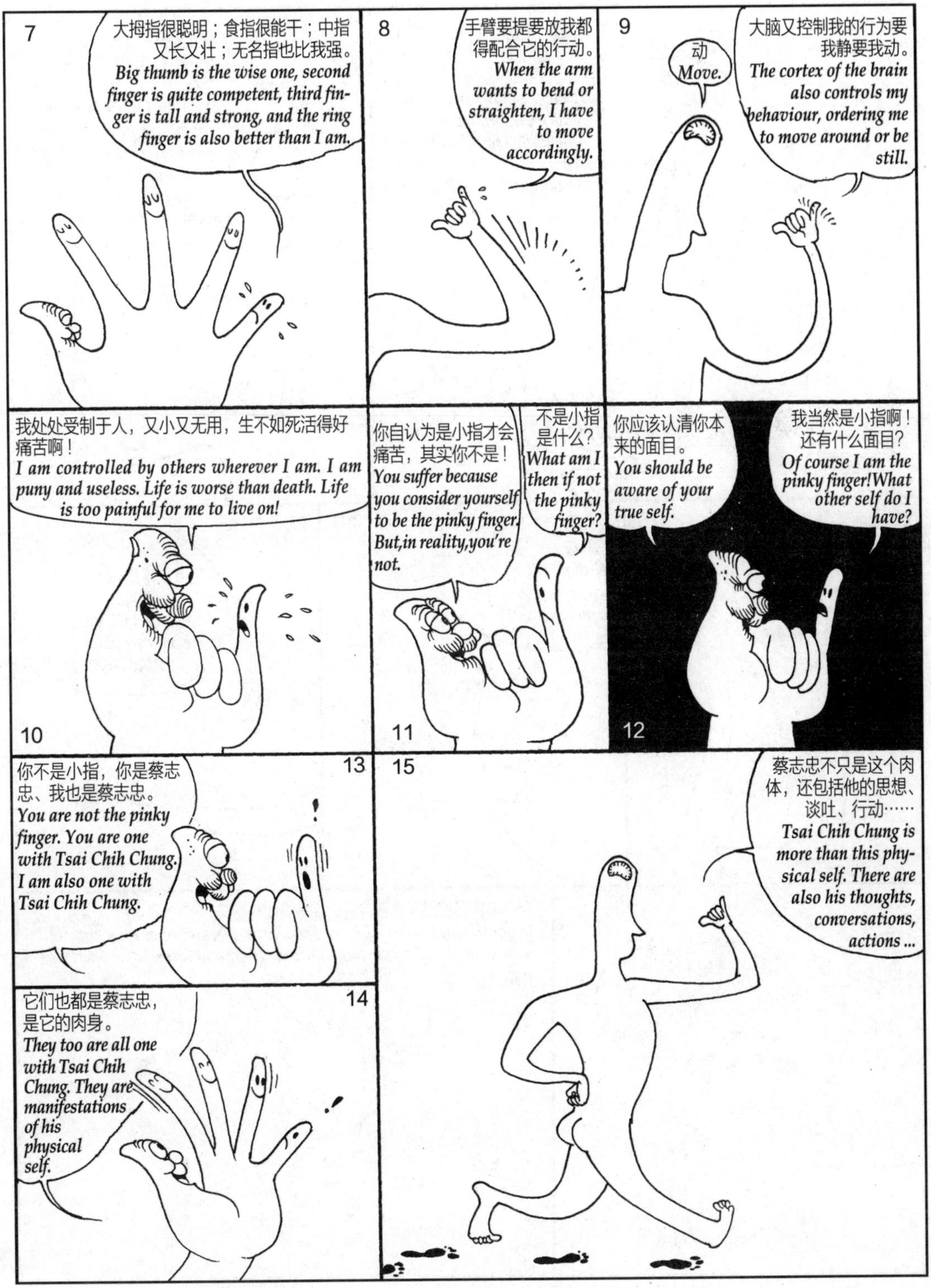
7
大拇指很聪明；食指很能干；中指又长又壮；无名指也比我强。
Big thumb is the wise one, second finger is quite competent, third finger is tall and strong, and the ring finger is also better than I am.
8
手臂要提要放我都得配合它的行动。
When the arm wants to bend or straighten, I have to move accordingly.
9
动
Move.
大脑又控制我的行为要我静要我动。
The cortex of the brain also controls my behaviour, ordering me to move around or be still.
10
我处处受制于人，又小又无用，生不如死活得好痛苦啊！
I am controlled by others wherever I am. I am puny and useless. Life is worse than death. Life is too painful for me to live on!
11
你自认为是小指才会痛苦，其实你不是！
You suffer because you consider yourself to be the pinky finger. But,in reality,you're not.
不是小指是什么？
What am I then if not the pinky finger?
12
你应该认清你本来的面目。
You should be aware of your true self.
我当然是小指啊！还有什么面目？
Of course I am the pinky finger!What other self do I have?
13
你不是小指，你是蔡志忠、我也是蔡志忠。
You are not the pinky finger. You are one with Tsai Chih Chung. I am also one with Tsai Chih Chung.
14
它们也都是蔡志忠，是它的肉身。
They too are all one with Tsai Chih Chung. They are manifestations of his physical self.
15
蔡志忠不只是这个肉体，还包括他的思想、谈吐、行动……
Tsai Chih Chung is more than this physical self. There are also his thoughts, conversations, actions ...

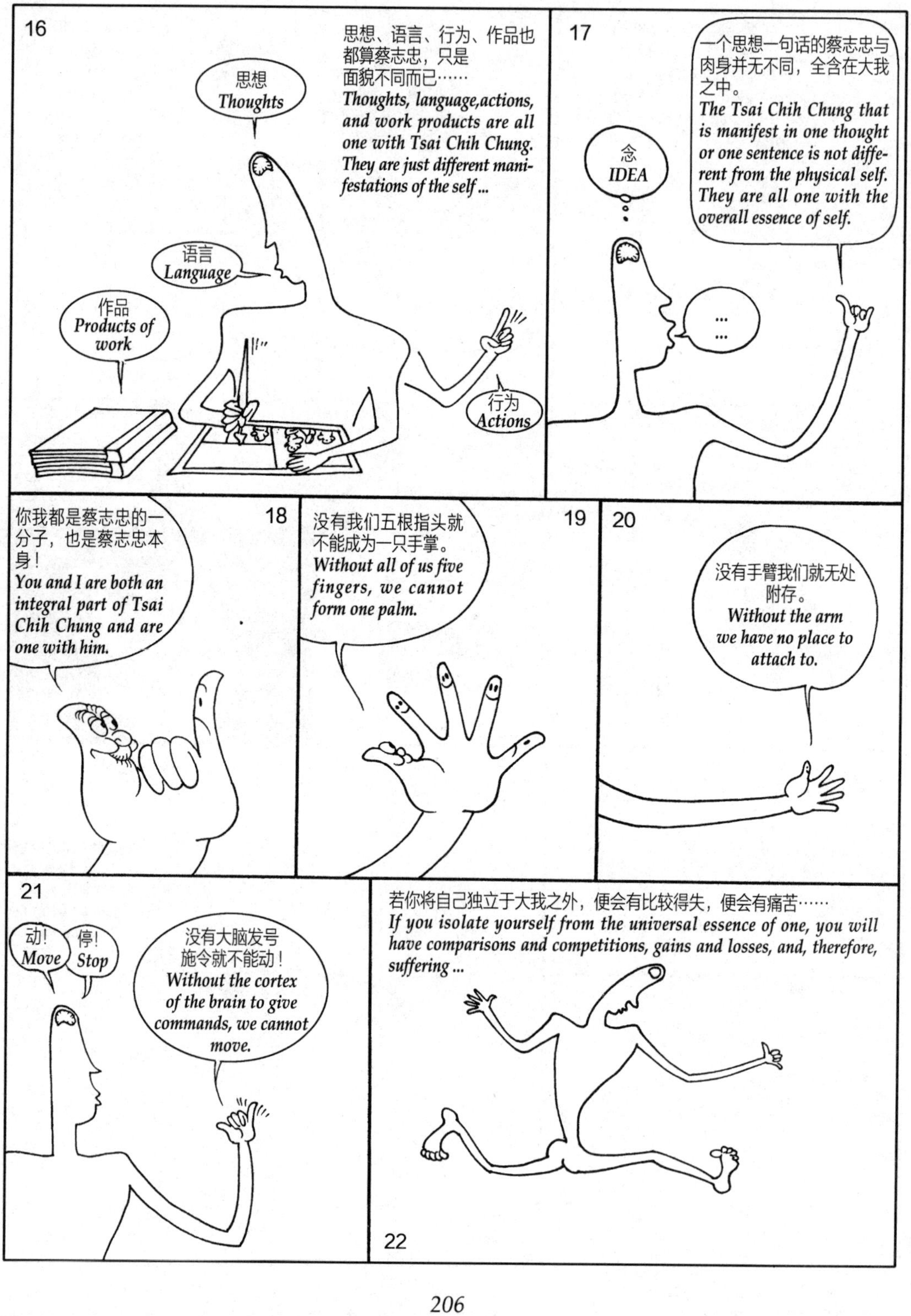
16
思想、语言、行为、作品也都算蔡志忠，只是面貌不同而已……
Thoughts, language,actions, and work products are all one with Tsai Chih Chung. They are just different manifestations of the self ...
思想 Thoughts
语言 Language
作品 Products of work
行为 Actions
17
念 IDEA
一个思想一句话的蔡志忠与肉身并无不同，全含在大我之中。
The Tsai Chih Chung that is manifest in one thought or one sentence is not different from the physical self. They are all one with the overall essence of self.
...
...
18
你我都是蔡志忠的一分子，也是蔡志忠本身！
You and I are both an integral part of Tsai Chih Chung and are one with him.
19
没有我们五根指头就不能成为一只手掌。
Without all of us five fingers, we cannot form one palm.
20
没有手臂我们就无处附存。
Without the arm we have no place to attach to.
21
动！ Move
停！ Stop
没有大脑发号施令就不能动！
Without the cortex of the brain to give commands, we cannot move.
若你将自己独立于大我之外，便会有比较得失，便会有痛苦……
If you isolate yourself from the universal essence of one, you will have comparisons and competitions, gains and losses, and, therefore, suffering ...
22

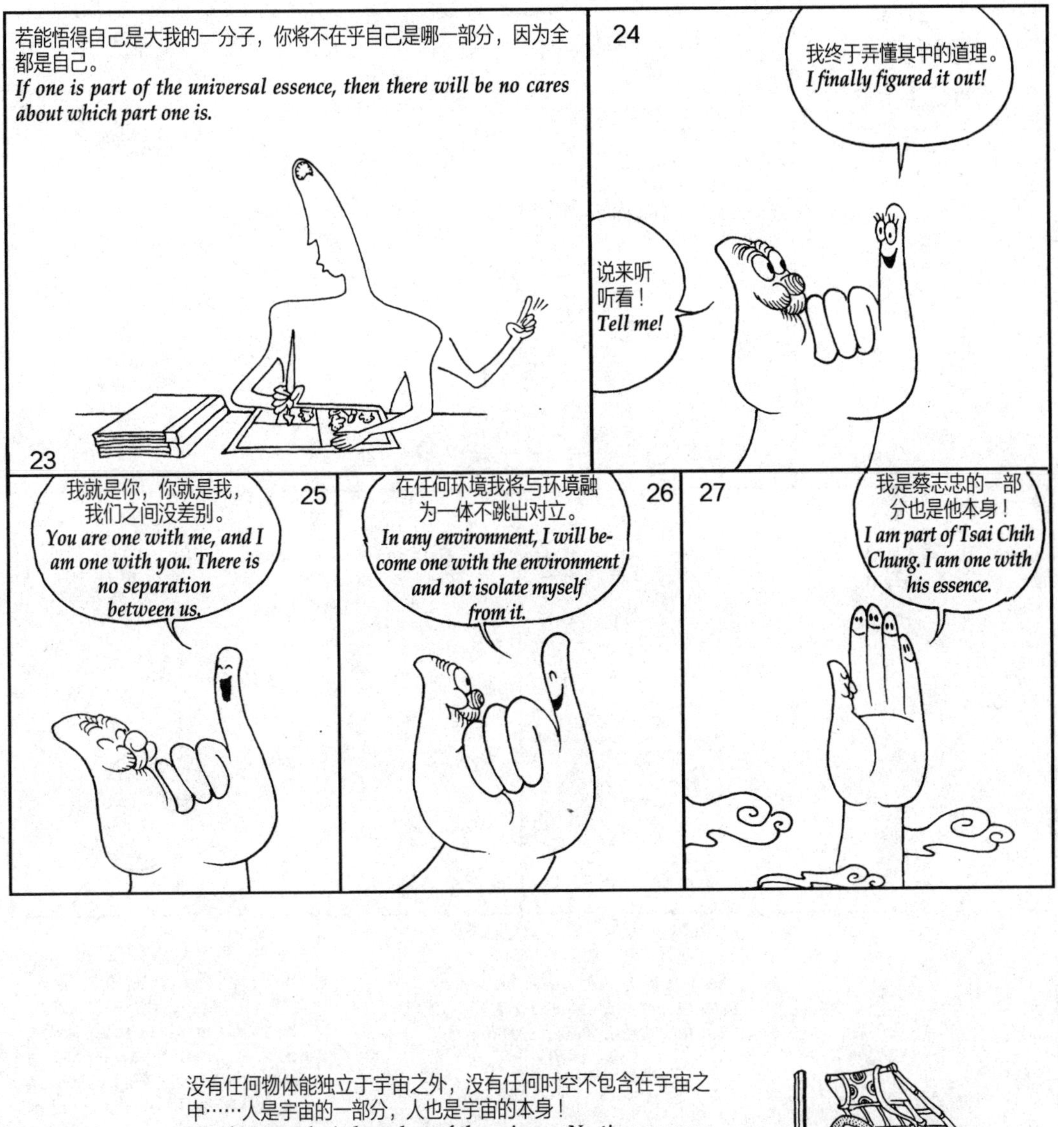
若能悟得自己是大我的一分子，你将不在乎自己是哪一部分，因为全都是自己。
If one is part of the universal essence, then there will be no cares about which part one is.
23
24
我终于弄懂其中的道理。
I finally figured it out!
说来听听看！
Tell me!
25
我就是你，你就是我，我们之间没差别。
You are one with me, and I am one with you. There is no separation between us.
26
在任何环境我将与环境融为一体不跳出对立。
In any environment, I will become one with the environment and not isolate myself from it.
27
我是蔡志忠的一部分也是他本身！
I am part of Tsai Chih Chung. I am one with his essence.

没有任何物体能独立于宇宙之外，没有任何时空不包含在宇宙之中……人是宇宙的一部分，人也是宇宙的本身！
No object can be independent of the universe. No time or space is not included in the universe ... Humans are part of the universe. Humans are also one with the universal essence!

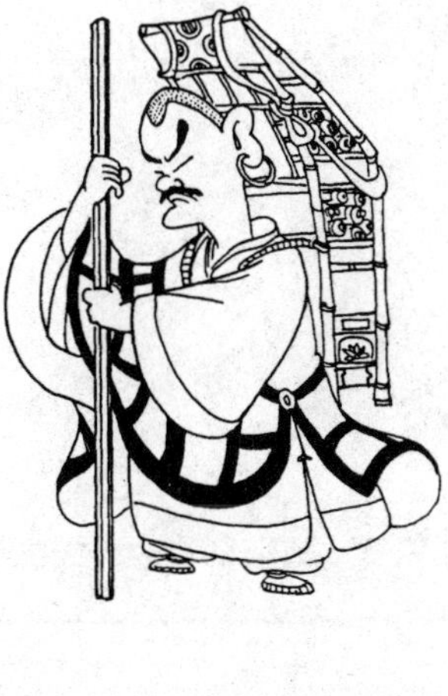

佛与粪
Buddha and a Pile of Shit
1
苏东坡与佛印禅师是很好的朋友，有一天他问佛印禅师说：
The infamous poet Su Dong Po (A.D.1037-1101)was a good friend of Dharma Master Fo Yin. One day, he asked Master Fo Yin:
大师，你看我坐在这里像什么？
Master, what do you think I look like sitting here?
看来像一尊佛！
You look like a sitting Buddha.
2
但我看你倒像一堆大便！
But you surely look like a pile of shit to me.
哦……是吗？
Oh... Is that right?
3
你尊我为佛，而我说你是大便你不生气吗？
You respect me as a Buddha, and I refer to you as a pile of shit, Aren't you mad?
我应该高兴才是，怎么会生气？
I should be thrilled. How could I be mad?
哈！
Ha!
哈！
Ha!
哈！
Ha!

4
因为自己是佛，看别人也会像佛，自己是大便，看别人也会像大便。
Because if the self is Buddha, the self sees others as Buddha-like; if the self is full of shit, the self sees others as shit-like.
哈！哈！
Ha! Ha!
哈！
Ha!

世界是依每个人的眼而呈现，什么样的人，会看见什么样的世界；什么样的心，会生出什么样的结论。

The world presents itself according to the viewpoint of each person. Whatever kind of person one is, one will see that kind of world; whatever kind of mindset one has, one will derive that kind of conclusion.

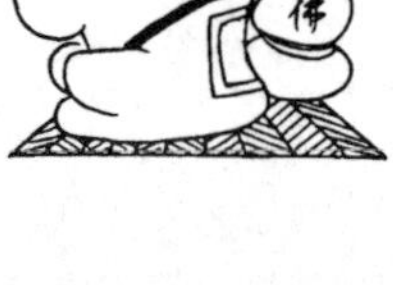

八风吹不动，一屁过江来

The Eight Types of Emotional Winds Could Not Move Him;Yet, One Passing of Gas Blows Him across the River

1
有一天苏东坡写了一首佛偈，彰显自己通达佛理……
One day, Su Dong Po wrote a Zen poem to express how thoroughly he understood the wisdom of Buddhism ...
他很得意地派人将这篇佛偈送到江北给佛印禅师看。
He proudly sent someone to deliver this poem to the north bank of the river, where Master FoYin lived.
老师请你过目这篇偈子。
Master, please take a look at this poem.
我瞧瞧！
Let me see ...
2
3
敢自称自己八风吹不动？放屁！
He dares to claim that he is immovable in front of the eight types of emotional winds! This nonsense is like passing gas!
4
大胆的老和尚，敢在我偈子上批个屁字，看我找你算账。
This outrageous old monk!He dared to write"fart"on my poem. I'll teach him a lesson!
注：八风是得、失、毁、誉、称、讥、苦、乐。
The eight types of emotional winds are:gain, loss, slander, fame, praise, sarcasm, sadness and happiness.
苏东坡啊！你不是自称八风都吹不动你吗？怎的一个屁字就把你吹过江来了呢？
Su Dong Po! Didn't you claim that all eight types of emotional winds could not move you?How come a simple word like "fart"has blown you across the river?
…
5
禅是一种层次，一种境界，一种实践。而只落入语言、文字的禅是野狐禅、口头禅，跟真正的禅沾不上一点边。
Zen is a state of mind, a level of consciousness, a way of living. Zen that focuses on semantics and playing with words is a Zen of lip-service and cult Zen. It has nothing to do with real Zen.

蜕变自己
The Transformation of the Self
1
小蛇问大蛇说：
The young snake asked the senior snake:
你活得这么久了，应该知道什么是人生的意义？
You have lived a long life. Would you tell me what is the meaning of life?
2
童年时快乐活泼，青年时发现自我，壮年时朝前奋斗，老年时安逸任游。
During your childhood, be happy and lively. During your middle age, strive for your goals. During your later years, be peaceful and enjoy life.
3
就是童年时童年过，青年时青年过，老年时老年过？
Does that mean, living your childhood in childhood style, living your youth in youth style, and living your later years in the style of later years?
4
不错！一个人如果一生只有一个自己就太可怜了，不会蜕皮的蛇即将死亡！
That's right. If one is stuck with the same persona all life long, that is very pathetic. The snake that does not know how to shed old skin will face death soon.
不变就是死亡，生就是变化不已。人应随着成长随时蜕变重新化生出一只新的蝴蝶来。
No change means death, for life is ever-changing. One should continue to evolve with the growing process. The soul can always be reborn as a new butterfly.

谈禅令人呕吐
Discussion of Zen is Nauseating

有一位年轻的书生，滔滔不绝地与禅师论说禅理……
Once there was a young intellectual who talked on and on about the wisdom of Zen with a Zen Master ...
1

2
你的禅味太重了。
Your Zen flavour is too heavy.
!
3
老师，你为何不喜欢谈禅？
Master, why don't you like to discuss Zen?

4
因为谈禅令我反胃！
Because the discussion of Zen makes me nauseous.

食物是用“吃”的；景色是用“看”的；音乐是用“听”的；而禅是用“体会实践”的而不是用来空谈的。

Food is to "eat". Scenery is to "see". Music is to "hear". Zen is to "appreciate and practise" and not for empty talk.

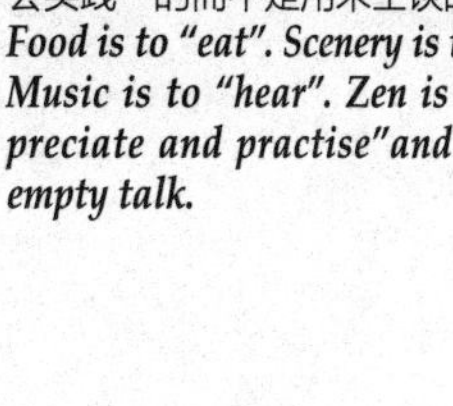

"是"而非"有"

"Being" and Not "Having"

1
儒说：
Confucianists say:
我追求有！
I seek having.
有为
Accomplishment
成就
Achievement

道说：
Taoists say:
我追求无！
I go after nothingness.
2

3
禅说：
Practitioners of Zen say:
我不追求有或无，我只是实践！
I do not seek having or not having. I only practise being.

我登上高处，并不是为了极目远眺；我走下山谷，并不是因为孤寂已极。我不追求掳获的占有，我只是完全融入地认同。

I climbed to the top of a mountain not to see as far as I can; I walked down into the valley between the hills not because I felt extremely lonely. I do not seek the possessiveness of ownership. I only dissolve into the oneness completely.

拥有与融入
Ownership and Being A Part Of

1
有一位艺术家到可港去画画……
Once an artist went to paint at the harbour of a river ...
2
他发现一切都很美，美得无法下笔！
He found everything to be extremely beautiful – too beautiful for him to start his painting!

3
于是便买下一栋房子，
Therefore, he bought a house there ...
售
SOLD
4
收拾起画具，永远不再画画了……
... put away his painting supplies, and never painted again ...
5
从此就在可港住下，把自己融入美的画面里……
From then on, he settled down at the river harbour and dissolved himself into the beautiful scenery ...

人不应只追求时空的一点……人应融入任何时空，于是便能真正拥有任何时、任何空……

Human beings should not seek after one point in time and place ... We should dissolve into any space and time. That is how we can truly own any time and any space ...

蜕　变
Metamorphosis

1
有一天早晨，我一觉醒来……
One morning I woke up from sleep...
2
我发现自己变成一只怪兽，我惊慌不已地躲在床底……
I found myself turning into a monster. I panicked completely and hid under the bed...
……
3
我变成了一只一百只手五十张嘴的怪物，不晓得到底出了什么问题……
I had turned into a monster of one hundred hands and fifty mouths. I had no clue what went wrong or where ...
4
猫儿说：
Pussy Cat says:
这才是真正的你自己！
This is your real persona, the role you are really playing these days.
5
一百只手是你的"贪"；五十张嘴是你的"欲"！
One hundred hands are manifestations of your "greed"; Fifty mouths are manifestations of your "desire".
……
每个人的外表只是个假面具，撕开表皮，内在的才是真正的自己！你可曾真切地揽镜自照，瞧瞧真正的你？
The outward appearance of everyone is only a mask. It is only after the surface skin is torn off that the real persona comes out. Have you ever sincerely looked into your own eyes in a mirror? Looked into the real persona you are playing out now?
禅

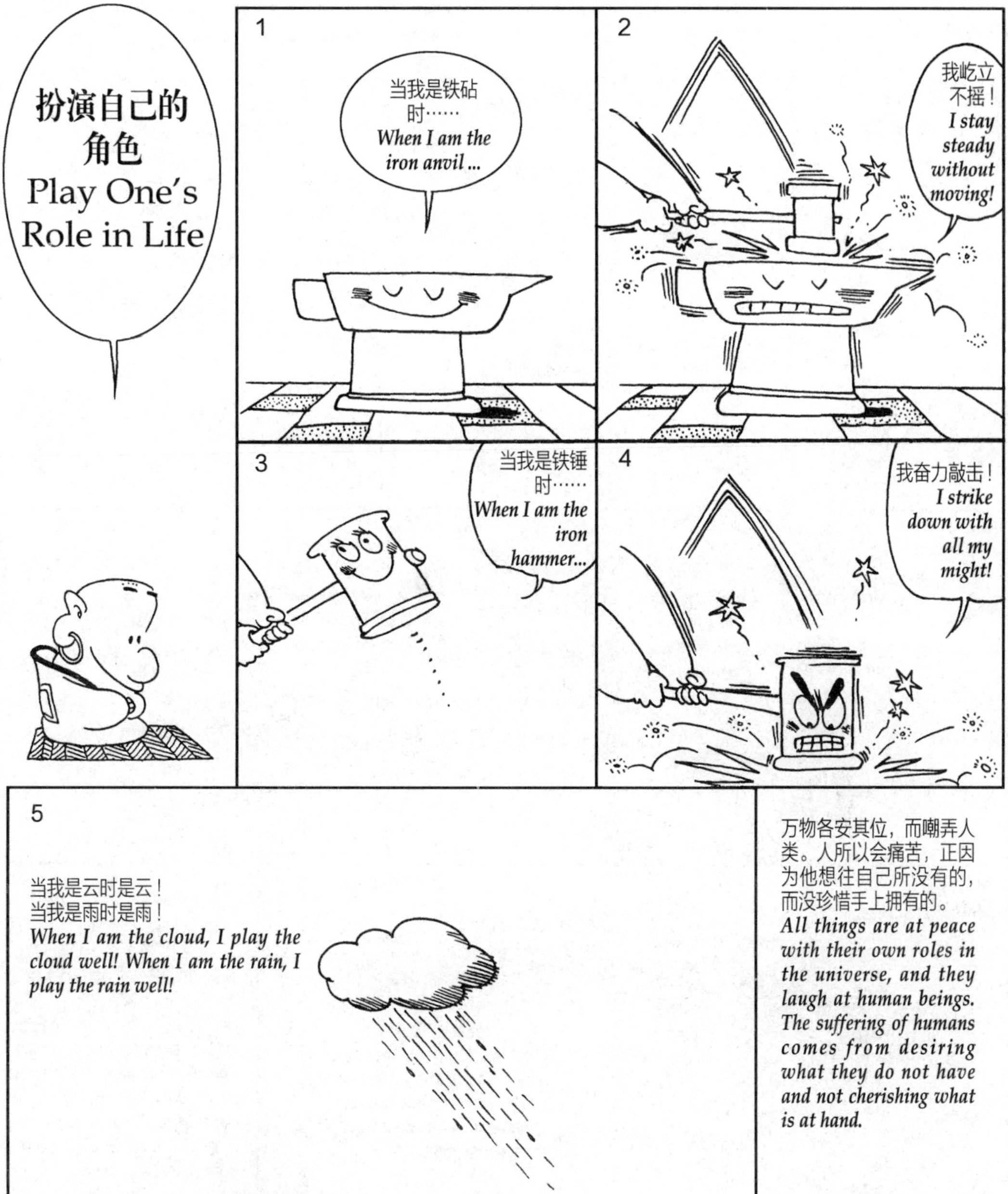
扮演自己的角色
Play One's Role in Life
1
当我是铁砧时……
When I am the iron anvil ...
2
我屹立不摇！
I stay steady without moving!
3
当我是铁锤时……
When I am the iron hammer...
4
我奋力敲击！
I strike down with all my might!
5
当我是云时是云！
当我是雨时是雨！
When I am the cloud, I play the cloud well! When I am the rain, I play the rain well!
万物各安其位，而嘲弄人类。人所以会痛苦，正因为他想往自己所没有的，而没珍惜手上拥有的。
All things are at peace with their own roles in the universe, and they laugh at human beings. The suffering of humans comes from desiring what they do not have and not cherishing what is at hand.

尽情做自己
Be All You Can Be

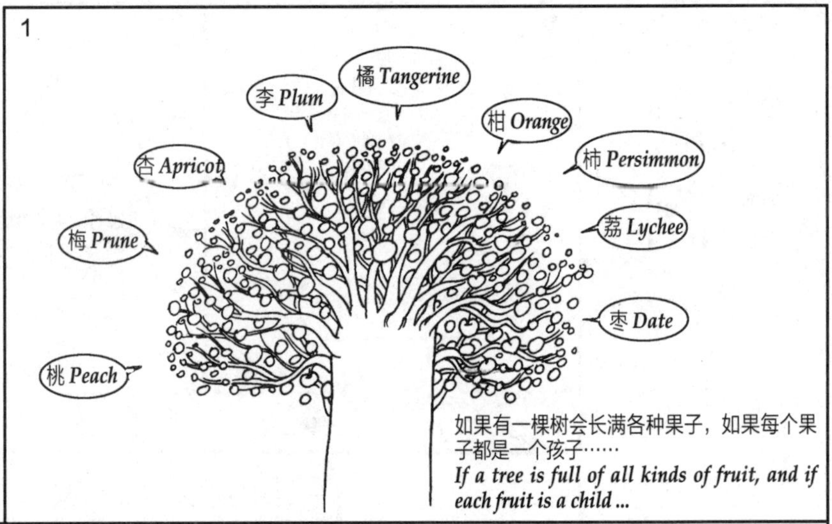
1
李 Plum
橘 Tangerine
柑 Orange
杏 Apricot
柿 Persimmon
梅 Prune
荔 Lychee
枣 Date
桃 Peach
如果有一棵树会长满各种果子，如果每个果子都是一个孩子……
If a tree is full of all kinds of fruit, and if each fruit is a child ...

2
我是荔枝，肉最丰腴！
I am Lychee and have the richest taste!
我是苹果，营养最好。
I am Apple, and I'm the most nutritious.
我是樱桃才美丽珍贵呢。
I am Cherry, the prettiest and most precious.
我这柿子风味才佳呢！
Look at me. I am Persimmon with the best flavour!
我是柑，最甜！
I am Orange and proud to be the sweetest!

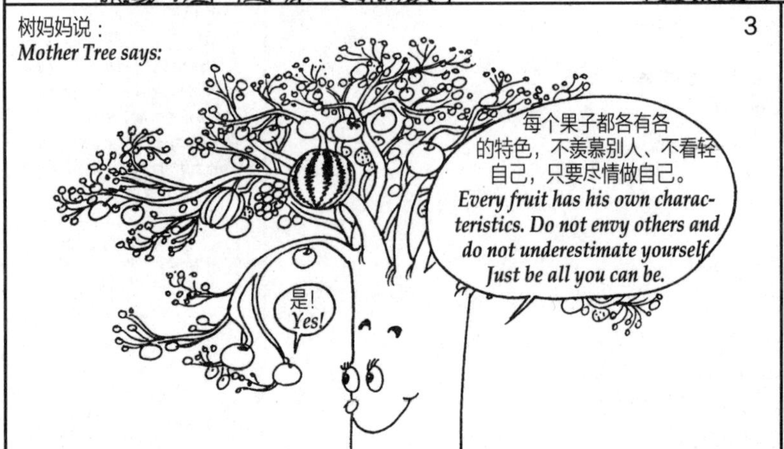
树妈妈说：
Mother Tree says:
3
每个果子都各有各的特色，不羡慕别人、不看轻自己，只要尽情做自己。
Every fruit has his own characteristics. Do not envy others and do not underestimate yourself. Just be all you can be.
是！
Yes!

人各有所长，每个人有每个人的价值，何必在乎别人的尊重或轻视？以别人的价值生活，一定也死于自己的不满之中……

Everyone has his own strengths and unique qualities. Why care about other people's respect or disdain? If one lives according to others' values, one is guaranteed to die in one's own dissatisfaction...

诞生自己
Recovery of the Soul
1
一个人里面有好多层皮，覆盖着他内心深处。
A person has many layers of skin covering his heart deep inside.
2
人认识很多东西，但却不认识自己……为什么？为什么？
He often knows many things except for his own heart... Why?Why?
3
因为有三十层牛皮或熊皮那样坚厚的皮掩盖着他的灵魂。
There are usually thirty layers of cow skin or bear skin-thick layers of tough leather that cover up his soul.
4
探索你的本源，去认识你自己吧。
Go search for your original heart. Get to know your own heart.
人类生命的主要目标，是让自己诞生！一个人若能真正知道："我是什么？"他便能知道"我能做什么！我要什么！"
The major objective of human life is to let the essence of the soul be recovered! If a person can really answer the question:"What am I?", he would also know "This is what I can do! This is what I need!"

应无所住而生其心
Do Not Be Attached and Let the Essence of the Heart Emerge

1
你和我站在这儿，各以不同的地位，你打算做什么？
Here we are, you and I. Each of us has our own place in life. What kind of plan do you have?
一颗星俯视着对我说：
One star gazed down at me and said:

2
我尽我所知地等待，等待……
I do my best to be patient in the process of living.
3
然后，让时间经过，直到我的变化来临。
Then I let time take its course until it is time to change and move on.

4
我也是这样想，我也是这样做。
I also think the same way. I also do the same thing.

人是宇宙的一部分，也是宇宙的本体。只要打开心灵将自己与所处的时空融为一体，时时没有对象、没有自己，不自外于宇宙，不自外于生命。

Human beings are part of the universe and one with the universal essence. All we need to do is to open our hearts and allow the self to become one with the time and space of being. Constantly live without distinctions between our egos and the rest of the world. Don't isolate ourselves from the universal essence. Don't separate ourselves from the force of life.

真空妙有
Ultimate Kong and Special Being
1
我画画——喜欢缤纷五彩旁的留白；
I paint—and like the blank space left beside the busy strokes of rainbow colours;
2
我生活——喜欢繁忙后的无事；
I live fully—and enjoy the free time after business;
A
3
我吟唱——喜欢狂欢悲壮前后的静默；
I sing loudly—and like the silence before and after the extreme emotions of joy and sadness;
4
我爱多彩多姿，但……我也爱孤寂！
I like colourful and varied moments, but ... I also enjoy solitude!
插花——没有花的那部分空间也属于插花本身。画中——没有画的那片留白也是画面之一。对谈——无言沉默的那一段也是话语的一部分。有人爱缤纷五彩，我独爱留白！
Flower arrangement—the space not occupied by flowers also belongs to the overall design. Paintings—the piece of space left blank also belongs to the overall presentation. Conversations—the period of quietness without words is also part of the entire communication. Some people like busy and colourful places, but the space left blank also can be cherished.

输与赢
Losing and Win-ning
1
...
...
我要征服这座山！
I'm gonna conquer this mountain!
2
是你无法抵抗山的诱惑。
But you are unable to resist the call of the mountain.
3
我赢了电脑机器！
I beat the computer!
BOOM
4
是你输了你的意志力。
But you lost your will power.
不复习功课还打电动玩具！
What are you doing with videogames? You should be reviewing your homework!
BOOM
人生的挑战说穿了只是内在的自己挑战外在的自己。若是赢得全世界也先别高兴，因为你可能真的输了自己。
The challenge of life—to see through it all—is the spiritual self inside challenging the external ego-self. Don't be too happy, even if you have won the whole world, because you may have truly lost yourself.

人生的牢狱
The Prison of Life

禅

1
每个人都自以为自己是个鸟笼，
在捕捉他生命中的鸟……
Everyone considers himself to be a bird cage trying to catch the blue bird of life ...

2
其实每个人都是一只鸟，在寻找关自己的鸟笼……
In reality, everyone is a bird, looking for a bird cage to keep himself locked up ...
名利
Fortune

3
权势
Power
成就
Achievement

4
失的误以为是得，被猎的还自以为是猎人。
What is loss is mistakenly considered gain; the hunted still thinks of himself as the hunter.

人耗尽一生追求一切，其实是被一切所埋葬。人生所追求的难道只是一重重的牢狱而已？

People spend their whole life pursuing everything. Indeed, their spirits are buried alive by everything. How can it be that layers of prison are what we pursue in life?

鱼与鸟
The Fish and the Bird
1
如果你这世不是生为人，你愿意自己是只翱翔苍穹的鸟？还是条悠游水中的鱼？
If you were not born as a human, would you rather be a bird that soars freely in the grand sky?Or would you prefer to be a fish that swims without a care in the flowing water?
2
我希望年轻时是只自由翱翔的鸟，年老时是条安逸任游的鱼。
I wish that when I am young, I would be a free flying bird. When I get old, I wish to be a peaceful fish just enjoying myself. That would be nice.
很好。
Fine.
3
老师，那你呢？
Master, how about you?
4
是鱼是鸟没有关系，是鸟时是鸟，是鱼时是鱼。
It doesn't matter whether I am a fish or a bird. When I am a bird, I'll be a bird.When I am a fish, I'll be a fish.
人总是做得到的不想做，想做的却做不到。珍惜你拥有的，别想望你所没有的。是鱼时尽情悠游，别妄想要飞；是鸟时尽情翱翔，别妄想着潜水。
Many of us don't feel like doing mediocre things like others, but we aren't able to do what we dream about doing. Cherish what you have and don't hunger for what you don't have. When you are the fish, enjoy yourself swimming to your heart's content, and don't fantasize about flying; when you are a bird, enjoy soaring to your heart's content, and don't even think of wanting to dive.

大与小
Big and Small
1
一团泥对陶工说：
One batch of clay said to the potter:
请将我塑成个小小的陶瓮就好。
Please make me into a small clay urn. That would be great.
2
人人都求大，何独你求小?
Everyone asks to be big. Why do you alone ask to be small?
3
因为小好过大。
Because small is better than big.
4
怎么说?
How do you explain that?
5
因为小器易盈，大器老是不满。
Because a small vessel fills up easily, while a big one is never fulfilled.
一点点我就满足了。
A little bit will bring me satisfaction.
我老是不能满盈……
I am always lacking and unsatisfied...
世人皆说大的好，唯独我愿宁为小；我富有乃因我的欲望比我的能力小，我贫穷正因我的欲望大过我的拥有。
Everyone in this world says that bigger is better. I, alone, would rather be the small one; I feel rich because my desires are smaller than my capabilities. I would feel poor if my desires are larger than what I have.

前生今世
Past and Present

泥土终于如愿地被烧成一个小小的陶瓮……
As wished, the batch of clay finally was fired into a small clay urn ...

2
小陶瓮说：
The little clay urn said:
从前我是一团泥，可塑成瓶、成壶、成瓮、成砖，充满各种可能性……
My past was a batch of clay. I was full of all sorts of potential to be made into a bottle, a vase, an urn, or a brick ...
酒
liquor

3
如今我是小陶瓮，但还是充满各种可能性，可以装香水、装水、装药、装金银财宝。
Now that I am a little urn, I am still full of possibilities. I could be filled with perfume, water, medicine or monetary treasures.
财宝
Treasure
水
Water
香水
Perfume

不要背负着过去，不要企盼着将来，只要真真切切地过着现在，现在是什么就以什么面目过着现在。当我是铁锤的时候，奋力敲击，当我是铁砧的时候，稳如磐山。

Do not carry the burden of the past; do not live in the future. The only important thing is that one lives in the present authentically and fully. Whatever your current life presents you, be the most you can be by living in the moment. When I am the iron hammer, I strike with all my might. When I am the anvil, I stay grounded and stable, like a rocky mountain.

有与无
To Have and Not to Have
1
大酒瓶对小陶瓮说：
The big liquor bottle said to the little clay urn:
我是大器皿。
I am a big container.
XO
伏特加
VODKA
我是小器皿。
I am a small container.
2
我装满好酒一大瓶。
I am filled with a large quantity of fine liquor.
XO
伏特加
VODKA
我里面空无一物。
I am empty inside without a thing.
空！空！
Konk! Konk!
3
满盈使人充实，
空则是虚无。
Fullness makes one feel solid and satisfied. Emptiness gives the feeling of being totally insubstantial, like a void.
XO
伏特加
VODKA

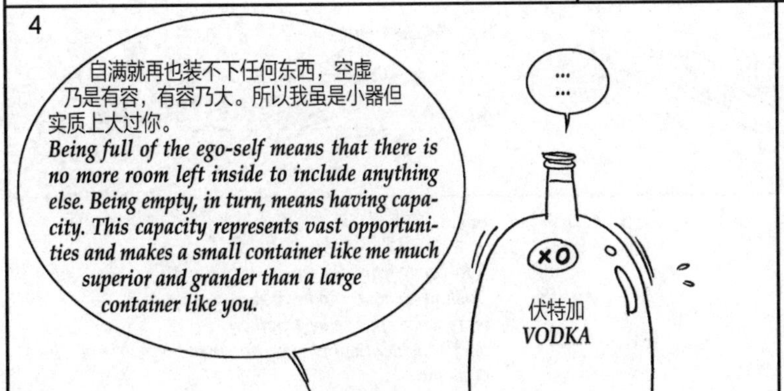
4
自满就再也装不下任何东西，空虚乃是有容，有容乃大。所以我虽是小器但实质上大过你。
Being full of the ego-self means that there is no more room left inside to include anything else. Being empty, in turn, means having capacity. This capacity represents vast opportunities and makes a small container like me much superior and grander than a large container like you.
…
XO
伏特加
VODKA

空虚才能有容，自满就再也装不下任何东西；满盈看似充实，但其实正因为满盈而再不能加入任何可能性。

Emptiness allows for unfulfilled capacity, while fullness of the ego-self does not allow for anything more to be added. Fullness appears to be concrete, but because of its full nature, it no longer allows for the possibility of anything more to be added.

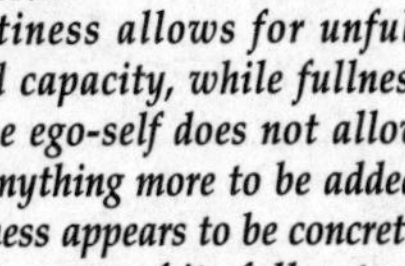

孤寂与唠叨
Loneliness and Nagging

婚姻是："一艘寂寞的船……
Marriage is "A lonely boat ...
…
…

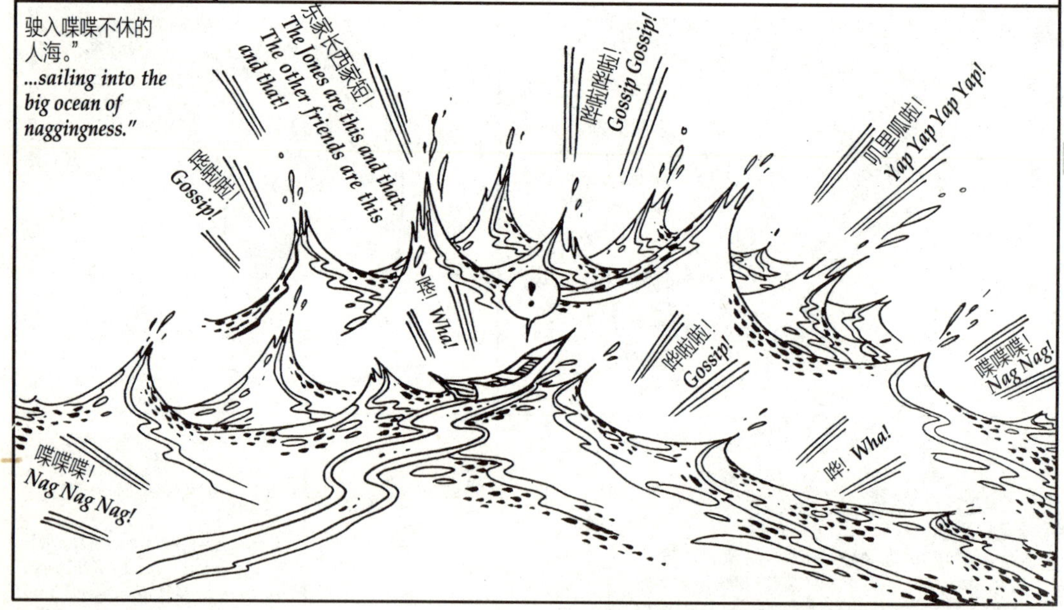

驶入喋喋不休的人海。"
...sailing into the big ocean of naggingness."
东家长西家短！
The Jones are this and that.
The other friends are this and that!
哗啦啦！
Gossip!
哗啦哗啦！
Gossip Gossip!
叽里呱啦！
Yap Yap Yap Yap!
哇！
Wha!
!
哗啦啦！
Gossip!
喋喋喋！
Nag Nag!
喋喋喋！
Nag Nag Nag!
哗！
Wha!

船歌："酒要温的才好，鱿鱼要烤的才好，女人要静默的好。"

A folksong from boat people:
"Fine wine is warm,
fine squid is roasted,
a fine woman is quiet."

海唱："鱼要有水才活得愉快；水要有鱼才活得实在；男人要体贴细微才值得女人的爱。"

A folksong from the seashore:
"Fish needs water to be lively;
water needs fish to be genuine.
only considerate and sensitive men are worth the love of women."

山不长脚，人长
The Mountain Has No Feet, I Do

1
先知有一天向大众宣布，他要表现一个奇迹……
A prophet once announced to the public that he was going to demonstrate a miracle ...
明天中午我要那座山走到我的身边。
By noon tomorrow, I am going to have that mountain come to me.
2
哇！ *Wow!*
哇！ *Wow!*
哇！ *Wow!*
3
快啊！ *Hurry up!*
快去看先知表演奇迹！ *Hurry to see the prophet demonstrate a miracle!*
快去看。 *Let's hurry to watch.*
4
第二天，众人由四处赶来争睹这一奇迹的出现……
The second day, the crowd showed up from everywhere in a rush to witness the miracle ...
5
喂！山呀！到这边来！ *Hello! You, Mountain. Come over here!*
6
山动了没有？ *Did the mountain move?*
没有动静啊…… *Nothing has happened yet...*

7
喂！山啊！到这一边来！
Hello!Mountain! Come, be at my side.
8
喂！山啊！到这一边来。
Hello! Mountain! Come to my side.
9
还是没动静……
Still no movement...
山一点也没有动呀！
The mountain has not moved a bit!
10
各位，你们也看到了，我向那座山叫喊了三遍可是山还是没动。
Everyone! You have seen it too. I yelled three times to that mountain, but that mountain still did not move.

11
山不动，我动！同样能使山到我的身边。
However, even though the mountain does not move, I can move!This can also make the mountain be at my side.

世事并非皆能如人所愿，转不动外面局势转动自己同样能达目的。山不动，人动！水不弯，船弯！

Things in this world are not always as we wish. When we cannot change circumstances outside of us, we can still change ourselves; and that, often, can help us reach the same goal. The mountain doesn't move; people can move! The water doesn't turn; the boat can turn!

自在地做一只都市的熊
Be a Carefree Urban Bear

1
从前有一只熊住在森林边缘，它的屋前有花有树林也有草原……
Once there was a bear who lived at the edge of a forest. In front of his den were flowers, forests, and meadows ...

2
当叶子变黄变红纷纷飘落之时它就进洞里冬眠……
When leaves turned yellow and red and started falling he would return to his den to hybernate...
3
冬天的几个月它都一直睡着没有改变……
During the months of winter, he slept without any change...
4
它虽不变但洞外的环境却在这时起了大改变……
Although he did not change, the environment around his den was going through a major alteration...
5
人们在熊冬眠的期间将森林夷平，建造了一个大都市……
While the bear was sleeping, people chopped down the forest and built an urban community ...
隆！
Krak!
隆！
Krak!
隆！
Krak!
6
噢！睡了一个冬天，好舒服哦！
Ah! How comfortable it is to have slept through the winter.

7
啊！森林哪里去了？树木哪里去了？花草哪里去了？
Oh, my goodness! Where is the forest?Where are the trees?Where are the flowers and the grass?
8
这是怎么回事？我身在何处？
What's going on? Where am I?
9
是不是还没睡醒，还在做梦？
Am I still sleeping? Or am I dreaming?
痛！
10
是梦？是真？我真搞不清楚……
Is this a dream? Is this for real? I am really confused...

从此这只熊无法适应新环境得了焦虑症，日子过得很不安稳。
From then on, the bear could not adjust to the new environment. He fell prey to anxiety syndrome, and his days were always nerve ridden.
11

人的一生也常像熊的境遇一样，虽然自己没有改变，但不能否定外在客观条件改变的事实。生命的实相是随时与时空融入，所以应该进入这事实，而不要自以为那是梦。

Our lives are often like the fate of the bear. Although we have not changed, we cannot deny changes in external factors. The essence of living is to continually dissolve into the space and time in which we happen to be. Therefore, we should face reality instead of fooling ourselves in daydreams.

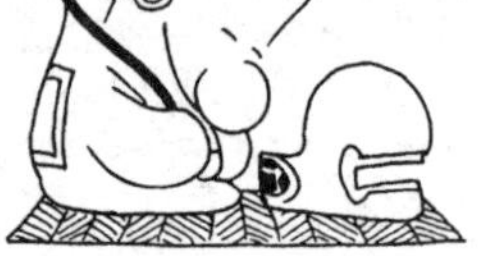

实相看不见
Not Able to See the Heart of Things

1
首吠多迦陀苦心研究《吠陀经》十二年……
Shvetuketu studied the Vedas Sutra for 12 years ...
2
哈哈！终于全部读通了。
Ha! Ha! Finally I understand it all.

3
爸爸，我已懂得《吠陀经》中的含义和真理。
Father, I have figured out the meaning and truth of the Vedas Sutra.
我教你一些书本没有的知识。
Let me teach you some knowledge not covered in the texts.
4
摘一颗榕树的果实给我。
Pick a nut from the banyan tree.
是，先生。
Yes, sir.
5
把它剥开。
Open it up now.
剥开了。
It's opened.
6
里面有什么东西?
What's in there?
几粒很小的种子。
Several tiny seeds.

7
剥开一粒种子看看。
Now open up a seed and take a look inside.
是。
Yes, Father.
8
种子里面有什么东西?
What is in there?
里面什么也没有!
Why, there is nothing inside!
9
儿子啊!大榕树的生命是藏在种子里面，而里面却什么也没有。一切存在者的自我都在那微妙的本质里面，那是最真实的自我，而你也就是那个东西。
My son, the life of the big banyan tree is hidden inside that seed, even though there is nothing visible. Every self of any living being is inside that subtle heart. That is the truest self, and you are that too.
10
请父亲再多教我一些。
Father, please teach me more.
11
把这袋盐放进水桶中。
Put this bag of salt into a bucket.
是，爸爸。
Yes, Father.
12
盐放进水桶了。
The salt has been put into the bucket.
13
再把盐拿出来给我。
Now, take the salt out and give it to me.
是，先生。
Yes,sir.

14
盐统统不见了。
The salt has completely disappeared.
15
尝尝水桶表面的水味。
Taste the water at the surface of the bucket.
是咸的。
It's salty.
16
尝尝水中央看看什么味道?
Taste the water in the middle. What is it like?
17
也是咸的。
It's also salty.
18
尝尝水底的味道看看?
How does it taste at the bottom of the water?
19
还是咸的。
It's still salty.
20
儿子啊！这桶水像你的身体，而最真实的自我就像咸味一样微妙地藏在本质之中。那是真实，那是自我，而你也就是那个东西。
My son, listen! This bucket of water is like your body. The truest heart is hidden inside, as subtly as the salty taste of the water. That is the truth. That is the heart of everything. And you are also that thing.

真理藏于微妙的本质里，虽然看不见但事实上确有这东西。就像榕树的生命实相里面是空，就像盐溶于水中。从里面看不见，从表面也看不见，你只能体会、实践。

Truth is hidden in the subtle nature of the heart of everything, although it is invisible. The appearance of life is kong, like the inside of a banyan seed and like salt dissolved in water. One cannot see it from inside and neither from the surface. One can only live and experience it.

两种观点 Two Points of View

1
有一个宋国人，带着帽子和衣服到南方的越国去贩卖，他以为可以大赚一笔
A long time ago, when China was divided into many small countries, there was a merchant who lived in Song, a country in northern China. He brought men's hats and shirts to the country of Yue, in southern China, thinking that he would make a great fortune ...

2
买衣服哦！漂亮又新潮的衣帽呀！
Come! Buy new clothing here! I have shirts and hats that are handsome and fashionable!
3
但是，越人的风俗是留短头发，文身，赤裸着胸膛，都不穿衣戴帽。
However, the fashion in the Yue area was for men to keep their hair short and tattoo the naked upper body. They didn't wear shirts or hats at all.
4
于是，他写信给他的老婆说：
Therefore, the merchant wrote to his wife:
很惨，这儿的人全都赤身不穿衣戴帽，我马上回去……
This was a total disaster. No man here wears any shirts or hats. They keep their upper bodies naked. I am coming right home.
5
又有一郑国人也同样带着衣帽来到越国做生意……
There was another merchant from Zheng(another country in northern China) who also brought men's shirts and hats to do business in the country of Yue ...

6
来买衣帽呀！
漂亮又新潮的衣帽呀！
Hey, come and buy new shirts and hats! Gorgeous fashionable outfits.
7
他也发现了越人的习俗是赤身不穿衣戴帽的……
He also discovered that the custom of Yue men was to keep the upper body naked ...
8
咱们这里的人，从来都不穿衣戴帽的。
We guys here never wear shirts or hats.
这也是我来这里的原因。
That's exactly why I came here.
9
太棒了！找到一个衣帽行销的处女地。
Great! Virgin territory for selling shirts and hats.
哈！Ha!
哈！Ha!
哈！Ha!
10
于是，他也写一封信回郑国给他的老婆……
Therefore, he also wrote a letter back to his wife in Zheng ...
这里没有人穿衣戴帽，是个最佳的市场，速寄大批衣帽到越国来。
No man here wear shirts or hats. It's the best market! Please send a large quantity of shirts and hats to Yue by mail.
相同的状况，悲观和乐观的看法却是两极。事情没有绝对的好、坏、善、恶，要怎么想？要怎么做？完全在于自己！
Under the same situation, the viewpoint from pessimism and optimism are extreme opposites. Things usually are not absolutely good or bad, nice or evil. How do we perceive? What do we do? It entirely depends upon ourselves.

你拥有自己吗？
Do You Own Yourself?

1
诸法空相，世间的一切皆属虚幻。
All phenomena we observe are based on our viewpoint and are really kong. Everything that exists in this world is illusionary and not absolute.
2
怎么会皆空呢？最少我自己是存在的，不容怀疑。
How can it all be kong? At least I am physically here. That is without doubt.
3
你真的自认为拥有自己的存在?
Do you really think you own your existence?
难道不是?
Don't I?
4
精神上的我思故我在没错，肉体上的拥有自己却是有问题……
Mentally, I think;therefore I am. That is correct. Physically, it is questionable whether we own ourselves ...
5
就像这只白蚁，白蚁吃木屑为生，但它无法分解木屑成为可吸收的蛋白……
For example, let's look at this termite. The termite feeds on sawdust from wood, but it cannot directly digest sawdust into nutrients for absorption ...
它依靠的是大肠里的鞭毛虫提供酶，使木屑变成可以吃的碳水化合物……
It depends on the flagellates in it's large intestine to provide enzymes which break down sawdust into digestible carbohydrates ...
6

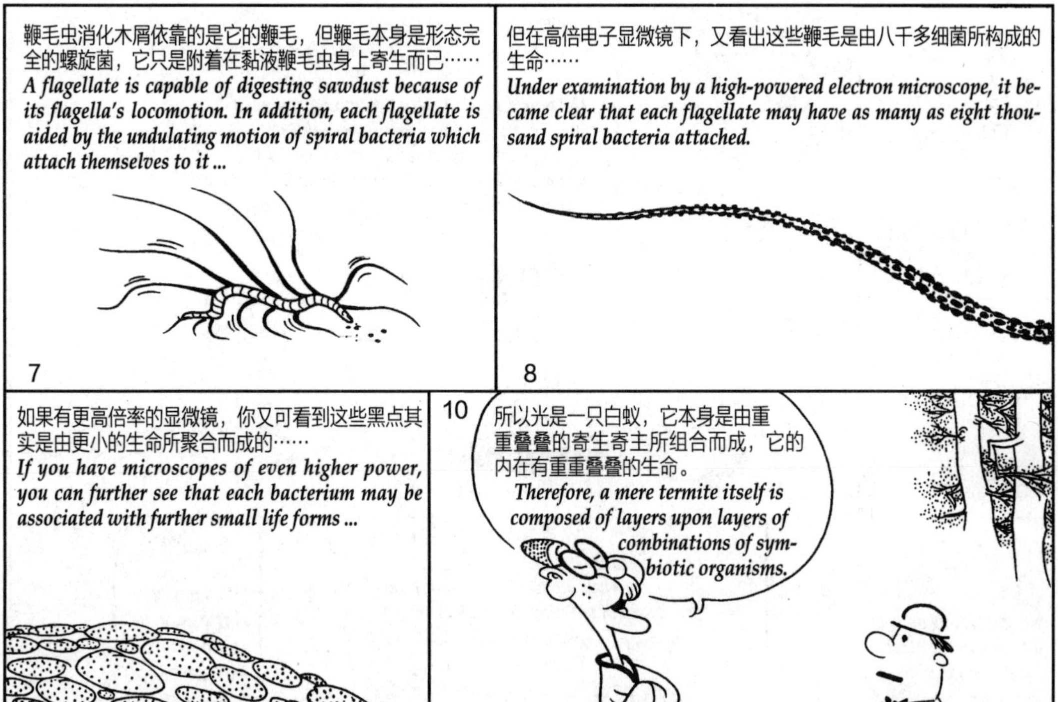
鞭毛虫消化木屑依靠的是它的鞭毛，但鞭毛本身是形态完全的螺旋菌，它只是附着在黏液鞭毛虫身上寄生而已……
A flagellate is capable of digesting sawdust because of its flagella's locomotion. In addition, each flagellate is aided by the undulating motion of spiral bacteria which attach themselves to it ...
7
但在高倍电子显微镜下，又看出这些鞭毛是由八千多细菌所构成的生命……
Under examination by a high-powered electron microscope, it became clear that each flagellate may have as many as eight thousand spiral bacteria attached.
8
如果有更高倍率的显微镜，你又可看到这些黑点其实是由更小的生命所聚合而成的……
If you have microscopes of even higher power, you can further see that each bacterium may be associated with further small life forms ...
9
10
所以光是一只白蚁，它本身是由重重叠叠的寄生寄主所组合而成，它的内在有重重叠叠的生命。
Therefore, a mere termite itself is composed of layers upon layers of combinations of symbiotic organisms.
所以，你怎能证明你真正拥有自己的存在？
Therefore, how can you prove that you can own your existence of self?
11
12
生命不只是一个生命，而是一个团体、一个集合，每个人都是很多生命聚合的存在。
I see now. Life is not only one life. It is a group entity, a collection. Everyone of many lives gathered together.

每个人都只是生命旅程中的一个脚步而已，而在这小小的一步中还聚合着重重叠叠的生命。我从太初洪荒来，要走向未知的未来！我所拥有的仅仅是“现在”。
Everyone is simply a footstep in the journey of the life force. While only a tiny step, it still connects layers of symbiotic life forms. I came from the unknowable origin of space and time, and I'm heading toward the unknowable future! All I own is the "present".

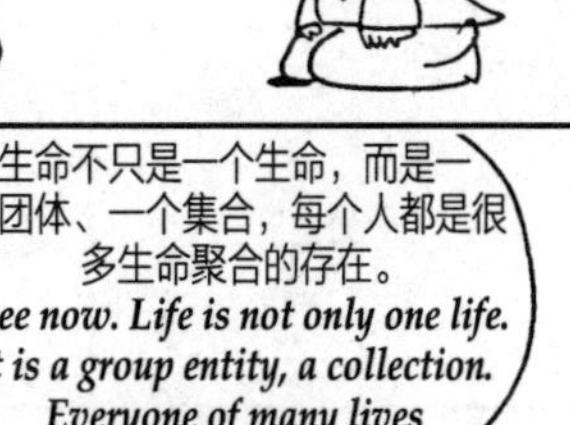

大、小、多、少
Big vs. Small & Abundant vs. Scarce

1
世界是以你自己的观点呈现，其实天下万物没有好坏善恶多少大小，一切都是你自己的意识所定下的偏见。
The world presents itself from your point of view. In reality, everything under the sun has no distinction between being abundant vs. scarce and big vs. small. Everything depends on the prejudice defined by your ego-self.

2
万物有大有小有坏有好，怎么会无大小好坏高低？
No, everything must be one way or the other. How could there be no difference whatsoever?
3
好吧！那么请告诉我一微克的一粒盐是大还是小，是多还是少？
OK! Then please tell me about one grain of salt which weighs 1 microgram! Is it big or small? Abundant or scarce?
4
一粒盐当然是小是少！
Of course, a single grain of salt is small and scarce!
5
一粒盐中间含有 10^16 个原子数，10 的 16 次方就是 1 后面跟着 16 个零，就是一万兆！
One grain of salt contains ten to the power of 16 atoms. That means there are 16 zeros following the first numeral. That's ten zillion!
6
这一万兆原子有五千万亿颗氯原子，有五千万亿颗钠原子。
Among these ten zillion atoms, half are chloride and the other half are sodium.

7
氯是具有致命毒性的气体，两次世界大战曾被用来制作毒气弹；钠是具腐蚀性的金属，遇水便会燃烧。
Chloride is a deadly poisonous gas which was used as a chemical weapon during the World Wars. Sodium is a corrosive metal which starts burning when in contact with water.
8
然而这两种致命的氯和钠合在一起，便成为一种稳定无毒的物质——氯化钠，也就是食盐。
However, when these two lethal elements, chloride and sodium, are combined together, they become a stable and safe compound called sodium chloride-table salt!
9
现在我再问你一次……
Now, let me ask you one more time ...
10
一粒盐是多还是少？是大还是小。
One grain of salt. Is it abundant or scarce? Big or small?
!
11
一粒盐不能说它多不能说它少，不能说它大不能说它小。
One grain of salt–We cannot say it is abundant or scarce. We cannot say it is big or small.

人生的意义
The Meaning of Life

1
有一天，禅师和他的弟子到一处风景区……
One day, the Zen Master and his disciple came to a scenic spot ...
2
风景好美好漂亮哦！
What beautiful scenery!
是啊！
Yes, indeed.
3
师父，我可不可以请教一些问题？Master, May I seek your wisom in answering some questions?
4
人死后又将到哪里去？
Where do people go after they die?
如何看待分合问题？
How should we treat the one or two China issue?
什么是人生的意义？
What's the meaning of life?

5
人生的真谛是融入任何时空，体会实践每一个此时此地。
The essence of life is to dissolve into any space and time you are in, to experience and practise in every space and time.
6
你远来寻求湖光山色，但对眼前的一切为何如此盲目呢？而净想着别的问题！
You came all the way to seek natural beauty. Why are you blind to all the gifts of life right in front of your eyes? All you think about are questions irrelevant to the present moment!
!
7
生命就像拥有一张八十年的旅游券，在这八十年中每个人可自行安排自己的旅程到何处去。
Life is like owning a travel coupon valid for eighty years. During this time, everyone can arrange his schedule voluntarily and go wherever he wants to go.
8
但可别拿着旅券只站在原地，而一味地想着八十年以后票券失效之后的问题。
But don't just stand in place holding your travel coupon, only obsessed about the problems that will occur when the coupon is no longer valid—eighty years from now.
是。
Yes.
别为整个宇宙烦恼，别自寻烦恼地去追问创造世界的终极目的是什么，生命与爱就是生命与爱；一束紫罗兰就是一束紫罗兰，不必去寻求答案。
Don't worry about the whole universe. Don't worry compulsively about the ultimate reason for creating this world. Life and love is life and love; a bunch of violets is a bunch of violets. It is not necessary to be obsessed about further answers.

万物的本质
The Spirit of Everything
1
2
这是郑板桥的真迹！
This is an authentic copy of the infamous calligrapher Zheng Ban Qiao!
3
写得太好太棒了！
What wonderful and amazing work!
4
站在这里好像看着他正在写这幅字一样……
Standing here I could almost feel him in the middle of doing the calligraphy ...
5
别被感情骗了！这幅字是后人的仿冒品！
Don't be fooled by your emotions! This copy is actually an imitation by someone of a later time!
既是仿冒品就一文不值了……
Well, then, if it is just an imitation, then it's not even worth pennies ...
6

7
别又被自己的主观意识骗了！再真正地把这幅字仔细看一遍！
Do not be fooled by your subjective judgment this time. Take another careful look at this work!
是！
Yes!
8
……
9
不管是真迹或仿冒品，不管是郑板桥还是别人写的，这幅字写得真好！
Whether this copy is authentic or imtative, whether it's done by Zheng Ban Qiao or somebody else, this is a very fine piece of work!
的确如此！
Indeed so!

经验累积成人的主观意识，意识又左右了人的感官世界……
人，一有了立足点便看不真眼前的万象了。不要用己目看世界，世界便会以全新的面貌真实地呈现在你眼前！

Experiences accumulate into people's subjective awareness. Awareness, in turn, preconditions people's sensory world ... Once people have a point of view, they are not seeing everything as it truly is right in front of their eyes. Do not observe the world from the limitaiton of your old viewpoint. The world will then present it's true spirit in brand new ways in front of you.

自省为先
Self-Reflection as the First Priority

1
没有目标的船，不是出不了海，就是靠不了岸……
A boat without destination is either stuck at the dock forever or not able to reach the coast of choice ...

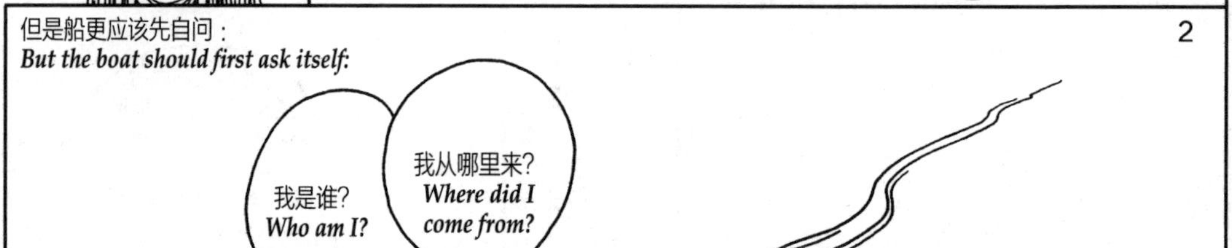
但是船更应该先自问：
But the boat should first ask itself:
2
我是谁？ Who am I?
我从哪里来？ Where did I come from?
3
我要去哪里？ Where do I want to go?

人生像似马拉松跑道，大家人挤人地一味往前跑。虽然好像有个共同的目标，但是这目标是由别人反射出来的，并不是你的真正需要。

人应先退出跑道自问：我是谁？我想做什么？我有什么能力做什么？然后再定下自己的目标加入跑道。

Life is like a track for marathon runners all crowding together and rubbing each others' shoulders while heading forward with a "one track mind". Although it appears like there is a common destination, the destination is only reflected through others and not necessarily what each runner needs. We should first back ourselves out of the racing track and ask: Who am I? What do I want to do? What am I good at doing? Then, after one has set one's own destination, one can join the race track that fits.

佛

云想衣裳花想容

The Clouds Desire Pretty Attire and the Flowers Desire Pretty Faces

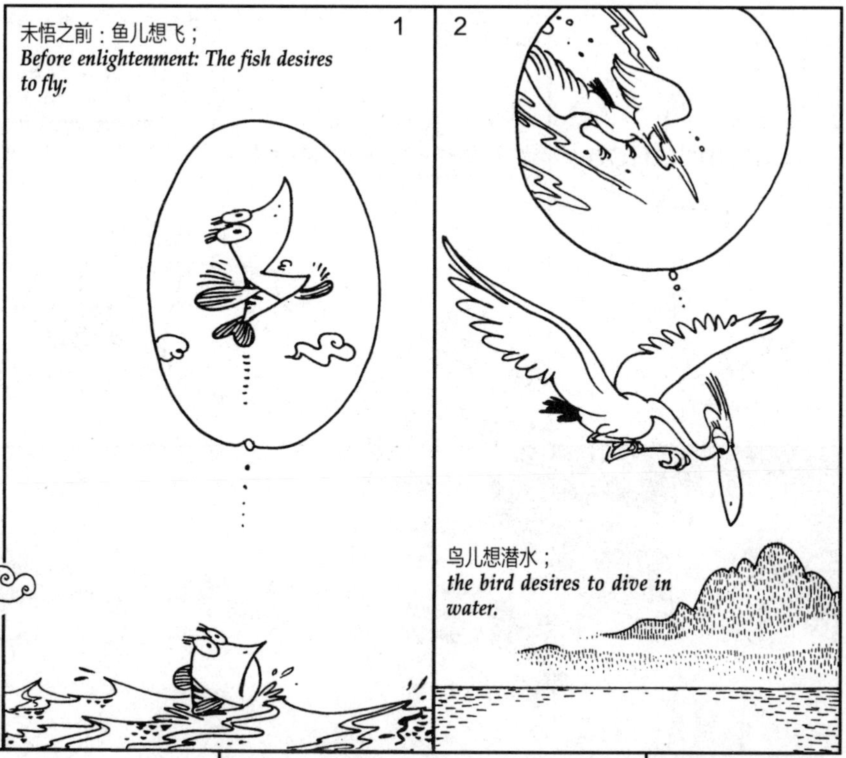
1
未悟之前：鱼儿想飞；
Before enlightenment: The fish desires to fly;
2
鸟儿想潜水；
the bird desires to dive in water.

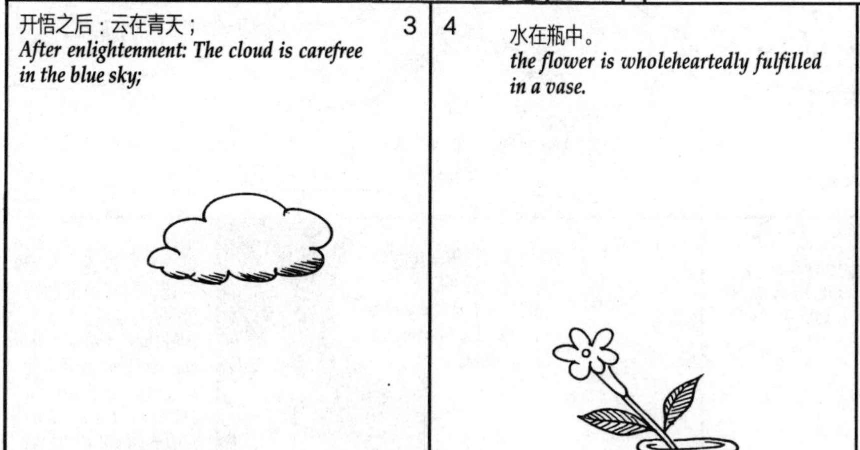
3
开悟之后：云在青天；
After enlightenment: The cloud is carefree in the blue sky;
4
水在瓶中。
the flower is wholeheartedly fulfilled in a vase.

你是铁砧时，应屹立不摇；你是铁锤时，应奋力敲击。你是鱼时，畅游水域；你是鸟时，翱翔天际。

When you are an iron anvil, you should stand steady without moving; when you are the iron hammer, you should strike down with all your might; when you are a fish, enjoy swimming around in water; when you are a bird, fly freely in the sky.

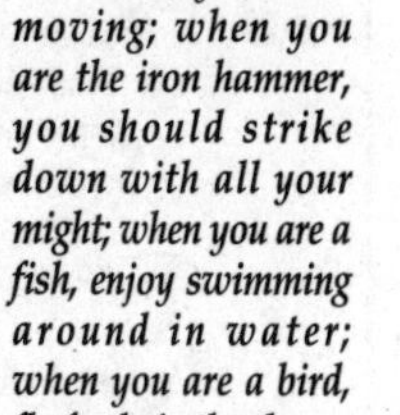

轮回
Reincarnation
1
枯木将死，但它死得很安宁……
The dried up tree is about to die, but he is dying quite peacefully ...
这是树的死，这也是炭的生，只是法相不同。
This is the death of a tree; this is also the birth of charcoal. They are just different manifestations of being.
2
当我是树的时候，我荫凉人们的身。
I provided shade for people, when I was a tree.
当我是炭的时候，我温暖人们的心。
I will provide warmth for people when I am charcoal.
3
烧成灰烬之后又如何？
What happens then, when you are burned down to ashes?
!
4
我将还原再化为尘土，滋养树木。
I will be reduced to soil again to nourish trees.
是树、是炭、是尘、是土各有际遇，不问生死，只问是否活在当时……
Whether it is a tree, charcoal, or soil, life has its own terms. Do not ask whether I will be dead or alive; ask only if I am living my life to the fullest in the present.

失即是得
Loss Is Gain
1
师问弟子说：
A teacher instructs his pupil:
桌上有三个苹果，你拿一个去吃！
There are three apples on the table. Go ahead and grab one to eat.
谢谢老师。
Thank you, teacher!
2
3
真好吃。
Yummy.
4
三个苹果被你吃了一个，现在有几个？
One of three apples was eaten by you. Now, how many apples are there?
三个！
Three!
5
怎么还会有三个苹果？
How can there still be three apples?
6
一个在肚子里，两个在桌上。
One in my tummy; two on the table.
人太看重得失，更往往把得失看错得离了谱。吃下肚的苹果不正是真正的“得”吗？哪叫做“失”？
People often take gain and loss too seriously, and even more often judge them entirely wrong—to the point of being ridiculous. Isn't the apple that is already in the stomach a true"gain"? How could that be a "loss"?

1的故事
The Story of 1

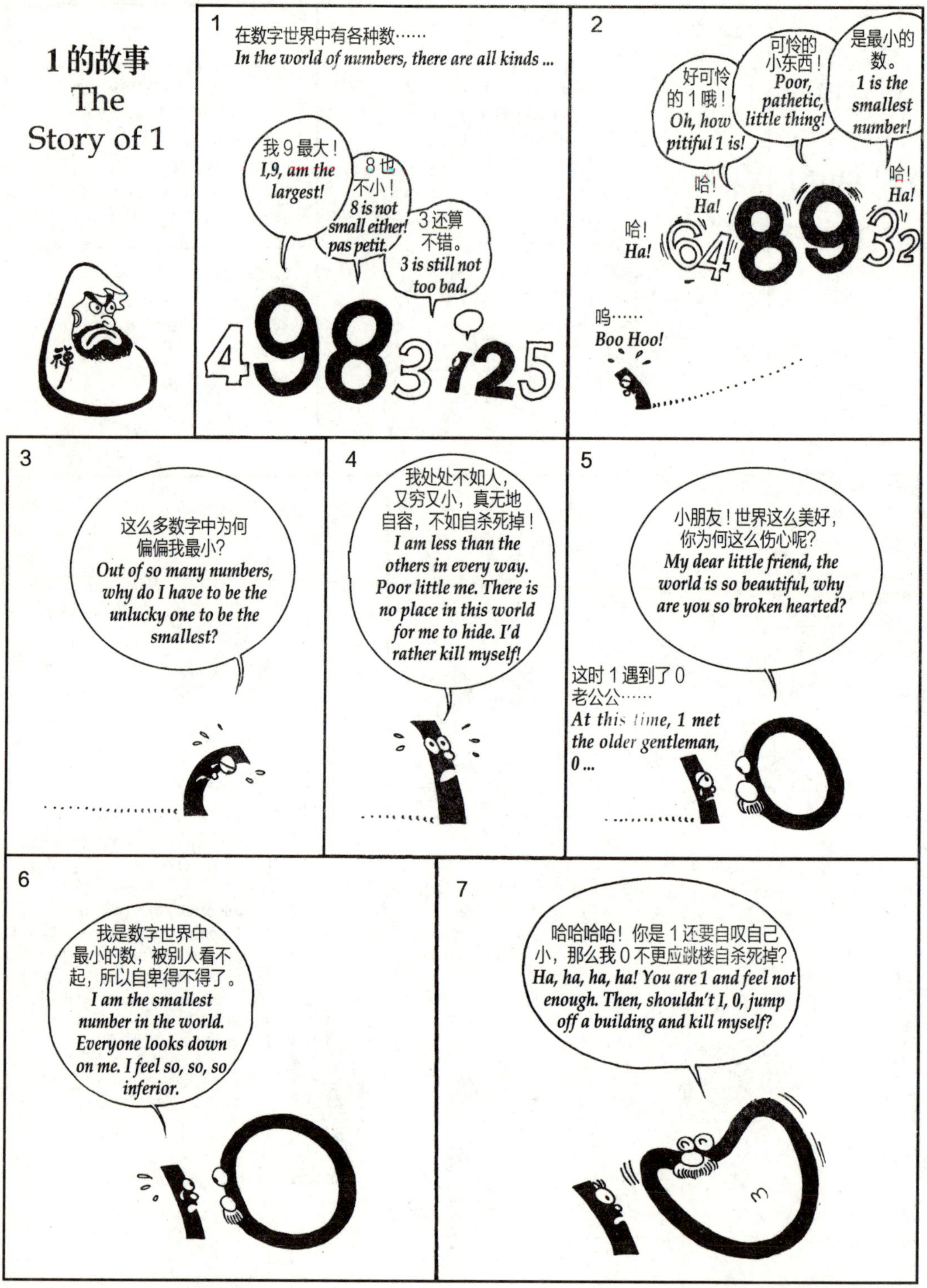
禅
1
在数字世界中有各种数……
In the world of numbers, there are all kinds ...
我9最大！I,9, am the largest!
8也不小！8 is not small either! pas petit.
3还算不错。3 is still not too bad.
2
好可怜的1哦！Oh, how pitiful 1 is!
可怜的小东西！Poor, pathetic, little thing!
是最小的数。1 is the smallest number!
哈！Ha!
哈！Ha!
哈！Ha!
呜……Boo Hoo!
3
这么多数字中为何偏偏我最小？Out of so many numbers, why do I have to be the unlucky one to be the smallest?
4
我处处不如人，又穷又小，真无地自容，不如自杀死掉！I am less than the others in every way. Poor little me. There is no place in this world for me to hide. I'd rather kill myself!
5
小朋友！世界这么美好，你为何这么伤心呢？My dear little friend, the world is so beautiful, why are you so broken hearted?
这时1遇到了0老公公……At this time, 1 met the older gentleman, 0 ...
6
我是数字世界中最小的数，被别人看不起，所以自卑得不得了。I am the smallest number in the world. Everyone looks down on me. I feel so, so, so inferior.
7
哈哈哈哈！你是1还要自叹自己小，那么我0不更应跳楼自杀死掉？Ha, ha, ha, ha! You are 1 and feel not enough. Then, shouldn't I, 0, jump off a building and kill myself?

8
其实你很不错，从外表来评估 1 长得单纯又正直。
In fact, you are quite nice yourself. Judging from your appearance, 1, you look clean cut and straightforward.
9
若由实质评估，1 不多也不少，不坏也不好。
If we judge by your true quality, 1 is not many or few, not bad or good.
10
1 只是一个数，本身并没有好坏善恶与大小。站在 9 的右边是他大你小！
1 is only a number and in itself implies no value judgement. When you stand on the right side of 9, 9 is big and 1 is small.
大 *Big*
小 *Small*
11
但若站在 9 的左边则反变成你大他小。
But if you stand on the left side of 9,then in turn you are big and 9 is small.
大 *Big*
小 *Small*
12
所以与其他数字在一起时你不需要自卑，但也不必要自傲。
Therefore, when you are together with other numbers, you don't need to feel inferior. But also there is no need to feel arrogant.
这话怎么说？*What do you mean by that?*
13
老子《道德经》说："道生一，一生二，二生三，三生万物。"所以 1 也是宇宙生成的开始。
The famous Chinese philosopher Lao Zi once said in his "Book of Morality": The universal essence gives birth to 1, 1 gives birth to 2, 2 gives birth to 3, 3 gives birth to everything else. Therefore, 1 is also the beginning of the formation of the universe.

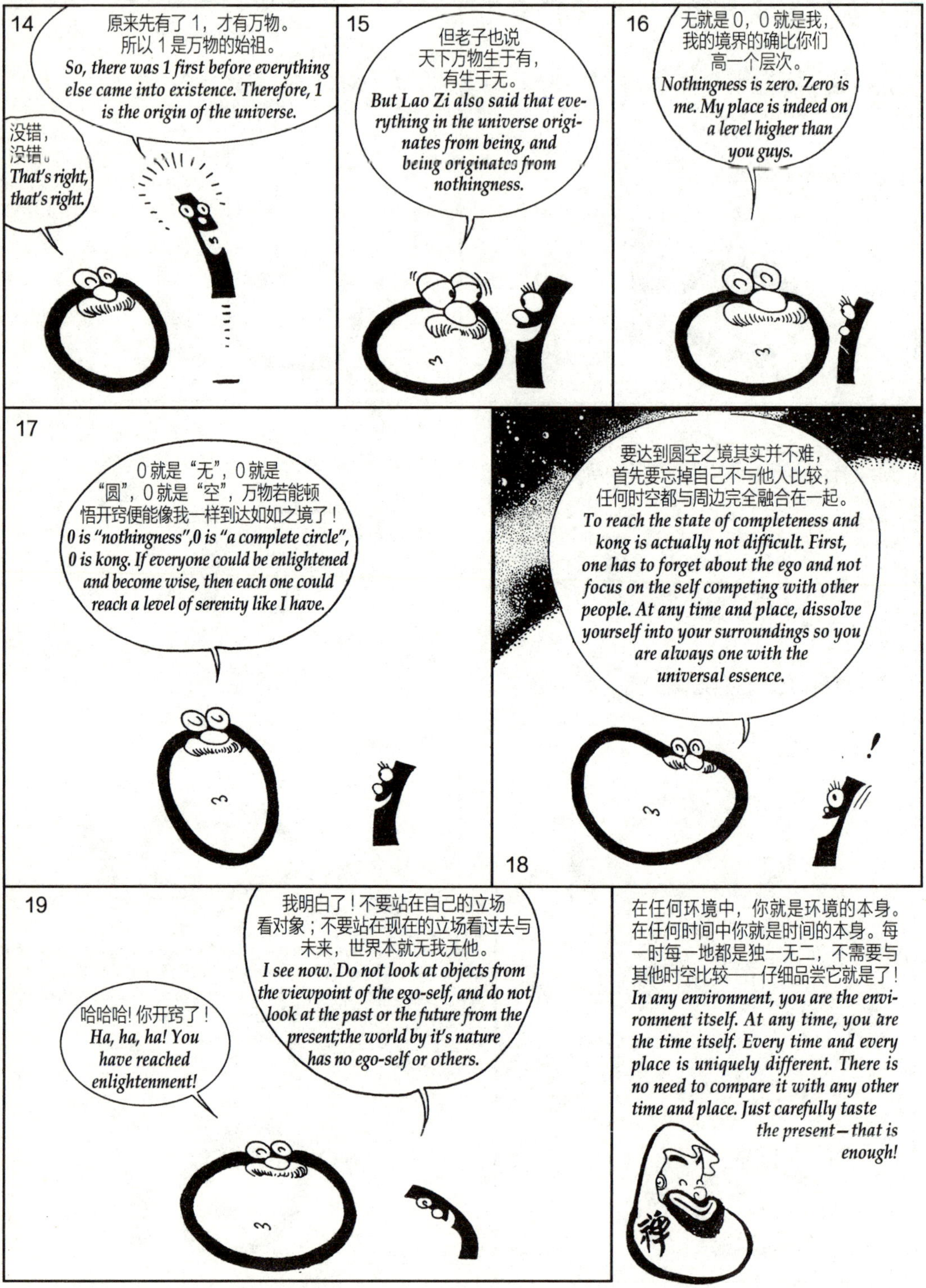
14
原来先有了1，才有万物。所以1是万物的始祖。
So, there was 1 first before everything else came into existence. Therefore, 1 is the origin of the universe.
没错，没错。
That's right, that's right.
15
但老子也说天下万物生于有，有生于无。
But Lao Zi also said that everything in the universe originates from being, and being originates from nothingness.
16
无就是0，0就是我，我的境界的确比你们高一个层次。
Nothingness is zero. Zero is me. My place is indeed on a level higher than you guys.
17
0就是“无”，0就是“圆”，0就是“空”，万物若能顿悟开窍便能像我一样到达如如之境了！
0 is “nothingness”,0 is “a complete circle”, 0 is kong. If everyone could be enlightened and become wise, then each one could reach a level of serenity like I have.
18
要达到圆空之境其实并不难，首先要忘掉自己不与他人比较，任何时空都与周边完全融合在一起。
To reach the state of completeness and kong is actually not difficult. First, one has to forget about the ego and not focus on the self competing with other people. At any time and place, dissolve yourself into your surroundings so you are always one with the universal essence.
!
19
我明白了！不要站在自己的立场看对象；不要站在现在的立场看过去与未来，世界本就无我无他。
I see now. Do not look at objects from the viewpoint of the ego-self, and do not look at the past or the future from the present;the world by it's nature has no ego-self or others.
哈哈哈! 你开窍了！
Ha, ha, ha! You have reached enlightenment!
在任何环境中，你就是环境的本身。在任何时间中你就是时间的本身。每一时每一地都是独一无二，不需要与其他时空比较——仔细品尝它就是了！
In any environment, you are the environment itself. At any time, you are the time itself. Every time and every place is uniquely different. There is no need to compare it with any other time and place. Just carefully taste the present—that is enough!
禅

附录·延伸阅读

APPENDIX Further reading

此部分为本书图画页的延伸阅读，
各段首所示的页码与图画页对应。

P138-P140 《般若波罗蜜多心经》

这八个字是一经的总题，全名为《摩诃般若波罗蜜多心经》，是佛教近万卷的经典中，字数最少义理最丰的一部经典。其释义如下：这是教导世人依照“般若”妙法修行，便可以度脱茫茫生死苦海，达到究竟安乐的彼岸，而亲证不生不灭之真心实相的一部经典。

P141 观自在菩萨行深般若波罗蜜多时。

圣者观自在菩萨，修习深妙般若，功行到了极点，能够观察了解诸法实相之真理，得到大自在，不为境界所转，又能救度迷途众生，具有“自觉觉他”的精神的时候……

P142 照见五蕴皆空。度一切苦厄。

观察到色、受、想、行、识五蕴，都是缘生无性，当体即空。这一切众生造业受苦的根源既空，自然而然就没有一切苦厄的产生了。

P144 舍利子，色不异空，空不异色，色即是空，空即是色，受想行识亦复如是。

舍利弗呀！物不能离开精神而存在；相对地，精神也不能离开物质而独立。你要知道，缺了物质就失去了现实的作用；少了精神则失去思想的活动。

P145 换句话说，物质的本体就是空，空的现象就是物质。除了色蕴之外，五蕴中的受想行识等四蕴也是相同的道理。

P146 ●番外

从姚秦宋代的六百年间，《心经》一共有十一种译本，到今日多已散失无存。其中流传最广的是唐代玄奘大师于贞观二十三年所译《般若波罗蜜多心经》。玄奘法师俗名陈祎，河南洛阳人，十三岁便在净土寺出家，二十六岁时下定决心冒险西行取经，经戈壁大沙漠，穿过葱岭到印度。经过十余年的旅游参访学知识，终于带回大量梵文佛经。他所译的佛经中以《大般若经》最为杰出。

P148-P149 舍利子，是诸法空相，不生不灭，不垢不净，不增不减。

舍利弗啊！五蕴、十二入、十八界、四谛诸法的现象虽然是假的，然而它的本体却是真空实相，真常不变、至圆至极的，本来就没有所谓的缘聚为生，缘尽为灭；也没有出障为净，入流为垢；悟时为增，迷时为减等虚妄之假象。

P150　是故空中无色，无受想行识，无眼耳鼻舌身意，无色声香味触法，无眼界，乃至无意识界。

依照前面所说——“是诸法空相”的道理来看，在真空实相的理体中，本来就空寂，不生不灭，不增不减，没有色受想行识等五蕴，也没有眼耳鼻舌身意六根，色声香味触法六尘，以及眼识、耳识、鼻识、舌识、身识、意识等虚妄之法。

P151　无无明，亦无无明尽，乃至无老死，亦无老死尽。

因此，依据真空实相的理体来说，不但没有凡夫流转门的生死轮回之相状，由迷而成凡的十二因缘；同时也没有圣者还灭门的解脱生死的法门，由悟而入圣的十二因缘。这样一来既没有无明（烦恼），也就不会有老死，自然就没有无明灭，乃至老死灭了。

P153–P154　无苦集灭道，无智亦无得。

总而言之，本经彰显般若真空理体，所以没有生死“苦”的感觉，没有贪爱的“集”因可断，没有寂 “灭”的涅槃可证，更没有解脱的“道”法可修。因为自性本来解脱没有生死可舍，本来清净没有烦恼可断，本来空寂没有涅槃可证，本来俱足没有菩提可修，此为佛陀修证的结果。

P155–P156　已无所得故，菩提萨埵，依般若波罗蜜多故，心无罣碍，

因为般若之智能照见诸法实相，本来就是“无所得”，所以菩萨依了般若波罗蜜多修行，证得真空理体、心境一如、解脱自在的道理，真心便不会被无明烦恼蔽盖，而事事妄为执着，导致外在环境阻滞，心中便无法自在了。

P157–P158　无罣碍故，无有恐怖，远离颠倒梦想，究竟涅槃。

由于心无罣碍，便不受世间利衰毁誉、称讥苦乐所动，或因为生老病死、忧悲苦恼而心生恐怖。到了那个时候，心中光明坦荡，没有任何胡思乱想存在，便远离了一切虚幻不实的妄想，最后无明全破，大梦全醒，而证得大灭度、大解脱的“究竟涅槃”。

P159–P160　三世诸佛，依般若波罗蜜多故，得阿耨多罗三藐三菩提。

不仅菩萨们依了般若，而获致究竟涅槃；就是现在、过去、未来的三世诸佛，也都是依般若波罗蜜多之真空妙智照见五蕴皆空，明白缘起性空之真谛，而证得“无上、正等、正觉”的圆满佛果呢！

P161–P162　故知般若波罗蜜多，是大神咒，是大明咒。

按照前面所说的，依了般若而修可以得证菩提涅槃，那么毫无疑问的，般若不但有理论上的思想力，而且有彻底改造人生的功能，能令受持者驱除烦恼，解脱生死之苦，从凡入圣，是一种大神力的咒呀！能使受持者远离颠倒虚幻之妄想，打破无明烦恼而成光明之大觉，是一种大光明的咒呀！

P163–P164　是无上咒，是无等等咒，能除一切苦，真实不虚。

同时此经能使受持诵念的人，直达无上涅槃灭寂之境，不迷于凡小之执着，不落入圣人之空，人世间再也找不到任何一法可超过它。所以，它是一种至高无上的咒呀！是一种超绝无比的咒呀！它的功力能除去所有的苦，这些都是真实而没有半点虚假的，大家要绝对相信啊！

P165-P166　故说般若波罗蜜多咒，即说咒曰：揭谛，揭谛，波罗揭谛，波罗僧揭谛，菩提娑婆诃。

所以说，般若波罗蜜多咒不但能自度且能度人，不但使自己了脱生死，更能令广大群众同度生死之深渊；不但自己度出生死到达涅槃真理彼岸，而且能与大众共度同时脱离生死，到达彼岸。即安乐彼岸之邦，不应该个人独享，而应与众人同乐，那么请大家共同迅速启程吧！

《般若波罗蜜多心经》

P167 ●番外

《心经》只有三百六十个字，却是浓缩了《大般若经》庞大的内容要义，将大乘、小乘的思想都包括在内了。在简洁有力的文字中阐明“般若皆空”的道理，否定一切分别心；同时也阐述了人的自性本妙真清净，不生不灭，具有一切功德智慧，凡世出世间的一切法，都由此“真心”而生，所以称之为《心经》。

P169-P172　至道无难，唯嫌拣择。但莫憎爱，洞然明白。毫厘有差，天地悬隔。欲得现前，莫存顺逆。违顺相争，是为心病，不识玄旨，徒劳念静。圆同太虚，无欠无余。良由取舍，所以不如。莫逐有缘，勿住空忍。一种平怀，泯然自尽。止动归止，止更弥动。唯滞两边，宁知一种。一种不通，两处失功。遣有没有，从空背空。多言多虑，转不相应。绝言绝虑，无处不通。归根得旨，随照失宗。须臾返照，胜却前空。前空转变，皆由妄见。不用求真，唯须息见。二见不住，慎莫追寻。才有是非，纷然失心。二由一有，一亦莫守。一心不生，万法无咎。无咎无法，不生不心。能随境灭，境逐能沉。境由能境，能由境能。欲知两段，元是一空。一空同两，齐含万象。不见精粗，宁有偏党。大道体宽，无易无难。小见狐疑，转急转迟。执之失度，必入邪路。放之自然，体无去住，任性合道，逍遥绝恼。系念乖真，昏沉不好。不好劳神，何用疏亲。欲取一乘，勿恶六尘。六尘不恶，还同正觉。智者无为，愚人自缚。法无异法，妄自爱著。将心用心，岂非大错。迷生寂乱，悟无好恶。一切二边，良由斟酌。梦幻虚华，何劳把捉。得失是非，一时放却。眼若不睡，诸梦自除。心若不异，万法一如。一如体玄，兀尔忘缘。万法齐观，归复自然。泯其所以，不可方比。止动无动，动止无止。两既不成，一何有尔。究竟穷极。不存轨则。契心平等，所作俱息。狐疑尽净，正信调直。一切不留，无可记忆。虚明自照，不劳心力。非思量处，识情难测。真如法界，无他无自。要急相应，唯言不二。不二皆同，无不包容。十方智者，皆入此宗。宗非促延，一念万年。无在不在，十方目前。极小同大，忘绝境界。极大同小，不见边表。有即是无，无即是有。若不如此，必不须守。一即一切，一切即一。但能如是，何虑不毕。信心不二，不二信心。言语道断，非去来今。

《信心铭　三祖僧璨大师》

P173-P174　竺土大仙心，东西密相付。人根有利钝，道无南北祖。灵源明皎洁，枝派暗流注。执事元是迷，契理亦非悟。门门一切境，回互不回互。回而更相涉，不尔依位住。色本殊质象，声元异乐苦。暗合上中言，明明清浊句。四大性自复，如子得其母。火热风动摇，水湿地坚固。眼色耳音声，鼻香舌碱醋。然依一一法，依根叶分布。本末须归宗，尊卑用其语。当明中有暗，勿以暗相遇。当暗中有明，勿以明相睹。明暗各相对，比如前后步。万物自有功，当言用及处。事存函盖合，理应箭锋拄。承言须会宗，勿自立规矩。触目不会道，运足焉知路。进步非近远，迷隔山河固。谨白参玄人，光阴莫虚度。

《参同契　南岳石头和尚》

P175-185 君不见，绝学无为闲道人，不除妄想不求真。无明实性即佛性，幻化空身即法身。法身觉了无一物，本源自性天真佛。五阴浮云空去来，三毒水泡虚出没。证实相，无人法。彼那灭却阿鼻业。若将妄语诳众生，自招拔舌尘沙劫。顿觉了，如来禅。六度万行体中圆。梦里明明有六趣，觉后空空无大千。无罪福，无损益。寂灭性中莫问觅。比来尘镜未曾磨，今日分明须剖析。谁无念，谁无生。若实无生无不生。唤取机关木人问，求佛施功早晚成。放四大，莫把捉。寂灭性中随饮啄。诸行无常一切空，即是如来大圆觉。决定说，表真乘。有人不肯任情征。直截根源佛所印，摘叶寻枝我不能。摩尼珠，人不识。如来藏里亲收得。六般神用空不空，一颗圆光色非色。净五眼，得五力。唯证乃知谁可测。镜里看形见不难，水中捉月争拈得。常独行，常独步。达者同游涅槃路。调古神清风自高，貌悴骨刚人不顾。穷释子口称贫。实是身贫道不贫。贫则身常披缕褐，道即心藏无价珍。无价珍，用无尽。利物应时终不吝。三身四智体中圆，八解六通心地印。上士一决一切了，中下多闻多不信。但自怀中解垢衣，谁能向外夸精进。从他谤，任他非。把火烧天徒自疲。我闻恰似饮甘露，销融顿入不思议。观恶言，是功德。此则成吾善知识。不因讪谤起怨亲，何表无生慈忍力。宗亦通，说亦通。定慧圆明不滞空。非但我今独达了，河沙诸佛体皆同。狮子吼，无畏说。百兽闻之皆脑裂。香象奔波失却威，天龙寂听生欣悦。游江海，涉山川。寻师访道为参禅。自从认得曹溪路，了知生死不相干。行亦禅，坐亦禅。语默动静体安然。纵遇锋刀常坦坦，假饶毒药也闲闲。我师得见燃灯佛，多劫曾为忍辱仙。几回生，几回死。生死悠悠无定止。自从顿悟了无生，于诸荣辱何忧喜。入深山，住兰若。岑崟幽邃长松下。优游静坐野僧家，阒寂安居实潇洒。觉即了，不施功。一切有为法不同。住相布施生天福，犹如仰箭射虚空。势力尽，箭还坠。招得来生不如意。争似无为实相门，一超直入如来地。但得本，莫愁末。如净琉璃含宝月。既能解此如意珠，自利利他终不竭。江月照，松风吹。水夜清宵何所为。佛性戒珠心地印，雾露云霞体上衣。降龙钵，解虎锡。两股金钚鸣历历。不是摽形虚事持，如来宝杖亲踪迹。不求真，不断妄。了知二法空无相。无相无空无不空，即是如来真实相。心镜明，鉴无碍。廓然莹彻周沙界。万象森罗影现中，一颗圆明非内外。豁达空，拨因果。漭漭荡荡招殃祸。弃有著空病亦然，还如避溺而投火。舍妄心，取真理。取舍之心成巧伪。学人不了用修行，真成认贼将为子。损法财，灭功德。莫不由斯心意识。是以禅门了却心，顿入无生知见力。大丈夫，秉慧剑。般若锋兮金刚焰。非但能摧外道心，早曾落却天魔胆。震法雷，击法鼓。布慈云兮洒甘露。龙象蹴踏润无边，三乘五性皆惺悟。雪山肥腻更无杂。纯出醍醐我常纳。一性圆通一切性，一法遍含一切法。一月普现一切水，一切水月一月摄。诸佛法身入我性，我性还共如来合。一地具足一切地，非色非心非行业。弹指圆成八万门，刹那灭却阿鼻业。一切数句非数句，与吾灵觉何交涉。不可毁，不可赞。体若虚空勿涯岸。不离当处常湛然，觅则知君不可见。取不得，舍不得。不可得中只么得。默时说，说时默。大施门开无壅塞。有人问我解何宗，报道摩诃般若力。或是或非人不识，逆行顺行天莫测。吾早曾经多劫修，不是等闲相诳惑。建法幢，立宗旨。明明佛敕曹溪是。第一迦叶首传灯，二十八代西天记。法东流，入此土。菩提达摩为初祖。六代传衣天下闻，后人得道无穷数。真不立，妄本空。有无俱遣不空空。二十空门元不著，一性如来体自同。心是根，法是尘。两种犹如镜上痕。痕垢尽除光始现，心法双亡性即真。嗟末法，恶时世。众生福薄难调制。去圣远兮邪见深，魔强法弱多怨害。闻说如来顿教门，恨不灭除令瓦碎。作在心，殃在身。不须怨诉更尤人。欲得不招无间业，莫谤如来正法轮。栴檀林，无杂树。郁密深沉狮子住。境静林闲独自游，走兽飞禽皆远去。狮子儿，众随后。三岁即能大哮吼。若是野干逐法王，百年妖怪虚开口。圆顿教，勿人情。有疑不决直须争。不是山僧逞人我，修行恐落断常坑。非不非，是不是。差之毫厘失千里。是即龙女顿成佛，非即善星生陷坠。吾早年来积学问，亦曾讨疏寻经论。分别名相不知休，入海算沙徒自困。却被如来苦诃责。数他珍宝有何益。从来蹭蹬觉虚行，多年枉作风尘客。种性邪，错知解。不达如来圆顿制。二乘精进勿道心，外道聪明无智慧。亦愚痴，亦小骏。空拳指上生实解。执指为月枉施功，根境法中虚捏怪。不见一法即如来，方得名为观自在。了即业障本来空，未了还须偿宿债。饥逢王膳不能餐。病遇医王争得差。在欲行禅知见力，火中生莲终不坏。勇施犯重悟无生，早时成佛于今在。狮子吼，无畏说。深嗟懵懂顽皮靼。只知犯重障菩提，不见如来开秘诀。有二比丘犯淫杀，波离萤光增罪结。维摩大士顿除疑，还同赫日销霜雪。不思议，解脱力。此即成吾善知识。四事供养敢辞劳，万两黄金亦销得。粉骨碎身未足酬，一句了然超百亿。法中王，最高胜。河沙如来同共证。我今解此如意珠，信受之者皆相应。了了见，无一物。亦无人，亦无佛。大千世界海中沤，一切圣贤如电拂。假使铁轮顶上旋，定慧圆明终不失。日可冷，月可热。众魔不能坏真说。象驾峥嵘谩进途，谁见螳螂能拒辙。大象不游于兔径，大悟不拘于小节。莫将管见谤苍苍，未了吾今为君决。

《证道歌　永嘉真觉大师》

P186–P188　至道本乎其心。心法本乎无住。无住心体，灵知不昧，性相寂然，包含德用，该摄内外，能深能广，非有非空，不生不灭，无终无始。求之而不得。弃之而不离。迷现量则惑苦纷然。悟真性则空明廓彻。虽即心即佛，唯证者方知。然有证有知，则慧日沉没于有地。若无照无悟，则昏云掩蔽于空门。若一念不生，则前后际断，照体独立，物我皆如，直造心源，无知无得，不取不舍，无对无修。然迷悟更依，真妄相待。若求真去妄，犹弃影劳形。若体妄即真，似处阴影灭。若无心忘照，则万虑都捐。若任运寂知，则众行爰起。放旷任其去住。静鉴觉其源流。语默不失玄微。动静未离法界。言止则双亡知寂。论观则双照寂知。语证则不可示人。说理则非证不了。是以悟寂无寂，真知无知。以知寂不二之一心，契空有双融之中道。无住无著。莫摄莫收。是非两亡。能所双绝。斯绝亦寂，则般若现前。般若非心外新生。智性乃本来具足。然本寂不能自现，实由般若之功。般若之与智性，翻覆相成。本智之与始修，实无两体。双亡正入，则妙觉圆明。始末该融，则因果交彻。心心作佛，无一心而非佛心。处处成道，无一尘而非佛国。故真妄物我，举一全收。心佛众生，浑然齐致。是知迷则人随于法，法法万差而人不同。悟则法随于人，人人一智而融万境。言穷虑绝，何果何因。体本寂寥，孰同孰异。唯忘怀虚朗，消息冲融，其犹透水月华，虚而可见，无心鉴象，照而常空矣。

《五台山镇国大师澄观答皇太子问心要》

P189–P190　观心空王，玄妙难测。无形无相，有大神力。能灭千灾，成就万德。体性虽空，能施法则。观之无形，呼之有声。为大法将，心戒传经。水中盐味，色里胶清。决定是有，不见其形。心王亦尔，身内居停。面门出入，应物随情。自在无碍，所作皆成。了本识心，识心见佛。是心是佛，是佛是心。念念佛心，佛心念佛。欲得早成，戒心自律。净律净心，心即是佛。除此心王，更无别佛。欲求成佛，莫染一物。心性虽空，贪嗔体实。入此法门，端坐成佛。到彼岸已，得波罗蜜。慕道真士，自观自心。知佛在内，不向外寻。即心即佛，即佛即心。心明识佛，晓了识心。离心非佛，离佛非心。非佛莫测，无所堪任。执空滞寂，于此漂沉。诸佛菩萨，非此安心。明心大士，悟此玄音。身心性妙，用无更改。是故智者，放心自在。莫言心王，空无体性。能使色身，作邪作正。非有非无，隐显不定。心性离空，能凡能圣。是故相劝，好自防慎。刹那造作，还复漂沉。清净心智，如世万金。般若法藏，并在身心。无为法宝，非浅非深。诸佛菩萨，了此本心。有缘遇者，非去来今。

《心王铭　傅大士》

P191–P198　心性不生，何须知见。本无一法，谁论熏炼。往返无端，追寻不见。一切莫作，明寂自现。前际如空，知处迷宗。分明照境，随照冥蒙。一心有滞，诸法不通。去来自尔，胡假推穷。生无生相，生照一同。欲得心净，无心用功。纵横无照，最为微妙。知法无知，无知知要。将心守静，犹未离病。生死忘怀，即是本性。至理无诠，非解非缠。灵通应物，常在目前。目前无物，无物宛然。不劳智鉴，体自虚玄。念起念灭，前后无别。后念不生，前念自绝。三世无物，无心无佛。众生无心，依无心出。分别凡圣，烦恼转盛。计校乖常，求真背正。双泯对治，湛然明净。不须功巧，守婴儿行。惺惺了知，见网转弥。寂寂无见，暗室不移。惺惺无妄，寂寂明亮。万象常真，森罗一相。去来坐立，一切莫执。决定无方，谁为出入。无合无散，不迟不疾。明寂自然，不可言及。心无异心，不断贪淫。性空自离，任运浮沉。非清非浊，非浅非深。本来非古，见在非今。见在无住，见在无心。本来不存，本来即今。菩提本有，不须用守。烦恼本无，不须用除。灵知自照，万法归如。无归无受，绝观忘守。四德不生，三身本有。六根对境，分别非识。一心无妄，万缘调直。心性本齐，同居不携。无生顺物，随处幽栖。觉由不觉，即觉无觉。得失两边，谁论好恶。一切有为，本无造作。知心不心，无病无药。迷时舍事，悟罢非异。本无可取，今何用弃。谓有魔兴，言空象备。莫灭凡情，唯教息意。意无心灭，心无行绝。不用证空，自然明彻。灭尽生死，冥心入理。开目见相，心随境起。心处无境。境处无心。将心灭境，彼此由侵。心寂境如，不遣不拘。境随心灭，心随境无。两处不生，寂静虚明。菩提影现，心水常清。德性如愚，不立亲疏。宠辱不变，不择所居。诸缘顿息，一切不忆。永日如夜，永夜如日。外似顽嚚，内心虚直。对境不动，有力大人。无人无见，无见常现。通达一切，未尝不遍。思惟转昏，汩乱精魂。将心止动，转止转奔。万法无所，唯有一门。不入不出，非静非喧。声闻缘觉，智不能论。实无一物，妙智独存。本际虚冲，非心所穷。正觉无觉，真空不空。三世诸佛，皆乘此宗。此宗毫末，沙界含容。一切莫顾，安心无处。无处安心，虚明自露。寂静不生，放旷纵横。所作无滞，去住皆平。慧日寂寂，定光明明。照无相苑，朗涅槃城。诸缘忘毕，诠神定质。不起法座，安眠虚室。乐道恬然，优游真实。无为无得，依无自出。四等六度，同一乘路。心若不生，法无差互。无念为宗。无作为本。真空为体。妙有为用。夫真如无念，非想念而能知。实相无生，岂色心而能见。无念念者，即念真如。无生生者，即生实相。无住而住，常住涅槃。无行而行，即超彼岸。如如不动，动用无穷。念念无求，求本无念。菩提无得，净五眼而了三身。般若无知，运六通而弘四智。是知即定无定，即慧无慧，即行无行。性等虚空。体同法界。六度自兹圆满。道品于是无亏。是知我法体空。有无双泯。心本无作。道常无念。无念无思。无求无得。不彼不此。不去不来。体悟三明。心通八解。功成十力。富有七珍。入不二门。获一乘理。妙中之妙，即妙法身。天中之天，乃金刚慧。湛然常寂，应用无方。用而常空。空而常用。用而不有，即是真空。空而不无，便成妙有。妙有即摩诃般若。真空即清净涅槃。般若是涅槃之因。涅槃是般若之果。般若无见，能见涅槃。涅槃无生，能生般若。涅槃般若，名异体同。随义立名，故云法无定相。涅槃能生般若，即名真佛法身。般若能建涅槃，故号如来知见。知即知心空寂。见即见性无生。知见分明，不一不异。故能动寂常妙，理事皆如。如即处处能通。达即理事无碍。六根不染，即定慧之功。六识不生，即如如之力。心如境谢。境灭心空。心境双亡。体用不异。真如性净，慧鉴无穷。如水分千月，能见闻觉知。见闻觉知而常空寂。空即无相。寂即无生。不被善恶所拘。不被静乱所摄。不厌生死。不乐涅槃。无不能无。有不能有。行住坐卧，心不动摇。一切时中，获无所得。三世诸佛，教旨如斯。即菩萨慈悲，递相传受。自世尊灭后，西天二十八祖共传无住之心，同说如来知见。至于达摩届此为初。递代相承，于今不绝。所传秘教，要借得人。如王髻珠，终不妄与。福德智慧二种庄严行解相应方能建立。衣为法信。法是衣宗。唯指衣法相传，更无别法。内传心印，印契本心。外传袈裟，将表宗旨。非衣不传于法。非法不受于衣。衣是法信之衣。法是无生之法。无生即无虚妄，乃是空寂之心。知空寂而了法身。了法身而真解脱。

《心铭 牛头山初祖法融禅师》

P199–P229 有大禅师号希运。住洪州高安县黄檗山鹫峰下。乃曹溪六祖之嫡孙，百丈之子，西堂之任。独佩最上乘离文字之印。唯传一心。更无别法。心体亦空。万缘俱寂。如大日轮升于虚空中，照耀静无纤埃。证之者，无新旧，无浅深。说之者，不立义解，不立宗主，不开户牖。直下便是。动念则乖。然后为本佛。故其言简，其理直，其道峻，其行孤。四方学徒，望山而趋，睹相而悟。往来海众常千余人。予会昌二年廉于钟陵。自山迎至州。憩龙兴寺。旦夕问道。大中二年廉于宛陵。复礼迎至所部。寓开元寺。旦夕受法。退而纪之。十得一二。佩为心印。不敢发扬。今恐入神精义不闻于未来，遂出之，授门下僧太舟法建，归旧山之广唐寺，请长老法众，问与往日常所亲闻同异何如也。时大唐大中十一年十月八日谨记。

诸佛与一切众生，唯是一心，更无别法。此心无始已来，不曾生，不曾灭，不青不黄，无形无相，不属有无，不计新旧，非长非短，非大非小，超过一切限量名言踪迹对待，当体便是，动念即差，犹如虚空，无有边际，不可测度。惟此一心即是佛。佛与众生更无差异。但是众生著相，外求转失。使佛觅佛，将心捉心，穷劫尽形，终不能得。不知息念忘虑，佛自现前。此心即是佛。佛即是众生。众生即是佛。佛即是心。为众生时，此心不灭。为诸佛时，此心不添。乃至六度万行河沙功德本自具足，不假修添。遇缘则施。缘息则寂。若不决定信此，而欲著相修行以求功用，皆是妄想，与道相乖。此心即是佛。更无别佛。亦无别心。此心净明，犹如虚空，无一点相貌。举心动念即乖法体，即为著相。无始来，无著相佛。修六度万行欲求成佛，即是次第。无始来，无次第佛。但悟一心，更无少法可得，此则真佛。佛与众生一心无异。犹如虚空，无杂无坏。如大日轮照四天下，日照之时，明遍天下，虚空不曾明。日没之后，暗遍天下，虚空不曾暗。明暗之景，自相凌夺。虚空之性，廓然不变。佛与众生心亦如此。若观佛作清净光明解脱之相，观众生作垢浊暗昧生死之相，此人作此解，历河沙劫终不得菩提。即是著相之故。唯此一心，更无微尘许少法可得，即是佛。今学道人不悟此心体，便于心上生心，向外求佛，著相修行。皆是恶法，非菩提道。供养十方诸佛，不如供养一无心人不可得。无心者，无一切心也。如如之体，内外如木石，不动不转。内外如虚空，不塞不碍。无能无所。无方所。无相貌。无得失。趣者不敢入此法，恐落空，无栖泊处，故望涯而退。文殊当理。普贤当行。理者真空无碍之理。行者离相无尽之行。观音当大慈。势至当大智。维摩，净名也。净者，性也。名者，相也。性相不异，号为净名。诸大菩萨所表者，人皆有之。不离一心，悟之即是。今学道人不向自心中悟，乃于心外求，著相取境，皆与道背。恒河沙者，佛说是沙。此沙，诸佛菩萨释梵诸天步履而过，沙亦不喜。牛羊虫蚁踏践而行，沙亦不怒。珍宝馨香，沙亦不贪。粪溺臭秽，沙亦不恶。此心即无心之心。离一切相，众生诸佛更无差殊。但能无心，便是究竟。学道人若不直下无心，累劫修行终不成道，被三乘功行拘系，不得解脱。然证此心有迟疾。有闻法一念，便得无心者。有至十信十住十行十回向乃得无心者。有至十地乃得无心者。长短得无心即住，更无可修，更无可证，实无所得，真实不虚。一念而得与十地而得者，功用恰齐，更无深浅。只是历劫枉受辛勤耳。造恶造善，皆是著相。著相造恶，枉受轮回。著相造善，枉受劳苦。总不如言下自认取本法。此法即心，心外无法。此心即法，法内无心。心自无心，亦无无心者。将心无心，心即成有。默契而已，绝诸思量，故曰言语道断，心行处灭。此心是本源清净佛，人皆有之。蠢动畜生与诸佛菩萨一体不异。只为妄想分别，造种种业。果本佛上，实无一物。虚通寂静明妙安乐而已。深自悟认，直下便是，圆满具足，更无所欠。纵三僧只精进修行历诸地位，及一念证时，只证元来自佛，向上更不添得一物，却观历劫功用，总是梦中妄为。故如来云，我于阿耨菩提实无所得。若妄有所得，然灯即不与授记。又云，是法平等无有高下，是名菩提，即此本源清净心，与众生诸佛世界山河有相无相遍十方界一切平等，无彼无我相。此本源清净心，常自圆明遍照，世人不悟，只认见闻觉知为心，为见闻觉知所覆。所以大见精明本体。但直下无心，本体自现。如大日轮升于虚空遍照十方更无障碍。故学道人惟认见闻觉知为动作。空却见闻觉知，即心路绝无入处。但于见闻觉知处认本心。然本心不属见闻觉知，亦不离见闻觉知。但莫于见闻觉知上起见解，莫于见闻觉知上动念，亦莫离见闻觉知觅心，亦莫舍见闻觉知取法，不即不离，不住不著，纵横自在，无非道场。世人闻道诸佛皆传心法，将谓心上别有一法可证可取，遂将心觅法。不知心即是法，法即是心。不可将心更求于心。历千万劫终无得日。不如当下无心，便是本法。如力士额珠，隐于额内。向外求觅，周行十方，终不能得。智者指之，当时自见本珠如故。学道人迷自本心，不认为佛。遂向外求觅，起功用行，依次第，证果位，历劫勤求，元不成道。不如当下无心，决定知一切法本无所有，亦无所得，无住无依，无能无所，不动妄念，便证菩提。及证道时，只证本心佛。历劫功用并是虚修。如力士得珠时，只得本额珠。不关向外寻求之力。故佛言，我于阿耨菩提实无所得。恐人不信，故引五眼所见，五语所言，真实不虚，是第一义谛。

学道人勿疑四大为身。四大无我。我亦无主。故知此身无我亦无主。五阴无我亦无主。故知此心无我亦无主。六根六尘六识和合生灭，亦复如是。十八界即空，一切皆空。唯有本心，荡然清净。有识食。有智食。四大之身，饥疮为患，随事给养，不生贪著，谓之智食。恣情取味，妄生分别，唯求适口，不生厌离，谓之识食。声闻者，因声得悟，谓之声闻。但不了自心，于声教上起解，或因神通，或因瑞相语言运动，闻有菩提涅槃，三阿僧只劫修成佛道，皆属声闻道，谓之声闻。佛惟直下顿了自心。本来是佛。无一法可得。无一行可修。此是无上道。此是真如佛。学道人只怕一念有，即与道隔矣。念念无相，念念无为，即是佛。学道人若欲得成佛，一切佛法总不用学。惟学无求无著。无求则心不生。无著则心不染。不生不染即是佛。八万四千法门对八万四千烦恼，是教化接引门。本无一法。离即是法。知离者是佛。但离一切烦恼，无法可得。

学道人欲得知要诀，但莫于心上著一物。言佛法身犹如虚空，此是喻法身即虚空，虚空即法身。常人将谓法身遍于虚空处，虚空中含容法身。不知虚空即法身，法身即虚空也。若定言有虚空，即虚空不是法身。定言有法身，即法身不是虚空。但不作虚空解，虚空即法身。不作法身解，法身即虚空。虚空与法身无异相。佛与众生无异相。生死涅槃无异相。烦恼菩提无异相。离一切相即是佛。凡夫取境。道人取心。心境双忘，乃是真法。忘境犹易。忘心至难。人不敢忘心，是恐落空，无捞摸处。不知空本无空，唯一真界耳。此灵觉性，无始以来，与空虚同寿。未曾生，未曾灭，未曾有，未曾无，未曾秽，未曾净，未曾喧，未曾寂，未曾少，未曾老，无方所，无内外，无数量，无形相，无色象，无音声，不可觅，不可求，不可以智识解，不可以言语取，不可以景物会，不可以功用到。诸佛菩萨与一切蠢动众生同大涅槃性。性即是心。心即是佛。佛即是法。一念离真，皆为妄想。不可以心更求于心。不可以佛更求于佛。不可以法更求于法。故修道人直下无心默契。拟心即差。以心传心，此为正见。慎勿向外逐境为心。是认贼为子。为有贪瞋痴，即立戒定慧。本无烦恼，焉有菩提。故祖师云。佛说一切法，为除一切心。我无一切心，何用一切法。本源清净佛上，更不得著一物。譬如虚空，虽以无量珍宝庄严，终不能住。佛性同虚空。虽以无量智慧功德庄严，终不能住。但迷本性，转不见耳。所谓心地法门。万法皆依此心建立。遇境即有，无境即无。不可于净性上专作境解。所言定慧鉴用历历寂寂惺惺见闻觉知，皆境上作解，暂为中下人说即得。若欲亲证，皆不可作如此解。尽是境缚。法有没处，没于有地。但于一切法不作有见，即见法。

自达摩大师到中国，唯说一性，唯传一法。以佛传佛，不说余佛。以法传法，不说余法。法即不可说之法。佛即不可取之佛。乃是本源清净心也。唯此一事实，余二则非真。般若为慧，此慧即无相之本也。凡夫不趣道。唯恣六情，乃行六道。即学道后，一念计生死，即落诸魔道。一念起诸见，即落外道。见有生，趣其灭，即落声闻道。不见有生，唯见有灭，即缘觉道。法本不生，今亦不灭，不起二见，不厌不忻，不切诸法唯一心是，然后乃为佛乘也。凡人皆逐境生心，心随欣厌。若欲无境，当忘其心。心忘则境空。境空则心灭。不忘心而除境，境不可除，只益纷扰耳。故万法唯心。心亦不可得。复何求哉。学般若法人，不见一法可得。绝意三乘。唯一真实。不可证得。谓我能证能得，皆增上慢人也。法华会下拂衣而去者，皆斯徒也。故佛言我于菩提实无所得。默契而已。凡人欲修证，但观五蕴皆空，四大无我，真心无相，不去不来，生时性亦不来，死时性亦不去，湛然圆寂，心境一如。但能如此直下顿了，不为三世所拘系，便出世人也。切不得有分毫趣向。若见善相诸佛来迎，及种种现前，亦无心随去。若见恶相种种现前，亦无畏心。但自忘心，同于法界，便得自在。

凡言化城者。二乘及十地乃至等觉妙觉，皆是权立接引之教。并为化城也。言宝所者，乃真心本佛自性之宝。此宝不属情量，不可建立，无佛无众生，无能无所。何处有城。若问此既是化城何处为宝所。宝所不可指，指即有宝所，非真实所也。故云在近而已。在近者，不可定量言之，但当体会契之即是。阐提者，信不具也。一切六道众生及至二乘，不信有佛果，皆谓之断善根阐提。菩萨深信佛法，不见有大乘小乘佛与众生同一法性，乃谓之善根阐提。大抵因声教而悟者名声闻。观因缘而悟者名缘觉。若不向自心中悟，虽至成佛，亦谓之声闻佛。学道人于法上悟，不于心上悟，虽历劫修行，终不是本佛。若不心悟，乃于法悟，即是轻心重法，遂成逐块，忘于本心。故但契本心，不用求法。心即法也。凡人多谓境碍心，谓事碍理。常欲逃境以安心，屏事以存理。不知乃是心碍境，理碍事。但令心空境自空。但令理寂事自寂。勿倒用心也。凡人多不肯空心，恐落空。不知自心本空。愚人除事不除心。智者除心不除事。菩萨心如虚空，一切俱舍。所作福德；皆不贪著。然舍有三等。内外身心一切俱舍，犹如虚空，无所取著，然后随方应物，能所皆忘，是谓大舍。若一边行道布德，一边旋舍，无希望心，是谓中舍。若广修众善，有所希望，闻法知空，遂乃不著，是谓小舍。大舍如火烛在前，更无迷悟。中舍如火烛在旁，或明或暗。小舍如火烛在后，不见坑阱。故菩萨心如虚空，一切俱舍。过去心不可得，是过去舍。现在心不可得，是现在舍。未来心不可得，是未来舍。所谓三世俱舍。自如来付法迦叶以来，以心印心，心心不异。印著空，则印不成文。印著物，则印不成法。故以心印心，心心不异。能印所印，俱难契会。故得者少。然心即无心，得即无得。佛有三身。法身说自性灵通法。报身说一切清净法。化身说六度万行法。法身说法，不以语言音声形相文字。无所说。无所证。自性灵通而已。故曰无法可说，是名说法。报身化身皆随机感现。所说法亦随事应根以为摄化。皆非真法。故曰报化非真佛，亦非说法者。所言同是一精明分为六和合者。一精明者，一心也。六和合者，六根各与尘合，眼与色合，耳与声合，鼻与香合，舌与味合，身与触合，意与法合，中间生六识为十八界。若了知十八界空无所有，束六和合为一精明，一精明者即心也。学道人皆知此。但不能免作一精明六和合解。遂为法缚，不契本心。如来现世，欲说一乘真法，则众生不信兴谤，没于苦海。若都不说，则佛堕悭贪，不为众生普舍妙道。遂方便说三乘。乘有大小，得有深浅。皆非本法。故云，惟此一乘道，余二即非真。然终未能显一心法。故召迦叶同法座坐，别付一心离言说法。此一枝法令别行。若能契悟者，便至佛地。

《黄蘗希运禅师传心法要　河东裴休集》

P230–P239　大道常在目前，虽在目前难见。若欲悟道真体，莫除声色言语。言语即是大道，不假断除烦恼。烦恼本来空寂，妄情递相缠绕。一切如影如响，不知何恶何好。有心取相为实，定知见性不了。若欲作业求佛，业是生死大兆。生死业常随身，黑暗狱中未晓。悟理本来无异，觉后谁晚谁早。法界量同太虚，众生智心自小。但能不起吾我，涅槃法食常饱。

妄身临镜照影，影与妄身不殊。但欲去影留身，不知身本同虚。身本与影不异，不得一有一无。若欲存一舍一，永与真理相疏。更若爱圣憎凡，生死海里沉浮。烦恼因心有故，无心烦恼何居。不劳分别取相，自然得道须臾。梦时梦中造作，觉时觉境都无。翻思觉时与梦，颠倒二见不殊。改迷取觉求利，何异贩卖商徒。动静两亡常寂，自然契合真如。若言众生异佛，迢迢与佛常疏。佛与众生不二，自然究竟无余。

法性本来常寂，荡荡无有边畔。安心取舍之间，被他二境回换。敛容入定坐禅，摄境安心觉观。机关木人修道，何时得达彼岸。诸法本空无著，境似浮云会散。忽悟本性元空，恰似热病得汗。无智人前莫说，打你色身星散。

报你众生直道，非有即是非无。非有非无不二，何须对有论虚。有无妄心立号，一破一个不居。两名由尔情作，无情即本真如。若欲存情觅佛，将网山上罗鱼。徒费功夫无益，几许枉用功夫。不解即心即佛，真似骑驴觅驴。一切不憎不爱，这个烦恼须除。除之则须除身，除身无佛无因。无佛无因可得，自然无法无人。

大道不由行得，说行权为凡愚。得理返观于行，始知枉用工夫。未悟圆通大理，要须言行相扶。不得执他知解，回光返本全无。有谁解会此说，教君向己推求。自见昔时罪过，除却五欲疮疣。解脱逍遥自在，随方贱卖风流。谁是发心买者，亦得似我无忧。

内见外见总恶，佛道魔道俱错。被此二大波旬，便即厌苦求乐。生死悟本体空，佛魔何处安著。只由妄情分别，前身后身孤薄。轮回六道不停，结业不能除却。所以流浪生死，皆由横生经略。身本虚无不实，返本是谁斟酌。有无我自能为，不劳妄心卜度。众生身同太虚，烦恼何处安著。但无一切希求，烦恼自然消落。

可笑众生蠢蠢，各执一般异见。但欲傍鏊求饼，不解返本观面。面是正邪之本，由人造作百变。所须任意纵横，不假偏耽爱恋。无著即是解脱，有求又遭罗网。慈心一切平等，真如菩提自现。若怀彼我二心。对面不见佛面。

世间几许痴人，将道复欲求道。广寻诸义纷纭，自救己身不了。专寻他文乱说，自称至理妙好。徒劳一生虚过，永劫沉沦生老。浊爱缠心不舍，清净智心自恼。真如法界业林，返作荆棘荒草。但执黄叶为金，不悟弃金求宝。所以失念狂走，强力装持相好。口内诵经诵论，心里寻常枯槁。一朝觉本心空，具足真如不少。

声闻心心断惑，能断之心是贼。贼贼递相除遣，何时了本语默。口内诵经千卷，体上问经不识。不解佛法圆通，徒劳寻行数墨。头陀阿练苦行，希望后身功德。希望即是隔圣，大道何由可得。譬如梦里渡河，船师渡过河北。忽觉床上安眠，失却渡船轨则。船师及彼渡人，两个本不相识。众生迷倒羁绊，往来三界疲极。觉悟生死如梦，一切求心自息。

悟解即是菩提，了本无有阶梯。堪叹凡夫伛偻，八十不能跋蹄。徒劳一生虚过，不觉日月迁移。向上看他师口，恰似失你孩儿。道俗峥嵘聚集，终日听他死语。不观己身无常，心行贪如狼虎。堪嗟二乘狭劣，要须摧伏六府。不食酒肉五辛，邪眼看他饮咀。更有邪行猖狂，修气不食盐醋。若悟上乘至真，不假分别男女。

《大乘赞十首　梁宝志和尚》

P240–P250　菩提烦恼不二，众生不解修道。便欲断除烦恼。烦恼本来空寂，将道更欲觅道。一念之心即是，何须别处寻讨。大道只在目前，迷倒愚人不了。佛性天真自然，亦无因缘修造。不识三毒虚假，妄执浮沉生老。昔时迷日为晚，今日始觉非早。

持犯不二　丈夫运用无碍。不为戒律所制。持犯本自无生，愚人被他禁系。智者造作皆空，声闻触途为滞。大士肉眼圆通，二乘天眼有翳。空中妄执有无，不达色心无碍。菩萨与俗同居，清净曾无染世。愚人贪著涅槃，智者生死实际。法性空无言说，缘起略无人子。百岁无智小儿，小儿有智百岁。

佛与众生不二　众生与佛无殊，大智不异于愚。何须向外求宝，身田自有明珠。正道邪道不二，了知凡圣同途。迷悟本无差别，涅槃生死一如。究竟攀缘空寂，惟求意想清虚。无有一法可得，翛然自入无余。

事理不二　心王自在翛然。法性本无十缠。一切无非佛事，何须摄念坐禅。妄想本来空寂，不用断除攀缘。智者无心可得，自然无争无喧。不识无为大道，何时得证幽玄。佛与众生一种，众生即是世尊。

凡夫妄生分别，无中执有迷奔。了达贪瞋空寂，何处不是真门。

静乱不二　声闻厌喧求静，犹如弃面求饼。饼即从来是面，造作随人百变。烦恼即是菩提，无心即是无境。生死不异涅槃，贪瞋如焰如影。智者无心求佛，愚人执邪执正。徒劳空过一生，不见如来妙顶。了达淫欲性空，镬汤炉炭自冷。

善恶不二　我自身心快乐。翛然无善无恶。法身自在无方，触目无非正觉。六尘本来空寂，凡夫妄生执著。涅槃生死平等，四海阿谁厚薄。无为大道自然，不用将心画度。菩萨散诞灵通，所作常含妙觉。声闻执法坐禅，如蚕吐丝自缚。法性本来圆明，病愈何须执药。了知诸法平等，翛然清虚快乐。

色空不二　法性本无青黄。众生谩造文章。吾我说他止观，自意扰扰颠狂。不识圆通妙理，何时得会真常。自疾不能治疗，却教他人药方。外看将为是善，心内犹若豺狼。愚人畏其地狱，智者不异天堂。对境心常不起，举足皆是道场。佛与众生不二，众生自作分张。若欲除却三毒，迢迢不离炎殃。智者知心是佛，愚人乐往西方。

生死不二　世间诸法如幻，生死犹若雷电。法身自在圆通，出入山河无间。颠倒妄想本空，般若无迷无乱。三毒本自解脱，何须摄念观禅。只为愚人不了，从他戒律决断。不识寂灭真如，何时得登彼岸。智者无恶可断，运用随心合散。法性本来空寂，不为生死所绊。若欲断除烦恼，此是无明痴汉。烦恼即是菩提，何用别求禅观。实际无佛无魔，心体无形无段。

断除不二　丈夫运用堂堂。逍遥自在无妨。一切不能为害，坚固犹若金刚。不著二边中道，翛然非断非常。五欲贪瞋是佛，地狱不异天堂。愚人妄生分别，流浪生死猖狂。智者达色无碍，声闻无不恛惶。法性本无瑕翳，众生妄执青黄。如来引接迷愚，或说地狱天堂。弥勒身中自有，何须别处思量。弃却真如佛像，此人即是癫狂。声闻心中不了，唯只趁逐言章。言章本非真道，转加斗争刚强。心里蚖蛇蝮蝎，蜇着便即遭伤。不解文中取义，何时得会真常。死入无间地狱，神识枉受灾殃。

真俗不二　法师说法极好。心中不离烦恼。口谈文字化他，转更增他生老。真妄本来不二，凡夫弃妄觅道。四众云集听讲，高坐论义浩浩。南坐北坐相争，四众为言为好。虽然口谈甘露，心里寻常枯燥。自己元无一钱，日夜数他珍宝。恰似无智愚人，弃却真金担草。心中三毒不舍，未审何时得道。

解缚不二　律师持律自缚，自缚亦能缚他。外作威仪恬静，心内恰似洪波。不驾生死船筏，如何渡得爱河。不解真宗正理，邪见言辞繁多。有二比丘犯律，便却往问优波。优波依律说罪，转增比丘网罗。方丈室中居士，维摩便即来诃。优波默然无对，净名说法无过。而彼戒性如空，不在内外娑婆。劝除生灭不肯，忽悟还同释迦。

境照不二　禅师体离无明。烦恼从何处生。地狱天堂一相，涅槃生死空名。亦无贪瞋可断，亦无佛道可成。众生与佛平等，自然圣智惺惺。不为六尘所染，句句独契无生。正觉一念玄解，三世坦然皆平。非法非律自制。翛然真入圆成。绝此四句百非，如空无作无依。

运用无碍　我今滔滔自在。不羡公王卿宰。四时犹若金刚，苦乐心常不改。法宝喻于须弥，智慧广于江海。不为八风所牵，亦无精进懈怠。任性浮沉若颠，散诞纵横自在。遮莫刀剑临头，我自安然不采。

迷悟不二　迷时以空为色，悟即以色为空。迷悟本无差别，色空究竟还同。愚人唤南作北，智者达无西东。欲觅如来妙理，常在一念之中。阳焰本非其水，渴鹿狂趁匆匆。自身虚假不实，将空更欲觅空。世人迷倒至甚，如犬吠雷吅吅。

《十四科讼　志公和尚》